WELCOME TO THE GATHERING PLACE

The Erato Club, Mayfair: a decadent Sixties playground for London's rich and famous. But the Erato's pleasures are nothing compared with those on offer at the 'club within the club' known as The Gathering Place. A Futuristic penthouse lair where money buys you all the sex, drugs and murder you could want. This is the world that undercover journalist Sophie Boyd must infiltrate if she is to investigate tycoon Hugo Summers' connection with the disappearance of a wartime spy. A world that will threaten her sanity, her soul and her life.

Find out more about the author and *The Gathering Place* at www.trevorjohnson.co.uk

The cover image of The Plaza Hotel in New York is by James Maher. See www.jamesmaherphotography.com

ISBN-13:
978-1502909749
ISBN-10:
150290974X

The Gathering Place

By Trevor Johnson

SIXTIES

PROLOGUE

Gipsy Hill, south London
Friday, November 14 1969
7.15pm

He could see her standing in the rain on the other side of the door, her body distorted by the coloured glass design of Joseph at his carpenter's bench. In the darkness of the hallway, he made a minor, unnecessary adjustment to his tie and took a deep breath before opening up.

Rain danced violently around the woman's buckle side boots. She was in her early thirties now, no longer quite the late twenties sexpot he remembered but still very easy on the eye. Different perfume.

"It's Challoner," she said. "He's been in touch. Says he can prove he didn't kill the nurses."

His perfectly white hair was swept back from the forehead to cap a pale, smooth-skinned face. A patrician nose supported heavy tortoise-shell glasses, through which he was now inspecting her.

"Come in," said Bernard Littlechild.

He fully opened the door and Sophie Boyd stepped into the hallway.

"I'm sorry I couldn't tell you more on the phone," she said. "It seemed quicker just to come round."

He made no reply but shut the front door and led the way into what appeared to be the only heated and lit room in the three-storey house.

"Now it's just me living here I tend to base myself in the one room for the winter," he said. "I do like a bit of cosy."

Here was the unlovely domain of the widower, furnished in little but a cream leather sofa and armchair (facing an imposing Ibbotson TV cabinet), Belling electric fire (furiously pumping out heat) and a violent clash of purple floral curtains and blood red deep-pile carpet. On the walls, rugby trophies and signed team photos competed for space against a dozen or so British Esso road maps.

"I've got them all," he said, in his gentle Geordie voice. "Except for Southern Scotland. But I'll get her."

Sophie gasped as she saw three people standing off to her left, near the front windows. Then she laughed at her foolishness: mannequins, decked out in various World War Two uniforms.

She removed her cap and shook free her shoulder-length blonde hair, which, despite the headgear still flicked up good-naturedly at the end.

Suddenly they found themselves facing each other. Sophie Boyd the delicate bird, modern in her swingback raincoat, wool trousers and rollneck sweater. Bernie Littlechild the size and shape of a coffin, a coffin dressed in a brown zip-up cardigan and striped nylon tie.

"You haven't got any taller, then," he said, smiling down at her.

"That's the closest you've ever come to a joke, Bernie."

"I've had five years to work on them." He removed his glasses, frowned at the raindrops that speckled the lenses, and put the specs aside. "Take a seat, pet. Drink?"

"Whatever you're having. Cheers."

He gave one of those beatific smiles that was half grandad, half executioner. Probably a good mix in a copper, she had always thought.

Not hurrying – he had never hurried, she remembered – he removed the stopper from a glass decanter and poured them a couple of fingers of Scotch each.

"Go on, then," he said.

"I got a note from Challoner," she began, perching on the settee and removing her suede shoulder bag. "Asking me to call him. He must have remembered my byline from the time of the murders and thought he could trust me."

Five years ago, two nurses were strangled outside staff accommodation at The Royal London Hospital, Whitechapel. The first: Kay Lofthouse-Jones, aged 19. Ten days later, and despite an increase in hospital security: Sheila Bartram, aged 21. The same spot. Clearly by someone who relished the thrill of being caught, or narrowly avoiding it.

Michael Challoner, a 23-year-old porter at the hospital, was questioned twice without being charged. When the cops went to pick him up a third time, he had disappeared, never to be seen again. A few days after this came the first of four letters sent to Detective Inspector Bernard Littlechild, revelling in cruelty and relishing the fact the writer knew key details about the case that had been withheld from the press.

Sophie continued: "The only real evidence against Challoner was that he did a runner. Your lot pretty much stopped investigating any other leads after that."

"That's not true," said Littlechild in a harder voice. "We followed every lead. But yes, of course Challoner incriminated himself by vanishing. If he's innocent he only has himself to blame."

"He was scared out of his wits just being in a police station, Bernie. He's from a strict Catholic family – he was terrified his drug addiction would come out."

"So why has he come out of hiding? What's this evidence he has?"

"The letters. After the murders came the letters, right? Four of them. Taunting the police for being useless, the hospitals for not protecting their staff and the families of the nurses for, well, no reason other than sheer cruelty."

Cruelty. The cruelty in the letters had shocked the public more than the actual murders.

"The letters had London postmarks but Challoner says he had fled to Madrid by the time the first letter was sent. Holed up in a squat. Says he was picked up by the Civil Guard on the first day for possession but they didn't want to deal with the hassle of extradition and let him go. He says that if their paperwork still exists in Madrid, it can prove he didn't send the letters."

"It's unlikely there will be paperwork," scoffed Littlechild, still standing. "And besides, samples of Challoner's handwriting from the hospital showed similarities with the handwriting in the letters."

"Oh come on. Challoner was practically illiterate. The samples you guys studied were a few ticks and scratches on deliveries he'd signed for. Plus your handwriting expert was under immense pressure – the whole country wanted him to say there was a link. It stank, Bernie."

Littlechild looked down at his black slip-ons. The only sound was the loud gurgling of a drainpipe struggling with the downpour.

"So you called Challoner back?"

"Yes. He rambled on, protesting his innocence. And then he just came out and told me where he was staying and asked me to come round. I said no, of course. But I did agree to meet him in public tomorrow afternoon. He says he'll give me the whole thing. For me to do with as I wish, as long as I promise to tell his story honestly."

"So what do you want from me?"

"I trusted you when I was reporting the case for the *Mirror*, Bernie. You were always straight with me. I need a sounding board. I'm out of my depth."

"I should say so. Turn him in now or face jail for obstructing justice. In fact, you're already halfway there for not reporting your contact with Challoner to the police. And I'll be in the you-know-what, too, if this gets out. You're a stupid girl, Sophie."

He went to a cupboard and returned with a thin hand towel.

She looked at it blankly for a second, still lost in thought, then began rubbing her hair at the nape. "Thank you."

"Let me pop next door and see if I still have any files."

**

Bernie Littlechild didn't bother to turn the light on in his office but stood in the dark. He just wanted time to think. Eventually he took a few steps into the blackness and bent down, placing his hands on the nearest edge of an ornate, camphor wood trunk his grandfather had brought back from India. Now it contained the dead body of Michael Challoner, who lay in there in a mess of congealing blood, the back of his head bashed in with a large wrench.

Why did he want to open the lid? He had suddenly felt the need for reassurance. To see the body, to know that he was safe.

Pull yourself together, Bernie. You were right to let the girl reporter come here tonight. You needed to know whether she had any evidence. Well, she doesn't. The only person who can get you in trouble is lying cold in the box. Just go with the girl to King's Cross tomorrow, and when Challoner doesn't show up you can roll your eyes and tell her to forget all about it.

Tomorrow – maybe even tonight – he'd get rid of the body. All in all it was a good thing. Because now Challoner was dead he was forever unable to prove that the Whitechapel murderer was still at large.

**

"I must have been a good detective inspector and handed everything in when I left the force," he said, startling her.

"I'm sorry about all this, troubling you..."

"It's all right. If Challoner is innocent it would be mad to just hand him over to the police again."

"So what should I do?"

Littlechild rested his thumbs in the cardigan's slash pockets.

"Who knows about all of this?"

"Nobody. Just my husband and he's sworn to secrecy."

"No-one at the *Mirror*?"

"I don't work there any more. I'm a freelance features writer now."

"Have you told friends? *Anyone?*"

"Nobody."

Littlechild was straightening the hat on a mannequin sporting a Gurkha's dark green dress uniform.

"Go to the meeting," he said. "I'll come, too. Safe distance."

"Yes, okay."

"I doubt Challoner's planning to do you harm. A good journalist is about the only person who might be able to help him. And if he wanted to hurt you he wouldn't have picked a busy spot like King's Cross."

A deep and unsettling silence fell over the room. Littlechild made some clicking sound with his mouth, something to supply some noise.

Sophie felt dizzy as the meaning of what he had just said spread through her like a fast-acting drug. She got to her feet, knowing she had to do something before it was too late. She placed the towel on the sofa and walked to a black and grey uniform hanging on a dummy next to the TV.

"This guy has intrigued me since I got here," she said.

"Luftwaffe pilot," replied Littlechild. "The badge is one of my treasures. Manufactured by Wilhelm Deumer. Look at that craftsmanship."

She touched the cap's metal badge, with its huge swooping eagle clutching a swastika in its talons. She sensed that Littlechild was right behind her.

Turn round. You must face him or you're dead.

"A terrible thing, to be born with such a curse," said Littlechild. "Not wanting to hurt people but at the same time wanting to. I don't know what it is about cruelty that's so appealing – the power, probably. So try to forgive me when I tell you something I've found out."

"You've lost me, Bernie. Could you pass my drink?" Her voice cracking.

He didn't move.

"I didn't want this, Sophie, but I made a stupid mistake just now. You never mentioned where the meeting was going to be, did you? But that didn't stop me blurting out 'King's Cross'. Silly Bernie."

"Perhaps I should go," said a distant voice.

"Oh please, not before you've filled in the blanks for me."

"Blanks?"

"Who is Saffron Honey?" he asked.

Hearing this name suddenly threw open a new door of possibility, that there had been some logical reason for him knowing the King's Cross information.

"A friend of mine. A freelance features writer, like me. We went to journalism college together..." When had he moved his hands behind his back? "What about her?"

"Saffron called here just this afternoon. Very apologetic but asked if she could speak to me in confidence. About the two murders. She sat down and

I gave her half an hour of my time. She'd swatted up on the basics but didn't know the case inside out, like you did. But she did know all about Challoner's return."

"Saffron knew...?" Sophie's mind was frozen with fear and confusion.

"She tried to buy me up. Wanted to take me along to meet Challoner. Said she thought she knew where he was staying. Wanted a big exclusive of some sort. Some confrontation. She knew you were going to meet Challoner at King's Cross tomorrow and wanted to beat you to it. An ambitious girl. I said no, of course. Bugger off. And now that I know she's a friend of yours, I'm glad I did, because that was very poor behaviour on her part, eh?"

"So Challoner went to Saffron, too?"

"Not exactly, Sophie."

"How did she have any idea where he was staying?"

"This is where I am the bearer of bad news."

He had been taking tiny steps towards her, no more than a couple of inches at a time.

"Bad news...?"

"Yes. You see, I followed Saffron when she left here, just in case she was off to meet Challoner. I thought I could deal with him myself. In fact, she went to a pub not far from here. She did meet someone, but it wasn't him."

"Who was it?"

"It was the person who'd given her the tipoff. The only person apart from you who knew Challoner was back on the scene. The only person you'd told where Challoner was hanging out. I recognised that person because we'd met before. It was a Christmas party at the nick or your newspaper, I don't remember which. With all that wild hair he's not a chap you forget."

In that sentence, Sophie's life fell apart. She uttered a terrible sound of despair, one palm going to her stomach like she'd been kicked.

"David..."

"Yes. Phuket, wasn't it? The honeymoon? You're the only person I'd ever known who'd been there so it's always stuck in my mind. I had to keep my distance, of course, but even spying in from outside the pub it was clear they were very close. But they had an argument and she flounced off, a bit teary eyed. And then I really did get lucky because her next port of call *was* Challoner. A row of squats in Camberwell – he did enjoy the high life, didn't he? I'm guessing that's what the tiff was about – she'd told her lover that I didn't want any part of her plan but that she would go round to find Challoner anyway. Paying house calls on a double killer? Risky business for a girl on her own. I bet her lover didn't like that, what do you think, pet? You know him better than anyone.

"And when she left, I went home, and came back to Camberwell in my van. Waved some cash around at the first junkie who opened the door and told him to send Challoner out on some pretext or other. It was already dark and spiriting him away was easy. It always is when they're dead. It's been quite an afternoon, I tell you.

"As you can appreciate, given my predilections, telling you that your husband is having an affair with Saffron Honey is a terrible, exquisite pleasure."

He moved incredibly quickly towards her, bringing his hands out from behind his back at the same time. Something flapped from his right fist and then his left hand grabbed the other end and she saw it was some kind of cord.

Now.

Lunging forward, the Luftwaffe badge clutched tightly in her right fist, the pin poking between her

13

fingers, she aimed a punch perfectly into Littlechild's left eye socket.

He dropped to his knees, his scream filling the room, deafening her.

Within a few heartbeats, Sophie was at the stained glass, screaming to the street for help, her fingers turning one key but then desperately scrabbling to find the others – one more? Two? How many had she heard him unlock?

Then the impossible happened and she heard Littlechild getting to his feet and coming for her. She turned just in time to see him stagger out of the living room, blood and clear liquid flowing down one side of his face, saliva flying from his mouth as he barked obscene oaths about what she was and what he was going to do to her. He grabbed her in a bear hug but before he could bring her down, out of sight of passers-by, she kicked back hard against the door, sending them both flying back and thumping to the bare boards. He didn't relinquish his grip and now she lay on top of him, facing the ceiling, her hands just free enough to go to her throat in time to block the cord he was pulling back on. She bashed her head back into his face, once, twice, and was spurred on by the sound of his nose breaking and the sight of the cord whipping away into some dark corner. But still he maintained the bear hug. Now it became an awkward, mismatched wrestling match, their bodies twisting and bucking on the narrow strip of carpet, Sophie's continued survival made possible only by the advantage of age and her attacker's ruined eye. The hallway was almost peaceful except for their intermittent grunts and cries and the gentle slooshing of rush hour traffic but then Bernie Littlechild began hissing a litany of gleeful profanities about the treachery of Sophie's husband and his lover and this seemed to fill him with a terrible strength...

CHAPTER ONE

Chichester Harbour, West Sussex
Five weeks later

The short, balding man in the waisted wool overcoat rounded the latest turn in the saltwater channel, winkle pickers in hand, trousers rolled over kneecaps, face creased in disapproval of the multiple indignities of the silt, the cold, the wildlife, in fact the whole notion of *being outdoors*.

He stopped to make some adjustment to his yellow paisley cravat and looked around helplessly at the rows and rows of pontoons with their day boats, family boats, race boats and cruisers all sunken in the low-tide mud. He'd been walking for what seemed forever, through endless vistas of saltmarsh and geese and woodland, the winter sun blinding him the whole way. He was starving, angry and his feet were *frozen*.

"Hopeless," he said. "Absolutely bloody hopeless."

But then a sound carried on the wind did give him hope: a generator – and wasn't that the smell of paint or varnish? Maybe he hadn't taken the wrong turning back there after all, maybe he was nearing the boatyard, where they said she'd be...

He began trudging with a renewed sense of purpose and spotted her almost immediately, sitting on a raised area of marshy grassland, wrapped up in a camel-coloured leather jacket and knitted hat, watching the marina from a bench, pen poised above a notepad on her lap. She didn't see him until he stepped out from behind a French yacht with a cluttered, jumble sale of a deck.

"*What*, may I ask," he began, tilting up at her, "is the *point* of the fucking seaside? It stinks, there are no good-looking men and judging by my journey from the station, the cabbies are all Sussex hillbillies who 'don't mind a trip to London every now and then but wouldn't want to live there'. People even appear to catch their own fish. In the name of God, why? There are some excellent fish restaurants in the West End. And then there's all this mud. How does anyone ever sail anywhere?"

She just let him stew for a bit. An icy gust of wind blasted across the flat, sending the halyards *clap clap clapping* madly against the masts.

"There's this thing called 'the tide'," said Sophie. "It goes in and out. Hello, Scottie. I wondered when you'd find me."

A minute later he'd wound his way up to her and they were hugging. Scottie's bay rum aftershave brought back all of Fleet Street's terrors and joys.

"What are you doing out here?" she said. "You know it's dangerous for you to stray outside Old Compton Street, you madman."

"Madman? I'm not the one in the loony bin."

"The place back there is not a loony bin, Scottie. It's a retreat."

"Yes, I say retreat as fast as possible. So why didn't you phone me? I've been desperate to come and see you."

"I wasn't exactly in the state of mind for banter. I'm sorry."

"But you didn't mind *Rachel* coming? I'll never forgive her – it took me six phone calls to get her to tell me where you were."

"Rachel is my best friend and was deemed less likely to get me over-excited."

"And I can guess who did the 'deeming'. Your witch of a mother. God, she's awful. 'Are you married yet, Ralph?' I had a good mind to give her a graphic description of my exploits at the steam bath."

"Well, *anyway*," said Sophie. "Thank God you're here. If I have to attend one more group session on

17

'embracing my inner dove' I'm going to murder someone."

"And what's that you're writing, hmmm? Out of interest? Fairytales?"

Scottie had always found it amusing that she liked to write stories for her nieces and that she'd harboured vague ideas about having them published. She tore the top sheet from the pad and stuffed it in a pocket. "A letter to my brother, if you must know."

"Ah," he said, as if he didn't quite believe her. He'd always had a knack of reading her mind.

It was certainly a joy to hear Scottie's camp, theatrical tones again. He seemed more like a teddy bear these days than the growling monster who had terrified her as a 17-year-old trainee at the *Mirror*. She'd barely been at the paper for a month when the newsdesk had shifted her to the crime desk, which meant doing his typing when he was too pissed to see the typewriter.

He'd ranted and raved about the decline of the public school system every time she'd hit a wrong key. One day she'd stood up and shouted at the top of her voice that she had not gone to public school, she had gone to the bloody secondary. The newsroom had been stilled. Scottie turned to the news editor, shrugged, and said: "All right, I tried to break her like all the others. I failed. She can stay on crime."

From that day on they'd been friends and had remained friends as she'd thrived at the *Mirror*. Not just thrived but *blazed*. Those *Daily Mirror* campaigns for women's rights and employment rights and housing rights and whatever rights happened to be in short supply had done some good in their time, hadn't they? Her photo byline splashed across millions of newspapers, her stories riling government ministers and captains of industry and the Church of England

and... and whoever all those enemies had once been. It all seemed so long ago.

On hitting thirty, she'd gone freelance and the old insecurities had surfaced when she'd sat down with nothing but a typewriter and a contacts book. But hadn't it all worked out again? Hadn't she hustled and sweet-talked and written her little socks off to become magazine editors' number one writer?

Well, number two. Nothing would ever have toppled Her Royal Highness Saffron Honey from her throne.

Now, shivering in the harbour, Sophie filled Scottie in on everything from how she'd met the bastard David to the night Bernie Littlechild had nearly killed her.

"So David had been having it off with Saffron for months..." said Scottie. "I never liked her. I always thought she was a bit unhinged."

"Well, me too but not so unhinged that she'd steal my husband and then try to steal my exclusive on Challoner."

"So David must have tipped her off about Challoner?"

"Yes, the pillow-talking shit. Told her two things: where Challoner lived and that I was going round to see Littlechild. When Littlechild snubbed her she went straight to see Challoner, not knowing Bernie was tailing her."

"The cow tried to steal the story right from under you. Did she succeed?"

"We'll never know. She claims in all those bullshit first-person stories she wrote that Challoner agreed she could be his confessor but you know Saffron – that could be lies. Still, you've got to hand it to her – she really knows how to walk all over a friend in the name of a story. She even went to see Bernie Littlechild to try to buy him up so he could add some spice to any interview she got with Challoner. She probably thought that by getting Littlechild on her side he could talk me out of the whole thing on her behalf – you know, put me off the scent. She knew I'd always trusted Bernie and would listen to him."

"Hmm, killers and adulterers, you're a lovely girl but an *appalling* judge of character, Sophie."

"Tell me about it."

"How did she hope to get away with it?"

"God knows. By selling it for some huge sum to *The Sun* and writing it under a false byline, maybe. But it would have been sub judice. Legal poison. Unprintable. Or maybe she was just going to grass him up to the Old Bill and then bask in the glory. I don't know what her plan was – she often has mad ideas that she pulls off and gets in print. That's why she's so good, the bitch."

"And she thought you'd never find out it was her? My God, she's stupid as well as evil."

"Maybe she didn't care. She knew I'd find out about her and David one day and would hate her for that, too. In for a penny..." Sophie rested her head on Scottie's shoulder. "Oh, why did we drift apart, Scottie?"

"You got married and my friendship was expendable."

"God, I really got that the wrong way round, didn't I? What a bitch. I'm so sorry."

"Never dump your friends."

"Sorry, sorry, sorry."

"Oh, sod it, life's too short. *Accepted*."

"Thank you, thank you. So how's the *Mirror*?"

"Don't ask. They stripped me of my crime correspondent title and gave it to some Oxbridge foetus. I can't wait to see what happens when *he* has to go and play snooker with the Krays."

"The Krays are banged up, Scottie. They won't be playing *any* snooker."

"No, and neither will he with a cue shoved up his arse. Anyway, I don't care, I've got much bigger fish to fry..." He started humming and pretended to focus on something in the distance.

"And that would be...?"

"Hmmm?"

Sophie had forgotten all the game playing that went with Scottie. "What is this new thing that's so exciting?"

"Oh, *that*. Well, darling, now is probably not the time or place. We don't want you getting over-excited, do we?"

"Scottie, tell me or I'll throw you to the geese."

"All right." He lowered his voice. "For the past six months I've been writing a biography of Abigail Wilman."

"Wartime spy, right?"

"Special Operations Executive, to be precise. Mad bunch of men and women, though it's mainly the women that get remembered these days. They were up detonating railway bridges while the rest of the world was still deciding whether to have boiled egg or toast. What happened to her after the war is one of the great British mysteries, of course. Or rather, it has been until now." Scottie had gone puce with excitement. "The only theory anyone's ever had is that the enigmatic little madam had a secret boyfriend and he did her in. But there's never been any evidence for that and frankly it's just bollocks. But I've cracked it, Sophie. I'm sure I know who did it. This story's got everything – a very rich man, a very dead spy and a very naughty club."

"Naughty?"

"Oh yes. We're talking filthy, depraved, orgiastic fucking by the richest, most powerful, most beautiful people in christendom. The problem with my investigation is that the trail goes cold for me at the club: *I can't get in*. These places are strictly for the powerful – or hot ladies."

"Bugger. There must be a way round it. It's tricky though. Maybe you could..." Sophie leapt to her feet. "You utter shit! You didn't come to see how I was at all. You came all the way out here to get me to be your stooge, didn't you? Same old Scottie."

Scottie was suddenly very nimble as Sophie stalked him around the bench.

"Now listen," he said. "It's not like that at all, you ridiculous girl. Of course I didn't come here for that. I came because I heard about you, because I was worried."

"Bollocks. You came here to see if I was up to your job. What's wrong with the girls at the *Mirror*, why can't *they* do it?

"Well, it's not a *Mirror* job, it's a book."

"So that *is* why you came! You bastard! I've had a breakdown, Scottie. A total bloody breakdown. What did you think I was going to say? 'Sure, I'll come back to London with you on the first train?' Then what? I'd waltz in to this club tomorrow night and say: 'Which of you wankers killed that lady spy?'"

"No need to. I *know* who killed her. But listen, that's not why I came here. Honest to God, Sophie, a friend wouldn't do that."

Sophie halted. The length of the bench was between them.

"Please don't hit me," said Scottie. "I'm feeling fragile."

Sophie turned her back on him. The breeze brought the sounds of trilling curlew, and T Rex's *Debora* from a cassette player in the boatyard. A cormorant landed on a DANGER sign next to her to dry its wings.

Scottie checked his watch and said in a quiet voice: "I have to start my trek back to the station. I'm meeting a friend in the steam room at Waterloo at half

22

six. I'm sorry I upset you. You must believe that it was a misunderstanding. I would never try to take advantage of you. All I want is for you to get better and for us to be friends again. It would be lovely if you give me a call when you're back home."

"You can't just leave. Not without telling me who did her in."

"Not now," said Scottie, putting his shoes back on. "You're not ready. You must get back to normal first. You were always so strong. Fearless."

"That was an act! This breakdown has been me being normal for once. Anyway, I'm bored with talking about me – tell me how I'd get into this club. I can't remember how Abigail died either."

"Ah, you were just pretending you knew," he said, whipping the cravat over his face like a bandit's mask and backstepping into the long grass. Just before he disappeared, he said: "Well, she didn't die as such. Just went missing after the war: February, nineteen forty-seven. Never heard of again…"

Sophie sat there, just watching the tide come in and asking herself how strong she really felt now. Physically she was fine – miraculously the Littlechild incident had left her with nothing worse than a small cracked bone in the back of her skull and a load of painful bruises. Littlechild had not been so lucky – after passing out from a combination of blood loss and having his head repeatedly bashed against the floor, he came round to find that Sophie had fled the house. He made his getaway (in the same van he had transported Michael Challoner's body in) but was rumbled two days later after checking in to a bed and breakfast in Brighton. With a patch over his injured eye and his face in every newspaper and TV bulletin he wasn't hard to identify. When armed police went up to his room, he opened the door and started firing with his Webley Revolver. He was killed within seconds.

A search of Littlechild's house found a drawer containing a variety of items which would have made effective garottes. It wasn't long before he was linked to the murders of the nurses as well as four other stranglings in London, not to mention the death of his own wife ten years earlier.

That Littlechild was no longer alive was of some comfort to Sophie, and comfort was in short supply. Friends would barely recognise the Sophie of old – her hyacinth blue eyes had lost their sparkle long ago and now stared listlessly from her heart-shaped face. She touched her fingers to the black circles beneath her eyes, then ran her hands through her blonde hair. What had she become?

The psychological after-effects of that night – and to a greater extent the revelation that David and Saffron had been having an affair – had tipped her over the edge, and as she recovered in hospital a huge depression had set in. When the physical wounds were healed, the mental ones grew deeper and she found herself tranked up on Valium, an addiction she had only beaten by coming to the retreat, run by a charity that helped addicts of all types get clean. It had saved her life. But she couldn't stay here forever. For a start, she hated fucking mung beans.

The cold was starting to bite through her mittens. She took the piece of paper that she'd hidden from Scottie out of her pocket and unfolded it. In her handwriting were the words: "Once upon a time there was a..." That was all there was. The plan to move to Ibiza and write fairytales for kids wasn't going to work if she didn't have any fairytales in her. Writing them used to be the easiest thing in the world.

Yeah, back when you thought life might still be a fairytale.

She was about to put the page back in her pocket when a gust of wind tugged it from her fingers and it danced away high into the darkening sky.

CHAPTER TWO

The cold snap had brought a kind of Dunkirk spirit to the Portobello Road street market.

It was as if the Saturday shoppers had resolved to make the best of things by dressing up in their winter finery, meeting friends for lunch and whiskey macs and splashing out on indulgent *objets d'arts*.

There was something else, too – a sense of community. It was like there was room for them all: the hippie survivors, the new Mods, the Jamaicans with their bluebeat and reggae, and the white kids who made the rock that blared from the record shops. The sixties had started a revolution that the Seventies would take to a new level.

Or so it seemed to Sophie.

Yeah, right, Polyanna, never mind the Mansons or that the Yanks just turned the world over to Nixon or that Scottie's going to suck you into something dangerous just as you've crawled back from meltdown...

Well, at least she had a takeaway double egg and bacon sarnie and cappuccino. Now she just had to get home and scoff it before Scottie showed up. She'd phoned him as soon as she'd got back from Sussex the previous night and asked him round for coffee (she didn't say that she was dying to know more about his Abigail Wilman book but he would have guessed that much).

It was madness to think that she could throw herself straight into a big story – the people at the retreat had told her that a relapse was highly likely if she didn't take things easy. It had been hell coming off the Valium – no way was she ever touching those things again, or putting herself in situations where she might want them.

But it wasn't like it was her *work* that had sent her off the rails, was it? It had been Littlechild. And David.

Mainly David. And she hadn't offered to be Scottie's partner in this, not yet. She could just pretend that she was simply being nosy about-.

"Hey, Sophie! Sophie!"

Oh God. She plastered on a smile and spun to face Moog, the goateed owner of Turned-On Records, who was leaning out of his shop. Moog was the worst kind of hippie – his heart bled for every cause in the world but rarely for anyone he actually knew.

"Hey, Moog. Long time, no see."

"It's been forever. Where've you been?" He removed his pink John Lennon glasses and squinted, as if not believing his eyes. "Everyone's been frantic – you've been gone months. Jake heard a rumour you'd gone to cover the war and blown your mind on acid."

"Acid? No way, not after that night."

Moog had witnessed Sophie's one run-in with LSD, when she and David had gone to a friend's house to watch the moon landing in July. She had innocently accepted a drink of "punch" before embarking on the trip from hell. David had set upon the guilty party – spiking of any sort was an enormous crime – and the TV had got smashed just as Neil Armstrong was about to make his giant leap for mankind.

"So what happened?" said Moog. "You said you were coming to hand out those war flyers at the Tull gig and you never showed."

"I was?" She had only the vaguest memory of that promise, which she must have made just before her world caved in.

"Forget it, it's just good you're okay. We all heard about that fucking maniac and then, well, you know, you and David..."

"Thanks... Yeah, bad times. But I thought I'd told Sheila I was going to look after my brother's house on the Sussex Downs for a few weeks. I needed some space and the city's just too uptight sometimes, you know?" This was the cover story she'd decided upon for people she didn't want knowing the real one. "I started writing a book and stayed longer than I planned."

"Cool. What's the book about?"

"Oh, it's early days. It's a freeform kind of thing, Kurt Vonnegut meets, er, John Fowles, perhaps? It's about these, you know, these *people*."

"I love people books. Come into the shop and I'll dig you out some new sounds that are going to blow you mind."

"Not more Beatles?"

"You mean you didn't like *Abbey Road*?"

"I haven't even heard it yet. *The White Album* was bad enough: *Revolution 9* and lift music? What was wrong with *Twist and Shout*? I'm a Bury St Edmunds girl, Moog – we know what we like. Listen, I've really got to run but I'll stop by next week. Let's go for a drink."

Moog was just nodding, some enigmatic smile on his face, like he knew more than he was letting on. Did he know about the retreat? Did everyone in Notting Hill Voices Against the War know? And how about all the other causes she belonged to? Hotbeds of gossip, every one.

"You're always running, Sophie," he said. "Sometimes you have to stop and *see*. Did you read about Fred Hampton?"

"Who?"

Moog shook his head. "He was a Panther. The Feds gunned him down in his bed last week and we're going to send his family some dough. Can you come along on Tuesday and take minutes – it looks like we'll be drafting some protest about those Hell's Angel pigs at Altamont, too."

"What's Altamont?"

"You haven't seen the papers?" he said, waving that day's *Guardian*.

"Give me a break, Moog – I've had stuff on my mind," she said, walking backwards along the crowded pavement. Her foot clipped a wicker basket outside a shop, spilling wooden pipes that rolled away down the pavement.

"Four kids go to a Stones gig and they wind up dead."

"Four dead? Jesus. Listen, I'll get back to you about Tuesday. I've got to go."

"Do you know what Altamont is?" called Moog, who was nearly obscured from view now. "I mean, do you know what it *really* is?"

"No, what is it, Moog? *I've got to go…*" She dropped the last of the pipes back into the basket.

The market traders' cries and the riffs from a shop called "Guitars and Sitars" combined into such a discordant din that Sophie wasn't sure of Moog's reply, but it sounded like: "Altamont is the *seventies*."

***

CHAPTER THREE

She dug the house keys from her coat, let herself into the Victorian townhouse and scooped up the solitary item of post, another letter from her solicitor about the impending divorce, which would see her effortlessly take David to the cleaners.

Sophie struggled up to the first-floor flat, whose living room was undergoing a difficult transition from hippie trail to *2001*, meaning beaded fabric lampshades and Indian-style rugs clashed with Bridget Riley prints and lava lamps.

Today there was the added problem that half the contents of Sophie's suitcase lay in a trail from the living room's pod chair to her bed, where it climaxed in a volcano-shaped pile. She'd been too busy popping in to see friends, making phone calls and opening her post this morning to put everything away. Maybe she had time to just scoop everything up now and dump it on the bed before laughing boy arrived. But then the doorbell rang.

Five minutes later, they were raucously exchanging stories in the kitchen as Sophie made coffee. Her tales were of the other addicts at the retreat and Scottie's were of his exploits at the steam room. Just when she thought that if she laughed any more she'd pull a muscle, Scottie excused himself to use the toilet. But when Sophie brought the coffees through to the living room a minute later, she found him covering the table in photos, maps and a stack of notepads.

"Make yourself at home," she said.

"Just a few things about this Abigail Wilman story. I thought you might find it interesting."

He opened a hardback book at a photo of six French Resistance fighters and placed a finger on a woman on the right of the group.

"Abigail," said Sophie.

"Correct. Born May 1919. Lives just outside Cambridge. Father dies when she's two, mother when she's six. She goes to live with an aunt and uncle in France. Uncle is some kind of banker. When Abby's fourteen the aunt and uncle separate. The aunt and Abby return to England. Abby goes to grammar school and is booted out for nearly blinding another girl in a fight."

"Nice."

"She manages to get into another grammar. Secretarial college after that. Her first job's at a food importer's in The Strand, and then she goes to *The Affairs*, a small magazine for commies, pacifists and general weirdos. Here."

Scottie pushed a yellowing bundle of papers to Sophie. *The Affairs* had clearly been produced on a shoestring. It was abysmally printed and had no illustrations, just acres of tiny, closely spaced print. Sophie sniggered as she read out the main heading: "Why Germany deserves the benefit of the doubt."

"Indeed. Abby only stayed for six months. We don't know why she left. After that, she basically temped for a few months and then joined the First Aid Nursing Yeomanry."

"The FANYs. I've heard of them."

"The SOE used the FANYs as one of its hunting grounds. They came calling, turned her into a killer and dropped her into France. At first she was ferrying messages between the SOE and the Resistance. Then she started *training* the French, mainly in explosives and small arms. They resented her at first but it wasn't long before they were queuing up to die for her. Every circuit she took charge of went crazy – bridges blown to hell, convoys wiped out, Nazis brass assassinated. But you can swot up on all that for homework."

Scottie slid Sophie a book called *Avenging Angel: The Life and Disappearance of Abigail Wilman*.

"After the war she got a job with a map maker's in Holborn. Hardly anything's known about her life at this point, except that she took lodgings in Clapham and the landlady didn't think she had many friends. In February '47 her employers report she hasn't shown up for work for a couple of days. And no-one ever sees her again. We can be pretty sure that whatever happened to her, happened around February 16, 1947."

"So what are the theories?"

"Someone from the map firm claims he saw Abby and a man in the back of a swish motor in Pall Mall shortly before she vanished. That suggests she might have been bumped off by someone important, and there *have* been theories that she knew too much about the SOE. That has some credibility: sabotage and murder don't always look so clever when wars are over. And the SOE's Baker Street HQ *did* burn down rather suspiciously in 1946. Nearly all the records on the FANY agents were destroyed."

"What do you think – that someone from the SOE killed their own girl?"

"Not quite, but you're close." He reached for a map of central London. Four streets in St James's were speared with red pins. "What I'm about to say is common knowledge. It's in the police reports, and the bloke who wrote *Avenging Angel* couldn't add to it. Okay: there were three known movements of Abby outside of work in the week before she vanished. The first was the sighting by this colleague, who saw her in the car in Pall Mall. That was around 6pm on Saturday, February 8. The following Saturday she had lunch at Lily's Restaurant in St James's Street nearby. The police knew this because the manager came forward – Abby had paid by cheque and he recognised her name in the papers when she vanished.

"The next day, she was back at Lily's. She asked to sit in the window and had Sunday lunch. She stayed for almost two hours – quite a long time for a gal on her own. This time she paid by cash but a waiter remembered her. Two days later, the map firm contacted Abby's landlady, who said she hadn't seen her for three days. That's when the Old Bill were called in.

"What Abby was up to in St James's in her spare time is the mystery no-one has ever been able to crack." Scottie delved into a folder and passed Sophie a sheaf of papers. "Until now."

She scanned the letterhead: "Page-Hoare, Carlier and Fahy?"

"Solicitors. *Very posh* solicitors. What you're holding is some dull correspondence between the firm and Tom Havelock about a loan. Havelock owned *The Affairs*, as much as you can own something that's worth nothing. The letters grow increasingly nasty, with the firm threatening to start proceedings if he doesn't pay their client the whole lot back. Their client was none other than Hugo Summers."

"As in Summers Steel?"

"As in." Scottie passed Sophie a newspaper cutting. Staring back at her was a handsome man with a manicured moustache and an impressive mop of slicked-back hair.

"Well, *hello Hugo*," said Sophie, lighting a cigarette.

"Must you act so post-coital? Though I do admit he's rather dashing. Not bad for fifty-five, anyway. Last year *The Times* declared Hugo the twenty-third richest man in the UK. But let's start from the beginning. Hugo had his 'flicking towels in the showers' days at Lancing College before poring over the Classics at Oxford, where he blossomed into quite a sportsman – he rowed against Cambridge two years running and won more boxing trophies than any student before or since. And then there was the *real sport*: a string of very rich girls and all the cash he won at poker. He's lethal at seven-card stud and would host backgammon parties at the Ritz for his chums, fleecing them for twenty quid a point.

"After graduation, daddy got him cutting his teeth on some trivial part of the empire. Then war broke out and MI5 got their claws into Hugo. He excelled as a case agent but resented being seen as a pen pusher by his charges and insisted on doing all the training *they* had to do. The upshot was that he's now also lethal in unarmed combat. Some jewel thieves tried to break into his house one night and he gave them a right pasting. Trussed them up and called the Old Bill – they both got eight years.

"Our Hugo could have gone far in the Department but quit in '46 to take over the business after daddy popped his clogs. Ten years down the road and there was more than just steel to Summers Steel: there was tobacco and pharmaceuticals and a newspaper."

"*The Daily Post.*"

"Hugo turned it from a centre-left rag to a rabid, right-wing triumph; his personal mouthpiece on everything from immigration to the so-called Moscow Three."

Sophie recalled the infamous episode when the *Post* had all but accused three Cabinet members of spying for the Russians.

"The *Post* dropped the story to avoid a libel case," said Scottie. "It didn't have a choice, given that the claims were pretty much bunkum, but that didn't stop it from going on to wage smear campaigns against the union leader Jim Garwood and later Seamus Knutt."

"They wrongly linked Knutt to the IRA... Oh God, I remember that."

"Yes, he was just a gentle little poet and the poor sod killed himself. And as you can't libel the dead, the *Post* got away with that, too. After his wife Emily gassed herself in her car in 1954, Hugo had his biggest breakdown and took a year off. When he came back, he ordered that there were to be no more witch hunts and malicious fictions. He didn't have a choice – the paper had lost a lot of sales – but now it became a crusader, a champion of the people, fighting injustice and picking its targets with care. It quickly regained the lost readers and has put on half a million more since the bad old days.

"Now, Hugo had always been a depressive but Emily's death just made things worse and he stepped down as chairman of the *Post* to 'concentrate on writing'. It's true he *has* written a few biogs of obscure cricketers and military figures but my City insiders tell me that when Hugo's supposed to be away writing, he's actually sitting in some posh loony bin."

"So he's a manic depressive?" said Sophie.

"Probably just your common-or-garden depressive. When he's well, he's still the king of the stock market. They call him the Takeover Typhoon because he's always stripping companies down, hiving bits off and generally turfing out the dead wood. There was a bit of a hoo-ha a couple of years back when it looked like he was going to buy *The New York Journal.* The British unions were livid at the idea of him splashing out on foreign rags when he'd cut their own workers' pay and conditions to Dickensian levels but the deal fell through."

"The unions are never off Summers' back."

"Right across the empire. It's because he pares everything to the bone. Anyway, back to the money he lent Tom Havelock: in November '37, the demands just stop."

"So Havelock coughed up?" said Sophie.

"Maybe. Maybe not. But the point is that the police and all those other pretenders who've written books on

Abby *never went back far enough*. They looked at what Abby did *during* the war and *after* the war but never *before* the war. They've always assumed that her short time at *The Affairs* was irrelevant. But like a true genius, I tracked down Tom Havelock's sister. Got the 10.17 to Horsham and sweet-talked her into letting me poke around in her loft. She still hoards her brother's possessions, right down to back copies of his shitty mag. I told her a few white lies: that I had an interest in obscure left-wing periodicals blah blah. I didn't mention Abby, didn't want her to think her loft might hold the key to a famous mystery."

"Havelock's possessions? So he's dead?"

"Topped himself during the war."

"Another suicide?"

"Yes," said Scottie. "Hugo does seem to attract them. Which adds to the intrigue. But Havelock was a real mixed-up kid, according to sis. I went through everything in that loft, which is when I found those letters from the solicitors. And they got me thinking: why was Summers lending small amounts of cash to a poxy outfit like *The Affairs*? Were he and Havelock pals? In all the background reading I'd done on Summers, I'd never come across Havelock's name."

"Whoa, wait a minute," said Sophie. She pushed her chair back from the table and went to stand by the windows. Outside on the balcony, a pirate's plastic moustache from her summer party turned a slow circle in a puddle. "What's Havelock's loan got to do with Abigail's disappearance?"

"All right. We're into the final stretch − full concentration now. Summers' clubs are listed in his *Who's Who* entry. Among them − and this is my *piece de resistance* − are The Grenfield and Henry Q's."

It took the names a few seconds to register with Sophie. "My God. They're both in St James's Street..."

"Yes! And on the opposite side of the road, Lily's Restaurant is smack bang in the middle of the two."

Sophie gasped. "Abigail was waiting for Hugo."

"Waiting, or watching."

"It must have been waiting – she was spotted in a posh car, for God's sake. It had to have been Summers. Abigail was his bit on the side. He made her wait in the restaurant like his dirty little secret, until he'd stagger out of one of his clubs and pick her up!"

"Exactly the theory I'm working on."

"But I still don't see the link, between the loan to Tom Havelock and all this creeping around in St James's."

"Neither do I," said Scottie. "But it's all we have. Hugo Summers lends Tom Havelock five hundred pounds in 1937, possibly to keep the magazine afloat. Nearly a decade later, Havelock's former secretary sits in a restaurant spying on Summers. Then poof, she vanishes."

"God, Scottie, you're a genius. So what next? You said something about a sex club."

Scottie placed a business card on the table. Embossed in silver were the words *Erato Arts Club* and the address: 1 Arcadian Gardens, Mayfair. Entwined thorns and roses snaked up one side. A telephone number was listed for membership enquiries.

"Erato – the goddess of... erotic verse?" said Sophie.

"Correct. She was a goddess of music, song and dance. In Classical times she was named the muse of erotic poetry."

"I've heard of this place. How did you get the card?"

"Went there myself. Asked the doorman a few questions. Like some innocent tourist, you know. He wouldn't tell me much. Fobbed me off with the card, told me to phone up and ask about membership. But it was invitation only, he said. Bugger off, in other words. However, a few nights later I breezed past and there was a different doorman and I just knew that he was *one of us*."

"A journalist?"

"A poof, you stupid girl. Well, we got chatting and not only did he want my phone number but he wasn't averse to my cash either. For twenty quid he sneaked me in to the Erato on a Saturday night. I only got as far as the disco before some East End rough chucked me out among the dustbins. But the men, the women, the glamour! It was fabulous, Sophie."

"And Summers belongs to this joint?"

"His father *founded* it. It's still the juiciest chunk of property in Mayfair."

"And you want me to snoop around in there?"

Scottie shook his head. But then he said: "If you decide you're up to it. And I do not want you to do something you're not up to."

"What's in it for me?"

"Well, hypothetically you could infiltrate the club, get close to the guilty party and find out what you can about him and Abigail Wilman. *I'd* use anything you get for my biography, and you can use whatever *you* find out for a juicy article on the club.

"You'd have to get close to Summers. Undercover, like the old days. It won't be easy – it's probably easier to get close to the president of the USA than Summers. But apart from the occasional gambling trip to the Clermont, the Erato is his only haunt now, according to the gossip columns. A lot of naughty stuff seems to go on in there but security's tight and not many rumours leak out."

Sophie fell into her pod chair. "I don't know, Scottie. I promised everyone I'd stick to easy, girlie interviews until I was back on my feet."

"I understand, kitten," he said, pretending to be more interested in the Get Well cards on top of the

TV. "But there's a little something extra that might make up your mind."

Sophie had half expected something like this, some tidbit held back. This was a favourite tactic of Scottie's.

"After I'd searched the loft, I went downstairs and had tea with Havelock's sister. She clearly had no idea her brother once employed a famous spy-in-the-making and I wasn't about to tip her off – she's just the sort of curtain twitcher to get on to the tabloids with pound signs in her eyes. But she told me something fascinating about her sister-in-law: Tom's wife, Caroline. She was an ambulance driver. Lost her sight in the Blitz and went to live at St Dunstan's home for the blind on the south coast. She was found dead at the bottom of the cliffs. The date: February 17, 1947."

"The day after Abigail vanished..."

"No-one has ever made the connection between the deaths. Abby had no close relatives, apart from the aunt, who died of cancer during the war. And Caroline and Tom's relatives never knew Abby had been *The Affairs'* secretary; she wasn't there long enough. The author of that book on Abigail was so incompetent he never bothered tracking down anyone connected with the Havelocks, and the police investigating Caroline's plunge down the cliffs assumed it was self-inflicted, given what she'd been through. *No-one has ever made the link between the two deaths*. But *somebody* was very busy in those 24 hours."

"Summers..." said Sophie.

"We seem to hear a lot less about peace and love these days and I know how you believed in all that, in changing things. I admired you – I was always too jaded for that. What I'm saying is, maybe this is a chance to do some real journalism again. And if you don't want to do it for yourself, perhaps you should do it for Abigail, and Caroline Havelock..."

Keef – Sophie's fat ginger cat – hopped on to her lap and she hugged him close to her. Above the rooftops, the sun shone through a break in the scudding clouds, before the clouds blocked it out again. Light and dark, light and dark, as if locked in some duel.

***

CHAPTER FOUR

They arrived at Sophie's local as the doors were opening for the Saturday evening session. It was an old man's boozer with sticky seats and Henry Cooper memorabilia but the landlord was game enough to follow Scottie's instructions for making cocktails. These were drinks he'd invented over the years, using whatever spirits were in his desk.

"Tell me about this Erato," said Sophie, when they were settled. "Will I have to fuck ten guys or what?"

"Is that a problem?"

"I've so missed your wit. Come on – what's this place all about? I'm so excited!"

"Stop gushing. I never managed to kill off that awful head girl enthusiasm, did I?"

"We didn't have a head girl at my comp. Tell me about the Erato."

"It's decadence. Entitlement. Power. Everything we're not. But here's the story: in 1964, huge cracks were discovered down one side of the building. Summers couldn't stomach the bill and was thinking of selling up, or so the rumours went. And then everything went quiet. The club stayed shut. Memberships were not renewed.

"Then word started circulating that it was open for business again. But those people who'd lost their membership had to reapply – and a lot of the old guard were rejected. Those that were successful found the fee had trebled. It's about five hundred quid now. If they let you in, we'll go halves on it."

"I've got savings. And mum's been paying my mortgage while I've been off sick so I'm doing okay. What else?"

"Not so long ago the City hacks at the *Mirror* decided to get to the bottom of all these shenanigans at the Erato. They didn't get far, except for concluding that

Hugo has a new partner, possibly an unsavoury one. Whoever it is probably helped Hugo out with the repair bill and is now calling the shots. You see, the clientele is starting to change: there's a hipper, more dangerous crowd. Showbiz, high rollers, crooks, flash money in general."

"Scottie, this story sounds like it's going to be incredibly dangerous. Is it?"

"Quite possibly, but I thought you might relish the chance to put one over on the Establishment. It must be time to re-establish your credentials."

'What does that mean?"

"Darling, are you not aware that everyone thinks you sold out the day you ditched the *Mirror* to write about hemlines?"

"Who said that?" yelled Sophie, loud enough to briefly silence the pub.

"Well, it's true, isn't it?" whispered Scottie. "That's why you threw yourself into all those groups – Women against Rape, and Rapists Against CND, wasn't it? Guilt that you deserted the cause?" Before Sophie could explode, he placed a hand over her mouth and said: "Another G&T? Wait a minute – you shouldn't be drinking. Or should you?"

"Relax. It was Valium that was my problem, not booze."

"But your father…"

"He only drank so mum would kick him out. Why are you so concerned about my drinking now? You never tried to stop me tipping lager and lime down my throat when I was seventeen."

"How could one have stopped the party girl *par excellence*?"

"Well, indeed. It's my round – same again?"

Later, they stood on the cold street, embracing. Scottie dangled something before her eyes.

"Your keys!" she slurred, snatching them from him.

"Your own set, like the old days."

"You bastard – you had them cut because you knew I'd want in."

"Maybe. Sadly, fifty-five Spencer Street, Kilburn, is hardly the Belgravia pad you once knew as my residence. These days I have to share a *water closet* on a *landing* with *other people*, if you can imagine such an obscenity. But if this gets dangerous, you might need a safe house. And vice versa – get me some spares for your place, will you? And hide your notes somewhere very safe."

"Seriously?"

"Yes. Or somewhere the average housebreaker won't find them, anyway. I won't lie to you, darling – we're entering dark waters."

***

CHAPTER FIVE

Sophie opened her eyes. Her head was pounding and her mouth tasted like Keef's litter tray (she imagined). Damn Scottie and his cocktails. Then she remembered the Abigail Wilman project and found herself full of resolve. She parted the bed's sari drapes and padded through to the living room phone, dialling the membership number on the Erato card. Yes, she had heard about the club and just wanted to know how you went about joining... Nice and naive, that should do it. The worst they could do was say no.

Her heart was pounding like crazy as the number began to ring. No-one answered – instead there was a click and an answerphone message. A man who sounded as if he'd been born and bred at RADA said: "Thank you for calling the Erato Arts Club. For membership enquiries, please leave your name and number and we shall phone on the next Monday evening between eight and nine pm. Thank you."

There was a beep and she gave her name as Sophie Boyd, and her telephone number. She hung up.

It had been a good move, using her married name. She had always written as Sophie Miller, her maiden name, and it was the name she had been referred to in all the publicity following the Littlechild case. There had been some outdated photographs of her in the newspapers in the days after Littlechild's death but that was now six weeks ago. She'd be unlucky if anyone at the club made the connection.

Besides, she had forty-eight hours before they called back – more than enough time to work on her cover story.

She made some black coffee and curled up in the pod chair with *Avenging Angel: The Life and Disappearance of Abigail Wilman.* This was as racy as Saturday nights were going to get for the new, clean-living Sophie, so she might as well get used to it. Word had gone out among the old crowd that she was to be left alone for a while. Phone calls and scheduled house calls were fine but otherwise she was to rest.

It was hard to believe that it had only been a few months ago that this place would have been heaving with people. David's death-wish snappers (always just back from Vietnam or Aden in their quest for the big picture) would have been converting the bathroom into a dark room, turning every household object into a bong and rubbing Sophie's magazine friends up the wrong way, until the two tribes were so wasted that they paired off by the end of the night. It had seemed fun at the time... but not so much now she knew that her friend Saffron Honey and David were two of those who had been doing the pairing off...

Happy sodding times, Boyd. But they're over – read the book.

Abigail's childhood and the years in France proved a slog, with the author speculating endlessly about the Paris of the era. Sophie skipped chunks but found that things picked up when Abby was expelled for attacking a fellow pupil with a milk bottle.

The next time she checked her watch, she was amazed to see that it was nearly midnight. The flat seemed eerily hushed. For the first time, the likelihood that Abby had been murdered really hit home. It was still a long time ago – 22 years – but recent enough that the killer was in all probability still alive.

Sophie looked down at the rain-glistening street. A streetlamp illuminated a man standing in the entrance to a conversion across the road. The building itself was in darkness.

A Hillman Minx passed by, a slow wave of water growling as it struck the wheel rims. Everything seemed a little sinister. Had she really recovered from the setback enough to be-.

A creak on the landing made her jump out of her skin.

Oh come on, Martha Gelhorn, you'll have to do better than this.

After checking there was no-one outside her front door, she practised yoga for half an hour to the gentle, folky sounds of Simon and Garfunkel's *Bookends*. Splitting up with David hadn't been all bad – at least she didn't have to listen to his Hendrix and Led Zeppelin or justify her total lack of interest in reading *The Tibetan Book of the Dead*. He'd always made fun of her, saying she was a hung-up chick, a pretend child of the counterculture because she didn't take drugs (apart from the occasional joint, which always made her paranoid) or like her music much heavier than Joan Baez. Maybe he was right. Fuck him: she'd always been able to *drink* him under the table and that's all that mattered to a hack.

She scooped up Keef and looked down at the street again. The man was gone and the building's downstairs lights were on. Probably the same man, indoors now. Just a neighbour.

They're not coming for you, Boyd. Give your imagination a rest and start working your journalism. Firstly, what do you say when that plummy membership guy rings? That you're a single lady looking to get into group sex? That you're a nympho? What?

An early piece of Scottie's advice came back to her – if you must come up with a cover story, keep it as close to the truth as possible. Amateurs tried to get too clever and tripped themselves up.

Did she still have the guts for all this? She was a shadow of the seventeen-year-old Sophie who'd quit secretarial college in favour of a course at the London College of Printing. The livewire Sophie who hadn't thought much of the existing student magazine and with the help of new friend Saffron Honey started a new one with the fifty quid her dad had left her in his will.

She smiled at what a little madam she had been. But what a time: the earnest late-night debates, the romantic intrigue, the excitement at getting an interview with Sir Anthony Eden, just before he succeeded Churchill as PM... The mag had folded after five issues but the heat it created was enough to enable her to bluff her way on to the *Mirror* as a copy runner, a lowly messenger. It wasn't long before her enthusiasm won her a promotion of sorts – typing up Scottie's dictation.

She escaped Scottie's clutches five years later and carved out a niche running the paper's campaigns. Whether it was saving donkey sanctuaries or exposing slum landlords, she always got a result, and as the clamour for rights and equality grew stronger in the sixties, the campaigns got bigger. After tiring of news, she switched to the features desk, and then aged 30 went freelance for a new challenge and, if she was honest, more money. The liberal in her felt guilty at quitting for cash but a string of magazine exclusives soon got her over it, including the last interview with folk legend Mary Sharpe and an undercover investigation into a religious cult.

And then there were those controversial think pieces such as *Why You Should Leave Your Husband* that so enraged the right-wing press and made Sophie the hottest magazine writer in the country – well, possibly after Saffron Honey. Saffron's success had run in parallel with Sophie's. Instead of the *Mirror*, she had worked her way up the ladder at *The Daily Mail* and then *The Sun*, before quitting to become a freelance features writer just six months after her friend had done the same. Rivals again, something that had irked Sophie and made her wonder whether it was coincidence or instead a deliberate ploy of Saffron's to ensure she could keep competing with her contemporary. After all, Saffron had always been insanely competitive, prizing a great exclusive above personal relationships, and this had caused friction on more than one occasion. Still, they remained good friends. Never best friends (that would always be Rachel) but good ones.

Life was good, and in the summer of 1968 it got even better. Sophie and Rachel went to the Isle of Wight Festival and had come back from Jefferson Airplane's headlining set to discover several of their tent pegs missing. Sophie – who was drunk – accused their neighbour of having stolen them. He said that he had but that the women had more than enough pegs to do the job anyway, whereas he'd forgotten all of his. A huge argument blew up, encompassing ownership, property, capitalism and idiots who brought tents to music festivals but no tent pegs. It ended with Sophie ripping up her tent's remaining pegs and throwing them at him, saying she hoped he got struck by lightning. A month later the sexy, impossible, wild-haired photographer had moved into her flat. Four months after that, they were married.

Now, in that same flat, the phone was ringing. Sophie grabbed it, glad to be shaken from the memories.

"Hello?"

"Miss Boyd?"

"Speaking."

"Miss *Sophie* Boyd?"

"Yes, that's me."

This had to be them – but why were they phoning a day early?

"This is Edward Venn, from The Erato Arts Club. You were enquiring about membership."

For a moment she struggled to put a sentence together. "Yes, hello. I wasn't expecting your call. I thought you said Monday. I mean, not that this is inconvenient."

"Well, I'm very glad I haven't inconvenienced you. We don't always call when we say we will. Otherwise there's a danger that people with ulterior motives will have too much time to think up... cover stories?"

"Cover stories?" she said. "You mean, the press?"

"Yeah. Snoopin' around with their long lenses. Our members expect privacy, a high level of it, and I make sure they get it."

"I'm pleased we're talking the same language, Mr Venn; I expect complete discretion." Good. That sounded like the old, confident Sophie.

"It's a pity, then, that someone told you about the club."

"Well, a friend of mine is a member."

"Who would that be?"

"I'd rather not say."

"Was it a man or a woman?'

"A woman." Sophie was inventing stuff now. Why did he care how she knew about the club? It was famous and the number was clearly displayed on its business cards. And why was she having to deal with this Cockney bully, rather than the nice RADA guy?

"Your friend is a woman?" said Venn.

"Yes."

"And this card... where did she get it?"

"It's hers. She got it when she joined." *He can't put the frighteners on me. He knows nothing about me. He can't know that the card came from Scottie.*

"She got it when she joined?"

"Yes. I'm sure of that. She told me."

"Then something doesn't add up, Miss Boyd. You see, that card you've got, it's what we call an Alarm Card. It's what we give out to people we don't want to join. Mainly it's single blokes we give 'em to. Let's say I'm out on the town and some geezer I've just met

48

starts bending my ear, *begging* me to let him in to the club. Because there are lots of pretty ladies at the club and words gets round and you know what men are like. So I fob him off with the Alarm Card and when he calls up the next day on that phone line, we know that whoever's on the other end is an undesirable, and we politely tell 'em where to go. So I get curious when a young lady phones up on this number. And I don't like mysteries. So why don't you tell me how you *really* got hold of it?"

Sophie's palm was clammy around the receiver. She was used to posing the hard questions, not facing them. "Look, Mr Venn... Okay, you've got me. What happened was that I went to a party and this guy told me about the club and what he got up to there. He was trying to impress me, I guess. He gave me the card. Now I see that he had one of these Alarm Cards. He's probably never set foot in the Erato. I'm sorry I... I'm sorry I lied to you."

A very long silence followed, with Venn letting her hang there as he took a draw on a cigarette. "So what have you heard about us?"

"That there's a lot of fucking."

To her relief, he gave a genuine rather than a mocking laugh.

"We're an arts club, Miss Boyd."

"Yes, of course."

"Have you got a pen?"

"Yes."

"Come to the New Regency Hotel, 105 Hereford Road in Bayswater at ten o'clock tomorrow night. Tell the geezer on the door you have an appointment with Venn. Got that?"

"Ten o'clock, 105 Hereford Road. Mr Venn."

"It's just Venn. There used to be a Tommy Venn. A rival of mine, in fact. Well, we couldn't both be called

Venn and me being the junior man I lost out. So I was Eddie. But now I'm Venn. The only Venn."

"So what's your rival called?"

"He's not called anything any more. Good night, Miss Boyd."

And he hung up on her.

CHAPTER SIX

The next night, Sophie took a cab to Bayswater. Her heels seemed to resound the length of the street as she walked up to the white-fronted New Regency Hotel.

A thick-set Arab stood in the open doorway, smoking and barking to someone inside the building. At Sophie's approach, he ran his eyes up and down her Zandra Rhodes print dress, and nodded approvingly. She should have been pleased that her undercover guise was already passing muster, but his attentions just made her more nervous. What the hell was she getting into?

"I have a ten o'clock appointment with Venn."

The man flicked his cigarette past her on to the path and with a jerk of the head ushered her into a shabby foyer crowded with crates of whiskey and champagne and rails of fur coats. The man made some strange tutting/whistling noise, as if displeased by Sophie's interest in the merchandise.

"Follow, please," he said.

He led the way up the staircase's thinning carpet, past a gallery of cheap prints: a Mediterranean seascape, movie star portraits and a boy riding a horse along a shore.

Sophie was relieved she had given Scottie the New Regency's address because alarm bells were ringing – this dive didn't seem the kind of place someone like Summers would be seen dead in.

The doorman led her into a crowded bar, which on first impressions seemed to be hosting some exotic fashion show, with the models mingling among the patrons, who were mostly Arab men.

She was shown to a secluded table while her escort went to fetch her a G&T. It took all of a few seconds of observing the women flirting and caressing to reach the conclusion that this place was a brothel. There was

51

something for every taste – Nazi uniforms and caps, Chinese silk robes and cone-shaped bras, Moulin Rouge showgirls, simple cotton T-shirts and bikini panties, good old-fashioned stockings and suspenders, even a white cotton afternoon dress and bonnet for those with a *My Fair Lady* fetish... Sophie didn't know whether to run or laugh.

Jesus, am I about to be sold into the white slave trade?

She ran through the cover story again: that she was a freelance copywriter but occasionally wrote articles for the medical press (this was what Rachel did, and although Sophie hadn't told her about the Erato yet, she would confide in her if it became necessary to flesh out the cover story).

The doorman returned with her gin and tonic. As soon as he'd turned his back, Sophie took a big gulp.

It was then that she noticed the woman.

Although the bar was packed, she had a sofa to herself. No-one even stood near her, as if they were deliberately giving her space. She had black, feathered hair, olive skin, sparkling blue eyes and fabulous beestung lips. She smoked and scowled and generally gave the appearance that acid ran through her veins but Sophie couldn't take her eyes off her, she was a genuine beauty.

Even so, there was something not entirely right with her face – some kind of disfigurement, perhaps – but it was on the side that was turned from Sophie.

Into the woman's space ventured a man, some silver-haired chancer who ran a hand down the front of her silk, bias-cut gown and gestured to the red door. The next instant he was staring down at his white jacket, and the glass of wine that now covered it.

The woman leapt to her feet and let rip a volley of abuse in Spanish. The jilted punter's friends surged forward as if to attack but stopped when they saw who they'd taken sides against. The wine-stain man was shouting in some language Sophie didn't recognise and stabbing his finger in accusation but he, too, kept his distance.

The rest of the room just watched as the stand-off continued. And then the red door was flung open and everyone fell silent.

A mid-thirtyish man with a sandy-coloured crewcut stepped into the bar. Deep-set eyes slowly took in the scene. Sophie recognised the same mad stare from psychos she'd encountered when working the crime desk with Scottie. The man couldn't have been taller than five eight but there was something about his composure – and the way his broad shoulders filled out a Blades-tailored, dark blue suit – drew a portrait of power. The Spanish woman appeared to recoil, as if he could cause her violence from where he stood.

And then he headed for her, fast. Sophie expected some protest from the woman but she allowed herself to be hauled away towards the exit. As the pair passed by, the woman caught Sophie trying to make out that imperfection on her face, and snapped her head to one side to show off a scar that trailed from the left-hand side of her mouth to her ear. Evenly spaced along its length were a series of puncture marks.

And then, with a bestial hiss just for Sophie, the woman was gone.

A wave of nervous laughter restored the bar to normality. Sophie was still wondering what the hell she had just witnessed – and what could have caused that scar – when the crewcut was suddenly in front of her.

"Sophie," he said. "I'm Venn. Nice to meet you. Apologies for the amateur dramatics. Ana's very beautiful – but very Spanish. Follow me, please."

As they crossed to the door, a platinum blonde in a sequinned dress fell in with them.

"Hi," she said, in a dreamlike voice. "I'm Amber."

"Sophie."

"Hi, Sophie. I've always loved that name. I think we're going to be really good friends." Her eyes were glassy and as round as cartwheels.

The door opened on to what appeared to be a shabby hotel corridor. Only one lightbulb was working and most of the doors had lost their numbers, leaving ghostly outlines.

"My mate Ali owns the place," said Venn. "I sold it to him in sixty-four. The lazy A-rab's let it go to seed but he still lets me use it as and when."

He led the way, making a left and then a right through a rabbit warren of murky passages. Fire doors were padlocked shut and the walls leaned in at worrying angles. Sophie glanced behind her and caught Amber smiling vacantly.

The trio reached a dead end.

"Shit," said Venn. He turned on his heels and pointed back the way they'd come. "Get lost in here myself."

More turns brought them to an arch knocked through a wall. Plaster and brick hung loose around the edges.

"Mind your clothes," said Venn, taking Sophie's hand as they crossed a series of wooden boards into another hotel corridor. To Sophie's relief, this one was brightly lit and adorned with a smart, navy blue carpet.

"Ali's just bought this place an' all," said Venn. "He hasn't got round to knocking them together proper." After another short walk, Venn unlocked a door and they entered a large, modern hotel suite with its own bar. "But he *has* finished customising a couple of rooms..."

Amber drew the curtains. There were curtains on the opposite wall, too, but those were already shut. Even though Sophie was disorientated, she was sure that wasn't an exterior wall.

Of more concern was the bed that dominated the room. It was a king size... plus at least a half again.

"Super, super king size," said Amber, bouncing up and down on it.

"Cost a fortune, they do, then some wanker always breaks 'em," said Venn. He had his arm stuck into the ice-box.

Amber patted the bed. "Come here, Sophie. Stay close, like a school trip. We can hold hands when the show begins."

"Show?"

Amber winked and put a finger to her lips. Sophie sat beside her.

"What do you fancy, Sophie?" said Venn. "Someone's had a stock-up."

"Cocktails!" said Amber.

"It ain't stocked with miracles," said Venn, removing his jacket. "There's red and white and bubbly or I can do you a rum and something."

"Surprise me with the rum," said Sophie. "I'm sure you're very creative." Did that sound flirty? It was meant to. Why was she so crap at flirting?

"Rum surprise, comin' up. We'll all have one."

"So Sophie, what do you know about the club?" said Amber.

"That it's the place to come for a good time."

"A good time, eh?" said Venn. "Someone's been pulling your leg. We're an arts club. We just sit around reading."

Amber sniggered.

Sophie said: "That's a shame. Because I wanted the ultimate. And forgive me for saying, but you don't strike me as a man of the arts."

"Maybe not," said Venn. "But I'm full of other surprises."

"The kind of surprises the existing membership like?"

Venn gave Sophie a look that made her look away. The thought popped into her head: *this man has killed people.*

"Not always," said Venn. "But they can't do much about it."

"And why's that?"

"Let's just say it's in my interest to make the club run smooth. That's why I take security so personal. I do all the screening myself. We don't like it when people go round blabbing about the club. But it does go on. The screening protects us from *too much* gossip, and from stuff we don't want to read about over breakfast."

"Screening?"

"Yeah. That's why you're here tonight."

"I thought this was a membership interview."

Venn brought over the drinks. "Same thing. Here, you two get your laughing gear round that. Cheers."

The three of them clinked glasses and Sophie took a sip of the rum surprise. It tasted pretty good.

Amber was pulling a sad face at Venn. He reached into a pocket and threw her something that she caught before doing a backwards roll off the bed.

"If I don't think someone is right for membership at this stage, it's best they haven't seen the club at Mayfair," said Venn. "That's why I do the screening here. Not all our members are spring chickens but they're good looking and they keep themselves in shape. No fatties, no pigs. We don't do equality at the Erato, we're not politicians. Anyway, looks aren't going to be a problem in your case."

Amber started chopping up coke at the bar. The drug was unknown in Sophie's circle and she'd encountered it only once – while trailing a Hollywood actress around London for a big interview. As stars went, she'd been down to earth and likeable, but one night her coterie brought out the powder and she'd turned into a shrieking monster.

Venn looked at his bracelet watch and opened the curtains to reveal a two-way mirror. Beyond it was an identical room with an identical bed. Bustling around were two couples: two white women in their late twenties, and two Arab men Sophie recognised from the bar. One was about her age and the other was maybe late forties. It looked like they'd just arrived: the women were still slipping out of mink coats and fixing their make-up in silver compacts. The men were shouting at each other and spinning shot glasses over their heads to catch behind their backs. Their voices were just murmurs.

The walls must be soundproofed, thought Sophie.

Venn drew the curtains again.

"They've usually got going by ten. So tell me what you do, Sophie," he said. "Are you married?"

"Separated. The divorce is going through."

"Yeah? Sorry to hear it. Job?"

"Freelance writer. Mostly ad copy, but I do the occasional legit article for the medical press. That's just a sideline."

"Sounds like you're a frustrated hack. Never fancied Fleet Street?"

"You've got to be really hungry for that. I wouldn't appreciate being called out at three in the morning to doorstep some poor sod who's lost his wife. And besides, I need my beauty sleep."

Need your beauty sleep? This guy wants wild nymphos, not the Queen Mother. Play the part.

"So you're a journalist?" said Venn. "Is that why you're here – to write a story on us? Because the screening would make that very difficult for you."

What the hell was this screening he kept on about?

"Yes, I understand," she said.

"I'll be honest with you, Sophie. Most of our members are very powerful or very famous or just plain very rich. A lot of business gets done at the club, which is why privacy is so important. Now, you're clearly not rich or famous and you haven't been introduced by an existing member. Normally that would rule you out but there is sometimes one exception. Amber, tell Sophie what the exception is."

"If we think you're fuckable," said Amber, who was back on the bed. She kissed Sophie on the nape of the neck. Then she sniffed loudly and pinched her septum.

"Where's mine, then?" said Venn.

"On the bar, Major Tom."

Venn went to snort his lines. Sophie was surprised by his indiscretion. Did he trust her already, or did he just not care?

"Fancy a toot, Sophie?" he called.

"No thanks," she said. "Not my bag." *Enough with the Queen Mother.*

Still sitting behind her, Amber put her arms around Sophie's waist, hooked her legs under hers. "Is *this* your bag, babe?"

She ran her hands over Sophie's breasts, peppered her neck with tiny kisses. Sophie closed her eyes and tried to go with what was happening. She just hoped she wasn't expected to go much further or she'd be too compromised to write so much as a paragraph, let alone an exposé.

But then Venn said: "And now on BBC1," and whipped open the curtains again.

"Plastic fantastic!" squealed Amber.

Afterwards, Sophie could not remember how long she had watched. It could have been a few minutes, could have been half an hour. But what she couldn't forget was that she had been mesmerised; shocked and thrilled at the same time.

"Is this something to do with the club?" she said at last.

"No," said Venn. "This is just some geezers with a couple of tarts." He gestured as if about to rap on the mirror.

"Venn, no!" hissed Amber.

"I wasn't going to, woman. Beats the test card, dunnit?"

Amber pulled him to the bed by his belt. He slid his hand into her dress and roughly caressed a breast as he kissed her. Amber tugged at his shirt so hard that the top button flew off.

"For fuck's sake," said Venn, and shoved her back on to the bed. He opened a bedside cabinet and removed a Polaroid camera. "We didn't used to have to do this, but the gutter press are getting more desperate to poke around at the Erato." Seeing Sophie's worried look, he added: "Is this a problem?"

"It's just not what I expected."

"There's nothing to worry about unless you're out to cause mischief. These pictures stay in my safe. I'm not interested in blackmail, Sophie. I've got nightclubs, gaming clubs, restaurants, snooker halls, demolition firms, all working for Eddie Venn. Do you think I'd risk a ten stretch to blackmail a few quid out of a writer, no offence?"

"No. I guess you wouldn't. But like you say, you're full of surprises."

"Well, believe me, I don't do *this*" – he gestured to the swarm of bodies beyond the mirror – "for anything more than the buzz." He drummed his fingers on the camera. "We don't have to go through with this – you can leave now. Some people do."

Amber pulled her sad clown face.

"It's okay," said Sophie. "I want in."

"The club's held together by trust, Sophie," said Amber. "We're all guilty together."

Amber leaned in to Sophie and they kissed. The camera bulb flashed and popped.

"My little movie stars," said Venn. Out of the corner of her eye, Sophie saw him waving the photo to dry it. Again, she felt the need to flee. She had been kidding herself if she thought she could go along with this. Even if she got some story out of it, she would never dare offer it for publication – Venn would simply post the pics to everyone in the industry and ruin her.

Amber untied Sophie's belt and pushed the dress from her shoulders.

"Watch them," said Amber.

And Sophie watched. She watched the mirror show and let Amber kiss her neck. If she wanted to get into this club, she told herself, she had no choice.

"Ladies," said Venn.

Amber gently but firmly pushed Sophie away and got to her feet.

Venn was popping the camera back into the cabinet. Three photos dried between his fingers.

"Was that the screening?" said Sophie, rearranging her clothing.

"Yeah. That qualifies you for a look round the place. If we like you, you'll be invited to join. It's five hundred quid for the year. We're open seven days a week. If you need a lift, phone this number for one of the cars." He passed her a card. "Try to give a couple of hours' notice."

He opened the door and stood there, waiting for Sophie as she fumbled with her belt.

"Mr Venn, Mr Venn, one moment, please," called a man in the corridor.

"Yusef, you done that job yet?" said Venn.

A tiny man wearing huge milk-bottle specs had appeared in the doorway. He unfolded a piece of cloth in his hand for Venn to inspect something. "I've been looking for you all evening. These are the stones."

"Handsome. Have 'em set like we discussed."

"They'll be ready tomorrow lunchtime."

"Good. When it's done, give it to Ali. He's coming to the club tomorrow – he can give 'em to me then."

Sophie tried to sneak a look at what was in Yusef's hand – did stones always mean diamonds? – but in a flurry of thank yous, he scampered away. A few moments later, the screening trio retraced their steps to the bar, where Venn gave a curt goodbye and disappeared into another room.

Amber giggled. "Well done, Sophie. We're going to be the best of friends. I just know it."

Sophie was about to try to engage her in conversation – she wanted to find out more about Venn's "stones" and get a handle on what other stuff he might be in to – but Amber blew a kiss and ran off.

Sophie stood alone in the middle of the bar, feeling foolish and used. No wonder Venn hadn't cared that she'd seen him doing coke – he knew that after the screening she'd be putty in his hands. He'd probably suspected her since she'd phoned up using the "Alarm Card". It looked as if he was going to play a game, keep her close, see what she was up to. He wasn't stupid. But maybe she was.

Sophie hurried to the exit, desperate not to be in this place a minute longer.

***

CHAPTER SEVEN

As the taxi pulled up to Sophie's building, she was already pressing a banknote on the driver. She would die if she didn't speak to Scottie within the next sixty seconds.

The ride home had been a torture: endless prattle from the cabbie when all she'd wanted to do was re-play the evening: "Ana" – the woman with the scar – and the foursome and the diamonds and what she should tell Scottie about her and Amber. Had she kind of enjoyed the thrill of that world? Had she just made some terrible mistake that would ruin her?

As she entered the downstairs hallway, she heard her phone ringing. Damn Scottie. He couldn't just wait for her to call – he had to be the centre of attention. Sophie burst into the flat and skidded to the phone.

"I didn't go!" she screamed into the handset. "I had to see *The Golden Shot* in colour and I missed the whole bloody thing!"

In a broken voice, a woman said: "Is that... Sophie Boyd?"

"Oh shit." Sophie cleared her throat. "Yes, yes, this is Sophie Boyd."

"I'm sorry to call you at this hour, but... I have some bad news."

"Who is this?"

"I'm Eileen Williams. We haven't met. I'm Ralph Scott's sister."

Scottie. Sophie felt sick. "What's happened?"

"Oh God, Sophie, there's been an accident. I don't really know why I'm calling you but he spoke of you the other day and I found your number in his address book."

"Eileen, what's happened?"

"We don't know. It doesn't make sense. I spoke to him just two days ago and he seemed happy. This new writing project. He wouldn't tell me anything about it but he was happy for the first time in ages."

"What's happened to Ralph?"

"The police called me. His neighbours went out to the front. Ralph fell from his window. He's dead, Sophie. Ralph is dead."

***

CHAPTER EIGHT

The mourners emerged from St Bride's into a churchyard swirling with snowflakes.

Eileen held tightly to Sophie's arm as the pair left the "journalists' church" for the bustle of Fleet Street. Eileen was a good ten years older than Scottie and afflicted by all manner of ailments that Sophie didn't dare ask about. At several points during the service, she had seemed on the verge of fainting.

Half an hour after Eileen's devastating phone call, the police had paid Sophie a visit. She'd had just enough time to change out of her "screening" outfit and shove all the Abigail Wilman books into a cupboard before they arrived.

She denied knowing anything about Scottie's new writing project. She guessed she'd be in the clear – at first, anyway – as it didn't sound as if Eileen knew much about it. Playing dumb was a big risk but there was no reason Scottie would have written Sophie's name down in any of his notes on Abigail. And if he'd been murdered by a jilted lover or burglar, it wouldn't matter.

Keep kidding yourself. Of course it matters. You've lied to the police and hampered a murder investigation.

The fuzz had fired questions at her. They wanted to know why Scottie had come to see her in Chichester but it had been easy to persuade them it was because they had once been close friends and he'd heard about her suicide attempt.

Sophie couldn't picture Scottie holding out under torture – he was the biggest coward she'd ever met. That meant he'd either told his killers what they wanted to know, or his heart had given out before he could. Either way, someone had thrown him headfirst out of his window.

"Ralph walked his own path," said his brother Ted, as a slide projector beamed an image of Scottie dressed as a tart.

Sophie had never seen Ted before – Scottie had rarely talked of "the black sheep of the family", so labelled for having got married. What had family man Ted made of his deviant brother?

Sophie looked around at the other mourners – a motley collection of jowelly men, vampish women (had Scottie swung both ways?), ageing queens and familiar faces from the *Mirror*.

It was hot in here and Sophie wanted to get out. She might have tricked Eileen and the boys in blue but there would be questions from people here, too.

"Even as an eight-year-old, Ralph was a precocious talent," said Ted, as the next slide showed an impossibly young Scottie sitting at a typewriter, an image that was greeted with fond laughter.

After the eulogy, Sophie stayed with Eileen as the guests queued to pay their respects. When there was a break, Eileen leaned in to Sophie and said: "I know you must be tired of me asking this, but I think it's important… Are you sure that Ralph said nothing about having worries? Money worries, maybe, or a feud, or, you know, difficulty with a man? It can be a violent world, that world…"

"I've racked my brains, Eileen. He just seemed very happy."

"And this book he was writing?"

"He was writing a book? He didn't mention it to me."

"He was very secretive about it. But it had lifted his spirits – he was very upset when those vile people at the *Mirror* took away his title. I wondered if it was the thing with the title that tipped him over."

"I wouldn't like to guess. We'd only met a couple of times recently and mostly we talked of the old days. He seemed as happy as he ever got. Tell me what the neighbour said again."

"The man downstairs said Ralph had been playing classical music loudly all evening," said Eileen. "Then at about ten there had been some thumping and what he thought were shouts. But this chap says Ralph was always shouting to himself or if a cat jumped in or... at whoever he was with at the time. He had a lot of arguments with his men friends, I understand. And then the music went up very loud and the shouting got louder and then it stopped with this terrible crash..."

To Sophie's relief, a barrel-chested man was hovering next to Eileen, waiting for an audience. Eileen smiled at him, but then whispered to Sophie: "I've decided I owe it to Ralph to take another look through his things tomorrow. The police and I only had the briefest look through all those papers. They seem happy to write it off as some homosexual thing, some pick-up gone wrong. But I'll never have peace of mind if I can't rule out it was anything more suspicious."

Sophie gave a sympathetic smile. This was where she was supposed to offer to help with the search, but there was no way she could become Eileen's buddy. Her job was to put Eileen off the scent.

In the ladies, Sophie splashed water on her face. She needed a plan.

Maybe she should simply tell Eileen and the police the truth. *Hey guys: I lied. What really happened was that Scottie said there might be a link between a sex club and the disappearance of Abigail Wilman and so I popped along and did some mildly lezzer stuff while a gangster took pictures, okay?*

No, there was no going back. She had to keep quiet about her role as Scottie's assistant. Cover it up, even. If someone connected to Hugo Summers or the Erato

Club *had* murdered Abigail and Scottie, they wouldn't stop at two corpses.

What was it Eileen said? *I owe it to Ralph to take another look through his things tomorrow. The police and I only had the briefest look through all those papers.*

Sophie paced back and forth in the tiny space. Snow frosted the windows.

Keep your notes somewhere safe, Scottie had told her. That implied he had done the same. She had to search his place, and fast.

Back at the wake, Sophie discreetly claimed her coat and bag and slipped away without saying anything to Eileen. What excuse could possibly have sounded plausible?

She wasn't thinking straight, couldn't remember where she had left her car, and soon she was lost in the maze of streets between Fleet Street and the river. Every time she tried to piece her thoughts together, all she could picture were Venn's henchmen pushing Scottie to his death, at the same time as their boss was "screening" the dead man's accomplice. And the chances were, Venn hadn't even realised that's what she was. Hadn't made the connection.

Fuck Venn. He was clever – his screening had already worked and he didn't know it. She couldn't go to the police. Couldn't go to anyone.

She'd blackmailed herself.

***

CHAPTER NINE

Half an hour later, Sophie's '58 Roadster was crawling along Scottie's road in Kilburn.

As she drew close to the house number, she noticed a parked panda car. In the street, a uniformed police officer was talking to a man in plain clothes. Sophie drove on. Her only hope was that those boys were finishing their crime scene investigation and might be gone the next day – before Eileen showed up.

Back home, Sophie took the phone off the hook, drank a large Scotch and went to bed. The next thing she knew, it was 10am. She dressed quickly and drove back to Kilburn, where she parked in the street next to Scottie's. When Sophie had last known Scottie, he had lived beyond his means in a huge flat in Belgravia, so she was saddened to find that number 55 was a flaking building with an upended sofa by the dustbins.

"Oh, Scottie..."

She tied her hair back in a scarf, slipped on her Jackie O sunglasses and turned up the collar of her Afghan coat. Now if anyone glimpsed her poking around, they wouldn't be able to describe her very well. She looked up and down the street and was relieved not to see any marked police cars.

After a struggle to open the warped front door, Sophie entered a dark hallway. There were two letters for Scottie on the mat but both appeared to be from banks and she left them where they were.

The two remaining keys that he had given her were marked number 12. Stealthily, she made her way to the first floor. The building was split into tiny flats, each fronted by a plywood door with a padlock. From behind them came a cacophany of clashing sounds: television, a budgerigar having a fit, two men talking loudly in French.

She climbed to the second floor and took a careful look both ways along the corridor. No sign or sound of the boys in blue. She crept down the passage. None of the doors was numbered – except for Scottie's. His number 12 was announced with stick-on gold letters, sitting amidst some fancy crest.

A piece of paper plastered over the door read: "METROPOLITAN POLICE CRIME SCENE. DO NOT CROSS."

With one rip it was gone. To her relief, the second key fitted the padlock and she entered the final home of Ralph Douglas Scott.

The room was only slightly bigger than her own bedroom, but this had been his whole life. There was a sink, a bed, a tiny wardrobe and a stack of exotic spirit bottles lined up on a shelf. Every other square inch was packed with documents, newspapers and books.

Now, where to start looking. The desk? The bookshelf? Those tower blocks of paper?

No. Scottie was sharp. If he said it was well hidden, he meant it.

There was no way she could search that lot. And surely she didn't need to – by the sloppy arrangement of the piles, it looked like the police had already done that. If Sophie's name had cropped up in that lot, she'd have known about it by now.

There was a row of box files on the desk. She opened each one and was soon satisfied they contained nothing more interesting than bank correspondence, cuttings of Scottie's own stories and some letters begging people for money. Next she went through the desk drawers but again there was nothing relating to the Abigail story. She removed the drawers and searched under each one.

Yeah, like the murder squad wouldn't have looked under there.

Perhaps the police *had* found the notes and her name simply hadn't been in them.

Scottie had always been very paranoid about people stealing his work. There had been that time at the *Mirror* when he thought he was going to get the sack and he'd hidden his notes (on a nutter who kept following Prince Charles) so the newsdesk couldn't pinch his exclusive.

Sophie smiled at the memory. Only Scottie would have thought to hide his notes in...

She leapt to her feet and grabbed one of the spirit bottles on the bookshelf. Empty. She grabbed two more. One was a cheap brand of vodka and was a third full. The other was a black plastic bottle containing some exotic liqueur.

She just knew that was the one.

And there was the proof: the telltale line around the middle, where he had sliced through it. Her hands shook as she pulled apart the same contraption she'd seen him make fifteen years earlier. Glued into the base were three spirits miniatures, each full of liquid to add a convincing weight and sound.

Scottie, you genius.

Packed into the top section was a thick wad of paper, which Sophie was about to remove when she heard a woman in the street say: "He was such a hoarder. Who knows what's buried up there?"

Eileen.

Sophie peeked through a gap in the curtains and saw Scottie's sister being helped out of a car by a man from the funeral.

Shit. Great timing, Miss Marple.

She snapped the top back on to the bottle and made for the door. Was there any route out of here other than the way she'd come in?

Back on the landing she eased the door shut and refastened the padlock. Eileen and the man were entering the ground-floor hallway. They were deep in conversation: something about checking for post. Good. They could study those bank letters.

All Sophie had to do was go up a floor and wait for the visitors to enter Scottie's flat and then she could-.

Shit. There *was* no third floor.

There were two doors opposite Scottie's. An idea – knock on both and see who answered. She could bluff some story – that she was a friend of Ralph Scott's, could she come in and have a word?

Sophie rapped on both doors at the same time. Probably a mistake – if both opened at the same time it could kick off a three-way conversation on the landing when all she wanted was some sanctuary.

Maybe she could just breeze past – Eileen probably wouldn't recognise her in her headscarf and sunglasses. But if she did...

Eileen was saying: "I feel guilty taking you up on your offer to help but if there's some clue we're missing..."

Sophie waited. And waited. No-one was going to open their door. Great. She'd picked the only two households in the building to have jobs. She flipped her sunglasses on and adjusted her headscarf. She was going to have to make her charge.

Eileen appeared at the top of the stairs. She stopped to catch her breath. Peered towards Scottie's flat. Saw someone lurking in the shadows. Someone with a strange bottle tucked under their arm.

"Hello there," said Eileen.

Sophie kept quiet.

Shit. Shit. Shit.

Eileen started moving down the corridor.

She'd have to be blind not to see me now.

Sophie hammered on the doors again, hoping she could keep her back turned and just ignore Eileen. And then she noticed that only the door on the right had a padlock. Something Scottie had said came back

71

to her: *These days I have to share a water closet on a landing with other people.*

She threw open the door on the left and stepped into a tiny, filthy toilet and thought nowhere had ever looked so sweet.

CHAPTER TEN

For the next week, she threw herself into work and completed two articles – *Connery Or Caine?* and *So, Did The Pill Change Our Lives?* – and got out of the flat as much as possible, lunching with friends she hadn't seen while she was in hospital, and getting drunk with Rachel in the evenings. Sophie was still shaken up about Scottie and needed to talk about it, but was careful not to reveal anything about Summers or the Erato.

She had decided to drop the story altogether, bury it. It was preposterous to think Scottie's death had anything to do with Summers, and even more preposterous to think she could link someone as powerful as him to Abigail's disappearance.

And then the unexpected happened.

On Saturday morning, eight days after the funeral, Sophie awoke with one neon-bright thought burning in her mind: *I am going to the Erato tonight.*

She had to. To abandon the story now would be to abandon Scottie.

Sophie showered and drove to Mayfair. The Erato was in Arcadian Gardens, between Hay's Mews and Hill Street, and was flanked by an upmarket antiques dealer's and an antiquarian bookshop. The club's ground floor was taken up by a restaurant, Arcadia, that was preparing for lunch.

It was a bright day but Arcadian Gardens' stately buildings blocked out the sun, creating a chill that seemed in keeping with the club's three storeys of Portland stone. Sophie felt the suspicious gaze of the doorman as she tried to squint into the lobby, and was relieved to get back to Piccadilly. The Erato was as formidable as she had feared but that just made her want to get in there.

Back home, the afternoon passed at a daunting speed but she kept her resolve: she was going.

At 8.30pm, she called the club and requested a car. At 10.30pm, half an hour before it was due, she was pacing her living room and taking large gulps of a G&T. A final look in the mirror gave her a lift – there were no two ways about it, she was looking sexy. It's amazing what a backless, white Paco Rabanne dress could do for you... Had she gone too far? Would she be ravaged as soon as she walked in to the place? And how easy would it be to avoid any more sexual come-ons?

The clock had raced round to 10.55pm. Five minutes until her lift arrived. She shut her eyes, tried to meditate; failed.

The Abby biog on the table had fallen open at the photo section. A picture of Abby Wilman with her Resistance comrades gave her a boost of courage. The caption read: "Saint-Lô, 1944." A handsome young man stood behind Abby, a Sten Gun strapped across his chest. This was Charles Le Harivel. He and Abby had briefly been lovers. Charles had been married, although no-one in his circuit had known this. Not even Abby, who had only found out the truth at his funeral.

Sophie placed the book, her Abigail notes and the notes she'd uncovered at Scottie's flat into a large box file, which she hid in a cardboard box full of Christmas decorations in her wardrobe. Once she'd covered the file with a layer of tinsel and baubles, Sophie positioned the box at a certain angle – if anyone moved it so much as an inch, she'd know.

The doorbell blasted the silence. With trembling hands she put on her Persian lamb coat, picked up her bag and left the flat.

A uniformed chauffeur held open the back door of a Black Bentley T with tinted passenger windows. Just as she was thinking that she could use the drive to hone her false identity, she saw Venn, dapper in a camel-hair coat, sitting on the rear-facing seat. Amber reclined in the corner, a coke-frosted mirror on her lap. Her black, pure silk evening gown was in disarray, as if Venn had already been pawing her.

"Look at her," said Venn. "The queen of Notting Hill."

"Princess," said Amber. "She's a princess, not a queen."

"Princess, queen, she knows what I mean."

Sophie issued some confident greetings and eased herself into the velour interior, at which point a champagne cork popped and ricocheted off the windows. Venn poured for all of them.

"Get this down your throats," he said. "Here's to Sophie's first night at the Erato."

"Sophie's first night!" said Amber.

As they clinked glasses, Venn tapped Sophie's wedding ring.

"So where does hubbie think you are tonight – bingo?"

"Like I said at the screening, I'm separated."

"Oh yeah, so you did. Sad when that happens."

Sophie wanted to tell him to mind his own business but she kept her cool.

Amber placed a hand on Sophie's thigh. "Are you excited about tonight?"

"Abso-fucking-lutely," said Sophie, feeling a rush at her own bravado. Thank God for G&Ts.

"Steady, girls," said Venn. "I've just had the upholstery cleaned." He laughed so violently at his own joke that he spilt champagne on his lap. "Oh shit, I've pissed myself."

"You're a real dope, Venn," said Amber.

Venn raised the back of his hand and Amber flinched.

"Enough lip," he said.

"Oh, keep your face on, *Jase-on*," she said, before snorting a line of coke with a little gold tube. She offered it to Sophie, who shook her head.

"Our Sophie's a nice girl, don't go offering her the nose-up," said Venn.

Sophie nearly took the bait but again stopped herself. Why was he so keen to rile her?

"Hey, Sophs, you see that building in the dark over there, with that little row of lights at the top?" said Venn. "That was the King's Valet cigarette factory. My dad worked there for thirty-eight years. I'd go out and meet him sometimes. His body was beaten at the end of the shift. His face lit up when he saw me but each day he died a little bit. Work wore him down, you know? He knew a poem for every occasion: sonnets, Kipling, Wordsworth, the lot. And he could carve you anything out of a piece of wood. He made all my toys. He and mum lived in council houses their whole lives. He died at fifty-nine. Lung cancer. All them free fags. He had dignity and he always kept his nose clean. He thought that would be enough in life. It was the one thing he got wrong.

"Now look at this place on the right, where the kids are queuing. What's it called now? The Trip. God 'elp us, it was Rio's when I bought it. My first club. I was twenty-four. And now I hang out at the Erato. I'm sure the Erato won't seem much to you – you've been brought up on art galleries and hobnobbing, right? But every time I walk into the building, it's a palace to my eyes."

"Please don't assume you know the first thing about me," said Sophie. There. She'd bitten. *You idiot.*

Venn pulled an expression of mock amazement. "Don't tell me your old man worked at King's Valet, too?"

"My father was head waiter at a hotel in our town. When he left us, mum brought up me and my brother pretty much on her own, with what she made in a shop. Now, we can play working-class heroes all the way to the club, or you can just shut up and pour some more champagne."

Amber burst into shrill laughter and Venn held up his hands in surrender.

"She's got me bang to rights!"

After freshening drinks, he said: "Okay, club rules: respect other members. If someone comes on to you and you're not up for it, just say no thanks. Courtesy's paramount – anyone being abusive is given a warning. Next time they misbehave, they're out, and we don't do refunds. It don't matter how rich, how famous – if they act like a wanker, they're out.

"Next: guests. We don't have any. It's members only. Drugs: policy is none allowed. Of course, if you do come across them, I'm sure you'll be discreet. We police ourselves. Talking of which, those Polaroids from the other night – and very nice they are, too, I might add – remain with us, or should I say, *me*. We didn't used to have to be so careful. But since my relationship with the Erato has grown, the gutter press have become much more interested in what goes on at the club. Which is why trust is so important. Members trust us, and we trust the members."

Venn put a hand on Sophie's thigh. She tensed, and the hand slid away.

Stupid. Stupid. What kind of sexual adventurer are you trying to play – the frigid type?

Venn opened the partition to address the driver. "Ronald, I think we're being chased by Russian agents. Step on it, will you?"

"Yes, Mr Venn."

"I hate it when he does this," said Amber, as the Bentley surged forwards. Suddenly all three of them

77

were rolling around in the back, with Venn laughing maniacally as the car sped along a Mayfair backstreet. Sophie clamped her palms to the edge of the seat and just as she thought she was going to be sick the driver braked sharply and eased the Bentley into an underground car park.

"I think you lost 'em, Sir Ron," said Venn.

"Yes, sir."

"Do you know how many cars you've got through playing these stupid games?" said Amber.

"You sound like my accountant," said Venn. "Right, we're there."

The Bentley pulled into a space and Venn led the way to a small doorway, which was opened for them by a stocky man in a dinner jacket. They entered a low-ceilinged tunnel.

"We're in Hill Street," said Venn. "This tunnel takes us under the road to Arcadian Gardens. The passage was built at the same time as the clubhouse. Gave the first owner's guests a discreet way in. And out, of course."

"He had gazillions of mistresses," said Amber.

"Yeah, old Bill Raven couldn't keep it in his trousers. I've got plans for a nuclear bunker down here. That missile business in Cuba shit me right up, I tell you."

Upon reaching a small lobby, Venn wrenched open an elevator's mesh doors and Sophie and Amber got in.

"Halten sie!" barked a man's voice in a mock German accent.

A middle-aged couple were entering the lobby. The man was fiftyish and well maintained, even if the tight white trousers and deep tan smacked of the oldest swinger in town. The woman was starved nearly to the point of anorexia, the little flesh on her face stretched back in a vicious facelift.

"Jerry! Pippa!" called Venn. "How was the Cap Whatsit…?"

"Cap Ferat," said Jerry. "Bloody marvellous. Pippa's brother's just bought this new cruiser and he took us all along the coast."

"You flash bastard! I wouldn't mind a bit of sun right now − it's 'taters out." He hit a button and the lift jerked to life.

"Jerry, Pippa, this is Sophie. It's her first night."

"Sophie, hi," said Jerry, shaking her hand. "Pleased to have you on board."

"It should be a good night," said Venn. "The ballroom's heaving."

The lift passed a ground-floor lobby and Sophie glimpsed the front doors she'd peeked through earlier that day.

On the first floor, their group of five stepped into a wide marble lobby that resounded with the sounds of a riotous party nearby. Adrenaline pumped through Sophie. She felt that she was on the threshold of some fantastic, forbidden place that was going to change her life. Back in the chase again.

Amber grabbed her hand and they entered a grand hallway overlooked by a mezzanine gallery. Venn's arrival sent a frisson through the clusters of people lounging on leather couches.

Sophie craned her neck to admire the high, gilded ceiling with its mythical beast friezes but Amber was dragging her towards the music.

"Let's go to the ballroom," said Amber. "I want to dance."

"Hold on to your hats," said Venn. "It's Saturday night at the Erato."

And then Sophie was thrust into a room with a great coffered ceiling decorated with painted panels and which was so tightly packed that she didn't see how they could ever set foot in there. Against one wall, a four-piece pop group in a grey military uniform were ploughing through some instrumental freak-out, the kind of improvised cacophany that Sophie usually hated but which at this moment seemed exactly right. Sweat flew from the drummer's head as he lurched back and forth, long gone to whatever raced through his bloodstream. Suddenly he brought the sticks down hard on the skins and released them. As they flew high above him he winked at one of the two podium dancers, girls who were eighteen at the most, before catching them above his head and launching back into the jam. The swirling logo on his drums read Pitchfork Sunday.

At the back of the stage an obese black man in a kaftan carefully tipped the contents of a test tube on to some slides resting on a projector lamp. The lamp warmed the liquid and the effects were beamed on to the crowd, turning them into melting, endlessly metamorphosing beings. An avant-garde film was being screened on another wall: black and white images of Greenwich Village intercut with footage of American bombers dropping their payloads on to a jungle. Acid heads stood around, freaking out or happily mesmerised, and for those who weren't into LSD it was clear that the place was awash with amphetamines because everywhere that Sophie looked, jaws were grinding round and round, complexions were grey and clammy, conversations shouted, intense...

Amber dumped her and Sophie's coats and bags on a drinks waiter and barged on to the dancefloor. Boogying with Amber gave Sophie a chance to check out the clientele: golden-haired Sloanes twirled by rich Greeks and richer Arabs; elegant debs in full evening dress rubbing shoulders with lithe Japanese girls. And then there was an older set in dinner jackets and evening dress, who were pissed enough to keep up but obviously bemused by the scale of the excess.

Clothes were coming off; everywhere the floor was littered with designer garments shredded by stilettoes. In a corner, two couples had sex beside a solemn-faced alabaster statue, their hands straying across to the others' partners. Next to Sophie, two TV actors pressed up against a pop starlet, one from behind, one in front, in a dance that was barely still just a dance.

Sophie felt hands around her waist and stubble on her neck. She turned and lashed out with slaps at her pug-faced admirer, who just laughed and waggled his tongue. She shoved him backwards into the throng.

"Good for you!" said Amber. "But you'd better get used to it. Hey, you won't believe who was in here last week."

"Who?"

"Casey Judd!"

"No way!" said Sophie. "I interviewed him for…"

"You what, honey?" said Amber, cupping her ear.

"I said I think he's really cute." *I interviewed him once? You're supposed to be a copywriter, not a features writer, idiot.*

"Me, too! Casey really digs the scene. Where else can a movie star get his rocks off without having to worry about the paparazzi?"

Sophie was terrified of being groped again and shouted to Amber that she needed a drink. After battling across the dance floor, they reached the bar and grabbed champagne from a waiter's tray.

Venn appeared beside them, a blob of white powder in one nostril. Amber pointed to her own nose and Venn sniffed it away.

"So how do you keep the staff from selling their stories to the press?" said Sophie.

"They all go through the screening, just like you did," said Venn. "Take that girl behind the bar: Jane. In my safe, I've got a lovely snapshot of her with her legs at ninety degrees. Does my back a mischief just to look at it. The same for the rest of them. We check 'em all out thorough, make sure they're decent people with roots, families, ambitions. People who really wouldn't want their screening pics plastered around their parents' village. People who know they'll go a lot further *with* Eddie Venn than *against* him."

"And if the members want real secrecy they can go to the top floor," said Amber.

"That's enough," snapped Venn.

A man was storming up behind Venn. There seemed to be such anger in his face that Sophie was half expecting him to pull a gun, but he merely tapped Venn on the shoulder.

"Can I have a word?" he bellowed.

"Jesus, Charlie. *I'm busy.*"

"Clearly. Or you'd have found time to sort out the new membership cards as we discussed."

"I told you I was taking care of some new people tonight. Not that I'm accountable to you. This is Sophie. Why don't you introduce yourself, Charlie? It'll probably be more flattering than what *I'd* come up with."

The man glowered at Venn, then snapped his heels together and offered his hand. He was probably in his mid-fifties but looked quite dashing in a blue silk two-piece Italian suit and bow tie.

"Sophie, the name's Dryden. Charlie Dryden. I co-manage the club. How do you do?"

"Here, why don't you manage my coat?" said Venn, dumping the camel hair on Charlie.

"Don't you think there's rather a lot to be done for you to be playing chaperone, Venn? I can't handle the membership cards on my own."

"Sod the cards. We'll send the bloody things by pony express, Charles."

"I wanted to give them to people *tonight*. It's called professionalism."

Venn looked at Sophie. "Excuse me." He slapped a hand on Charlie's shoulder and moved him away for a private word. Sophie caught Venn's opening line: "Listen, old boy, you're forgetting your place in the hierarchy, know what I mean?"

This seemed to take the wind out of Charlie's sails. In a less fiery tone, he said: "I'm just saying we both have a responsibility to manage the club."

Venn stabbed Charlie's lapel with a finger. "I do *screenings*. Any other help I give you is a bonus. And before we forget, I have a stake in this place. *You* are staff. And if you want some free advice from someone who's made something of himself without a public school education, it's that shambolic attitude you've just shown that's kept you broke all your life."

Venn said something else that Sophie didn't catch. Charlie nodded, puffed out his chest and returned to the women.

"Sophie, I'd like to apologise for my rudeness," he said.

"There's no need," she said. "It must be difficult, running a place like this."

"Yes, it can be. It can be."

Amber caressed Sophie's neck and slunk back to the dancefloor. "Catch you later, honey," she said, blowing a kiss.

Time for a coke top-up, thought Sophie.

And then, less pleasantly, Venn's hand was on Sophie's backside.

"And I'll catch you later, too," he said.

Now Sophie was alone with Charlie, whom she had guessed was the posh bloke on the Erato's answerphone. Did he know all about Venn's "Alarm Cards"?

"Have you had a look around?" he asked.

"No. I've just got here."

"Fine. I'll give you Charlie Dryden's Grand Tour. Let's get out of this infernal place."

Charlie threw open a door and ushered her into another long room. The only people in here were grouped at the far end, reclining on four couches pushed into a loose square.

"I can't stand that music," he said in a gravelly tone. "I suppose you like all that: the Beatles and Hendrix and Pink Fred, is it?"

"Not as much as I used to."

"It's no wonder Glenn Miller crashed his plane. He saw this racket coming."

Charlie was greeted warmly by the small crowd and some banter was exchanged about an imminent theatre trip. This bunch were clearly more bohemian than business – and older than anyone on the dancefloor. Did Charlie take care of these members, while Venn schmoozed with the younger set?

"This is the Members' Lounge," said Charlie. "There aren't many artists and writers left at the Erato, but this is where they come. They're the kind of people William Raven had in mind when he designed this place."

"I've not heard of him."

"He was the third earl of Ambresbury. An architect, poet, dreamer. He had the notion that his Neo-Classic masterpiece would be where the scientists, thinkers and artists of the day could meet for the advancement of the human race. Unfortunately there's not much money in advancing the human race and after three years the project bankrupted him.

"The masons bought it off him and finished it in 1790. A century later they sold it to the New Regal Tobacco Company, and then they flogged it to Joe Summers. I take it you've heard of *him*?"

"Yes, of course."

"And his son Hugo inherited it. You'll have heard of him, too. Hugo encouraged a more arty set than his old man, and the place soon flourished with bohemians. Rich bohemians, anyway."

"So it was Hugo who brought in the fun and games? Is he here tonight?"

"I don't know. He's rarely seen, to be honest. He's a great man – I will personally be indebted to him for life – but he's ever so private."

"Does the Erato take up the whole building?"

"Yes. We lease the ground floor to a restaurant called Arcadia but it's all owned by the club, all one thousand square feet of it."

Back in the grand hallway, Charlie pointed to some double oak doors. "Over there is our own restaurant – one of the best-kept secrets in London, believe me. To the right of that is the gaming room if you fancy your luck at chemin de fer or roulette. And the portrait over the doors is of Raven himself. There are some quite valuable pieces in the club. Just here in the hallway you have that witches picture by Salvator, and those decadent characters are by Fragonard. And that over there is a clock that says it's nearly party time."

So far, Charlie had put Sophie at ease but now she felt nervous again as they climbed the main staircase to a mezzanine gallery.

At the top, her guide pointed out various ornate mirrors and Classic busts and reliefs but she was more interested in watching two women hurrying into a darkened side room, carrying candles and cushions. Two men appeared at the opposite end of the gallery, carrying candelabras. They, too, scurried into the side room.

Charlie put a hand on Sophie's elbow and guided her away.

"Still a bit early for lantern city," he said.

"What's lantern city?"

"All in good time. Now, I reckon we could sneak in a quick reviver at the cocktail bar – my favourite place in the joint. Joint! Listen to me! I fled Hollywood six years ago and I'm still talking like a bloody Yank."

"So what were you doing in Ho-. My God, what's that smell? Is that chlorine?"

Charlie threw open a door to reveal a balcony overlooking a swimming pool. Silvered acrylic bubbles surrounded the walls of the baths, reflecting and refracting the water and swimmers.

"Permanently kept at 82 degrees. Look at that, it's a work of art. And just behind it is the fencing salle. Venn paid for that to be restored – it was being used as a store room until he came on the scene. And over on that side of the gallery are a dozen suites that members can stay in."

Sophie stared down at the half dozen swimmers idling through the water.

"So what *were* you doing in Hollywood?"

Charlie looked at his watch. "Now that's a story I definitely can't tell without a cocktail."

***

CHAPTER ELEVEN

After the Paladian grandeur of the rest of the club, Sophie was surprised to find that the cocktail bar was decidedly Art Deco. Charlie ordered strawberry daiquiris and explained how the Erato's styles had evolved with each owner's taste.

He asked Sophie about her job and as there was no way of knowing if he would later cross-check her story with Venn she kept to the same version she'd given at the screening: that she was a freelance advertising copywriter who occasionally wrote for the medical press.

Charlie's face crinkled with ecstasy as he took his first sip. "This is what we used to drink on set. When the day's filming was done, and quite often before."

"So, from Hollywood to Mayfair – tell me about it, Charlie."

"Ye Gods. Well, I've been an actor all my life. My mother was a stage actress, quite a name in her time, and I travelled round the country with her. I barely had a proper day's schooling. Then I squeezed into RADA when I was 18 and after that I had a relatively easy time getting work in the West End. When war broke out I persuaded British Pathe that I was a cameraman because I quite fancied that. They sent me to North Africa and then Normandy for D-Day and I got into some right scrapes but nothing too fatal.

"After I was demobbed my stage career really took off. In the late forties I was playing the lead in what turned out to be a big hit and that's when I met Hugo: he was one of the angels. He's always loved the arts, worshipped the theatre. We hit it off at once and became good friends.

"When TV came in, I was one of the first actors on the box, and they let me direct some *Play for Today*s, too. Then a good friend of mine took over as head of production at King's International Pictures and asked me to direct a pet project of his, a comedy war film. He'd written the script and hell or high water weren't going to stop him from putting it on the silver screen now that he could. The shoot was very smooth considering I didn't know what I was doing. We even came in under budget. Anyway, the movie was called *They Might Be Heroes*."

"I saw that! A boyfriend took me to see it. War movies aren't usually my thing but it was great."

"Bless you for that. And God bless all the others who paid to see it because it turned into a little goldmine. After *Heroes*, the offers flooded in. The next thing I knew I was on the plane to the West Coast, where my ego grew so inflated that I started to believe I could remake *Citizen Kane* and get it right this time!"

Sophie narrowly avoided spluttering a mouthful of drink over Charlie.

"What *actually* transpired was a romantic comedy that closed within the fortnight," said Charlie. "But Hollywood is very forgiving and when I said I was going to revive the big, old-fashioned musical, they couldn't throw enough money at me. And that was *So Julie Bronstein, Is This Your Life?* I bet hubbie didn't take you to see that one."

"It didn't do too well, did it?"

"Only in so far as it was a bloody disaster. I lost my nerve and came back to London. Just when I'd found my feet directing adverts I invested in a pyramid scheme. Lost everything. Then I started boozing and, well, it seemed the Charlie Dryden luck had finally run out. And then out of the blue, Hugo phoned and asked me to run the Erato. We hadn't spoken for many years but word had got back to him about my troubles. That was in 'sixty-two. And here I am, seven years later. I'm a lucky man."

"And there's a new decade coming," said Sophie. "Here's to your luck holding out."

"*Our* luck," said Charlie.

At that moment, an American woman's booming voice silenced the bar. "That Venn is a vile little man; *a repugnant beast!*"

A heavily overweight woman in a cream sequinned dress was bustling towards them. "Sometimes I think he'd walk right through me if he didn't know that one brush with my tits would knock him all the way back to Beffnal Green or whatever Cockney shithole he crawled out of. Barry, fix Mitzi a drink. Something big and obvious that's gonna put her in the mood for some action."

Charlie shook his head.

"Who the hell is that?" whispered Sophie. "And how did she pass Venn's audition?"

"That," said Charlie, spinning on his stool to face the woman, "is my wife."

"Charlie, there you are," said Mitzi, in a thick Brooklyn accent. "Chatting up the young girls as usual. She's young enough to be our grand-daughter, not that we could have any kids, er..?

"Sophie."

"His sperm or my eggs, depending on which quack you believe."

"My wife," repeated Charlie.

"Oh, do be quiet, Charlie. So what lies has he been telling you, Sophie?"

"I told her I'm the three times limbo champion of St Lucia," said Charlie.

"Ha! He tried to twist and shout in 1963 and put his back out for the rest of the decade. But he's always got a line for a beautiful girl and you're beautiful, Sophie." The barman handed Mitzi a turquoise cocktail. "Is this your first night? Haven't seen you around."

"That's right. I'm a virgin."

"We have so much in common. Is Charlie giving you the tour?"

"Yes."

"Make sure that's all he gives you."

"For Christ's sake, woman," said Charlie. "We were discussing *the arts*."

"The arts as in *Charlie's Life Story*?" said Mitzi.

"The woman is impossible."

"Maybe, but she's the only one looking out for you," said Mitzi. "Talking of which, Venn's been hollerin'. Says we're out of bitter again. Wants to know why you didn't order some extra barrels or something."

"Because I'm not going to help him turn the Erato into a working men's club. His primate pals will just have to slum it with champagne like everyone else."

"You be careful, Charlie Dryden," said Mitzi, hugging him. "Sophie, have a blast tonight. Catch up with you kids later. Maybe we can–. Hey, Julian!" Mitzi was making a beeline for a young waiter who'd popped his head round the door. "Freeze! You're taking Mitzi for a dance, and then a tour of lantern city."

When Mitzi had gone, Sophie said: "I'm sorry about my little comment when she came in."

Charlie laughed. "Forget it. You're right: Mitzi and I would never pass Venn's ridiculous screening. Luckily we don't need to: I'm staff and she's with me and besides, screening only applies to *new* members, not those who joined *before* Venn showed up." He looked at his watch. "It's time to move on. Bring your drink."

Back in the gallery, Sophie noticed a spiral staircase with a handrail that flared into a gorgon's mouth. She stepped closer and saw that the entire structure was made of glass. A doorman with the ears and nose of a veteran boxer stood guard by the velvet rope at the foot of the steps.

"What's up there?" she asked Charlie.

"The Gathering Place."

"Sounds interesting. Can we go up and... gather?"

"I'm afraid not. It's a private members' club."

"A private members' club within a private members' club? No-one could accuse this place of lacking intrigue."

Charlie smiled benignly and gestured to the guard.

"Sophie, this is Terry. He's in charge of security for both clubs."

Terry smiled but his eyes remained dead and black, like a shark's. Had it been him who'd pushed Scottie?

"So what does a girl have to do to join The Gathering Place, Terry?" asked Sophie.

"You have to be a member, miss."

"That's right," said Charlie. "To go up there you need a thousand pounds for the life membership, an invitation and... well, let's just say I don't think it's your kind of place."

A woman in a red cocktail dress was clopping down the staircase. As she came into view, Sophie recognised the Spaniard who had caused the commotion at the hotel on the "screening" night.

"Good evening, Ana," said Charlie.

Ana blew out a contemptuous cloud of smoke and flicked the butt away.

"Nothing is up there," she said, hands on hips. "No people."

"Well, it's still early. Ana, this is Sophie. She's a new member."

Ana gave a tiny nod and held Sophie's gaze – did Ana remember her from the other night? Sophie was dying to know the story behind that terrible scar that stretched from mouth to ear, with its evenly spaced indentations.

"Is all shit," she said, and flounced away towards the cocktail bar.

Charlie smiled weakly. "Don't worry about Ana. She's a funny one."

"Is she a member?"

"She helps to run the place."

"What happened to her face?" Sophie hadn't really meant to say it; it was the champagne talking.

"I've honestly no idea. Why don't you ask her?"

Sophie laughed. "Has *anyone* ever asked her?"

"As a matter of fact, they have. Last Christmas, one of our members was curious, and not a little drunk. We took bets on whether he'd have the balls. Well, he did. He walked up to Ana and asked her about the scar."

"And?"

Charlie shook his head at the memory. "Let's just say no-one's ever asked again. Let's press on."

They had gone just a few steps along the gallery when their path was blocked by an elegant young couple in evening dress. The man was placing the needle on a gramophone resting on the floor. He darted back to his partner and they stood frozen in an embrace, their faces nearly touching. And then, with a loud crackle, an Argentine tango burst from the speaker and the duo came alive.

"God, I love to watch these two dance," said Charlie. "That's Danny and Isabelle. Fantastic couple. He's Texas oil, she's old Paris money. Sometimes I remember why I've never walked away from this place: there's still just enough magic."

Some movement in the shadows caught Sophie's eye. Someone else had come to watch, but he was keeping out of sight behind a pillar.

Unfazed by the gallery's limited space, Danny led and Isabelle followed, their feet always close to the floor, their ankles brushing, their moves perfect and thrilling to Sophie's amateur eyes.

Danny kissed Isabelle and ran his hands down her back and lifted her skirt, revealing a flash of garter tops. She shouted for him to concentrate but he did it again and she laughed and threw her head back and screeched like some Latino temptress.

Then, a discordant rip as the needle slid across the record. Sophie's eyes darted to the gramophone and she saw a little ball of a man disappearing into a side room. Danny bolted after him but as if by magic the figure appeared from behind a pillar at the far end of the gallery. Then he was at the glass staircase and Terry was unhooking the rope for him.

"Goddamn weirdo!" shouted Danny. "Just because we wouldn't do your pervy show!"

"Honey, it's okay," said Isabelle.

"Danny, I'm sorry," said Charlie. "You know what I think of that SOB. As manager, I feel kind of guilty that he's a member but..."

Danny waved away Charlie's apologies. "Hey, Charlie, don't even... I know it's nothing to do with you."

"I'll have a word with Hugo..." Charlie didn't seem too sure of this promise. "But hey, you guys were looking great. When are the world championships?"

Isabelle laughed. "I wish you'd tell that to our teacher."

Charlie introduced Sophie, and after a little conversation, Danny and Isabelle headed downstairs.

"What was that all about?" asked Sophie.

"It's like any club," said Charlie. "Not all the members get on."

"Who was that funny little guy who ran off?"

"I call him Mr Toad but it's best not to ask too many questions. Or people might start asking questions about you."

"But Mr Toad's a member of that other club on the top floor?"

"Sophie, you're a lovely girl but you have to understand there are some things that go on here that it's not your place to know about, hmmm?"

"Yes. I'm sorry. I understand."

They were back at the top of the main staircase. Now that the tango music had stopped, Sophie was aware of some insistent noise from the darkened room. A woman's cry, the unmistakable sound of climax. Sophie was surprised to find it shocking.

"Lantern city?" she said.

"Yes. It's time."

A stream of partygoers was migrating up the main staircase and into the candlelit room. Charlie and Sophie fell in with them. The "lantern city" was a long room filled with a series of boudoirs divided by drapes that flowed from the ceiling. Each boudoir was furnished with banquettes, chaise lounges, sofas and custom-made beds similar to the ones at the screening hotel but designed for even more people.

"Don't be shy, they don't bite, most of them..." said Charlie, putting one hand on the small of Sophie's back just a little too long as he encouraged her onwards. Tiny Chinese lanterns bordered the narrow gangway that zigzagged its way through the action. Two giant Syrian-style chandeliers with coloured beadings cast an unearthly red glow over the beautiful people as they shed any remaining inhibitions.

Sophie ventured through it, this flesh playground, and it was almost too much for her senses: the bodies rearing up out of the dark to be frozen in a sliver of light before falling back into the shadows; the tinkle of shattering glass; the giggles of the guilty party; the glow of something – a pipe?; the scents of wax and patchouli incense; the vibrations on her feet from the disco downstairs; the hum of a sex toy as a man bent over a naked woman, her body slick with sweat; a wiry young black guy settling next to the woman, her hand reaching for him, closing around him...

And Sophie felt something else, too, something she'd felt at the screening: wasn't it the first stirrings of lust? Why the hell *wouldn't* she feel that?

"Much as I'd like to stay..." whispered Charlie. "I should get back to work. Will you be all right?"

"I'm sure I'll find ways to amuse myself."

"Sophie, it was a pleasure meeting you. I hope we see you again very soon."

"That's a promise."

"Excellent. Oh, and one word of advice: avoid Venn tonight."

"Why?"

"He's always very wary of new people. And you being a journalist."

"Just a low-grade scribbler," said Sophie, annoyed that her cover story had already aroused suspicion.

"Even so, the man's paranoid on coke."

Sophie remembered the menace of Venn's parting words: *I'll catch you later, too.*

"We'll let you know whether your application was successful," said Charlie.

"So I was being auditioned tonight?"

"Kind of. But as long as you didn't pinch any silverware, I fancy your chances."

And with a salute, Charlie stole away.

Sophie moved deeper in, occasionally stepping over a foot or around a hand when they fell into her path by accident or to draw her into an encounter. The musk of sex hung heavily in here. Already the lantern city was strewn with debris: shattered champagne flutes, overturned candles, discarded clothing, drained bottles of Veuve Clicquot, used condoms that spilled from the mouths of lion-shaped receptacles.

She saw an unoccupied armchair and sat down. The drink had gone to her head; it was time to remind herself what she was trying to achieve here. Number one had to be spotting Summers. Would she recognise him even if he was right under her nose?

She closed her eyes and felt herself starting to doze. Maybe that wouldn't hurt, just for a few minutes...

When she opened them again, she saw Venn, picking his way along the gangway towards her.

He knew who she was. Of course he did. He'd probably known since the night his thugs had tortured Scottie. Because Scottie *would* have blabbed, *would* have given away the name of anyone helping him with his investigation.

Sophie stood and pressed on along the path. She tried to lift one of the drapes but discovered they were weighted to the floor.

A quick look over her shoulder: Venn was closing the gap.

The only option was to keep going in the hope there was an exit or at least a hiding place. She sped up and caught a heel on something, causing her shoe to fly off into the shadows. No time to search for it. She removed the other one and tossed it in the same direction. She'd just have to take her chances amid the broken glass.

Lantern city came to a sudden end. Maybe it was her imagination, but it seemed as if the rules were different here. There were more bodies on each surface, the cries were louder, the orchestration of bodies more elaborate, the toys more sinister with their snubnosed chrome that glinted in the candlelight.

Is this how it worked? Was it an unspoken rule that the fewer limits you had, the further you headed down the gangway?

The lantern-lit path ended at an opening where mattresses formed one giant surface, swarming with bodies. Those who couldn't find room on it were entwined on the floor.

Venn was upon her. They locked eyes. He smiled. Sophie took a few steps backward, her foot caught the edge of the bed and she tumbled down among the bodies, eliciting cries of protest. As she started to get up, a powerful hand locked her in place. With his other hand, Venn was undoing his belt.

"The final screening, eh?" he said.

She looked around for someone who might come to her rescue but knew it was pointless; this was Venn's domain. She tried to cry "help" but as in some terrible nightmare it was no louder than a whisper.

The last hope was to get among the action, lose herself among the others. She could maybe clamber to the other side, slip under the drapes and make a dash for it.

She did it, fell in among them and the hands found her at once, a waterfall of caresses, a multitude of fingers tugging at her clothes. She resisted them, needed to stay dressed, and began to make her bid for the opposite side of the bed. Two hands grabbed her ankles and she fell on to her face. Her cry of fear was lost among all the other cries.

He flipped her over and straddled her, his weight immovable. He was naked except for the shirt he couldn't quite shrug off. She tried to slap at him but he grabbed her wrists and then something happened. It was as if all the oxygen had been sucked from the room. The ballet around them was slowing, people were whispering, their eyes were on someone just behind Venn, someone Sophie couldn't see.

And then a commanding voice said: "*Venn.*"

Venn froze. Pulled away from Sophie. Turned to face this newcomer.

"There's a situation," said the man. A cigar glowed at his side.

Venn was already getting dressed. "All right," he said. "Couldn't it have waited?"

"No. You have to deal with this now."

The stranger began retracing his steps, and Venn hobbled after him, still trying to get his trousers back on.

Sophie got to her feet. All around her, voices were whispering one word. A name she had already guessed.

Hugo. Hugo.

She followed the men at a safe distance and finally had some luck when she spotted one shoe, then the other. She left the room and was crossing the gallery when she nearly ran into Venn and Summers, who had stopped at the top of the staircase. She ducked behind a pillar.

"Well, she's your responsibility," Summers was saying. "*You* brought her here. *You* deal with her."

"I didn't know, Hugo. I didn't know the bitch was spying!"

Sophie got her first look at Summers and he was as impressive as his photo, with his salt and pepper hair swept back in a wave, the strong jawline, that powerful chest accentuated by an exquisitely well-cut dinner jacket. He'd lost the moustache and looked better for that, too.

"Don't worry, old friend," said Summers. "These things happen. But let's take care of it tonight, all right?"

Summers adjusted a cuff and made his unhurried way down the stairs. Sophie moved round the pillar to stay out of sight.

Her foot caught a champagne glass, knocking it on to its side. Venn's head spun in her direction. Behind the pillar, Sophie made herself tiny. The glass rolled back and forth, back and forth, with a sound that seemed to fill the gallery.

She waited a full, agonising minute, and then peeked. Venn had gone.

If they were going to "take care of" her, why had they wandered off? Were they waiting for her to emerge from the lantern room?

There was no time to stand around thinking. No time to even go and get her coat. Her luck surely wouldn't hold any longer tonight – it was time to get out of the Erato.

CHAPTER TWELVE

She was dashing across the ground-floor lobby and the doorman was about to let her into the cold night when she spotted Venn in the street, shouting orders at someone.

Sophie skidded to a halt. "Ooh – forgot my purse!"

The doorman offered to get it but Sophie was already halfway back up the steps, praying like crazy that Venn hadn't spotted her.

She stopped on the first turn. What the hell did she do now? How did she get out of here?

The best bet was to keep going down. Presumably the steps would lead to that underground passageway joining Hill Street and Arcadian Gardens. And that led back to the car park, and from there she could sneak out and make her way to .Park Lane, where there'd be plenty of cabs.

She made a run for it, not even looking in the doorman's direction as she passed him on her way down to the basement. Another stroke of luck – the man who had been acting as doorman for the underground passage was gone.

A squeal of tyres shattered the silence, followed by the sound of a man barking a command.

Sophie ducked down between two cars. There came the roar of a vehicle accelerating fast, followed by a bone-chilling crash; glass tinkling, metal shrieking. She peeked out: what looked like an Aston Martin had ploughed into the exit barrier. Terry, the guard from the spiral staircase, was racing towards it. He tried to open the driver's door but it was locked or buckled. As he looked around for something to smash the window, the car growled to life and began reversing.

The driver of the DB6 – it was too dark to make them out – slammed on the brakes and then went forward again to make a circuit of the level.

"It's no good!" Terry shouted. "I've put the barrier down. You can't get out of here!"

The car took another corner much too fast and for a heartstopping moment travelled on its offside wheels. And then the driver was gunning it down the lane again. It was suicide – too much steam was pouring from the bonnet for them to be able to see.

Sophie looked away the instant before the collision. What she couldn't block out was the sickening sound of the DB6's disintegration.

At that moment, Venn stepped out of the underground passage. He saw the crashed car and ran over to join Terry, who was attempting to wrench open its twisted doors.

Terry spotted a fire extinguisher mounted on a wall and used it to make quick work of caving in the driver's window. He pulled the limp body free of the vehicle and laid it down. It was a woman. Her face had been cut to shreds by the shattered windscreen but Sophie recognised the platinum blonde hair and black evening gown.

"Can you hear me, Amber?" said Venn, kneeling beside her.

There was a strange interlude of calm as Venn stroked her ruined face and said gentle things. And then Amber jerked alive and began coughing blood.

"Spunky little cow," said Terry.

"You'd have to be, wouldn't you? To anger me like this?" said Venn, easing Amber to a sitting position. "Do you know how much you've hurt me? I trusted you. Brought you in from the streets. You were my number one girl. And then Hugo, just now, he tells me you've been listening in upstairs, spying on him and the Yanks. He caught you sticking a bug under the bar, didn't he? Who's been paying you, eh? Hugo might forgive me if I can tell him that. Hmmm?"

Venn held out his hand and Terry passed him some object that Sophie couldn't make out, but Amber knew what it was and she struggled. Venn slipped the object on to his right hand and Sophie realised that it was a knuckleduster. Terry lifted Amber up and pinned her against the car. She shook her head and muttered no, and she was still shaking her head when Venn slammed his fist into her face. Her body slumped to the concrete.

"Pick her up," said Venn.

Terry hesitated. "Don't you think…"

"Just fucking do it, Terry."

Terry did as he was told. Sophie didn't watch now, just listened. She was powerless. There was the same terrible sound, as if every bone in Amber's skull was being crushed with a sledgehammer. Terry protested again, and his voice was trembling, but Venn shouted for him to hold her there.

There was a final, unforgettable punch.

"Go and get the Bentley," said Venn.

A minute later, Terry pulled up in the car that had brought Sophie to the club. He hoisted Amber's lifeless body into the boot.

"Get rid of it," said Venn. "The usual place."

"What about this lot?" said Terry. Sophie guessed he meant the wreckage.

"I'm going to lock this level. No-one'll see it."

"People are going to want to get to their cars," said Terry. "Not just from the club – other people use this place."

"I'll have Jack keep watch down here. They won't argue with him. And I'll get Lenny and the spade to tow it away first thing. Now get on the case."

Terry got in to the Bentley and pulled away. Venn examined what was left of the DB6. Next, he looked at the knuckleduster and turned his hand this way and that as if admiring some fine piece of jewellery. And then Sophie felt sick, because she finally understood Venn's discussion about the "stones" on the screening night, and what he had wanted them for. The five diamonds ranged across the knuckles sparkled so beautifully that for once his smile was not ironic or mocking but joyful.

***

CHAPTER THIRTEEN

After edging her way out of the car park, Sophie ran to Park Lane and flagged a cab. She got the driver to drop her off in a street next to hers and then just stood there, too scared to go home. What was to say Venn hadn't despatched one of his bully boys to come round and wait for her?

Eventually, she reasoned that Amber's death had given Venn and his soldiers more pressing matters to deal with than... than what? Had he been planning to rape and kill her because he knew she'd been Scottie's accomplice? Had he only allowed her into the club to exact some terrible revenge?

At the very least, he had to suspect her of being an undercover hack – all those questions he'd asked her at the screening night. It had been a mistake to adopt any kind of writer as her cover story. Scottie should have briefed her against it, should have helped her out with a different identity, should have been a lot more concerned with her safety than the glory his book would bring him.

Immediately, she hated herself for blaming Scottie. *She'd* done thirteen years on a national – if she didn't know how to look out for herself by now, then more fool her.

Holding the collar of the fur coat close to her neck, she headed off for her street. Reason had kicked in and told her that Venn and his boys would be too busy dealing with the Amber aftermath to come after her tonight.

Even so, after approaching her building it took another twenty minutes of listening and tiptoeing before she felt confident to enter the flat. She crept around (*Yeah, like they're not going to hear you if they're in here – get real, Boyd*), opening every cupboard, and when she was satisfied that she was alone, pushed the dining table up against the door, which she locked and chained. Next: a huge G&T: she needed oblivion.

God, what I wouldn't give for a couple of Valium right now.

Lying in bed, fully clothed and cuddling Keef, Sophie concluded that Venn had merely got the hots for her tonight. What she'd (almost) been on the receiving end of in their so-called lantern city was a grotty little gangster with the horn, not some punishment. There was no way he could know that she'd been in league with Scottie, unless Scottie had given her up. And on reflection, she didn't think that likely – it probably hadn't occurred to Venn to ask about accomplices. Scottie's assassination had in all likelihood been decided upon and ordered in a hurry.

There was one check she could make to set her mind at ease and with her last bit of strength, she switched on the beside light and opened the wardrobe. Pushed back the clothes on the rail.

And saw that the decorations box had been moved.

Oh my God.

Maybe she had moved the box when she'd first come in and started poking around. She didn't remember checking the wardrobe but she didn't remember *anything* she'd done when she'd walked in just now.

Her eyes kept shutting. Exhaustion was claiming her. Some mechanism in her was refusing to allow her to be more scared than she already was.

She passed out.

**

She clutches her seat, terrified, as black clouds roll in from the ocean, as lightning spears the water. Rainwater sweeps from the hills to the right, swallowing the road in places, making it seem impossible that they won't swerve from the cliffs at any second and plunge to where the Atlantic breakers pound the rocks.

She wants to cry but she can't repay Joe's kindness with cowardice. He's been good enough to bring her this far, driving her round and round Achill Island in search of an address she'd told him she could find but which in reality was nothing more than a vague scribble on a piece of paper.

Since it has become clear that she doesn't have a clue where they are going, Joe has turned silent, no doubt ruing the moment he bumped into her at Galway bus station. It was unfortunate he'd taken pity on the helpless English girl whose eyes had lit up at seeing "Achill" on the side of his electrician's van. Now he is on some kind of suicide run, and even if he survives it he'll probably be cut off from his family on the other side of the island...

She takes the letter again from her tartan shopping bag and unfolds it. In the most spidery hand, the address read simply: "Brennan's, Achill Island". No-one they had stopped to ask knew where it was or who Brennan might be. Almost as if the writer didn't really want to be found. They'd been the last vehicle allowed across the bridge before it was closed – now it looked like the luck had run out.

"I can't do much more for you, girl," says Joe. "It's a miracle the engine's brought us this far. We need to find some shelter 'til this blows over. I can't-."

He shoots his arm across her chest to brace her and she looks up from the letter to see a great bank of earth breaking free from the hill, propelled by a torrent of muddy water. It crashes into the van, jolting it sideways. Through the back window she sees they're just feet from the crest of a steep hill.

"Hold on!" shouts Joe, stamping furiously on the brakes but it's no good – the surge of water is taking them down the hill with it, too powerful for any brakes to resist. Her fingers claw at the door for the handle but it's too late to get out anyway because the van has begun its slow descent and she can do nothing but wait for it to be pulled from the road and disintegrate on the rocks. Sickening butterflies in her stomach as the torrent drags them downhill at speed, faster and faster, pushing them to the edge of the abyss, and now she screams...

CHAPTER FOURTEEN

Sophie gasped herself awake.

She sat up. It had been a while since she'd had that dream. Hopefully it would be the last.

The next morning, the urge to call Rachel was almost overpowering but she resisted: it would be unforgivable to put her friend at such risk. Instead, she took a stroll through Holland Park but didn't stay out long: brooding skies and a biting wind heightened her sense of fear.

There was something else she didn't want to face: families. Couples with pushchairs everywhere. And why did so many of the men remind her of David? She realised how much she missed him... Of *course* she missed him – they'd been married (they were *still* married, she reminded herself; the divorce was only just starting to grind into action). It was just that when he'd walked out, she'd quickly hit the pills, got tranked up, gone crazy. Only now that she was clean again could she see how life without him was going to feel. Not surprisingly, it felt like shit.

She pushed him to the back of her mind. There were more pressing matters, namely the fact that by attempting to fight off Venn in the lantern room, she had blown her chance of infiltrating the Erato.

Back home, she barricaded herself in using the table again and ate toasted crumpets until she felt sick. A pot of tea and *The Graduate* soundtrack completed the job of lifting her spirits. Her taste for melodic pop had often been mocked by her more musically adventurous friends but she didn't care: she'd never felt the need to run with the pack and wasn't going to start now.

She also wasn't about to start giving up on stories when they had ground to a halt... So what now? She didn't have a clue. Scottie would have shouted at her to be logical. She needed some more material to work with, some clues. Last night had been dangerous but pretty fruitless – all she'd learned was that Venn had a hard-on for her, that there was a club within the club and that Amber had been planting bugs there.

Why had Summers gone into business with a crook like Venn? Was Summers still calling the shots at the Erato? Who had Amber been working for, and who were the "Yanks" she had been listening in on?

Sophie made another black coffee and fished the box file from its hiding place. A close examination had convinced her that the decorations box *had* been moved but not searched: the covering layer of baubles and tinsel lay just as she'd arranged it. She must have moved it herself upon her panicky return to the flat.

Next, she removed *Avenging Angel: The Life and Disappearance of Abigail Wilman* from the box file and curled up on the bed with it: time for an Abigail refresher.

Abby had been at *The Affairs* magazine from February to September 1939, when she joined an agency and temped for a short period before joining the First Aid Nursing Yeomanry, working in canteens, hospitals and military headquarters.

One day in early 1943 she was summoned to a meeting in a dingy hotel in central London, where a man stumbled through some small talk before asking if she would consider dangerous work for her country. She replied immediately that she would and went to train with the Special Operations Executive, a rival of the Secret Intelligence Service (aka MI6), which regarded its antics with great suspicion.

Wait.

It had been MI5 that Summers worked for – the domestic intelligence service – not MI6, which handled the overseas operations. Sophie noted this in her pad and continued reading.

Over the next six months, Abby learned to become a self-sufficient killing machine, an expert in everything from contacting resistance circuits to setting up her own, from map reading to self-defence, from building bridges to blowing them to hell. She could duplicate keys, escape from handcuffs, repair radio transmitters, set boobytraps and had a fair understanding of German.

The training pushed the intake to their limits, but Abby was one of the best students the SOE had ever seen. "She was unstoppable; a fury, a natural killer," one instructor was quoted as saying.

Next came parachuting lessons, taught at a house in Altrincham, near Manchester, with practice jumps in the grounds of Tatton Park. For the final stage of training, she was sent to Bealieu Manor in the grounds of an old abbey in the New Forest. This was the SOE "finishing school". The rough and tumble was over – there were no longer any 3am wake-up calls for the trainees to be sent clambering up walls and shot at in the dark. Bealieu Manor taught the fine details that could mean the difference between life and death in occupied France. On the final night, the fledgling agents were treated to a slap-up meal and plied with booze. In the course of the evening, each of them was questioned on some seemingly innocuous subject, but one that they had been told to keep absolutely secret for the duration of the course, nonetheless. Those who revealed this information over dinner, or afterwards in the bar, were dropped.

Abby was not one of them.

Now she was officially a British officer with the rank of major in the First Aid Nursing Yeomanry. In reality, she was an SOE agent.

In November 1943, she was parachuted to a point near Le Mans, France, with her clothes and other belongings dropped in a separate container. Within an hour of the drop she had made contact with the resistance circuit. On the first few missions she acted as courier, relaying messages from the SOE to the resistants and then passing back their complaints and requests for guns and ammo. She would rendezvous with a three-seater Westland Lysander for the journey back to England.

Initially she found some of her contacts hostile but slowly won them over with her technical proficiency and the risks she took in moving between the two countries. She travelled around whichever region she had been assigned to using false ID papers, never staying in one house for more than two nights. If she was scheduled to stay in an area for more than a couple of weeks, she would find that secretarial or housekeeping work had been set up for her.

The rest of the time was spent recruiting resistants and training them in arms and explosives. It wasn't long before she started to make her mark – wherever she went, the number of roads, bridges and rail lines that were destroyed doubled, trebled. As a result, the Gestapo were always hot on her heels, raiding houses, bribing locals for tip-offs, torturing suspects in towns she had left just hours before.

One day in November 1944, while based in Normandy, she cycled to an isolated house for a meeting. Soon after it began, there was a raid by German soldiers. The resistants fought back and three were killed. Abby and one of her comrades, Charles Le Harivel, despatched two Germans with a burst from their Sten guns and escaped in a car. Charles managed to navigate to a farmhouse near Orléans that he had heard was owned by the leader of the local resistance circuit.

Charles was thirty-four, ten years older than Abby, and was generally a highly arrogant and difficult man (according to the former acquaintances that *Avenging*

Angel's author had tracked down in France). But he must have become smitten by the Englishwoman – and she by him – in the three days they were holed up, because when they made contact with the circuit, it was clear to their new allies that romance had blossomed.

Charles and Abby were officially fugitives now. He was given a new identity in Orleans, a room at a boarding house and work as a mechanic. The rest of his time was dedicated to sabotage and recruitment.

Abby remained hidden in the farmhouse. There was no readymade identity for her this time, and besides, she was too high on the Gestapo's wanted list to be wandering around in public any more.

Some nights, when he thought the danger level was acceptable, Charles would cycle out to her, she would make dinner and they would spend the night together.

After D-Day in June 1944, groups of resistance fighters increased in number, with up to thirty people involved in skirmishes. Abby took her chances and began moving around Normandy more freely. Her reputation was widely known among the circuits now, which was useful in that her orders were never questioned, but dangerous in that the Germans wanted her more desperately than ever.

Two months after D-Day, Abby, Charles and three other resistants were on a reconnaissance patrol when they ran into a retreating German convoy. After escaping the ensuing battle on a horse, Abby was nearly killed by American mortar fire but was saved when the injured creature fell on her, protecting her from the shelling. The Americans found her and told her that her comrades were dead. Abigail returned to England; her war was over.

The remainder of the book theorised on what happened to Abby next. It was known that she went to work for a map makers in The Strand, and that between December 1946 until her disappearance the following February, she rarely returned to her lodgings until late at night. The book then put forward the "mystery boyfriend" theory, that Abby had been seeing someone and he had murdered her.

The book ended by noting that in 1946, a month after the SOE was merged with the SIS, a fire broke out on the top floor of their Baker Street HQ and destroyed nearly all FANY records and operational files, including the field activities of SOE female agents and circuits that had been compromised by the enemy. Speculation on the fire centered on the suspicion that the blaze was arson − started deliberately to destroy sensitive material.

Sophie closed the book and flicked through Scottie's own notes. His big coup had been discovering that Abby had been waiting for − or spying on − Hugo Summers in December 1946, exactly the time that she stopped coming home. Three months later, Abby had disappeared, and Tom Havelock's wife Caroline was dead at the bottom of some cliffs.

Sophie backtracked down the timeline. She needed to get Summers' relationship with the Havelocks straight in her mind.

Summers had lent the Havelocks a small sum of cash before the war. How Summers had known the Havelocks, and why the Havelocks' former secretary ended up spying on Summers, were things Scottie hadn't cracked.

Abby must have stayed in contact with the Havelocks − or Caroline, at least, as Tom topped himself in 1941. Did something go on between the three of them? After the war, was Summers seeing Caroline and Abigail? Was it a menage a trois that went fatally wrong? Sophie began to warm to her theory − *Yes! That's why Tom killed himself; he found out about it.*

Sophie closed *Avenging Angel*. It was all just hopeless speculation.

"All that danger. I think you were *missing* the danger, Abby. That's why you started this thing with Summers after the war, whatever it was. He'd been in MI5, you'd been in the SOE. Different set-ups, but maybe you saw a kindred spirit."

The phone was ringing. Sophie answered it and had her ear blasted by a voice that still thought it was trying to reach the back row of the Old Vic.

"Sophie? It's Charlie Dryden, darling. I'm sorry I bent your ear the other night. All that crap about Hollywood — what an old fart. Now listen: firstly, did you leave your coat here? And secondly, the membership committee were keeping an eye on you the other night and they love you. You're in."

***

CHAPTER FIFTEEN

Over the next working week, Sophie kept busy by finishing a couple of articles for women's magazines ("I Married The Barnet Rapist" and "Why Everyone's Going Japanese"). But the going was slow – her concentration was shot to pieces by flashbacks of Venn stalking her in lantern city, and of what he'd done to Amber.

When Saturday came round, she chose her Andre Courreges sleeveless party dress (a couple of years old but it was the only posh frock she hadn't worn to the club yet) and took a cab to Arcadian Gardens. This time she entered by the main doors and was handed a membership card by the hall porter. Seeing her name printed neatly beside those trademark Erato roses and thorns gave her a tiny thrill.

Don't get seduced.

She took the lift to the first floor and was surprised to find the grand hallway deserted except for the pianist – plying his lonely trade – who gave her a smile.

And then Sophie looked at her watch and saw that it was only five to ten...

Great. The Girl Guide puts her foot in it again.

After ordering a kir royale she made a circuit of the floor in the hope of finding Charlie or some of his theatre pals. But the ante room where they had congregated that first night was empty. Next she tried the ballroom and found only the boys from Pitchfork Sunday – the band from the first night – setting up. There was no action in the Sussex Room, either, where three croupiers were being given a dressing down by the shift manager for not addressing the titled guests correctly.

Where now? Up to the gallery on the mezzanine floor? Was that safe? Surely Venn and that creepy guy whom Charlie had called Toad had better things to do than lurk up there on a Saturday night. She told herself to stop thinking and just act. Abby wouldn't have thought twice about doing it.

Yeah, and look what happened to her.

Sophie went up but again, there was no-one around except the staff preparing the lantern city for the night's entertainment. There was no point attracting attention with more swanning around – why not just check out the arrivals?

She leant over the balustrades and it wasn't long before the first identifiable social group drifted in – Charlie's theatre buddies, all done up in formal wear and exchanging droll one liners.

The next group she classified as "fixers". Snatches of their conversation suggested they were an assortment of loansharks, bookies, club owners, professional gamblers, fight promoters and God knew what else. They were clearly at the coalface of Venn's operations – they got him his money.

On the other side of the coin were the aristos, whom Sophie guessed to be Summers' buddies. They looked super rich but this was *old* money. There were no OTT tans and chunky jewellery. Generally, though, they looked no more at ease than Charlie's lot.

Then there were the women. They were either classically rich and high maintenance, dripping with Yves St Laurent or Gucci, or they were party girls, shrieking for attention in strapless, backless costumes with nothing underneath, or haute couture dresses held together by pins. As with the blokes, they were a real mix.

As well as money and sex, there was fame. Sophie recognised the bassist from a major pop group and the manager of a couple of other bands who were about to hit it big. Plus there were two up-and-coming British actors, one of whom had been featured in *Metropolitan Woman* (Saffron Honey had recently interviewed the cuter one, Sophie recalled sourly), a big record label honcho and an Oscar-nominated film director.

Charlie's friends made a hasty exodus for a quieter place as the music started up. Their days here were surely numbered and Sophie guessed there would be a lot of "membership application rejected" letters going out in the next year. Talking of which, when was someone going to ask her to write a cheque for the five hundred quid?

Just as she thought she had identified all the Erato's social groups, Venn and some hulking pal burst out of the lift in a riot of jokes and insults. Already off their heads.

The other guy was probably in his late forties and dressed more like a traditional gangster – black suit and pencil tie – than Venn in his Italian threads. The stranger shouted at a waiter to bring him a bottle of brown ale and a plate of cold tongue and Sophie remembered something Charlie had said: *"His primate pals will just have to slum it with champagne like everyone else."*

Venn was instantly mobbed by admirers, their eyes lighting up with the thrill of being in his presence. While he pressed flesh and kissed cheeks, his mate sloped off to lean against a wall, occasionally sneering when a well-to-do somebody passed by, or taking a swipe at some fleshpot's backside.

After making light work of the ale, the man – it sounded as if people were calling him "Tozer" – waved the empty glass at a waiter and, failing to catch his eye, hurled it at him. It caught its target on the back of the head and he fell unconscious to the marble floor. Tozer exploded with laughter and threw looks around the hall, as if daring someone to challenge him. Sophie pulled back from the balustrade: it was bad enough being the object of one madman's attentions; she didn't need another.

"You can't fucking do that!" said Venn, marching Tozer to the other end of the hall.

"You've gone soft, mixing with all these lord and lady lah-dee-dahs, Venny boy," said Tozer. "And I'll remind you that I'll do what I like in this gaff."

Sophie saw what looked like vulnerability in Venn's face. Was it fear? Was this guy Venn's boss?

It wasn't safe to continue spying: people were moving up to the mezzanine floor for cocktails. Sophie fell in with them and heard a familiar Brooklyn accent booming from the bar.

"Paul Newman is a *darling!*" Mitzi was gushing. "Such a genuine human being. Not like the trash you get in here these days. Paul said Charlie was the greatest British director he'd ever had the pleasure to work with. Or nearly work with. I mean, the project never actually took off but–. Sophie!"

Mitzi smothered her in a massive hug.

"How have you been, Mitzi?"

"Battling on, sweetheart. Mitzi always battles on. Barry, honey, another bottle of chablis, huh?"

With a grunt, Mitzi eased herself off the bar stool. "Come on, let's sit over in the corner. Girl talk demands privacy."

Half an hour later, Mitzi was still regaling Sophie with her life story. Sophie wondered how either Mitzi or Charlie got a word in edgeways at home.

"And we officially got divawwced on Valentine's Day," Mitzi said. "That was hubbie number two. And that's when I met Charlie and I knew the hunt was over. It was on the set of *They Might Be Heroes*? Or *They Might Be Heteros*, as we used to call it; there were so many fags on the set. I was costume designer. How about you, are you with someone, Sophie?"

"Separated."

"Oh, sad. No-one since?"

"No."

"The dating game's no joke. It's good you came here. Beautiful young thing, you want some action, right? No-one believes in all that lying back and thinking of England bullshit any more. We want orgasms! So have you had any fun yet?" She waved the latest empty wine bottle at the barman.

"No. I spent the first night just kind of looking around. Oh yeah, and then Venn tried to rape me."

"Jesus Christ. Are you serious?"

"Yeah, but it's okay. Fate intervened."

"Sometimes he just sees a girl and has to have her. And other times he likes to test new women. He has these helpers, like his molls, kinda?"

Sophie thought of Amber, and the Spaniard, Ana. Was Venn lining her up to be one of them? The thought sickened her.

"I wish I hadn't told him I was a journalist," said Sophie.

"You *did*? Oh my God, that was a mistake."

"All I do is write for arty magazines. I'm not here to blow the whistle on the Erato."

"Don't forget how paranoid he is. The hacks have been poking around since he moved in. There are ten thousand juicy stories at the Erato and they all want one."

"So Venn owns this place?"

"No-one knows what the deal is," said Mitzi. "It's not exactly in the company minutes, if you take my meaning."

"Why would Hugo Summers get involved with someone like Venn?"

"That's the million-dollar question, sweetheart. Nobody knows. But the point is this: stay away from Venn, okay? That doesn't mean you can't have fun. I mean, I'm ancient but even I still like to pop into lantern city and watch. Just hide in a dark corner and enjoy the show. Once in a blue moon I see Hugo in there. He just watches, too."

"Do you know him?"

"God, no. Nobody does. But I've met him many times. He and Charlie were good friends once. They still are, really, except Hugo's never around any more. It was through Hugo that Charlie got his job here."

"How come?" Charlie had already told Sophie this story but it would be interesting to see if Mitzi's story tallied.

"Hugo's always been into the arts. Not like all those bean counters he hangs out with. He ploughed some cash into a play Charlie was in at The Phoenix. This was years ago, just after the war. The play did good and Hugo stumped up for Charlie's next one, and then again when Charlie started directing. They became great friends, but my husband's a die-hard leftie and Hugo's more Establishment than Buck Palace so they were always falling out.

"Charlie did some stupid things a few years ago that sent us broke and Hugo offered him the job managing this place. God bless Hugo – they hadn't really spoken in years because Hugo was always so busy but he still thought of Charlie. It became Charlie's dream job, even better than making movies. But the fun only lasted a couple of years. Then Venn arrived and everything started to go to shit. I'm sorry – that's very indiscreet of me, seeing as you're a new member and all. But Venn's paranoid, a real controller. He thinks Charlie's some luvvie who doesn't know business, and in a way he's right... So you see why my Charlie gets so stressed out. He used to be the life and soul around here, but now his only allies are a handful of thesps, and they're all broke or queer."

Sophie remembered the heated exchange between Charlie and Venn: *"You're forgetting who you are and who I am, Charlie."*

"So what's the upstairs club all about?" she said. "This Gathering Place?"

"That was part of the deal when Venn bought in: the freedom to build his own club. There used to be some suites up there but he tore them all out and paid some crazy Spaniard to design a new place, a super-club. Venn doesn't realise that he's just a grubby little gangster; he thinks he's a visionary. They say it's like a Kubrick set up there."

"So what goes on?"

"Ha! You're asking the wrong gal. The only way I'm likely to get up that spiral staircase is with a machine-gun. Even Charlie's not allowed. It's strictly Venn's place."

"Is Hugo allowed?"

"It's the *only* place he goes when he's in the building. He rarely mixes with us mere mortals. We don't take it personal – Hugo's unwell a lot of the time."

"So Venn's running the whole place? The Erato and The Gathering Place? Why would Summers allow that?"

"You just gotta believe me: *I don't know*. No-one does. But you stay away from Hugo: you're just the kind of gorgeous young thing he likes. Someone he can connect with; that turns him on."

Sophie laughed. "And why is it called The Gathering Place?"

"Now *that* was Hugo's idea, apparently. Hugo was away on business a lot when Venn's upstairs was being built. But then we got word from the States – it would be The Gathering Place. Hugo had phoned to give his orders."

"*Hugo's* orders? But I thought it was Venn's place?"

"It is. Like I say, we never got to the bottom of it. Maybe you'll meet Hugo one day and you can ask him what it means. And there again, maybe you'll have quads with Liberace first."

Sophie's eyed wandered to the ceiling. She was itching to have a look up there.

"Wait a minute," she said. "All this screening that Venn does... That was his idea, right?"

"Right."

"So what happens with all the people who joined before he took over? All the old crowd?"

"Nothing. He can't do anything about screening them. But they're not here to cause trouble. It's only Venn's lot that might run to the press or do some dangerous stuff."

"*Dangerous*, this sounds good," said Venn. "What's dangerous?"

"Your goddamn aftershave," said Mitzi.

"I thought I was smelling rather nice. Evening, Sophie. How are you?"

"A little tired. I haven't slept very well since last Saturday."

"I'm sorry to hear that."

Venn seemed taken aback by her bold challenge; Sophie had even surprised herself. "Yes," she said, "some guy came on to me a bit strong in lantern city. So you see, I was a little scared about coming back."

Venn plopped a tablet into her drink. A shiver ran through her as she thought of the Valium addiction she'd kicked.

"This'll help your confidence," he said.

"What is it?"

"Very high-quality amphetamine."

"Thanks, but I don't want a week-long comedown."

"Why come down? There's plenty more where it came from. That stuff's a real buzz."

"Come on, Sophie, let's find some better company," said Mitzi. "Like out the back, where they stick the trash."

"Maybe the membership committee were wrong about you, Sophie," said Venn. "You don't like drugs, you don't like to fuck. What *do* you do like to do?"

"Maybe I just don't like to fuck *you*," said Sophie.

"Exactly," said Mitzi. "She's not some hack come to dig the dirt on your empire, Venn. You should swap those pills for bubbly, like Mitzi does."

Mitzi grabbed Sophie's arm but their exit was blocked by Venn.

"Do you want to see a show, Sophie?" he said.

"What sort of show?"

"Something I've put on just for you."

"You leave her alone," said Mitzi.

"Sophie'll be safe with me," he said. "This might even put a smile on her face."

Venn took Sophie's hand and sped her towards the exit so quickly that she thought she'd trip over her heels. They crossed the gallery towards the room she knew all too well.

"The lantern city?" she said. "You coward. Are you going to try to finish what you started?"

She wanted to call for help, cry rape, make any kind of noise but she knew nobody would challenge Venn. Mitzi was somewhere behind, shouting for Charlie.

"Why have you got it in for me?" persisted Sophie.

"It's the opposite, sweetheart – I'm looking for a new girl, someone special. These are just auditions."

"I'm not some brass, Venn. And I thought Amber was your girl."

"Amber's not around."

"What happened to her?"

Venn gave a tight little smile. "Who said anything happened to her?"

The smell of sex hung heavy in "lantern city". Venn's grip was painful as he guided Sophie along the gangway that threaded a path through the labyrinths of tents and beds, occasionally ducking below low-hanging Japanese paper lanterns with their *chochin moji* lettering. They halted at a crowd of spectators at the back of the room. Venn pushed Sophie forward until she had a ringside view.

On a four-poster bed were two men and a girl, who was sixteen at the oldest. She was on all fours. One man at each end, her body rocking back and forth like some obscene playground ride. Her arms fully outstretched to the sides as she used the bed frame to brace herself. Her eyes glassy and staring ahead, not focusing. Drugged up. Then Sophie noticed what the girl was wearing: a wedding dress. Some black, deathly feeling oozed through her like poison. She blinked away the tears that were welling up. Now she was starting to understand the depths of Venn's cunning. He'd read her well on that first drive to the club, sensing her fragility when she'd mentioned the separation.

The girl was wearing a strapless silk sheath dress. Too much of a coincidence. He'd looked for a weak spot and found it. Silk headdress decorated with organdie flowers. His goons had been in her flat. Yes, she'd been right: the box in the wardrobe had been moved. She knew they hadn't looked inside it, which meant they hadn't discovered the Abby notes, but they'd poked around the flat all the same. Found her wedding photos in a drawer. There was probably one missing right now. The man behind the girl cried out in climax, his face contorted in a grimace. He slumped back against the headboard. Venn gave the nod and a replacement moved in, ripped off the girl's headdress, flung it aside, tore the rest of the dress from her body. Runnels of perspiration soaked the white silk lingerie. The night that Venn's soldiers had been to her flat and moved the decorations box, they'd found the wedding album, stolen a photo, got a dress made; *an exact copy*. And now this sick show was Sophie's punishment.

123

Venn knew she had been working with Scottie. This was a warning to her, to *all* snoopers.

Loud voices shook her from her trance. New arrivals. A party of spectators whooping drunkenly. Four men, all American by the sound of it.

What was it that Venn had said to Amber in the car park? *"Hugo tells me you've been listening in upstairs, spying on him and the Yanks."* Were these the Yanks?

With the party was a fiftysomething man who watched impassively, his arms crossed, blue eyes probing every detail of the show. Sophie sized him up: six three; probably quite an athletic figure beneath that dinner jacket; imperious face a little stern but the features still handsome. And he was no doubt proud of that full head of hair with its streak of silver. It was the same man who had inadvertently saved her from Venn last week.

"He doesn't tend to mix with us mere mortals down here any more."

But here he was. This was her big chance to get close to Hugo and she was helpless, held captive by Venn. One of the men on the bed held two sets of handcuffs. He opened the bracelets in turn, left the key in them and slid them to one of his accomplices. Click. Click. The girl's ankles were secured to the bedposts behind her. The first man grabbed the girl's wrists and stretched them out in front her, locking her to the opposite bedposts. The Americans whooped louder. Couldn't they see what this was, that she was drugged? Sophie watched Summers for some reaction but he remained impassive.

Time to make some move. Sophie looked around for ideas. Beside her, a corpulent grandee sucked away on a fine-smelling Colorado-claro. Sophie looked at the burning tip and had a suicidal idea... Suicidal – but still the only one she had.

Do it.

She caught the man's eye and taking care that Venn didn't see her doing it, reached out her free hand as if seeking a puff. Happy to oblige, the smoker beamed at her and passed the cigar. Venn didn't see this – he was entranced by the perversity he'd orchestrated.

Sophie waited. Kept waiting. Was she really going to do this?

She lifted the cigar, hovered it over Venn's hand... and jabbed it down.

He was tough enough to swallow the pain with little more than a prolonged grunt.

The stunt worked – he released her.

The keys were still in the four sets of cuffs that tethered the girl's limbs to the frame. Finally some reaction as her eyes popped open wide in surprise. Sophie had time to unlock one set of bracelets before Venn stepped in to deal with her. He was in such a fury that the odds looked good he wouldn't even notice what she was up to. She offered her hand to him, as if regretting her brief escape, and as he reached out to take the bait she clapped the bracelets around his wrist.

Snap.

Nervous laughter rippled through the crowd as Sophie plucked the key free of the lock. The laughter died as Venn took a backhanded swipe at her face but Sophie had moved beyond his reach. She looked to Summers but he was ushering his entourage to an exit.

"Did your guests enjoy the rape show, Mr Summers?" she shouted, unable to stifle her anger any longer. "Is this how you run your club?"

Now the rest of the spectators were dispersing. They didn't want any part of this disturbance. The dark pleasures of the Erato existed on unspoken complicity. Venn raged against the cuffs that tethered him to the bedpost. "Someone fucking get me out of here!"

Those remaining on the scene were frozen with indecision: were they expected to grab this mad woman and wrestle the key from her? Meanwhile, Sophie was retracing her steps to the gallery, where she was just in time to see Terry securing the velvet rope across the spiral staircase. Hugo and the Americans were halfway up.

"Hey, Mr Summers!" she called. "I'd like some answers."

"That's far enough, miss," said Terry.

Summers paused in his ascent, his train of guests following suit. The men were muttering loudly among themselves about this mad woman.

Sophie was furious. Furious that this man who was so respected allowed someone like Venn to operate openly as his partner. "I don't know what kind of club you're trying to run around here, but..." Her voice was cracking. She wanted an eloquent rage but no words came.

And then Summers was gone.

"What's your bloody game, then?" said Terry.

"Nothing. I just wanted to meet the great Hugo Summers, okay? I'm really drunk. I'm just..." It was dangerous to dwell here. Soon Venn would be free, and then she'd be dead. "Well, even if I'm persona non grata up *there*, maybe someone in the cocktail bar will speak to me, eh?"

Sophie strode away towards the bar, just as Venn came haring out of the lantern room.

***

CHAPTER SIXTEEN

Five minutes later, Terry was thinking: *Venn's lost the plot.*

Venn was rushing around from one floor to the next, shouting that he was going to cut that stroppy bitch. Terry had already had a bollocking, both barrels, for letting her go after the little altercation at the spiral staircase just now. Like Terry was supposed to have *guessed* that she'd pulled a stunt with some handcuffs next door.

It was bad for business, letting all the members see Venn like that. Well, fuck him, if that's what he wanted. Terry would just stand here and do his job. He was doubly needed now that Jack Rickard had been called away to help with Venn's search. Jack minded The Gathering Place's lobby, checking the membership cards of those who went up there by the lifts. If he and Venn hadn't found that bird by now, they weren't-.

An immense crash followed by a succession of others sounded from somewhere off to Terry's right. The echoes told him the noise was coming from the staircase connecting the mezzanine, first and ground floors.

He removed a cosh from his jacket and approached the doors to the stairs. If it was Venn going crazy and chucking stuff around, Terry would turn on his heels and leave him to it.

He eased the doors open. No-one there... but whatever had made that racket was still rolling around. Something metallic.

"Who's down there?"

One of the fire extinguishers had been removed from its mount. Someone was drunk and playing silly buggers. It had to be that Sophie woman. Women always made the worst drunks.

Should he go down? It was risky to leave his post, especially as Jack wasn't watching the upstairs lobby. Erato members were always trying to sneak up to The Gathering Place, especially when they were half cut.

He went down to the first turn. Nothing. He went down to the ground floor and saw the extinguisher, dented but intact. Charlie wasn't going to be happy about the chunks it had taken out of the walls.

Terry stood there, his mind ticking over. He was better at following orders and dishing out violence than quick thinking. He never even heard the woman who'd been lurking on the stairs two floors above him nip back down to the mezzanine level. Never saw her check the coast was clear, eye the gorgon's heads at the end of the handrails and climb the glass staircase to The Gathering Place.

**

At the top of the staircase, two black doors purred open automatically and Sophie entered a large foyer decked out in stainless steel squares. Her image was reflected back to her thousands of times.

There was an empty chair by the lift doors. A guard's post? Was Venn's entire army out looking for her?

The only way out of the lobby was through circular acrylic glass doors operated by a keypad. Sophie pressed her face right up to them but a tint stopped her seeing in to what seemed to be a tunnel.

So this was the entrance to Venn's "Kubrick set". What the hell did he and Toad and Summers get up to in there?

A new noise. A low hum. *The lift.* Someone was coming up here.

She looked at the keypad. Get real. Millions of combinations. Run back down the staircase? Too late:

the lift had arrived. The muffled sound of Venn in mid-rant.

Without warning, the acrylic glass doors swished open and Sophie propelled herself through them. They closed moments before Venn and another of his goons tore up to them. Venn began stabbing at the keypad. Sophie pushed herself flat against one wall in this dark space, too scared to run.

Nothing happened.

The doors stayed shut.

Venn pressed his face to the doors but Sophie knew the tint would shield her.

Bang bang bang as he hammered on the acrylic glass doors.

In this dark chamber, she sensed that she was not alone.

"Who are you?" she whispered. "Why don't you come out of the dark?"

The flare of a match, followed by the pulsing glow of a cigar being lit.

"Now, there's a question," came a languid, upper-class drawl.

Venn and his helper were going back to the lifts.

"Probably gone to fetch an axe," said the man.

"Are you serious?"

"Don't get me wrong. I respect Venn in many ways. But he is undoubtedly a grade-A psychopath."

"I've had enough of this club. Can you let me out of here, please?"

"There's gratitude. I've just hit the override button to keep you *in* here. I can hit it again if you'd feel safer out there, with Edward Venn."

"Yes, please. Just open the doors so I can get out of the building."

"Why did you come up here in the first place?"

"I just came to complain about Venn. So please, tear up my membership but just let me out of here."

Her eyes were adjusting. She could see the man leaning casually against the wall, his back arched. Swirling smoke obscured his face but she had no doubt that this was Summers.

"You'll never make it to the street, of course," he said.

"I'll take my chances."

Summers clicked his fingers, the sound activating red and blue footlights that showed the way along a metal walkway. Now Sophie could see that they were indeed in a tunnel.

"What's down there?" she said.

"The Gathering Place."

Neither of them spoke for a while. Venn would be back soon. Her luck couldn't last forever.

"He broke into my flat," she said. Maybe it was time to play the bullied little girl. "Not him, but one of his men. Took a wedding photo from my album. That dress the girl was wearing tonight is an exact copy of *my* dress."

"Why would he do that?"

"I don't know." Panic was sweeping over her, destroying her power to make decisions. "So how do I open these doors again?"

"You've humiliated my business partner by handcuffing him, asked a lot of personal questions about myself and upset some important clients from the States. Not bad considering the ink on your membership card is barely dry, Miss Boyd."

She'd blown it, screwed up a gigantic story and probably signed her own death warrant.

"Come," he said.

There was such effortless authority in his voice that she followed. Another set of circular doors opened on to a stark, white foyer, decorated with a series of abstracts depicting an orgy. To the left, a corridor ran away into darkness and Sophie was relieved when

Summers went the other way, whisking her past a roof garden, restaurant and sauna. They were alone up here.

Summers stopped at the last of five doors, entered a code on another keypad and led the way into a vast suite. A floor-to-ceiling window looked out over the Mayfair rooftops and Sophie moved up for a closer look (and tried to ignore what she saw in the reflection: a bed that had clearly been designed for a multitude of bodies). She poured herself a brandy and checked out a wall of bookshelves. The predictable heavy tomes of Classics rubbed shoulders with some leftfield stuff: *Truffaut on Hitchcock*, *Walden*, *Tropic of Cancer*.

Summers had climbed some steps to a dimly lit office on a mezzanine level and perched on the edge of a writing desk. He gathered up the paper that spewed from a Telex machine and began striking something through with a pen.

"Incompetence," he muttered. "It's everywhere. You'd think twelve drafts would be enough for a simple contract."

"You're buying some more newspapers?" said Sophie.

A cold stare. "I'm buying a trout farm."

"Oh."

The phone on his desk trilled. "Summers. George, hi." A voice blared out of the receiver, but not quite loudly enough for Sophie to understand more than the odd phrase. Summers listened intently, offering the occasional *hmm* of acknowledgment. "Ungrateful fuckers. We should have sold them to Fenton's Press when we had the chance. They would have *really* taught them about pay and conditions." He started removing his bow tie. "No, we will absolutely not meet Hodgson, not even unofficially. He'll try to get you to some pub and act all chummy over darts: 'You and me, we're the same, mate' – that kind of crap. Come

131

on George, you know what these Scousers are like: it's death to give them an inch. If we show the slightest weakness, every one of our regional papers will be sabre rattling come the end of next week. We've never backed down to threats before and we're not starting now." He hung up.

"I felt myself becoming radicalised just listening to that," said Sophie. "Aren't you worried I'll report back to the workers?"

"And tell them I'm not backing down? Be my guest."

"I know someone who works on those Liverpool weeklies of yours. No pay rise for four years, isn't it? Newsroom numbers slashed by half? And didn't the chapel father get framed over some problem with distribution, which isn't even his department?"

"I have no idea of the local squabbles. What I do remember is that we saved those people's jobs when their previous owners went bust. Perhaps you'd have preferred to see them in the dole queue, shivering but with heads held high? I saw the notes on your membership application – copywriter, isn't it? Flogging dog food and toothpaste? My companies pay people's mortgages – what do *you* do for your precious workers?"

Sophie felt the bile rising. "Summers International has a terrible industrial relations record. You can't tell me that– ."

"You're a long way from the revolution here so I hope you didn't come to convert us. Ah, that's what that comedy was about downstairs, was it? The logical conclusion of the sexual revolution was staring you right in the face and you didn't like what you saw! Your so-called freaks never thought about where the permissiveness would lead, did they?"

"Maybe. But that girl downstairs didn't know what day it is. That's nothing to do with the sexual revolution."

"No-one made her come here. That girl knows the score. If that kind of thing shocks you, I'll give you a refund now because you are in the wrong place."

Sophie's heart was thudding. She hadn't intended to challenge Summers but his sense of entitlement had angered her, stirred up a sense of injustice that she hadn't felt so keenly for years.

"And what do I do with you now?" said Summers. "Turn you over to Venn? I want to, believe me. But I don't want a murder on the property. You knew what kind of a man he is, and yet you antagonised him. I find that a fascinating insight into human stupidity, into *women*. You think that because you are drunk tonight there will be no consequences tomorrow? Well, let me tell you: men like Venn *specialise* in consequences."

Summers re-lit his cigar. It was eerily silent up here. There was no sound of the band, no sound of anything. Sophie poured another brandy and lit a cigarette. Summers remained silent. The raised voice scared her but the silences did not. She could wait him out. Some arrogant, misogynist toff who'd had everything handed to him on a plate. Fuck him. She'd mixed with real lowlifes when she'd worked the crime desk.

But he seemed to have forgotten about her for the moment; his focus was on some distant place.

Something snapped him out of it and he came down to fix himself a whiskey and soda at the crescent-shaped bar. He pressed a button and barked in frustration as a plate of olives rose from the counter on a mechanised platform.

"I don't want bloody olives. I pressed the *ice* button. Here I am, in this so-called masterpiece of Futurism, and I can't even get my hands on an ice cube. This is where we are after two thousand years of architectural thinking. Look at it, the stark brutality: those spotlights

133

– I have to bring a torch if I want to read anything, because presumably this megalomaniac designer thinks nobody *reads* any more – and he cantilevers the bed before the windows as if I need to see the view when I'm asleep. The room's too hot in the summer and too cold in the winter and I can't even get a bloody ice cube."

"Does everything have to be functional?"

"If it's meant to *function*, then it should function, not prized for merely being different. I suppose you like it – as a writer, you think it's very *now*."

"Well, we can't all inherit Mayfair clubhouses and family piles, Mr Summers. If the Sixties scare you so much, just remember that they're nearly over – if the radicals are going to lynch the old guard, they're leaving it rather late."

"Yes. The Sixties." He removed some things from a row of books – a gold box and some kind of stick. "Bugger the Sixties. Follow." He opened glass doors on to a balcony. "All those centuries of art, all those geniuses, all that *reason*. And has any of it changed the world? Like hell it has – we're at the mercy of the Hitlers, the men with the atom bombs, the men who play the stock market."

"Aren't you one of the men on the stock market?"

"Yes. That's how I know."

"So why all those books in there, if none of this thinking makes any difference? If you don't care?"

"For their own pleasures. And when you realise how powerless you are, how futile, you can give yourself over to pleasure. Look at this city: it has so much of it."

Although she despised his values, when Sophie looked out across Nightingale Square, towards the West End, heard the hum of the traffic, caught the waft from a restaurant kitchen, heard the laughter of people leaving the clubs, she had to agree with him. Or was it just the *fear* that was giving her the buzz?

Either way, she was damned if she was going to tell Summers she agreed with him.

He passed the mystery object to her – a long, stick-stem pipe. He took a tiny amount of coffee-coloured flakes from the gold box and placed them in the bowl-shaped head, then took the pipe from her, lit the end and inhaled. When he straightened up, there was a softer look in his eyes.

He re-filled the pipe and held it while Sophie smoked. She thought her lungs would burst but she managed to hold it together. And then a wonderful sense of tranquility swept over her. Some distant voice reminded her to keep her wits about her, but crashing into it was another voice that said getting inside the world of Hugo Summers would be all about moments like these.

Inhale.

As she melted back against the balcony wall, Summers stepped into the suite and fiddled with something that triggered a mechanical whirring. Then he killed the lights and returned to re-fill the pipe.

"Opium?" she said.

Summers nodded and brushed the hair from her face as she leant over to suck down some more smoke from the pipe he held for her. She was trying not to think about what to do if – *when* – Summers made his move.

In the reflection of the open doors, Sophie saw what was making the whirring: a Super 8 film being projected on to a wall. She glimpsed a woman in a leopard skin, slit-to-the-waist gown entering the study of a large country house.

"Venn's testing you," said Summers. "He's always looking for women like you."

"Which is?"

"Intelligent, ambitious. You wouldn't have to screw anybody. Except him. He needs girls to help run his

135

operations: flattering clients, spying on people. He even has them running his casinos and bookies. He thinks they're more honest."

"Well, I'm very flattered you think of me that way, Mr Summers, but I really don't want to screw that man *or* run his casinos."

"It's unfortunate you showed such strength tonight. At the very least, he'll probably insist you join The Gathering Place."

"Isn't there still the question of the thousand pound membership?"

"Not if Venn thought you could be useful to him."

In the glass: the skin movie woman had walked in upon a couple on a couch: some neanderthal was being straddled by a slutty type in leather halter top and jeans. Sophie looked at Summers, into eyes as cold as glacial streams. He was offering the pipe again.

"Not my usual drug, but it has a certain exoticism," he said.

She shook her head. She'd had enough, and even the pleasant reveries of the opium couldn't block out the night chill. "So what's your usual drug?"

The pipe was at his mouth again and this time he sucked so hard that the burning opium cast an orange glow over his face. Sophie shuffled along to get a direct view of the film. The couch man's hand was inside the woman's skirt, working back and forth in a fast rhythm. Now the master of the house entered the room, saw the leopard-skin girl.

"I'll show you," said Summers, and led them back inside.

The master raised the leopard skin gown and tucked it into the band of her suspender belt.

Summers put the pipe back where he'd found it and hit a switch on the wall. Shutters purred down to cover the windows. In the shifting light of the film, he and Sophie stood facing each other.

A soft rhythmic chime sounded from somewhere near the doors. Summers swore under his breath and crossed to an entryphone, which he snatched from its cradle. Sophie followed his gaze and saw that he was looking up at a mounted TV monitor. It showed a ghost-like figure standing in the corridor. She would have recognised that squat figure anywhere: *Toad*. The weirdo who had sabotaged Danny and Isabelle's gallery tango.

"Gerald, I have company," said Summers. "No, I can't discuss it now. I'm sure it can wait. You're being paranoid, as ever. Those Americans are people I've known for many years. I can't help what the City pages are saying. They've been saying that for six months. Not that it's any of your business but I assure you nothing has changed." He listened some more. "And as for that matter, I won't accept any of your 'deadlines'. We can speak about this. Yes, that's what I just said. Why don't we have lunch tomorrow at-. Well, you call *me* when you can do it."

A bang of the handset terminated the conversation. "Gerald" was still standing there, eerie in black and white. Staring up at the camera. And then he ambled away, like some obese reptile.

"That man," said Summers.

He took a few steps towards her and then stopped. There was some distant look in his eyes – the opium? – that she had seen downstairs in the lantern room, and when he'd been sitting at his desk just now. Like he was suddenly transported to a dark land. She remembered Scottie telling her about Summers' secret bouts of depression.

He placed a fist to his mouth and dropped his head to his chest.

The screen filled with a reaction shot of the woman in the leopard-skin gown.

Summers' face crumpled and he sunk to his knees.

137

Sophie went to him, put her arms around him, muttered assurances that everything was all right but he made no response, just kept his head tucked in. She rushed away to find a switch but caught her heel on something and crashed into the bar, knocking bottles flying. Her head was swimming with the drug and in the dark her orientation was shot to pieces. What if Summers was having some kind of bad reaction? What if the same thing was about to happen to her?

"Where are the fucking lights?!"

She found a couple of switches and brought some light to the room. Summers had slumped into a foam armchair.

"Water," he said, the arrogant countenance replaced by a little-boy-lost look.

As Sophie brought him a soda water, she realised that she didn't feel so good herself; she was getting out of her depth. She sat on the edge of the bed and tried to read Summers' expression but his face was just ashen and blank.

"Hugo, are you okay?" she said.

"Yes. Just dizzy. Mixed opium with the pills and the booze. It's passing. I've been foolish."

"Is there anything else I can do?"

But he had shut his eyes.

Sophie propped a couple of pillows against the headboard and eased back. She was too scared to fall asleep in this room, or anywhere on this floor.

Some moving shadow startled her. It was coming from the monitor. A figure in the corridor breaking the screen's white glare.

It was Gerald again.

He approached the suite and she anticipated the door chime, but he merely stooped and placed something under the door. And then he was gone.

Sophie checked out Summers: sparko.

Silently she went to the door and picked up Gerald's offering: a photo. Taking care not to wake Summers, she ducked below the projector's beam and crept to the bathroom. Using just the light filtering in from an adjacent building, she examined her find: a colour photo of an old man in a wheelchair.

She could discern nothing else from the snap, except that it had been taken in the not-too-distant past, judging by the cars that could be glimpsed in the street outside the ground-floor room. The only other potential clues were in the bookshelf that was poking into the frame, but the titles were too small to be legible.

Sophie returned to the living room and concealed the photo deep in her handbag. Back on the bed, her attention alternated between Summers and the skin flick. By the time the film ended and the reel flapped round and round, she was too deeply asleep for it to rouse her.

***

CHAPTER SEVENTEEN

She awoke the next morning at 7.30am to find that Summers was gone. Whether he had slept in the chair or in the bed, she had no idea.

All that she knew was that she was desperate to get away from this place but as she was about to leave the suite, she noticed an envelope on the bedside table. Her name was inked on it in a rightward sloping handwriting. She tore it open and tipped out what she at first thought was a business card. When she turned it over she saw the familiar thorns and roses of the Erato, but instead of the usual white background of the club's membership cards, this one was black, and instead of the usual red roses, these were gold.

It was a Gathering Place membership card, signed by Summers himself.

Sophie performed a little spin of joy, and squealed with delight. It was a coup – she'd got the full membership, absolutely free.

Two nights later, The White Hart – known on Fleet Street as The Stab In the Back – proved to be exactly the same rollicking haven of alcoholic hacks that Sophie had known when she'd worked at the *Mirror*. If anything, the noise, alcohol and bullshit levels were even greater than she remembered.

As she walked in and heard the first belligerent debater, the first witty exchange about the day's news gathering, and heard the first execrable tune from the pianist, she was almost tearful with nostalgia. She had imagined that she would be a stranger in here and was flattered when she was hailed as a returning heroine.

Sophie spotted Eamonn Flynn at a table but there was five minutes of dealing with well wishers and the drinks they foisted upon her before she could reach him.

"Miss 'em?" said Flynn. He'd put on some weight and his nose had sprouted some veins but he was still dapper in his customary three-piece suit and blue silk handkerchief.

"Here, have one," she said, pushing him a drink from her tray.

"Port and lemon? What kind of crime correspondent do you think I am?" he said, knocking it back.

"So what's new?"

"Just these," he said, pinching his jowels. "And you? How did that thing with the maniac leave you?"

"Littlechild or David?"

"Ha. The copper."

"A few cuts and bruises. I'm fine. Apart from the nightmares for life. The David thing was worse."

"I'm sure. He was trash."

"I guess you heard about Scottie, too."

"Did it himself, the rascal?"

"Pills. Killers."

"Talking of killers, I was surprised when you phoned up asking for the short and curlies on Eddie Venn. I thought you wrote about eye shadow and lady feelings now."

"I'm writing a colour piece on hang-outs of the rich and famous. Well, maybe that's what it'll be. I haven't really decided yet, Eamonn, but I appreciate you coming."

"Stop talking to me like I'm some bloody government minister. This is Flynn." He finished one of the two pints before him and cleared his throat. "So. Eddie Venn."

Sophie pulled out her pad. She knew he would give this to her fast, and without notes. He was proud of his photographic memory.

"East End boy, one of six kids, did his national service in the army and proved a useful middleweight – won some silverware. He took over his uncle's scrap

141

metal business in Bow and was semi-legit for a while. Then he went into the protection game – gambling clubs, snooker halls – and got his fingers burnt with a couple of long firms, which landed him a short stretch at Brixton; he's got the scars from all those birchings to prove it, too.

"When he got out, he fell in with the Krays, became an enforcer, under the wing of a man called George Tozer. Old-school villain. Partial to electrodes on the knackers, and pliers on the teeth, though only on others. He and Venn teamed up and broke off from the Krays, while still paying their dues, of course. They led the Old Bill a merry dance, always slippery, always pulling some trick to scupper a prosecution. And since the Krays got banged up this year, the sky's the limit for Venn."

"And Tozer?"

"That's what's interesting. As soon as they turned the key on Ron and Reg, Venn got super-ambitious, super-*flash*. Bought himself a fleet of Rollers, a place in Spain, mixes with showbiz types... Rumour has it that he's breaking away from Tozer, who he looks on as a bit past it. And he may be right: Tozer was fairly small time until he met Venn; he doesn't have the brains or ambition to keep pace with his apprentice. Venn's made a lot of cash very quickly with his clubs and gambling and purple hearts operation, not to mention the legitimate stuff like property. And then there's the Erato."

Flynn was staring at her intensely. He'd guessed that the Erato was her angle. Sophie just raised an eyebrow, giving nothing away.

Flynn chuckled. "The Erato, as you may or may not know, is a swanky club in Mayfair. Opulent doesn't cover it. The club needed repairs a couple of years back and Hugo Summers – that rich bastard who owns Summers Steel – didn't want to stump up for it all by himself. Rumour is that Venn wrote him a fat cheque. He certainly spends a lot of time at the club, if you believe the gossip columns, and I know you do. And since the repairs got done, the crowd's become more like Venn's crowd. It used to be grey types from Barings and Lord and Lady Such and Such; now it's TV actors and gangsters."

"Venn's private playground."

"And what a playground; a lot of naughty stuff goes on there, they say. But Venn and Summers have got some very good lawyers and no-one's printed anything yet. Just to hint that Venn is Summers' partner would be libel, possibly *criminal* libel. And Venn's involvement is strictly off the record so nothing can be proved. And beyond that, I don't know much more about Mr Venn. Except he's still on the up, and he's a vicious bastard. There's at least two murders he's done himself and several more he's ordered. Police can't pin a thing on him. He's too damned slick."

It took a few moments for Sophie's shorthand to catch up with the briefing. She dipped into her handbag and found the photo that Masters had slipped under the door.

"Look, this is a long shot, but do you know who this is?" she said.

Flynn shook his head. "Nope... But he's not in Britain."

"Eh?"

"Look." He placed a finger on the two cars passing each other in the road beyond the old man's window. "They're on the wrong side of the road. That doesn't exactly narrow it down much but..."

"No, that's useful."

"So come on Sophie, tell me what this is all about because I don't believe you're doing an "At home with Eddie Venn" piece for *The Journal of Penal Reform*."

Sophie laughed. "Is that a real magazine?"

"It could be. You and me. We could run it from the Isle of Mull."

Sophie laughed and looked away. "Still a flirt. I think we're both too set in our ways to make that a goer, Eamonn."

There was some hurt in Flynn's eyes, like he'd been hoping she'd give him some positive signals. She bought him another drink and they chatted about the old days. It wasn't long before Flynn was checking his watch. "Well, I've got an appointment with a lady of the night."

"Business or pleasure?"

"She does it for the money, I'm sure."

"Hey, Eamonn, tell me just one thing: how come you guys never get out of Fleet Street?"

"The Street of Adventure? You don't need me to tell you that."

"I do. Getting out was the best thing I ever did. I love what I do now. I get up late, work from home. Easy. Healthy."

"Nah. You didn't get out, Sophie. We just loaned you for a while." He plumped his trilby back on and leaned in to her. "Colour piece, my arse. You take care now, and remember: *don't hunt what you can't kill.*"

Sophie remembered that she'd meant to ask him why he hadn't been at Scottie's funeral but he was out the door. She watched as he ducked his head against a driving rain and tapped his pockets to check for a hip flask or pills or whatever got him through each day, and she knew.

***

CHAPTER EIGHTEEN

The run-in with Venn had made her stronger, and the fearlessness with which she had pursued stories in the old days was back. It was like the four years she'd spent writing about marriage and fashion had never happened. She would do whatever it took to bring Venn down – and to find out if that bastard Summers was behind the disappearance of Abigail Wilman. No-one would be able to say she had sold out on her convictions.

Even the discovery that, as she had suspected, her wedding photos had indeed been rifled through, and one removed, seemed merely proof that she had successfully engaged the enemy. And when the "borrowed" wedding day snapshot arrived in the post, she didn't dwell on whether she should bin it, but simply slipped it back into the album. Even the new issue of *Serendipity* magazine, featuring an exclusive Saffron Honey interview with Paul Newman, didn't get her down.

In the week, Sophie went to Knightsbridge and bought two dresses. If she was going to do this Erato thing properly, she couldn't keep recycling the same three outfits, especially as she'd been promoted to The Gathering Place.

And on three occasions she evaded house calls from Moog (she was now in the habit of peering out the window when the doorbell rang). She simply wasn't up to throwing herself back into all those campaign groups yet, and those guys didn't take no for an answer.

The plan was to go to the club on the Saturday, but by the time Friday arrived she was so impatient that she decided to go that night. It was too dangerous to go to the upstairs but she could risk the Erato.

As the winter sun was setting, Venn phoned.

CHAPTER NINETEEN

He started off with some small talk, making no mention of the handcuffs incident, or how she had sneaked into The Gathering Place. But eventually he said: "I don't want there to be bad feeling between us. Especially now you're a member of the upstairs."

"I've been wondering how you feel about that."

"I like you, Sophie. You've got bottle. I'm pleased to have you on board. If I wasn't, I'd veto the membership. The upstairs is my club, after all. A lot of powerful people are members and I want to introduce you. We all work together at The Gathering Place. There's no room for petty games up there. So I was thinking, why don't you stop by for a few drinks tonight?"

"Actually, I was planning to."

"Attagirl. Come upstairs, then. Let's say around midnight? And don't worry, it's not some stitch-up. Hugo will be there. Or he says he will. He's a bit of an enigma is Hugo but you probably discovered that for yourself last week. Now, will you need a car?"

"No. I'll make my own way."

"Fine."

She thought he was going to hang up then, and wanted to beat him to it, but he added: "I'm sorry about the other night, Sophie. I'm very protective about security. Sometimes I have to test people, see how they respond. We get a lot of people snooping around. But after that thing you pulled on me, and the way you managed to get into The Gathering Place, well, no hack would stick their head that far above the parapet. In my eyes you're legit. So no hard feelings, eh?"

"No," she said, wanting to cry with relief. "No hard feelings."

And for the second time, he hung up on her.

CHAPTER TWENTY

At midnight, Arcadian Gardens shimmered with black ice.

In the lift, Sophie smoothed down her black satin wrap dress and regretted having been too nervous to eat because now she felt nervous *and* hungry. Mostly she feared that Venn would try to press drugs on her again, and she'd end up having to refuse. But there was no way she could go along with it – she'd been back from the halfway house barely three weeks...

The lift operator avoided her stare when she asked for the top floor, and looked down when she got out. A heavyset man with deep acne scars and a hangdog expression got up from his seat and asked for her membership card.

"I'm Jack, miss," he said. "Jack Rickard. I watch over this floor. If there's anything you need, just find me, okay? Or you can call me from any of the phones. Just dial 200."

She said that she would and was about to ask him how she got into the tunnel when the acrylic glass doors opened.

Great. So Venn's already watching you.

The red and blue footlights led the way to the doors at the other end and she emerged from the tunnel into the next lobby. Venn's laugh sounded from off to the left and she followed the dimly lit corridor that had scared her the previous week. She found herself praying that Summers would be here.

Praying that the man who probably killed Abigail was here?

The corridor opened on to a gigantic, Arctic-white lounge, done out in a Futurist style. Sophie stepped into it with her eyes and mouth wide open in disbelief. Venn spotted her and broke off from some lewd anecdote.

"Sophie," he said Venn, throwing his arms out as if embracing the incredible wonderland around him. "Welcome to The Gathering Place."

As he kissed her, Sophie tried not to recoil as his face – with its red raw nose and bulging eyes – pressed against hers. He escorted her towards a small group of people lounging on four giant black sofas, formed into a loose square.

"Wait a minute," she said, not even trying to hide her look of amazement. "Give me a minute to check this place out."

"It's mad, innit? You've got all night to look around. Come and meet the gang."

But she didn't hurry, she wanted to soak it all up. Dotted around was a variety of seating, from comfortable leather armchairs to reclining designer models and strangely shaped surfaces that fell halfway between chair and bed. Many had been customised with hooks, panels and buttons, their pleasures and pains only vaguely guessable to Sophie. All of the seats faced a screen on the far wall and Sophie spotted a projector, hidden among the exotic plants that flowed from a series of suspended trugs zigzagging overhead. These ran roughly parallel with an artificial stream coursing beneath a transparent perspex floor which was artfully cracked in places to give the impression of ice. Sophie felt the water burbling under her feet and saw the yellow marsh marigold petals being pulled in the current and thought: *this place is utterly insane.*

"That Spaniard really was mad," she said.

"Yeah, beats the pre-fab I grew up in," said Venn.

"So this is what a grand buys you."

"We like to think it's the company that the money buys you. And talking of which, can I introduce you to a couple of good associates of mine. Everyone, this is Sophie. Sophie, this is Gerald."

The man she knew as Toad waddled forward to pump her hand with a clammy palm.

"Sophie, I've seen you at the club. The pleasure's mine." A strand of Brylcreemed hair fell from his combover. He eased it back into place.

"How do you, do… I'm sorry, it's Gerald…?"

Gerald smarmed again. "Well, I think just Gerald's friendlier, don't you?" He fixed her with dead, grey eyes.

Nice try anyway, Boyd.

The other man, Tatsuya, was a Japanese maybe in his late thirties and wearing a dark business suit that was in disarray. He was unshaven and puffy looking and didn't bother to get up as he offered a half-hearted handshake and resumed his task of trying to get a gold lighter to work.

The four sofas faced in to a large glass coffee table covered in: canisters of Super 8 film; a slide viewer, some strange, chopped-up fruit, a carving knife; a tiny Buddha statue puffing incense; a wad of paper towels mopping up spilt booze; a multi-headed dildo; packets of assorted foreign cigarettes, their contents spilling out and slit down the middle; and several dozen amyl nitrite poppers emblazoned with Oriental symbols.

Tatsuya had got the lighter working and was melting a plastic blackjack shoe. His eyes were on a toy robot whose journey across the room had been halted by the playing cards that littered the floor. Its legs just trundled round and round.

Venn caught Sophie's anxious expression. "Don't mind Tat," he said. "He's had a bad day at the casino. And this," he said, gesturing to a young woman, "this is the beautiful Echo."

Echo was the girl from the wedding dress show. She was indeed beautiful, but how old was she? Sixteen? Eighteen at most. She wore a knife-pleated baby doll dress in poppy. One eye was hidden behind a pageboy hairstyle and there was strange white make-up around her eyes. Her lips were painted a garish red. A cigarette had burnt down to the butt and rested in her fingers. She sat motionless, gazing through the glass tabletop.

Echo. Amber. Sophie felt a fresh surge of disgust for Venn and his conveyor-belt of addicted playthings with saucer eyes and stag film names.

Sophie sat to her right, hoping Echo might still become some kind of ally in this threatening environment, but she was staring into space.

"Well, must be time for a crafty sherry," said Venn, moving to the bar. He stooped down and a second later music filled the room. A dreamy acoustic guitar low down in the mix. A tentative drum roll. A very English-sounding singer. *Ground Control to Major Tom...* His voice doubled, coming at her from unseen speakers. *3-2-1... Lift-off.*

"I bet you like Bowie," said Venn. "What do you think of the view?"

Sophie had already been entranced by the windows' panoramic aspect on the Thames but couldn't work out how it was possible all the way from Mayfair. Venn clicked a remote control and the windows flipped over in a series of cascading panels to reveal a different cityscape: Manhattan.

Tat threw himself back in his seat and slapped his palms on his knees, laughing furiously like this was the funniest thing he'd ever seen.

"He never gets tired of it," said Venn. "When I switch it to Tokyo, he gets all emotional."

Venn turned the shutters over again and this time the room seemed to double in size as a bank of mirrors appeared.

Something was moving under the coffee table. It was just the robot, whirring up to her and trying to mount her shoe. She turned it around.

150

Venn must have switched the panels to auto because they began rotating through their silent cycle, offering a seemingly endless variety of locations. Sometimes the view would be of a city or a desert, and sometimes the mirrors would show the room they were in, or the room upside down, or shown from one end.

"Round and round she goes," said Venn. "Where she stops, nobody knows."

Tat snorted coke from one of the mirrors inset into the table, then offered a gold tube to Sophie and pointed to a pre-cut line.

Oh well. So much for the plan.

And the stars look very different today...

"This little one here?" she said.

Tat grunted and moved the razor deftly around the mirror to draw in more powder. What the hell – there was a difference between OD'ing on pills because you were suicidal and doing a little bit of coke because you were undercover. So how did you take it? She'd watched the others – they just seemed to do it in one go. How hard could it be?

She leant over the table, held her hair back, and snorted half up one nostril – her eyes flicked up and saw the ash fall from Echo's cigarette – and then the rest up the other. Not so difficult.

Venn nodded approvingly, like she was his protégé. Maybe Summers had been on the money when he'd said that Venn would want her to work for him.

The song breaks into a sax and lush strings and nosedives with brass. *Though I'm past one hundred thousand miles, I'm feeling very still.* Too weird, the music was too weird, it was freaking her out. Was that the plan?

Venn sits to Echo's right and with no preliminaries clamps her head between his hands and kisses her deeply, slobberingly. On auto-pilot, she starts to undo his shirt. Venn's hands go to her breasts, his mouth to her throat. Sophie's heart is pounding – why did she

151

agree to come here? And where the hell was Hugo? *Shit shit shit.*

Gerald goes to the back of the room and returns with a Super 8 camera, which is already whirring.

Sophie is horrifed to see the birching scars that criss-cross Venn's back like a tangle of winter hedgerow but tries not to stare as he expertly removes Echo's dress. The girl wears no underwear and now her fragile body is naked on the leather. She sits on his lap, facing him, and starts undoing his belt buckle.

Tat barks something in Japanese and removes his shirt, revealing a muscular torso. Venn is struggling to remove his own trousers without standing up. Gerald takes a few steps in with the camera. Sophie feels cramped, threatened. Is it her turn next? Venn's tongue flickers across the little rings of Echo's nipples. Tat's eyes alight on Sophie, and he speaks his first words of English:

"Take them off. Take it all off."

He sits beside her and runs his hands down her stockings. She feels the first rush as the drug runs down her throat and hits her bloodstream. The music so loud it feels like it's crowding her in, feels like they've turned up the volume this high to knock out one of her senses, make her more vulnerable. Gerald eases his bulk on to the edge of the table for a better angle to film.

What do I do? What the hell do I do? Oh Jesus. I can't do this.

"I can't do this," she says.

"What do you mean?" says Venn.

Tat snaps something at her and she stares him down.

"I just… I've made a mistake," she said.

"Mistake?" says Venn.

She sees a way out. "I mean the coke."

"What about the fucking coke?"

"I've just had a bad reaction every time I've taken it," she lied.

"Jesus, so don't take it! Echo, get these fucking trousers off me!"

Gerald moves behind Sophie with the camera, making her nervous. Tat lunges, pulling her to him in a painful embrace, and tries kissing her. She turns her head to one side and he slobbers over her cheek. She hugs him tightly to her, pinning him there, playing for time. *I have to get away from him.* Over his shoulder, she sees Echo and an idea comes to her. She frees herself from the embrace and moves round to sit to the left of Venn and Echo. Now they act as a barrier between her and Tat. Her heart going frantic.

Venn grins. "Oh, looks like the girls want to say hello."

Sophie doesn't know how to get away from the situation and just gives in to it. Closes her eyes and they kiss. The song reaches a crescendo, a swirling mess of strings and beeps, fading in and out, jumping from speaker to speaker. Drug numbing her throat, heart pumping, blood pounding in her ears.

Echo screams. Her body convulsing.

Sophie rears back in horror.

Echo falling in slow motion. Her head striking the edge of the table. A hairline crack shooting across the glass. Some object flying from her neck and bouncing on to the carpet. With the hand that isn't holding the camera, Gerald scoops it up but Sophie's had enough of games, of not knowing what is going on. She pounces on Gerald and grabs his wrist just as he is pocketing the item. He pulls away from her but not before she has seen it is a hypodermic syringe.

Gerald breaks her grip and takes it back from her.

Venn is down on the floor where Echo has fallen. He feels for a pulse and begins giving her the kiss of life.

"Call an ambulance," Sophie yells at Tat but he just looks dazed. "Someone call a fucking ambulance!"

Venn lifts the limp body on to the sofa and attempts a heart massage, alternating it with mouth-to-mouth.

Eventually he says: "It's no good. She's dead."

"How do you know – you're not a doctor!"

"She's dead, Sophie. She is dead."

"This bastard killed her with whatever's in that syringe!"

Tat already had his shirt back on.

"If you don't call an ambulance, I will," she says.

"No you won't," says Venn.

Gerald puts a comforting hand on her back and she swats it away.

"You fucking murderers!"

"It's not like that, Sophie," says Venn.

"That's *just* what it's like. Gerald killed her for kicks. Who's next – me? Is that why you let me in here?"

"Echo was a mixed-up girl. A junkie. I saved her from the streets and brought her here, made her healthy again. I didn't mean-."

"You fucking liar! You brought her here to kill her because that's what creeps like them pay for!"

Bowie is on to the next album track. Venn goes to the music centre and switches it off.

"That's not how it is," he says, and nods to Gerald and Tat. Together they lift Echo's body between them and hurry from the lounge. "*Now listen*, Sophie. She didn't have any family, she was a runaway. *I'll* take care of this. *You* just have to forget it happened."

"She's dead because that bastard killed her with an OD."

"I didn't know he was going to do that. But it wasn't that fix that killed her, believe me. It was the one before and the one before that. I got her off that shit in the first place but some people can't be saved. What Gerald gave her was just the last straw."

"I don't believe a word of it. I want to hear what Hugo's got to say about this. Where is he, anyway?"

Venn blocks her way. "I don't know."

"You said he'd be here."

She tries to move around him but he shoulder barges her, sending her flying on to the sofa.

"I never said that."

The jolt winds Sophie. When she gets her breath back, she says: "Of course. You just wanted to get me here, to audition me for your army of whores. Well, Hugo's going to be very interested when I tell him about tonight."

"Don't think you're Hugo's friend just because you fucked him."

"Who said I fucked him?"

"Oh yeah, I'd *heard* that Hugo doesn't fuck any more. Depressives can't, can they? And anyway, the poor sod's fifty-five, what do you expect? You want to think about your loyalties, Sophie."

"What does that mean?"

"Hugo's not always going to be around. Even you can see who's in charge now. You could do well by me."

"Aren't I a bit old to be of use to you? I thought you only wanted models and bimbos."

"That's exactly what I don't need more of. I need people with brains, character. Thinkers."

"Great. So I join your gang and have to get it on with sleazy bastards like Gerald and Tat? And then get killed for a snuff movie?"

"Okay, okay, it was a mistake asking you here. But listen, the Echo thing was one in a million, a freak accident. I've got loads of work for good girls like you: in my casinos, schmoozing, keeping an eye on clients. You need to start trusting me. We're all guilty together here."

"I'm sick of hearing about trust. Echo trusted you and look what happened to her. Who paid to see her die – was it Gerald? Tat? Is that their thing? How many girls like her die up here, Venn?"

"It was an OD, Sophie. It happens to junkies all the time. She was begging me for a hit before you showed up. I told her no, over and over. Then Gerald gives her one little pick-me-up and... she'd obviously been doing it all day on the sly. That last hit just tipped her over. And you were right about the coke. You get a bad reaction. Stick to the booze next time."

Sophie grabs her handbag from the floor and stands up. "I'm going to the police."

"That wouldn't be so clever, given what was caught on film tonight."

"Me kissing a girl? I can live with that. It's Gerald that's got to worry: it's manslaughter at the very least. And it all happened in your club, so you should be worried, too."

"It's not just kissing the girl, Sophie. My guess is that Gerald was zooming in pretty close, close enough that if he gave her that jab, he won't have caught himself doing it."

It takes a few moments for the implications to hit Sophie.

"You set it up. The whole thing tonight wasn't a snuff movie, wasn't for Gerald or Tat. It was all done just so *you* could trap me into working for you..."

Venn shrugs. "You've got me all wrong."

"Then why did you get someone to search my flat?"

"They didn't search it, just had a poke around. I like to get information on people, Sophie. And I like you. I wanted to find out some more about you."

"And that thing with the wedding dress?"

"I wanted to see if you were strong enough to take it. Whether you had character. You did, and then some... And when you agreed to come here tonight, that just proved it to me all over again. Hook up with me, darling. I'm taking over London. The Establishment are shitting themselves right now, because they know that in ten years *we'll* be the new Establishment."

Sophie begins to laugh. "You're actually serious, aren't you? *The answer's no.* And you can't blackmail me: that film can't prove I gave her the injection for the simple reason that I *didn't do it.*"

"All the same, if I were you, I still wouldn't want that film out there. At the least it's going to mean a very messy police investigation. And what your friends and family and those nice little writing clients of yours are going to make of you being at an orgy when some under-age girl dies, well…"

"Where is it? Where's the film?"

"It looks like Gerald's taken the camera," he says. "I'll get it back. Believe me, I don't want that kicking about."

The second hammer-blow revelation hits Sophie. "And he took the syringe, too. My God, you've got me just where you want me. The film and the screening pictures."

"You're testing my patience, girl. Now tidy up, I'm calling you a car." He slips on his jacket and strides out.

Sophie sits down. She's shaking. That first kick of cocaine has worn off. She looks at the readymade lines and sees in them the confidence she needs to leave the club, with its risk of encountering Venn again.

She takes the razor and carves herself a line, just as she's seen the others do. A few minutes later, she's buzzing and feeling a whole lot less vulnerable.

Another line would help, but she doesn't want to start down that road.

The robot is at her feet again, blaring some Japanese phrase. She lashes out with a kick and sends it flying.

And then The Gathering Place is silent except for the gentle turning of the picture panels.

***

CHAPTER TWENTY-ONE

CRUUUUUNKKKKK!!!

An almighty crash. The contents of the cab fly around: a Virgin Mary statuette, tobacco tins and pipes, maps, tool box and coils of wire. The old man lying across her lap. Panicking, thinking he's dead, she wants to get out of the cab right now. Water is pouring in around the doors and splashes him in the face, jerking him to consciousness.

"Christ, someone was watching over us. All right, get out, girl!"

She hooks the handles of the bag over her head and with all her strength opens the passenger door against the weight of the water and drops down, landing up to her knees in the flood. The back of the van is wrapped around a couple of boulders on the cliff edge. Such relief that she doesn't even notice the sheets of stinging rain. In low-level shock, she stands in the road, staring blankly at the green hills, the smudge of the mountains, the barren heather.

Someone is calling her name.

She turns. A man stands with Joe.

"You wanted to find Brennan? That's Colm Brennan," says the stranger. "He's been gone a while but his yard's still up the lane. I think there might be someone living on the bus. I'll take you there later. Let's get out of the rain. Come down to my…"

He tails off because she is already wading towards the road he has pointed out… Joe is calling for her to come back but she won't be stopped.

She follows a stony track uphill and gets above the worst of the floods and it's not long before she sees what must be the scrapyard: a jungle of twisted black shapes silhouetted against the horizon.

There's nothing to stop her walking in. She finds herself almost tiptoeing, despite the cacophany of rain as it hammers down on a once-proud Leyland Lion bus, its racing green now dimmed forever, Gold Flake ad panels dangling by a screw. Her shoes are suctioned down by the mud and each step is an effort. She wanders the yard, threading her way slowly between oil-spattered Ferguson tractors; half chopped-up fishing boats; forgotten Standard Ten cars robbed of wheels, and in a space of its own, a mountain of radiator grilles, bathtubs, toilets, farm machinery and vehicle doors.

She spots a shack and for a moment holds out hope. It turns out to be a site office, long abandoned, with nothing inside but a stove and a chair.

Then, a tiny yellow movement catches her eye: she'd missed the red Leyland Lion up on cinderblocks at the back of the yard. Candlelight flickers between threadbare curtains that cover each of the windows. As she nears, she sees a pile of bottles and food cans dumped outside.

She listens. The white noise of a radio off the station, a presenter's voice occasionally audible. The smell of a paraffin heater. Suddenly this doesn't seem a good idea. Was he really here, in this awful place?

The choices are knocking or dying of pneumonia. She stands on a packing crate that doubles as a step and gives three thumps on what used to be the bus's single door, up by the driver. Instantly one of the curtains off to the right twitches but she's caught the side of a face – a haunted, waxy face.

A series of clunks and the door creaks open a few inches.

New smells waft out: boiled cabbage, stale beer, and above it all something terrible, something dark, something rotting. She has never experienced the smell before, but she knows what it is. She stands on the step and pulls the door open...

***

CHAPTER TWENTY-TWO

The next morning, in a pew at St Bride's Church, she sat with her head bowed. Still, hardly breathing, as if she hoped she could say her prayers, do her thinking and slip away unnoticed.

Every now and then, she would flinch at the sound of someone entering the church. She was particularly suspicious of people who sat at the back. If someone was following her, that's where they would be at this moment, wasn't it?

She opened her handbag and touched a wrap of coke that she had found on the coffee table before she left last night. It might just help her through this week: she had a lot of notes to make on events so far, and a lot of articles to write for her magazines.

Venn had stitched her up completely. He had her. The only way out of this was to go all the way in to his world, and the world of Hugo Summers. She owed it to Abby, and to Scottie, and all the other victims. And maybe she owed it to who she had used to be: the campaigner, the champion, the girl with fire in her belly. Moog was right when he said it was over. He wasn't the only one to feel it. Like the man said in *Easy Rider*: we blew it. The decade felt old, its heroes corrupted, the summer of love a very long time ago. But if Summers was guilty, you could bet your bottom dollar that it was his privilege that had protected him all these years. And that would be worth one last battle.

She said another prayer for the dead, and then hurried from the church. There was work to do.

***

CHAPTER TWENTY-THREE

In the fortnight leading up to Christmas, Sophie attended the Erato every Friday and Saturday night, as well as making a couple of appearances midweek to see what went on (the clientele was the same but nothing sexual took place). She hung around in the cocktail bar, where she felt safer, and where Mitzi was always splashing out on Krug and gossiping. The most interesting tidbit was that a famous interior decorator had been visiting the club to make drawings and take endless Polaroids. Neither she nor Charlie knew what he was up to.

Venn was coolly polite to Sophie but he wasn't around much. The only time she saw him do anything of note was when he broke up a fight on Christmas Eve between his mate Tozer and a young lord, the son of one of Summers' oldest friends.

As for Summers, she didn't see him at all. It was tempting to use her Gathering Place membership card to poke around upstairs but after the last occasion she was scared to. She considered writing Summers a note but what would it say? "It'd be nice to meet you again"? She'd just come across as some lovesick schoolgirl.

To really hammer home that she was no Queen Mother, she began taking a little coke when it was offered, but she chose to dab it into her gums rather than snort it. She needed confidence to seem at home at the club but didn't want to rely on booze, which would muddy her thinking and give her a hangover. She felt strong, hungry to go deep into these people's world, and that meant doing it properly.

One avenue for keeping tabs on Hugo Summers presented itself just before Christmas, when the City pages of the national press started buzzing with speculation that he was about to acquire *The New York*

Journal and its four sister titles. Summers was said to have long been seeking a foothold in the American media and was now eyeing the failing group. Whether it was to restore its fortunes or strip it down, no-one was sure, but it was the business pages' top story in an otherwise quiet week. These had to be "the Yanks". But then, frustratingly, any chance of the deal being resolved was scuppered by the arrival of Christmas.

Traditionally, Sophie had always quite enjoyed the Christmas Eve drive to her mother's house, nestling on the South Downs near Steyning. The back seat was usually stacked with wrapped presents for her two nieces but this year she couldn't go until Christmas Day as she hadn't wanted to miss the Erato's Christmas Eve party. This year she made the journey with her foot down while slurping from a flask of coffee and trying to ignore the fact that she hadn't bought many gifts, and that those she did have were still unwrapped.

Throughout Christmas Day lunch, she kept dashing off to jot down some thought, some line of enquiry she could pursue, and ended up having a blazing row with her mother's second husband. For the remainder of the stay, Sophie got blotto from midday to when she collapsed into bed at night. When it was time to go home, she blasted out the car radio and sang the whole way back to London. It was only a Sunday but it was still Christmas and that meant one thing: the Erato would be buzzing tonight.

When she stepped into the grand hallway, the first person she saw was Venn. His face lit up with what seemed genuine warmth.

"Evening, Sophie," he said, kissing her on the cheek. "And Happy Christmas."

"Happy Christmas."

"Talking of which, I've got a little Christmas box for you." He dropped his voice. "That crazy night, a few weeks back, well, I was closing a big deal."

"With the Japanese guy or Gerald?"

"Tat. Filthy rich. He wants to start a casino over here but he won't get a licence, not being a Brit. So I'm going in with him and – well, you don't need all the details but things are looking sweet. And that's what the upstairs is all about."

"Is that supposed to make everything all right? Because you made money out of it?"

"Listen, I cried for Echo. But if I'd gone to the Old Bill, would that have brought her back?"

What was she doing, arguing with him? *Stop bitching and play the role.*

"I appreciate it but I'd rather not take any money," she said. "I thought it was just going to be a few drinks. I didn't go there to make money."

"Have it your way. But at least let me supply the refreshments tonight, eh?" He placed something in her palm and closed her fingers over it. "If you want any more, Terry'll sort you out."

Sophie unclenched her fist and looked down at a small wrap of paper. Venn winked at her and was starting to walk away when Charlie began charging down the stairs.

"VENN! Your friends have been leaving broken glass in the sauna and terrorising the other members. What the hell is going on?"

"Who are you talking about?"

"I don't know their names. They're not even members, they've just started turning up with Tozer. I asked them to settle their gambling debts the other day and they threatened to cut my face open. What am I supposed to do?"

"Relax, Charlie," said Venn, walking Charlie to a secluded spot beside a giant Christmas tree. Sophie discreetly edged round to the other side of it. "You're making a scene. I'll have a word with them, all right?"

"They're morons, and dangerous ones at that. People have a right to come here and not fear a smack in the face. They're asking questions, too: about the designers, the planners, the lawyers who were in here every day before Christmas, making blueprints and whispering into dictaphones. What's going on?"

"None of your business."

"But I'm the manager, remember?"

"No, Charles, you're just an old friend of Hugo's. Some sad duffer who had to be rescued when a pyramid scheme went bust. Face it, Charles: there's one born every minute and you've had a lot of minutes. Now get back to work or I'll cut your face to ribbons myself."

Charlie drew himself up to his full height and looked down at Venn. "Threats, that's the only way you know how to communicate, isn't it? Let me remind you that Hugo was a great man until you drove him and his friends out."

Venn gave one of his rasping laughs. All other chatter in the hallway had long since faded out. No-one wanted to miss this.

"What's your deal with Gerald?" said Charlie. "Why don't you tell everyone here what-."

Venn tossed away his champagne flute and grabbed Charlie's shirt with both hands, slamming him into the wall, once, twice. Charlie flopped into a heap.

"That's enough!" shouted Sophie. She burst from her hiding place just as Venn was drawing back his foot.

Venn had had his fill. He shook his head and marched off. Charlie was already sitting up. When he was ready, Sophie guided him to an empty ante room, locked the door and sat him down.

"Jesus, Charlie. What was that all about?

"I'm really going to nail the bastard this time."

"What were you saying? About Venn having a deal with Gerald?" She spotted a decanter and poured them both a large Scotch.

"You don't need to know," said Charlie. "If I could only talk to Hugo, I could persuade him to get Venn out of here."

"Charlie, that's not going to happen."

"No, no, no. Hugo is reasonable. Intelligent. This was his father's club. The problem is that Hugo just doesn't know what Venn gets up to, the way this place is going to hell. Straight to hell..." Charlie was jabbering now. The resonant actor's tones had been replaced by the reedy voice of a sick old man.

"Just have a drink and calm down, Charlie."

"And what have you been doing up there, Sophie, in that place I've never even set foot in? You're a nice girl. Just stay down at the Erato, okay? Or better still, stay away from the whole building. It won't be long before even the Erato is ruined. Everything here is drawing to a close..."

Sophie hated herself for what she thought next: how weak Charlie seemed compared with Venn.

"He's wrong about the journalists," said Charlie. "He made that up just to make me look bad. I'm for the push, Sophie. And then what? Hugo won't rescue me again. There are no more little jobs for Charlie. I'm fucked, darling. Well, if that's the way it is, I'll just have to take him down with me."

"I think you should go home, Charlie. Where's Mitzi?"

"I've been a good manager. It's not easy, keeping this show going."

"Of course you're good, Charlie. Venn's just trying to undermine you, get you to leave so he can bring in his own people."

Charlie went silent for a minute. Then he said: "Tell me something, Sophie."

"I'll try."

"Are you good at what you do?"

"Yes, I think so... No, I'm sure I am."

"Really good?"

"Yes."

"But who's the *best* at what you do?"

"Magazine writer?"

"Yes."

Sophie was, as he said, keen to humour him, but she still surprised herself when she said Saffron Honey.

"I think I've heard of her," said Charlie. "Who does she write for?"

"The big glossies." Remembering her own cover story, she added: "She's in a different league from me: film stars and rock stars."

Charlie didn't seemed to have heard this last bit. He got to his feet.

"Why do you want to know, Charlie?"

"Just because... that's what I wanted to be. The best. That's all."

"Are you all right? You're still really white, and you're shaking."

"Dryden is made of sterner stuff. Now, things to do."

Someone was hammering on the doors just as Charlie reached them. He unlocked them and was nearly knocked over by Mitzi's entrance.

"Honey! What did that bastard do to you?"

"Nothing, just the usual barking. Charlie Dryden gave as good as he got, believe me."

Charlie shadow boxed a jab-jab-cross.

"I've been worried about him," said Sophie, trying to catch Mitzi's eye.

"I'm getting my husband to quit this foul place," said Mitzi.

"They'll quit *me* soon enough," said Charlie. "The only question is do I wait to be pushed, or go out with a little poetry?"

"He's not making sense," said Sophie. "Mitzi?"

"Yeah, I heard you, honey. Sit down, Charlie."

Summers entered the room with his usual poise. His eyes flicked around the room, quickly sizing up who was here and what the situation would require of him.

Charlie bellowed his name and locked Summers in a bearhug, which Hugo took awkwardly. Sophie realised it was the first time she had seen the two together.

"How are you, old mate?" said Charlie.

"Very well, Charlie. Busy. And yourself?"

"It's tough down here, Hugo. Tough. There are some things I'd like to talk to you about. Pretty urgent things. Shut the door and I'll pour us a couple of stiff ones."

"Now's not the best time."

"Fine. In fact, that's good, because I was thinking: you and I should catch *Guys and Dolls* at the Phoenix. I read the reviews and thought of you. I know how you love it. That young girl is supposed to be a sensation."

"She's *all right* – I saw her in *Hay Fever* – but she'll be miscast as Sarah Brown. No comic touch. They should have got Bloom or Plowright – both could have been free, apparently – but that fool of a director wanted to be a maverick, and the producer let him. And now the same producer's hunting round for a Lady Macbeth, and that girl would have been perfect. No wonder no-one's making any money; the producers don't have a clue."

"You're right!" said Charlie. "Hugo is always right. God, Theatreland needs him back. It's not too late, we could do it. We never produced that play of mine, the one set in Korea. I still think that could be big."

"Yes, I did like that," said Summers, noncommittally. "What I'd *really* like to see again is something we enjoyed in 1949."

Charlie made a big play of trying to remember. He was loving his moment in the sun, showing off to Sophie how well he knew Summers. "Lear?"

"No."

"Hmmm. Not that bloody Rattigan thing?"

"No, no… Something with a bit more… *legs* to it."

Charlie clapped his hands together. "The Folies Bergére!"

"Now, *that* was an evening at the theatre."

"Come on, Hugo, let's do it – jump in a car like we did then. Pack a hamper and a crate of Bolly."

Sophie was beginning to squirm: didn't Charlie sense, as she and surely Mitzi did, that Summers was just humouring him?

"The old days were indeed wonderful," said Hugo. "But alas, my schedule is rather more punishing now."

"Not everything has to be 'the old days' though? Surely you could squeeze in that new Ibsen one evening?"

"It really is punishing, Charlie. Sorry, old chap, but I'm going to have to get back to you."

"Oh, leave Hugo alone," said Mitzi. "You don't want him using his karate on you."

"Hugo's an expert," said Charlie. "He showed me some moves once. Lethal. Pity he never got to use it on the Bosch."

Charlie knocked back his brandy, and, perhaps finally sensing that he was getting nowhere, spun Mitzi away for an impromptu waltz. "You're a great woman, Mitzi Dryden," he cried. "You're my whole life."

Round and round they went, expertly dodging furniture, then vanished into the hallway, where a modest cheer and round of applause sounded.

Now it was just Hugo and Sophie.

169

"I'm sorry I had to leave in a hurry the other morning," said Summers. "An early meeting."

"Still putting together that deal with the Yanks?"

"If you believe the papers."

"Well, I hope you know what's going on in New York. They won't take too kindly to some rich Brit taking over their local rag."

Summers smiled wryly. "Well, I can find the Algonquin and I know a pretzel from a bagel. I'm hoping they'll see me as just one more immigrant looking to earn a crust. Now, if you don't have any more questions, I was wondering if you'd care to join me for a spot of late dinner."

***

CHAPTER TWENTY-FOUR

The Gathering Place restaurant's low arched roof and capacity for a mere dozen tables gave it an intimate – almost claustrophobic – feel. Suspended from the ceiling were clusters of mock icicles, which looked so real that Sophie had to reach up and touch one. Each tap elicited a brief red glow.

"Some drunk fool always try to steal one," said Summers. "Venn sends them the bill if he catches them."

While he perused the menu, Sophie excused herself and headed straight for the ladies'. Summers had taken her by surprise with the dinner invite and she hadn't had time to work out a strategy. Now, in the toilet, she tried to come up with one.

Well, he wasn't going to give anything away, he was too much of a cold fish. She would have to challenge him, rile him maybe, but that ran the risk of angering him and losing him for good.

Just be yourself. That's why he came to ask you to dinner. Because you're the only person he can talk arty stuff with. Now do it.

She opened the wrap of coke that Venn had given her and realised she didn't know what to do with it. Was it pure or cut? And how could she snort it? She moistened a finger and dabbed some into her gums. Perfect: a little sharpener to help her mind keep pace with Summers'. But she would need to be careful if she was going to be walking around with this stuff. The police had got heavier: there'd been the Stones bust and someone she'd known had got six months just for possessing grass.

On her way to the table, she passed the only other diner: Ana. The Spanish woman was pushing a piece of fish around her plate and smoking. A nearly empty bottle of Yugoslav Riesling rested on the table.

Summers had just finished ordering some Gevrey Chambertin from the white-jacketed maitre d', who left by a door in the far wall.

"That wine is very good," said Summers. "It's terrific with the shepherd's pie."

Sophie had forgotten his slow, arrogant delivery. This was a man who never expected to be contradicted. "You're having *shepherd's pie*?" she said.

"Of course. It's the best dish in the world. And you shall have it, too."

"I'm just not very hungry. I'll watch you."

"Coke," said Summers. "Kills the appetite."

"Oh, I forgot — you only approve of opium." Quickly changing the subject: "So where's the kitchen? I don't hear any action out the back."

"There *is* no back. That door leads to the corridor. We use the chefs from the Erato and the waiters bring all the food up. That's what the members pay for: total discretion. You can't have the staff just wandering around. By the way, I forgot to give you the keypad code for the tunnel. It changes every Monday. It's eight-one-eight-one this week."

"Does that mean I'll be able to override the doors, like you did when Venn was after me?"

"Why would you want to do that?"

"Who knows what I might get the urge to do. Women are impulsive — haven't you heard?"

"Sadly, only Venn and I have the override code. Unfortunately for him, it doesn't work from outside the tunnel, only inside. That's what saved your bacon that night."

The maitre d' had returned with the wine. After Summers had tried it he said they'd skip starters and ordered pie for both of them.

"Forgive me but this dinner date must be brief. My old friend Toby Judge is over from Zurich and we're hitting the town."

"So what's this Toby Judge into? Don't tell me: tarts and punto banco?"

"Something like that. These days I'd rather settle in for a dull Chekhov play but that's no way to entertain an out of towner, is it?"

"Charlie seems keen to get you back into the theatre."

"Isn't he. I wouldn't be any good. I've lost the passion."

"Did you ever act?"

"Briefly. I was a rather precocious seventeen-year-old Richard III. Insisted on sleeping with the hump still in. That came from mother's side. She'd been an opera singer but father was a philistine. He didn't get art at all. So when I grew to love the theatre, I began to see that he was wrong about everything else. He sort of unravelled before me."

"So why did you part ways with the theatre?"

"The business left no room for it. I have no desire to plough money into productions when I couldn't give them a hundred per cent. Since then I've invested my pocket money in charity instead. It salves the conscience, too."

"It's good that you have one."

"It's what men like Venn don't have. I often wish I didn't have one. But I do."

"It sounds like you have regrets."

"What kind of life would one have lived if there were no regrets? Yes, I have them."

"Emily?"

"Good Lord, you have some front. I loved Emily very much. Her death was very unexpected. Still a mystery, really. She could be unpredictable, emotional, but I never thought that she would..."

"Did her death bring on the depression?"

"I've always suffered from that. Emily's death just made it worse..."

173

Sophie waited for him to continue. What was going on behind those blue eyes?

"I'm sure you have regrets of your own," he said at last.

She almost mentioned her father then. Summers could have blanked her on Emily but he'd opened up a little and it was tempting to offer him some candour of her own to see where it led. But it would be crazy to volunteer secrets to men like Summers and Venn.

Instead she said: "About three years ago, some people came to me, said they were starting a new magazine for women. They wanted me to be editor. They had some good ideas and I thought it could work. And so we put it all together: the staff, the design, dummy copies, the office, everything. And the day before we were due to start work for real, it fell through."

"Why?"

"The directors had been telling porkies about the private loans that were going to fund it all. They'd sworn the investors were raring to go."

"But they pulled out?"

"Yes. The directors tried the banks but the banks had turned them down in the first place. And so it never happened."

"Leaving you in the shit."

"Not really. I just went back to writing. But it's definitely a big regret."

Summers topped up her glass. "From copywriter to magazine editor? That's quite a jump."

And that's why you should never give anything away.

"Well, I used to work for the *Mirror*. Many years ago."

"Reporter?"

The slightest pause. "Yes."

"How old were you when you started there?"

"Seventeen."

"Very young."

"I was very ambitious."

"You told Venn at your screening that you weren't the most ambitious girl in the world…"

She didn't know which way to go, which lie to tell. He was trapping her. Maybe there was one way out of the corner.

"I was back then. Something made me that way."

"Now you've got me hooked."

"Well, my mother kicked my father out when I was fifteen. He'd been hitting the bottle for years. He worked for the council planning department and they finally got round to giving him the boot. When Mum found out she did the same."

"Bad week for dad."

"He was a bully and a drunk and he only had time for my brother, which meant I spent my childhood playing the tomboy. Dad moved in with a friend of his, until that friend kicked him out, too. Dad went to Ireland, where he had a brother. He wrote to us but it became less and less frequent. That first Christmas, we got a card from the brother and his family. There was a letter inside, chatty family stuff, you know, but you could tell from the phrasing that they thought Dad was with us…"

"So he'd never gone to stay with them?"

"No. I think he'd been too ashamed. But I had to go and find him. Mum didn't want me to – I was just a girl. But one day I packed my bags and took the coach from London. I finally wound up in Galway in a storm, talked an old man into giving me a lift. I had some vague address but when we reached Achill Island nobody had heard of it. And then we crashed the van – almost went over the cliffs. This man came to help and he pointed me to the right place. Some scrapyard full of tractors; trucks; black, broken things. I thought: no-one could live here… And then I saw a light in the

175

window of a bus that had been converted into some sort of home. I knocked and the door opened and out came this smell and I knew it was the smell of death."

"Good God."

"There was nothing left of him, really. Just a walking skeleton with a yellow face and sunken eyes. He said: 'And where have you been, Sophie?' His first words. I said what do you mean? He said any other girl would have stopped their mother from kicking me out. He said that he was dying and I could have stopped it. Fifteen years old. I didn't know who was right or wrong. He said I had always been useless and I should just get married. I was a liability. I just listened as this vitriol came out. In the end he just fell on to the bed, exhausted, and I ran back to the road. I found out that he died the next day. Liver cancer. He'd never even been to see a doctor. I dropped out of secretarial college, decided to go into journalism and show the bastard exactly how useless I was."

'Why journalism?"

"I could write a little and I figured that if I could make it somewhere as tough as Fleet Street I'd know everything he'd said had been bullshit…"

Three thumps sounded behind Sophie as Ana punched the service button with one hand and poured out the last of the wine with the other.

"You've met Ana?" said Summers.

"I wouldn't say met."

The maitre d' appeared and hurried to attend to her. Passing him the other way was Gerald, who puffed up to Summers.

"I'd appreciate it if we could have that word now," he said.

"Gerald, isn't it obvious, even to you, that I am sitting here having dinner?"

"I apologise to Sophie, but not to you. You've been putting me off for *twenty-five years*."

"And I intend to put you off for another twenty-five, Gerald, because you have nothing coming to you. Now, do you mind?"

"Oh, of course. You don't want your embarrassing affairs brought up in front of the lady. Thank you for the tip – maybe it's the only way I can shame you into resolving this. Perhaps she'd be interested to hear how you steal from people, hold on to money that doesn't belong to you. Perhaps she'd be interested in-."

Summers got to his feet so abruptly that his chair tipped over. Gerald scurried away until he was halfway down the aisle.

"I'm giving you until the end of the year, Hugo. That's less than a week. And then I'm going to start making things very difficult for you. Because I've found him and I'm just *dying* to use him."

"Found who, Gerald?"

"You know who. You saw the photo I put under your door..."

"I've no idea what you're talking about. I've seen no photo."

Gerald raised an eyebrow and waddled away. "Of course. Toodle pip, Hugo."

"I do apologise," said Summers, righting his chair. "There's been a misunderstanding over some properties we own. It's a trivial matter but he does like a drama. I've been friends with him for a long time but I do wish he'd just drop dead now."

Sophie wrinkled her face in mock disapproval. "That's not very Sixties."

"I say bugger the Sixties."

"Who is he, anyway? I asked him his surname the other night and he wouldn't tell me."

"His name is Gerald Masters."

Gerald Masters rang a bell. Something from the news a few years back, some right-wing nastiness.

"What does he do?" she said.

"Apart from bring out my murderous side, he owns a publishing house. He was a Tory MP for Deershelter Plain in Suffolk. Not any more. They kicked him out. Even the Tories don't have the stomach for people like Gerald."

"Why?"

"The man's a fascist. He was tight with Mosley; helped out in his election campaign back in fifty-nine. They fell out over something."

"Isn't a fascist what they used to call *you*? The Moscow Three? Seamus Knutt? And all the other smear campaigns that the *Daily Post* used to love before..." Sophie remembered too late that it was Emily's suicide that had famously mellowed Hugo Summers.

"Before...?"

"Before you realised how expensive libel was?"

If Summers was irritated, he didn't show it. "My newspapers cover a range of politics, as I'm sure you've noticed. Anyway, as I say, there was some falling out just after Mosley lost, I believe. Gerald went off to do his own thing. Cruised into the seat at Deershelter Plain when the last chap died. He was doing quite well for a while until he ended up in stir."

"What for?"

"He paid a gang of thugs in balaclavas to set about some elderly Jamaicans playing dominoes in their club."

"Oh my God, I remember that."

"The bully boys couldn't keep their mouths shut and it all went tits up for Gerald. Eighteen months in Brixton. Now he devotes most of his time to his publishing house, churning out biogs of right-wing icons, not to mention the reports from his think tank. It's all disgusting bunkum. To give him his dues, he's a pretty decent seven-card stud player, though I can sometimes unstitch his game."

Churning around in Sophie's mind were angles, ideas for piquing Summers' interest. In poker terms, Gerald's appearance may have got the game out of the muck.

"Maybe I can help you," she said.

"How?"

"If Masters is bothering you. I don't know what this dispute is between you two but did you hear what happened up here before Christmas?"

"No."

Sophie dropped her voice low, so Ana wouldn't hear. "The night after I came to your suite, Venn invited me to the lounge. There was a girl called Echo. Masters was there, filming everything. They got me involved. I didn't know what to expect, what was going on. Gerald gave her a shot of heroin and she started convulsing. Venn tried to save her but it was no good."

Summers clanked his cutlery on to the plate and pushed the meal away.

"Are you serious?"

"Of course I'm serious." She wondered whether to mention Venn's threat that he could use the film to blackmail her but decided there was no point: look what had happened to Amber when she had crossed Venn. And besides, Sophie had reached a kind of peace with Venn.

"I knew nothing of this," said Summers. He looked irritated, as if he'd rather not have known about it.

"The point is that Masters was there, filming it all. He killed her and he filmed it. He could be done for murder or manslaughter or leaving the scene of a crime at the very least..."

Summers tipped his glass away from him, until the first rivulet of wine was about to slide down the bowl. "That's useful, but not entirely unexpected, given that Venn runs the floor."

"Aren't you going to do anything about it?"

"I wasn't there. Are *you* going to do anything about it? In any case, I don't think you should come back to the club again, Sophie. I'll arrange a refund."

"Not come back to The Gathering Place?"

"I mean this whole building. I should never have got involved with Venn and I can't guarantee your safety."

"I thought this was your club, Hugo. And your father's before you. How did you let him do this?" *Yes, get under his skin, challenge his pride, see what he gives away.*

"There are many things about me and this club you won't understand, Sophie."

"Or are you worried he'll make me one of his whores?" She took the table's single black tulip from its vase and twirled it between her fingers. "Is that it? Do you want me for yourself?"

"I wouldn't flatter yourself, Sophie. This is just dinner. Believe me, if there was anyone else in the Erato with whom I could hold a halfway intelligent conversation I'd be dining with them now. Unfortunately, that type of person has been driven out in recent times by persons who shall remain nameless."

"It's more than dinner," she said. "You're finding out what you think about me. What you feel. You think you can sit me down and 'unstitch my game', find out if I'm worth getting to know, or just worth taking to bed."

She was shocked to hear herself say it. That was a mistake. Wasn't it? A little wine trickled down the bowl of his glass and on to the stem.

"Oh, I know you're worth taking to bed," he said.

"So why didn't you the other night?"

"I wasn't well," Summers said curtly.

"I wondered if you pulled that on purpose, to try to get out of it. Because Venn said…"

"Venn said what?" A pool of red was crawling outwards across the tablecloth towards her.

Sophie held his stare and whispered: *"That you didn't fuck."* A voice in her head told her she wasn't trying to rile him any more, that she was in the grip of something else and it was nothing to do with Abigail or chasing a story. His look spoke of murder but Sophie had to continue. "That I should forget you," she added. "That *he* wanted me for himself."

Summers was nodding slowly. "Venn wouldn't touch you if he thought you were with me," he said. "That's one line even he wouldn't cross. East End code of honour..."

"I thought it would be *you* that was the interesting one around here, but the more I see of Venn, the more I think that *he's* where it's at. Look at what he's taken from you. I find that exciting, that kind of ambition."

"Absurd, the suggestion that I could fall for you," said Summers.

"I didn't say anything about falling for me. I know that's impossible because you're a bitter man, growing old." She'd had enough of his aloofness, his cool deflections of her attacking shots.

"Even if it were possible, I'm leaving..."

"Leaving?"

"Going away."

"This deal I keep reading about in the papers? *The New York Journal?*"

Summers gave no reply.

"Before you go, why don't you tell me what's on your mind?" said Sophie. "Why don't you tell me about this money of Gerald's that you've been holding on to?"

He stared intensely into her eyes. "I knew a girl like you once," he said.

"Oh… Who was that?"

Sophie's eyes flicked to Ana, who was blowing smoke rings.

Summers stood and came round to her side of the table.

"Sophie," he said.

He put his right hand on her shoulder before letting it graze distractedly over her exposed collarbone and come to rest on her right breast. His fingers circled her nipple through the silk.

With one arm, Summers swept everything away in an explosion of glass and china and steel. He grabbed her around the waist and hoisted her on to the table before hurling her chair aside, sending it tumbling down the aisle. He pushed her down on the tablecloth in a clear patch among the broken glass and pools of wine where the bottle had smashed against the wall. He ripped off her panties and pulled her hips close before unhurriedly unbuttoning his trousers and freeing himself.

He fucked her slowly, with a bruising force, and she let herself go. Now she knew the answer to the question she'd been asking herself about her real motivations for goading Hugo.

She arched her back and pushed into him.

When Summers finished it was suddenly and almost soundlessly. He withdrew abruptly and buttoned himself up.

"Toby Judge," he said, and left.

Sophie remained sprawled on the table, trying to work out what had just happened. She realised she was crying. The tablecloth started to slide and a moment later she found herself falling painfully to the carpet, bashing her head on the floor. She just lay there, arms and legs splayed at awkward angles.

Ana got up and ground her cigarette out under her shoe. She exhaled a fearsome jet of smoke as she strutted from the restaurant.

"Is all shit," she said.

Sophie watched the last drops of wine pitter-patter on to the carpet.

CHAPTER TWENTY-FIVE

She cried all the way home in the cab. She wasn't even sure whether it was mainly because she'd blown her chances of pulling off the big scoop she'd worked so hard at, or because she felt so used. Or just so stupid.

Back in the flat, she spent half an hour in the shower before curling up in the pod chair with a blanket. She was out of her depth and had been since making that first membership enquiry over the phone.

It was nearly 4am before she felt tired enough and brave enough to go to bed and shut her eyes.

There was something on the pillow.

An envelope. She opened it and found Venn's Erato business card, paperclipped to a wad of money. Sophie counted £300. She closed a fist around the notes. Clenched. Unclenched. She thought of the mortgage payments she'd be struggling to meet if this investigation went on much longer. And the clothes she was having to buy, and the drinks...

The cash was still in her grasp when she fell asleep.

The next morning, she headed for Notting Hill Gate Library, where she sat down with *Who's Who* and its sanitised version of the life of Gerald Masters, 57, of Deershelter Plain, Suffolk, and Cheyne Walk, Chelsea. After Eton and Oxford came the "Foreign Office" from 1940-47, and then presumably a period of cutting his teeth in business which led to his managing directorship of Five Trees Asset Management in 1948. Other key appointments were mentioned, namely chairmanships of Hemisphere Pharmaceuticals, Mercier Aerospace Group and Millennium Airlines. Interests included military history, shooting and fishing, and chamber music. Nothing about murder and voyeurism.

Sophie pondered the phrase "Foreign Office". Could that be a euphemism for MI6? That theory looked even stronger when she flicked to Summers' entry and saw that his war years were characterised simply as "Home Office".

Had Masters been doing the same kind of work as Hugo during the war, but for the overseas security department rather than the domestic one? Is that how they had met?

Sophie dug out the number of an old contact, a man who ran an anti-fascist organisation, and asked what he knew about Gerald. The contact didn't ask why she wanted the info and she didn't volunteer it. His most useful snippet was that Masters — whom he had been keeping an eye on for years — had lost all his directorships after the incident with the Jamaicans got him expelled from the Tory party in 1963.

"He's desperate for money and has thrown all his energies into Oak Tree Publishing, which he owns," said the source. "He's tied in with a gangster called Edward Venn, who seems to be doing his bidding. As far as I know, Venn has no interest in fascism, so maybe Masters is just paying him as a hired hand but frankly it's a mystery. I'll be interested in anything you get, Sophie."

She promised that she would reciprocate with information, while knowing she could do nothing of the sort. As soon as she put the phone down, it rang. With no introduction, Summers just said: "Last night."

"Yes?"

There was a pause. "I'm sorry I had to leave in a hurry. Are you coming tonight?"

"I haven't thought about it."

"Come along. Meet me at ten upstairs."

"I'll think about it."

"Yes, all right. But I'll be there from ten. If you need the code for my suite it's four seven zero zero. It would be nice to see you. I was thinking we-."

Sophie hung up on him.

CHAPTER TWENTY-SIX

Half past ten at The Gathering Place and Sophie was high.

She sat on the sofa with Jerry and Pippa, the nouveau riche couple she'd briefly encountered in the lift on her first night at the Erato. It unexpectedly turned out that they were great company, with Jerry's tales of thwarting an attempted pirate raid on his yacht being particularly entertaining. As accustomed to the high life as Jerry and Pippa obviously were, they were nonetheless very excited about the club's end-of-decade bash, just two nights away.

Sophie leant over the coffee table, snorted a thick line and tried not to ask herself whether she was starting to enjoy this side of coming to the club. And then she told herself that she was only taking it because she was shattered, permanently tired from all the late nights. Once this job was over, she wouldn't touch it again. She was still a G&T girl.

She sat back and waited for the drug to numb her throat. At first she hadn't liked this part of the ritual, but now she thought of it merely as the interval before the lovely rush.

And this story is going to make me rich. Why shouldn't I feel good for once? My Sixties were screwed up.

Yes, her 1960s started now.

Venn was bored with the Stones and jerked the needle from the record. Seconds later the room was blasted with a blistering guitar riff. Jerry and Pippa grimaced in unison, making him laugh, and he lowered the volume. "Jimmy Page! You must have heard Led Zep? Bona fide genius."

"I thought you'd be more of a Junior Walker kind of guy," said Sophie.

"That stuff was all right, but this is now."

Sophie sipped her champagne and surveyed the fifteen other people in the room. No-one famous, but plenty of money, judging by the talk of mergers and acquisitions and holiday villas in France. They were almost exclusively young, on the up, with not even a hint of the old money that still drifted around downstairs. For the first time, Sophie was seeing what a "normal" night at The Gathering Place was like. Just somewhere private for the high rollers to get together, get high and get laid (only one couple had gone that far and they did it quietly on a rug in the corner, while a Kenneth Anger film projected silently over their bodies). The business with Summers the previous night seemed a distant memory. She was more concerned that she'd walked into Summers' trap, made him suspicious by talking about the *Mirror*. Hopefully, what had happened on the restaurant table had gone some way to calming any fears and convincing him she was serious about wanting to be a member of the jetsetters' orgy that was The Gathering Place. It also occurred to her that he'd been claiming her as his own – Ana would no doubt have told Venn what had happened.

Maybe she was more capable of playing a hedonist than she had thought possible. She was even starting to dig Venn's psychedelic rock. The song was lost in a free jazz wilderness: guttural cries, a hissing percussion, revving sound effects: the kind of stuff that made her freak out when David had played it. And then the improv section was blasted away by that monster riff and thundering drums and the kick was awesome, almost sexual, and she finally saw what the music and powder was all about. The rush grew and grew, the coke heightening the music and the music heightening the coke.

"Wow!" she shouted to Venn. "This music's amazing!"

Behind the white patent leather-bound bar, shaking up cocktails, Venn broke into a cheshire cat grin and made the "okay" sign. The only slight dampener on the atmosphere was Ana, who sat at the bar, perfecting the arts of chain smoking and muttering.

Sophie took a long drag on her Marlboro and dabbed up some more powder from the table's inlaid mirrors. Venn saw what she was doing and called: "Good stuff, eh? I've got so much coming in for the party I don't know where to stash it all."

His "Last Days of the Roman Empire" party – his little joke about the death of the Sixties – was all he could talk about. He was proud of the elaborate props and food he had ordered, some of which was being delivered from overseas.

"How are the preparations?" said Sophie.

"Bloody nightmare trying to get my hands on all the costumes for the staff, all the special booze, all the kinky stuff. I told Charlie I wanted a snow machine and he still ain't managed it. The bloke reckons he was a film director and he still can't fix me some snow."

Sophie grimaced at the thought of Charlie running around after a snow machine. He was fragile enough without being given more impossible errands. Maybe she could track him down later and make sure he was okay, though her patience with him was pretty much exhausted.

Venn placed a daiquiri before her. He'd already plied her with three cocktails, but the coke just soaked them up. What the hell. She had nothing to get up for tomorrow. She was feeling so content that it was only when she caught sight of her watch that she realised it was eleven. Summers was already an hour late.

Feeling restless, she excused herself and went to the roof garden and looked out – not much of a view this side, just a blank grey building but she hadn't come for the view, she'd come to think. At last she was fitting in at The Gathering Place but getting to know Summers was frustratingly slow, and how long could she afford to keep trying? These nights were expensive; Venn's backhander was useful but she didn't want to start relying on that kind of money.

However many times she tried to concentrate tonight, her mind was racing in all the wrong directions. She just wanted to get back to the party.

On her way back to the lounge, she heard men arguing in the corridor ahead. She hovered in the shadows and identified the trio as Venn, Gerald and George Tozer.

"This was the agreement we had," Gerald was spluttering. "You should have said if-."

"Enough!" said Venn. "I'm not your lapdog. I didn't know Jean was going to catch the flu, did I?"

Gerald looked down at his feet a little too quickly to Sophie's eyes, as if he enjoyed being submissive to Venn.

"What's the rush, anyway?" said Venn. "We'll do it another night."

"But that's a pain in the arse – I've got all the gear ready," said Tozer.

"I very much wanted it done tonight," said Gerald. "Chowdry's out every day, rallying his people, collecting signatures, gathering strength. Where's Amber? She used to do these jobs for us."

Venn dropped his voice. "I had to get rid of her."

"In what sense?"

"In the sense that you're thinking of, Gerald. Hugo caught her bugging his conversations. I had to get rid of the treacherous bitch. Don't worry about it."

"Jesus Christ," said Gerald. "She was doing it *for me*, Venn. I paid her!"

Venn thought about this for a moment before slamming his heel into the wall. "Fuck!" he thundered. "What did you do that for? I thought she was working

189

for some company trying to get a bit of juice on Hugo's American deal."

"Well, she *wasn't*, old chap. Christ, when she went missing I thought she'd double-crossed me, done a runner with the cash without doing the surveillance job."

"Well, you should have told me what you were up to!"

"I didn't think you needed to know. We're on the same side, aren't we? I only told her to plant the bug if it was safe. I didn't think she'd balls it up."

Venn muttered a string of obscenities for what seemed an age. Finally he calmed down and said: "All right, all right, we'll do the job tonight. Happy? It's just Jean we're missing. Someone else can do it. It's only a bloody lookout we need."

"Who's around?" said Tozer. "How about Lenny?"

"Lenny's driving, ain't he?"

Sophie marched out of the shadows and breezed up to the trio. "Who died?" she said.

They all looked at her, dumbfounded, then laughed in unison.

"What's so funny?" she said.

"You've just got great timing, sweetheart," said Venn. "How do you fancy earning yourself a bit of pocket money?"

***

CHAPTER TWENTY-SEVEN

Five minutes later an Austin Morris JU van was pulling out of the underground car park with "Lanky Lenny" at the wheel. Along with Terry and Jack, he was another of Venn's private army. Sophie had only seen him at the club once before – he'd been pushing a gatecrasher down some steps.

Tozer sat opposite Sophie and Venn on the side-facing bench seats. The two men were wired, all darting eyes and deafening laughs. Sophie's fingers turned white gripping the edge of the seat as the vehicle made its way down Grosvenor Place. The van stank of petrol and made her feel sick.

"Gives me shivers, this thing," said Tozer. "It's like the Black Maria that took me to Dartmoor."

"Oh, I'm sorry, George, I'll have it painted pink."

Tozer bit the lid off a bottle of ale and dumped it on Venn's crotch. Venn leapt up, soaked, and set about hammering his antagonist with a flurry of blows to the arms. Tozer just laughed them off.

"Give up, son," sneered Tozer. "Your manicured mitts can't hurt me."

"Boys," said Sophie. "Why don't you tell me what this job's about?"

"It's a lookout," said Tozer. "You walk in and look out for this geezer. If you can't see him, you sit down, order a curry, see if he shows his Paki mug."

"Where are we going – a restaurant?"

"Yeah. Look." He passed her two crumpled cuttings from his pocket. The first was a story from a local paper about a curry house that had won some award. The short, white-haired proprietor stood proudly with three young men identified as his sons. "You're looking for the old geezer, right? His name's Chowdry – Amir Chowdry."

"What happens if I see him?"

"You come back to the van and leave the rest to us. I'll slip you a ton, all right?"

"Fine."

Sophie looked at the other cutting. This one was headlined: "CURRY HOUSE HERO DEFIES NAZI THUGS". The standfirst read: "Brick Lane businessman rallies support against blackshirts".

"What's he done to you?" said Sophie.

"Nothing," said Venn. "But Gerald – the fat bloke at the club? – well, he doesn't like Chowdry. And we help Gerald out now and then."

Tozer gave Venn a disapproving look.

"Relax, George. Like I told Gerald, she's one of us now. And besides, it's no secret that Gerald's a fascist."

"Yeah, relax, George," said Sophie. "I know the Tories booted him out for GBH. So do you two share his politics?"

"I don't have politics," said Venn. "I keep telling Gerald that, but he still thinks we're into the cause. I ain't putting no blackshirt on."

"It's not your colour, is it, sweetheart?" said Tozer, blowing him a kiss.

"How did you meet him?" asked Sophie.

"The Clermont Club," said Venn. "He said he'd heard I was a vicious little gangster and was it true? I was steaming, really pissed, and I thought about smacking him about. But he bought me a load of poker chips so I let him be. Then I pulled a few jobs for him. And I've never quite managed to get rid of him."

"Masters is always hinting he's got something on Hugo," said Tozer. "Something big. I reckon it's just a load of bollocks, Gerald's way of staying sweet with Venny Boy. Gerald put the heat on Hugo so he'd let Venn buy in to the club. Gerald even got his own way with the name – *The Gathering Place*. I mean, what kind of poofter name is that?"

"I thought that was Hugo's idea," said Sophie.

"Bollocks it was. When the upstairs was being built, Hugo went away on business to the States – some botched deal in New York – and while he was there, Gerald told Venn here some right porkies."

"That'll do," said Venn.

"What kind of porkies?" said Sophie.

"He told Venn that the new club was to be called The Gathering Place. *Hugo's orders,* said Gerald. Venn went along with it – he didn't have a better name for it anyway – and he thought it was part of the deal; you know, Hugo's condition for letting Venn in. So Venn prints all the cards up, sends out all the invites for opening night, and when Hugo gets back from America there's an almighty row between him and Gerald. Seems he never gave any instructions of the sort. It was some kind of private joke by Gerald. Hugo and Gerald didn't speak for about two months. But it was too late to change the name by then."

"So what *does* it mean?" said Sophie.

"Fuck knows. But another thing is-."

"Try not to spill all your guts, eh, George?" said Venn.

Sophie was dying to push Tozer a bit more but she could see that Venn was on the verge of an explosion. Tozer's story about the naming of The Gathering Place confirmed and elaborated on what Mitzi had said.

"What's this feud with Amir Chowdry about?" said Sophie.

"He set himself up in a cushy little business, then he started getting militant," said Venn. "Anti-racialist campaigner. Anti-housing laws, anti this and that. He's got 'em all marching, all the Pakis, signing petitions, waving banners. It's liberties. You might have different ideas; I don't know. You ain't got a problem with this job, have you?"

"No," she said, handing the cuttings back to Tozer. "I've got nothing against Pakis but you're right: it sounds like liberties. Anyway, I'm just in it for the cash. 'Cos you're not going to be slipping me free coke forever, are you?"

"You've corrupted her, Venn," said Tozer.

"Nah," said Venn. "It's Hugo what's done that."

So there it was – Venn's signal to her that he knew what had happened in the restaurant. Ana served him well.

Venn and Tozer stayed quiet as the van stop-started through heavy traffic into the East End. Lenny drove past Brick Lane and then made his way back to it and parked in a sidestreet.

Tozer was fiddling around with something on the floor. At first, Sophie thought he was taking another bottle of beer from a crate but then some terrible thought occurred to her. "I think you'd better tell me what this is all about," she said. "What's going to happen."

"Relax," said Tozer. "We're just here for a curry."

"Yeah," said Venn. "A chicken Molotov."

Tozer's machine-gun laugh filled the van. He sat up straight, having found what he was looking for. In each hand he held a wine bottle filled with liquid, and suddenly Sophie knew why the van smelt of petrol.

Just a lookout. Yeah: a lookout to a murder.

***

CHAPTER TWENTY-EIGHT

Venn and Tozer busied themselves tying lengths of rag around four bottles from the crate. When Venn was done, he pointed out a curry house with an illuminated yellow sign on Brick Lane. "That's the place – the Asha Balti House. Now, just nice and easy, all right? They're not goin' to know what you're up to. Apparently old man Chowdry sits at the back so you'll have to go right in. If you spot him right away, and you're *sure* it's him, just turn round and come out. If you can't see him, sit down, order some grub. Got some cash?"

"Yes."

"Good, but we don't want you scoffing a whole meal. If he *still* don't show up, ask one of the waiters if he's around. If it's a yeah, come back out to the van. If it's a no, do the same thing. All right?"

"Are you going to kill him?"

"Nah, we'll just give him a fright. Right, Lenny, let the lady out."

Sophie made the short walk as slowly as possible as she thought of ways to abort the job. It would be risky to try to enlist help – Brick Lane may have had a bustling street market but it was otherwise dogged by gangland crime and racists looking for trouble. If she tried to take anyone into her confidence, they'd probably suspect she was setting them up. She didn't believe that Venn just wanted to scare Chowdry – he wanted to kill him. Why else would they need Chowdry to be on the premises when they firebombed it?

She entered the Asha Balti House and was hit by the normally comforting smells of frying onions and curry powder. The place was busy with a mixed clientele of English and Bangladeshi customers but Sophie was relieved to spot a couple of empty tables. Good: the last thing she wanted was to have to return straight to the van just because the restaurant was full. Those evil bastards might just decide to torch the place anyway...

And then the first bit of bad luck: Chowdry himself coming to greet her.

She asked for a table for one and was shivering with nerves as she sat down, opting to keep her coat on for a quick getaway. She ordered a fruit juice and pretended to look at the menu. Chowdry disappeared and her attention wandered to the tiny details around her: the rusty brown flock wallpaper, the rural scene on the stitched tablecloth, the folk music playing over tinny speakers. She needed to think clearly but the coke had put paid to that.

Okay, a plan. Any plan to save this man and these people.

The plan... Buttonhole Chowdry when he came back with the drink? Yes, tell him what was going on and that he had to get everyone out. She would slip out the back and go to the police. To hell with the story – it was time to do the right thing, blackmail or no blackmail.

Chowdry returned with the fruit juice and asked if she'd like to order a starter.

Sophie pinched his shirt sleeve and pulled him close to her. "They're going to firebomb this place," she said. Her voice was weak with fear and the Saturday night crowd was raucous.

"I'm sorry, madam?"

She looked into his eyes and froze. What she was trying to say was so crazy that she couldn't believe it herself. She took a swig of water and tried again. "There's a van across the road."

Chowdry's eyes narrowed, as if he suspected her of being mad or pulling some con.

"You have to listen to me," she said.

He was about to reply when there was a blast of cold air as the door opened and half a dozen Pakistani men walked in. Chowdry's face lit up and he advanced towards them amid a noisy crossfire of greetings. Chowdry was standing right in the window. There was no way Venn and Tozer couldn't see him. Now they'd just be waiting for her to get out so they could burn the place down. And if she took too long, she didn't trust them not to burn it down while she was still inside.

Chowdry was locked into a loud exchange. The time for a quiet word had passed. If she said anything to him now, the boys in the van would see it.

The candle in the terra cotta candle holder on the table briefly sputtered. And an idea started to form. She made sure that it formed quickly.

Sophie tipped the menu towards the candle and almost set her own sleeve alight as she held it to the hem of the curtains. The other customers were too wrapped up in their conversations to notice what was happening.

Flames shot up the drapes with alarming speed.

Sophie dropped the menu and pushed back her chair.

"Fire!" she called, and this time there was no problem making herself heard.

The buzz of emergency swept from one table to the next in a domino effect, until all the customers were on their feet.

Sophie stepped away from the table.

"Fire! Everybody out!" shouted Chowdry. One of his sons was already storming out of the kitchen with a fire extinguisher. The customers were too drunk or blasé to get out; they were hoping the situation would be resolved without them having to shuffle into the cold.

Sophie made her way out the door and as she cast a last look back saw that the flames were out. The atmosphere had turned to one of relief. People were laughing. She'd blown it.

She hit the street at a run and climbed into the back of the van with no idea what she was going to say.

"Where the fuck have you been?" said Venn. "*We* saw Chowdry in there five minutes ago."

"Yeah, I saw him five minutes ago, too," snapped Sophie, clutching at a new plan. "But I didn't expect to get caught up in some D-Day reunion."

"You what?"

"Half a dozen old soldiers having a curry. The only free table was right next to them. They got so excited about my dress I thought they were all going to have heart attacks. But your man's in there all right."

Her only hope now was that Venn and Tozer were bright enough to take the bait.

"They were white, these old boys?" said Venn.

"No, they were Gurkhas. *Of course* they were bloody white."

"Fuck!" spat Tozer.

"What?" said Sophie, feigning exasperation. "Chowdry's in there. *I told you.*"

"Use some common," said Venn. "Gerald's not going to want to risk us killing six war heroes, is he?"

Chowdry and one of his sons were outside the restaurant, looking up and down the street.

"Waste of fucking time," said Tozer, putting his two bottles back into the crate.

Lenny didn't need to be told to start the ignition and head for Mayfair.

Sophie slumped back against the wall of the van, drained.

***

CHAPTER TWENTY-NINE

Sophie returned with Venn and Tozer to The Gathering Place to find that Summers had still not arrived. She let herself into his suite with a code he had given her. The phone was ringing. It was the head porter, explaining that Mr Summers had left a message to say he'd been detained on business and would not be attending the club tonight.

Relief washed over her. She was more in the mood for getting drunk on her own than playing mind games with Hugo.

Once again, she spent an age in the shower. However many times she told herself that she had probably saved some lives tonight, she still felt like a grubby crook.

When she came out of the bathroom wearing a towel, someone was sitting on the bed.

"Jesus, Ana, you scared the hell out of me."

"Sorry."

"How did you get in here?"

"I climbed." She gestured to the suite next door. "Over the balconies."

"What do you want?"

Ana shrugged. "To talk to someone."

It was only then that Sophie noticed a large swelling on Ana's cheekbone.

"Who hit you?"

"Who you think?"

"Venn."

"Yes. He wanted me to go with the Toad. Just now. I say no. I decide: no more. I hate Toad. Venn hit me."

"Let's get some ice on that. And while we're at it, could you manage some white wine?"

"Yes. That is my best drink."

"I know. I notice these things."

Sophie got busy making drinks and wrapped some ice cubes in a shower cap. Once Ana was holding the pack to her face, Sophie said: "What does Gerald get up to here?"

"Toad? Always bad things. Venn fix them to please him. Sometimes I go with him, other times not. He likes the camera. Sometimes the girls, they..."

"They get killed?"

Ana nodded and took a gulp of her drink.

"Why don't you just run away?" said Sophie.

"Is not so simple," said Ana, her eyes burning with anger. "Do you think I am stupid, that I would stay here if it was so easy?"

Sophie sat beside her on the bed. "Tell me why you're here."

Ana shook her head. "If he knows I tell you, things are worse for me."

"I won't tell him."

Some Spanish oath whistled under Ana's breath. "I trust no-one, Sophie. I am sorry. Maybe you are good, but..."

Sophie placed her hand on Ana's. "You tell me your story and I will tell you mine."

"Where is Hugo?"

"It's okay. He's not coming tonight."

"Okay. Deal." Ana lit them cigarettes and she began. "I am from the streets. You understand? A whore from the streets. My mother sold me on the streets. She was whore also. I did not know my father. We live in bad area of Madrid. Much violence. We went with the bad men, the crazy. They beat women. The only good thing is my daughter, Carmen. Her father, I do not even know who he is. That was my life. One day this man comes to the house. He was good to me. I think he fell in love that day.

"One day he comes and he gives much money to my mother. He says he buy me. He wants me to go with

200

him, be his wife. He say he has business, he is rich. That is why he is in Madrid. He wants us to go south to Andalucia, me and Carmen. He teach me read, buy me things, he says. A good life for us. My mother, she looks at the floor. She cannot see me in the eye when she takes the money, you know? She says this will be best for you. Ha. *Lies*. Because I know she means it is good for *her*. Because she takes the drugs, the heroin. And then he take me and Carmen in the car. Our new life." Ana actually spat then. "He take us in the car and we drive. We drive for many hours.

"The hacienda is in woods. You would never find the hacienda. Only he could find it. The gates are very high. Like a prison. Men with guns everywhere." She mimed the sweep of a machine gun. "Many men live there. He has many wifes. I know it before I arrive. Of *course* he will have many wifes. I do not believe the lies. The men fuck me. He does not care. The drug men come to bring the drugs from Morocco and I am just one more for them. He gives me to his friends. He loves Carmen, loves children and the other whores have their children, too. Many children. But me, I am a piece of meat. What can I do?

"Three years. That is how long. And then one day I decide: 'Enough!' You see, I have money. Money from the men. Sometimes they give me money. I hide it from him. And I know I can use this money to escape. I need a plan. And one day I have a dangerous plan. I know they will throw me to the dogs if I fail. I pick a night. We will go this night. Me and Carmen. I cannot stay one more summer. Because the world is beautiful in summer and all Carmen knows is this place. So, you see, it is the start of summer and this day I choose, it comes."

***

CHAPTER THIRTY

The woods seemed innocent enough.

Beautiful, even, especially at this time of year, when the short winter had passed and the blossoming flowers put on a dazzling show. The rutted track that led into the woods was lined with olive groves, and its verges flourished with poppies. The blood-red flowers followed the track from its beginning – where it met a hairpin road that wound round the mountains – to the point where it vanished into the woods. A neverending chorus of birdsong completed the idyll.

But few people ever came to this deep place of Spanish firs. It was not well known to hikers, who in any case would have struggled to reach it by foot (the twisting road was the only way through the landscape of soaring cliffs) and as for the locals... They knew what was in the woods, and knew better.

The track ended at a hacienda concealed behind a high wall of concrete and plaster. Men armed with rifles and machine-guns kept watch round the clock from towers at the front gate and back wall.

Visitors were admitted through a pair of thick, steel gates to the courtyard, the focus of hacienda life. It was here that the residents and their associates who delivered the drugs from Morocco were entertained with dog fights, bullfights, even the occasional knife fight when there was a score to settle.

The hacienda kept its dogs locked up in a filthy compound at the far side of the property. Apart from the rattling of their chains and their thumping against their stalls, the dogs made no noise because their voiceboxes had been removed. This made life bearable for the human inhabitants and meant that if some foolish party should try to break into the grounds, the dogs' attack was undetectable until the moment they pounced.

One time, after hearing that a large shipment of hashish had arrived, two chancers from Málaga climbed a tree overhanging the hacienda and slid down into the property. When the klaxon began to sound, they managed to clamber back again, only to be hunted down in the woods by dogs they never heard coming.

The pair's remains were left on their boss's doorstep in a dozen gift-wrapped parcels.

That had been the first and only attempted raid. And so the men in the towers had little to do. In days gone by, the whores had sometimes tried to escape, but they no longer fancied being ripped to shreds by the dogs, and besides, most of them had children at the hacienda, and they did not want to leave them to the mercy of Vicente Salvo. And so here deep in the mountains they kept whoring for Salvo, his men and their friends from Morocco.

One evening, at the start of summer 1966, just after the long shadows had blended into the night, the lookout in the front watchtower lit a cigarette and surveyed the miniature town. Lights were going on all over the main house, where Salvo lived with his wife and four children, not to mention his mistresses, who had a wing of their own. The sounds of dinner plates being scraped told the lookout that dinner was over. Salvo shuffled his bulk on to a first-floor balcony and shouted for his number two to show himself to play poker. Then he faced in the direction of the garage and called for his mechanic – the man who spent every day tinkering with Salvo's collection of twenty antique cars – to do the same.

The lookout nodded to himself. Not a bad boss. Not a bad life. And then he heard a key turning in a rusty lock, followed by a string of insults from a formidable-sounding woman, and chuckled because things were about to get even better.

How could he have forgotten that it was shower night? And not just any old shower night, but the *whores'* shower night, and he was in the perfect position to look down on all those lovely bodies.

A long line of the whores – the youngest being perhaps fifteen and the oldest in her mid-thirties – burst from their compound in single file, their children running at their sides. Salvo was a sentimental man and didn't mind when the whores fell pregnant; he liked having kids around.

The lookout always found this requirement to *dash* to the shower block amusing. It wasn't a requirement at all, of course; it served no purpose other than to satisfy the crazed standards of discipline demanded by the women's jailer and punisher.

Encarna.

Satan's mother.

Holy shit, thought the lookout, I'm up here with a rifle but still she turns my blood cold.

Encarna managed the whores' compound and relished every second of it. She was nearly as wide as she was tall (just under five foot), had never been seen in anything but shapeless black smocks (that stank to high heaven) and always wore her jet-black hair in a bun, almost as if she were proud to show off her gargoyle-like face with its clusters of moles. Her grim expression suggested that every second someone was not committing a punishable act was a second of life wasted. Around her neck was a whistle and in her hand a cane embedded with tacks.

Encarna was first out of the whores' living quarters, her stubby legs motoring across the courtyard to the stone building housing the shower block. She positioned herself on the top step and emphasised every insult with a thwack of the stick.

"Move, move, you silly bitch," she roared. "Stop again and it will be the last stop you make. Natalia, keep your children under control. This is your last warning. Look at me like that again and I'll gouge your eyes out!"

At the head of the line, dressed in handmade smocks and headscarves and clutching towels, were Ana and Carmen. Mother squeezed daughter's hand as they made their run beneath the gaze of a garish Franco portrait on the wall. Ana looked up at the stars and reminded herself why she was doing this – because there was a world beyond these walls that her seven-year-old daughter had never seen.

Carmen gave a brave smile. It broke Ana's heart, the risk she was putting them through. There was a very high chance that tonight they would both be dead, but wasn't that better than rotting away here?

Encarna unlocked the door, hit the light switch and began counting everyone in. To help achieve this, she dealt out a tap on each adult's shoulder. Sometimes Ana would growl at this – one time she had grabbed the cane and raised it at her tormentor, earning her a week in the wood shed. But tonight she averted her eyes from Encarna's and was the first to step into the musty interior. This was the plan that had been agreed with the other women: Ana and Carmen would be at the head of the line to give them more time to reach the far side of the room unnoticed.

They rushed past the communal shower areas along the sides and stopped at the last of three private stalls at the back. These were strictly for use by women with contagious diseases and Ana risked a beating *and* a week in solitary just for being near them.

Ana stared at the stall's saloon-style doors, too scared to open them. It was Carmen who found the courage to do it, to see if the man they had befriended, the mechanic, had been true to his word.

On the doorstep, Encarna was berating someone for asking to borrow another woman's soap.

The first protests of the children as the cold water rained down on them.

Carmen's little hand in Ana's.

Carmen opened the doors the rest of the way.

Squeezed in there: a motorbike.

Carmen's eyes sparkled. She and Ana crowded into the stall, just as Encarna turned from the front step to come in and supervise the showering.

Ana dropped the towels at the back of the stall. Breathed deeply to calm her nerves. Adjusted the headscarves that would keep the hair from their eyes.

And then a slow, careful balancing act followed as Ana eased herself on to the dirtbike's saddle while Carmen did her best to steady the machine. It all came back to Ana: riding motorbikes around the squares of her neighbourhood in Madrid. She'd always found it easy, always drove too fast. It was good news that this beaten-up Bultaco Sherpa was similar to those bikes from her youth. Perfect for rough, unpredictable terrain.

Carmen used the back wheel to step up and sit behind her mother.

Laughter rang out from the other women. They actually sounded joyful, as if anticipating their own liberation, for that was the deal: they would help Ana and Carmen escape and Ana would seek some way to free them.

But in the next heartbeat, Ana was convinced she'd made a terrible mistake as she felt Carmen's arms around her waist. She considered getting off the bike, creeping back down and falling in with the others but knew that Encarna would spot her. And then the bike would be found and she would be punished anyway. There was no going back.

Her hand was shaking as if afflicted by palsy as she checked her watch. Only three minutes past nine. There was one more step, one more moment of relying on someone: Alfonso, the food truck man. If he arrived at exactly ten past nine as he had promised – and it had taken all of Ana's secret savings to extract that promise – there was still another seven minutes to kill. They couldn't sit here like this for seven minutes. Only five minutes were allowed for showering and then Encarna would start the head count again...

The babble of voices from the showers was growing louder. Good. The women had promised to do what they could to mask the sound of the bike starting, and to turn on as many shower heads as possible to build a protective wall of steam.

Now mother and daughter waited.

Ana's calves already aching from balancing the bike. Balancing, barely breathing. Waiting for the cue: the singing that meant the truck was coming through the gates and that their tiny window of hope had arrived.

Steam swirled into the stall.

Slap slap as Encarna whacked the wall in some threat.

Carmen's fingers twisted deep into her mother's smock.

Both of them hoping for a miracle, that their saviour's watch was fast and he'd be driving through the gates early.

Encarna was shouting that shower time was over. Everybody out.

Heat building.

The groaning of the water tank.

"Where is Soler?"

Carmen shut her eyes. Sometimes you woke up from bad dreams.

Three blasts on the whistle.

"I said where is Ana Soler and her child?"

Slap slap of the cane, this time on flesh. An awful cry of pain.

"Somebody tell me where she is or you'll all be licking the toilet bowls for a month!"

The women began singing.

Ana walked the bike forward. It was wedged into the cubicle, and heavy. The wheels thumped the doors open. Ana's greatest fear was that she would not be able to make the turn to the right, that the bike would become wedged between the doors and the opposite wall. But it proved easy.

Now they faced down the aisle. There was nothing to stop Encarna spotting them if she moved a little bit closer through the steam.

With her left foot, Ana flicked the kickstarter. The bike growled to life. No singing, no children's fuss could hide the sound and the smell.

"What the hell is that?"

Ana twists the right-hand grip and is shocked at how fast they are suddenly jerked forward.

"Move!" she shouts to the women as she steers a terrifying blind path towards the showers. *"Move!"*

The singing has been replaced by cheers and Encarna's rapid-fire demands for explanations.

Ana expertly steers to one side of the benches running down the centre of the aisle. The women and children are safely out of the way in the showers, as planned.

Encarna appears out of the steam, her stick raised. One meaty arm brings it down and the cane catches the back wheel before flying from her hand and smacking Encarna in the face. But the touch has been enough to knock the bike off course and Ana can only watch and brace herself as the Sherpa hits the steps at an angle and instead of thumping down them one by one flies off the sides.

A short but terrible drop. The anticipation of flying over the handlebars. Of pain, failure.

The landing shakes rider and passenger to the marrow and must surely wreck whatever is left of the bike's shock absorbers.

But the machine stays upright.

Ana sees the food truck has already arrived and is parking over by the kitchen – and the electrically operated gates are closing. Shouts from the tower. The first volley of machine-gun bullets will ring out any moment. Ana sizes up the gap and wants to scream in fury as she estimates there isn't enough room for the scrambler to pass through.

She bangs upwards on the gear box with her foot and moves into second.

A hundred feet from the gates. Eighty. Carmen's grip crushing her abdomen, her hot little face pressed into her back. Just the smallest of gaps ahead, barely visible in the dim light from the bulbs strung over the courtyard.

The gap. Tiny. Impossible. They reach it.

And the Sherpa bursts from the compound.

Carmen's cry of jubilation is cut short as the bike dips into a rut and then does a wheelie out the other side.

"Hold on!"

Too late, Ana realises she has not switched the headlamp on and that they are heading down a rough track with only the moon to guide them.

As if hearing her thoughts, a searchlight turns night into day and the first blast from the machine-gun tears up the foliage just a few feet to their right. A klaxon rallies the hacienda to action. Ana knows the wild dogs will be unchained. Starved for days at a time, they will swarm through the woods until they find something to sate them.

Ana knows that all that stands between that mauling and freedom is how she handles this bike. She tenses her arms and squints hard as she tries to read the road. Machine-gun rounds pepper the trees to their left and to their right but so far somebody must be watching over them because not once are they hit.

A steep downhill run puts them out of the line of fire.

Distance.

Distance.

Ana puts another half-kilometre between them and the hacienda. The food truck man has told her to just go straight and she will hit the main road. If they can get that far, she fancies her chances at outriding any pursuers on the hairpin bends that wind around the soaring gorges of yellow and brown stone.

A distant rumbling means the pursuers are coming. Men who know the track well. Men with guns. She is exhausted from just trying to keep the bike straight and wonders if it would be better to pull into the woods and risk a getaway on foot. But a blast of headlights from behind tells her she has left that option too late. A pick-up truck is suddenly on their tail, its passengers jeering, wolf-whistling, firing into the air. This sport is too good to shoot the woman off the bike straight away.

The pick-up accelerates to within inches of the back wheel of the Sherpa and then slams on the brakes, skidding in the mud, bringing loud, drunken cheers. She's in top gear but there's no outracing them, even though she's using the back brake to accelerate on the turns, like the food truck man told her.

A gap in some firs to her right offers hope. It looks like it could be another track, something narrower where the truck won't be able to follow. But if it isn't a track...

She yells at Carmen to hold tight and swerves off the road, braking as sharply as she dares. The truck thunders past, deceived. The Sherpa enters the woods too fast and Ana brakes again and sees too late that the gamble has been foolish: there is no track, just a hill. Carmen screams as they plough a chaotic course through the straggly vegetation, rocks, fallen tree trunks. Ana can't quite believe it herself, how she keeps it all together, but the dirtbike does what it was made for. Still she brakes and still the wheels skid around, but then it seems they're in with a chance as she sees the end of the slope.

But then through a gap in the canopy of trees, moonlight reveals a barbed wire fence.

Ana swerves but it's too late: the bike slides out in front of her and drags her with it. Spinning wheels. Cold wet undergrowth on her body. The momentary scents of myrtle and rosemary as they are churned up by the runaway machine. Carmen's chilling screams behind her.

Ana shuts her eyes.

Barbed wire tears into her face.

***

CHAPTER THIRTY-ONE

With her fingertips, Ana gently traced the length of her scar from top to bottom.

"The dogs never reach us. We had gone too far. Carmen broke a leg, an arm, but she lived. Me... I bled. Almost die. They keep me locked up for months. I don't know how long. One day a man came to see Vicente. A drugs man. From London. This man likes sick things. They bring him to me. He likes this..." She placed a fingertip on the scar. "He says he take me. Vicente says good, she is ugly now. And so I go. I have no choice. I go with this sick man who likes my scar."

Suddenly everything made sense to Sophie. "Venn..."

"Yes. That was three years ago. He use me as his whore. And when he come to run this club, he keep me here. He buy me things. Sometimes he is okay."

"And Carmen?"

"Venn lets me send letters. He cuts them up if he thinks I try say where I am. He says he is not evil man, and that if I do what he says, one day I see her again."

"Why don't you go to the police?"

"Ha! You understand nothing. So I tell some English police and they fly to Spain and tell the police my story? They are all Franco's bully boys over there. You do not understand Spain. Vicente would know about it before anyone got near. He would have her killed. I wait."

Sophie wanted to ask more questions about Venn and Summers but she didn't know where to begin. And could she really trust this feral creature who would think nothing of betraying her to Venn if it might buy her a reunion with her daughter?

Sophie took Ana's hand in hers, and they sat in silence.

Ana never asked for Sophie's story. Sophie had never thought for a moment that she would.

***

CHAPTER THIRTY-TWO

That night, Sophie slept in the suite, with Ana beside her. In the morning, the Spanish woman skulked away with barely a word, her old self again. Sophie was coming out of the club to go home when she passed Jack Rickard, The Gathering Place's upstairs guard, signing for a delivery on the front steps.

"You haven't been giving mouth-to-mouth to your mate, then?" he said.

"What?"

"Charlie. Haven't you heard? He's had a turn."

"You're kidding?"

"No. He had a right barney with Venn this morning. Charlie was blue in the face. You know how he gets worked up. Venn went to smack him one and Charlie just fell down, all shaking. Mitzi was there and she's been nursing him."

"Where is he?"

"Sussex Room, last time I checked."

Sophie burst into the gaming room and found Charlie sprawled on a couch, with Mitzi stroking his forehead.

"Sophie!" called Charlie. "Come and join us, we're having tea."

"We're doing nothing of the sort," said Mitzi. "Sophie, he's had a bad turn, baby. It was that bastard Venn."

"What happened?" said Sophie. "Jack said you had an argument."

"Venn doesn't have the intellectual capacity to argue with a *chimpanzee*, let alone Dryden."

"We're taking you home and then we're calling Dr Shepherd," said Mitzi. She looked at Sophie. "The same thing happened last night. He just fell down. Wouldn't let anyone call an ambulance. He's heading for a breakdown."

"Rubbish! What happened, Sophie, was that I was dancing with these two girls – one Italian, the other French. Boy, could they move. And they weren't a little surprised that the club manager could match them every step. And then I slipped on a spilt drink and suddenly everyone thinks I'm having a heart attack."

"And what about this morning? There was *no spilt drink*. Venn was bawling him out, Sophie, about things Charlie has no control over."

"What kind of things?"

Mitzi dropped her voice low. "Someone's been spying."

"I don't believe a word of it," said Charlie. "The screening's too good."

"What do you mean, spying?" said Sophie. She felt sick.

"'Some facking hack's been poking their snout in where it's not meant to be,'" said Mitzi in her best impersonation of Venn.

"Who is it?"

Sophie felt the room zoom away from her.

"Venn doesn't know," said Mitzi. "He just got a tip-off that someone's out to write a big exposé on the Erato."

"And The Gathering Place?"

Mitzi shrugged. "Who knows? I doubt if they'd manage to get up there. Much easier for them to mingle with all the people down here."

"How about the screening? If they've been through that..."

"Maybe they don't care. That was always going to be the flaw in Venn's little idea – that one day someone would come along who doesn't give a shit if he leaks pictures of them all over town. It's nearly happened before: someone's misbehaved or stolen something or tried to run a racket here. But all Venn

215

had to do was mention the screening photos and that usually scared them off. But he thinks that some newspaper or magazine is gonna run the piece under some phoney byline and he'll never know who wrote it."

"It's just Venn being paranoid," said Charlie. "If he takes any more coke his nose is going to plop into his pie and mash."

Sophie's mind was racing. The only person she'd confided in was Eamonn Flynn.

Jesus, no. Not Eamonn.

She'd heard he had some gambling debts. And the other day, in the pub, when she had snubbed his advances... Had that really wounded him so deeply that he would do this? If so, why hadn't he given her name to Venn, too? Maybe that was how he dealt with the guilt. Maybe he'd offered Venn the tip-off that someone was poking around but not said who. That way he could pocket the dough and not feel too bad.

"It's all bullshit," said Charlie, sitting up and retrieving his tie from behind a cushion.

"Charlie, I need to speak to you alone," said Sophie. "Mitzi, do you mind?"

"As long as you don't get him all stressed I don't. Charlie, I'm going to call us a cab home. Sophie, can you bring him down in the lift in five minutes? No longer."

"I promise."

When Mitzi had left, Sophie said: "Listen, Charlie, there's something I need to tell you."

"I won't be short of work," he said. "I'll go back to TV. I'm quite excited about it already. There's not a week goes by that one of my old muckers from Unicorn doesn't beg me to shoot a bloody ad."

Sophie said nothing: even she knew that the production company Unicorn had gone bust the previous year. Charlie was on his feet and heading for a decanter of Scotch.

"Drink?" he said.

"No. And you shouldn't either."

"I forgot you're only into coke these days. Yep, word gets around, Sophie. The thing about that powder is that it never leads anywhere good. When I was a teenager, I used to watch my favourite film stars snort it from an illuminated dancefloor at this riverside club in Maidenhead. I watched them change before my eyes into grotesques. Killed them, too, some of them. Stay away from it."

"Yes, okay Charlie but listen… I have to tell you something. Can I trust you?"

"These young directors don't have a clue how to bring something in under budget. I might even get a feature straight off the bat."

"Charlie, this is important."

"I'm listening." He poured a huge whiskey that Sophie immediately confiscated.

"Will you sit down again, please?"

"No time. Errands to run. Big club to keep going. Venn doesn't understand the work involved."

She felt like she was losing him.

"Charlie, I haven't been entirely honest about who I am."

"Well, everyone here lies. We all pretend to be someone we're not. It comes free with the membership. All I need's a black coffee. This Roman party is the biggest nightmare ever. I've got just thirty-six hours to find togas for all the staff, not to mention a bloody snow-making machine." Charlie stepped up to Sophie and kissed her on the forehead before tottering towards the door, muttering about how useless all his suppliers had been.

Realising that her attempt to confess all to Charlie was a non-starter, Sophie caught up with him and escorted him to the lift.

CHAPTER THIRTY-THREE

Once the taxi had despatched the Drydens, Sophie decided to walk to Piccadilly. A five-minute stroll might clear up some of the nausea of too much booze and coke and too little sleep. She hadn't eaten more than a slice of toast in the last twenty-four hours; it was time to ease back on the powder and get her routines back to normal.

But the amble only succeeded in making her feel worse. All the leads bounced around in her head and the voices of Venn and Charlie and Hugo and Masters endlessly repeated their puzzling statements. She was no closer to cracking the fate of Abigail Wilman than Scottie had been. She'd failed him and achieved nothing more than a glimpse of Summers' and Venn's worlds.

So what now? *Go home and sleep, save yourself for tomorrow night.*

Tomorrow. The Roman party. Chaos she couldn't picture. Tozer's pals roaring with laughter, spitting threats, shoving the other guests around, Charlie challenging Venn over some trifling matter, Venn unveiling some sick fantasies for the elite at The Gathering Place. Images, like a string of flashbulbs: the outrageously OTT lines of coke that Venn would rack up; the sleek bodies of the couples in lantern city; the grinding hips of the beautiful men and women fucking...

She was ripped from the trance by a blast of car horns and found herself standing in the middle of the road in Piccadilly, with no memory of having stepped out. A cab was heading straight for her, honking madly. Her feet and head frozen, Sophie just watched it, her fate with the gods. The taxi squealed to a halt, inches from her.

The driver was winding down his window to shout at her but she was already climbing into the back and ordering him to go to Notting Hill.

At home, she made black coffee and then a new set of notes using felt-tip pens. Nice and simple, something she could follow. *A plan.* It came together quickly, and after two baby lines of coke (she had graduated from dabbing to snorting now, for a bigger buzz) the sheet of paper was filled with names, locations and her own scratchy drawings (the one of Venn made her laugh so much that she knew she shouldn't do any more powder today).

Sleep. She needed sleep... Or should she just push on through and sleep tonight? She had more than enough coke and the notes were going well...

Sod it. She could sleep throughout 1970 if she needed to. All she needed was a bit of a lift...

Ten minutes later she walked back through the door with the *Space Oddity* and *Led Zeppelin II* albums, two acquisitions from Moog's shop. For once she had impressed the old hippie. She cranked up the volume on Bowie and cut herself a generous line. This was the last time she would do this. The last time at home on her own, anyway. She'd broken the rules, there was no escaping that — taking drugs after you'd just weaned yourself off prescription medication was proof that she must have been mad in the first place. But things were different this time — she wasn't on the brink of disaster, but the verge of something special, something life-changing...

Back to the list, whose biggest question, spelt out in thick red marker pen was: what did Gerald have over Hugo?

Something massive.

The evidence? What was it that Tozer had let slip in the van? *Gerald put the heat on Hugo so he'd let Venn buy in to the club.*

And Hugo in the restaurant: *I intend to put you off for another twenty-five, Gerald, because you have nothing coming to you.* All this conflict, but always between Gerald and Hugo. Why had Gerald paid Amber to spy on Summers? Was he still on the lookout for fresh dirt?

And best of all, Gerald's parting remark at the restaurant: *I'm giving you until the end of the year, Hugo. And then I'm going to start making things very difficult for you. Because I've found him and I'm just dying to use him...*

The end of the year? That was tomorrow night. And who was "him"?

Sophie despaired at ever cracking the Hugo/Gerald intrigue, which in any case seemed unrelated to Abigail's disappearance. Gerald had accused Hugo of holding on to cash that wasn't his. That was hard to fathom: Summers wasn't hard up... Or was he? Was that why he'd sought a partner to share the repair bill?

And all the time, Venn circling like a buzzard, doing Gerald's fascist dirty work until Gerald could deliver him the rest of the club. That had to mean letting him buy in as an *official* stakeholder; at the moment it seemed that Venn just took some kind of cut.

Sophie looked at the photo that Gerald had slid under the door. She stared at the old man's blank expression... This had to be him – the man whom Gerald was "dying to use". Who the hell was he?

Late afternoon, Sophie popped some downers that Terry had given her and was relieved to fall into a deep sleep that took her through to the next morning. She woke up unsure whether to go to the club. If Venn still didn't know that she was the Fleet Street snoop, she'd be safe, but what if Venn had thrown some more money at Eamonn Flynn – or some kneecap-shattering violence – and extracted a name?

There was really no choice – she *had* to go tonight. Once Hugo had finalised this American deal he might be gone for ages. There was no way she could hope to inveigle her way into his circle over there. And besides, Abigail wouldn't have thought twice about going.

She took a shower, made more black coffee, then went back to pacing the living room. What was this sum of money that Gerald wanted from Hugo?

Still so many questions and there's just ten hours until the party and you don't have anything to wear. Plus you should get in touch with Eamonn Flynn, put the heat on him and find out what he's told Venn, find out if your life is in danger tonight...

The phone was ringing; had been for quite some while. She thought of answering it but what if it was her brother, giving her grief for her behaviour at Christmas?

She turned back to the piece of paper. What else? Charlie... Charlie... He needed to get out of the club. Venn would tear him apart as soon as Hugo the protector was out the way. Charlie was so naïve, he probably didn't even know of the murders that took place upstairs: Amber and Echo and God knew who else.

"Shut up!" she screeched at the phone, which she proceeded to bury under a house of cushions, the construction so meticulous that it gave her the giggles.

2pm. Her thoughts ricocheted from Hugo's crumpled, broken face to Abigail riding in a posh car in Pall Mall to the blood that had started leaking from one nostril.

That's enough of that stuff, your heart's going to quit even if your nose doesn't.

Hugo's takeover plans, his eyes on America. When would he go there? Soon. Soon soon soon. Which is why she had to go the club tonight, use all her guile to form some bond with him or force him into revealing something about Abigail.

3pm. Still no costume prepared, or even planned.

What else....? The designers with the plans and spirit levels that so annoyed Charlie. Charlie's snarl: *I'm really going to nail the bastard this time.*

The phone's buried cries were back. This time she decided to answer it. Mother. After some frosty platitudes she got stuck in, tearing Sophie off a strip about the way she'd acted at Christmas. Sophie hardly listened, just kept making notes, starting a new piece of paper, drawing increasingly spidery and surreal shapes, manically stroking Keef and practically slamming the phone down when she felt her mother had been granted enough time.

4pm. Too much energy (*drugs*) needed burning off. She went for a fast walk in the last light of the last day of the decade. People were already hurrying home from work, crowding into the pubs, excitement building. She found herself walking too fast, her heart racing.

She bought the final edition of the *Standard*.

The face on the front page was like a hook to the side of the head.

A Bangladeshi man in late middle age, pictured with his family.

Of course Venn was always going to finish the job.

Her own failings crushed her then. She could have tipped off the police, saved him... But she'd been too obsessed with her own plans to think about saving Amir Chowdry.

Under the headline: "ARSON ATTACK KILLS CAMPAIGNER", the standfirst read: "Racists hunted as equal rights hero dies in curry house firebombing".

***

CHAPTER THIRTY-FOUR

In the last minutes before one of the club's Bentleys arrived, she finished improvising a tunic from bedsheets, tied her hair back and put on a bronze choker for what she hoped was a Cleopatraesque look.

The next thing she was aware of she was in the car, vaguely listening to the driver's prattle about traffic and the best route. She made polite noises but when he started on about his family she couldn't face this taste of the straight world – it brought back Christmas and the arguments – and she switched on the back-seat tape player, cutting him off with *Abbey Road*.

The rest of the journey was a blur of coke dabbing and fretting and staring out at the swarming streets of the West End. Then she was in the lobby, where a shrieking horde of centurions and goddesses followed her in and swept her into the lift with them. What followed was a twenty-second torture of booze fumes, earsplitting laughter, mask swapping and hands on her arse. She swatted these away at first before anger spurred her to grab a handful of fingers and wrench them back, the resulting cry of pain coinciding neatly with the doors opening. But her escape across the grand hallway was blocked – by a triumphant Roman procession.

Hurling grapes and gulping from wine-filled pots were half a dozen Cleopatras riding in their own chariots, each of which was pulled by four bronzed male models, their grim smiles betraying that these circuits had been going on for quite some time. Marching behind the chariots were centurions, fully decked out with metal jackets, helmets and swords, and behind *them* was a jumble of men and women playing gladiators, fire eaters, philosophers, emperors, masked actors and a dozen women slaves who were chained and naked except for leather thongs and bras.

Drowning out the lyre and pipes of the Roman band in the gallery was Tozer's laughter. Sophie got her first view of what she guessed were his "associates", whose behaviour had so angered Charlie. There was a rake-thin man with nasty, squinty eyes; a very young Italian-looking guy with an ice-cream quiff and shiny grey silk suit, and a beaten-up, old-school type – even older than Tozer – with a scar across his chin. The three of them were fighting with swords and spears and bumping into the procession. Rat Eyes grabbed a helmet from a soldier's head and Venn rapped his blade on it; the Italian danced a jig with a pig's head held in front of his face.

Sophie pushed through to the ballroom, where a DJ was decked out in extravagantly flowing robes and false beard and the dancers were a bobbing sea of white togas and tunics. Brute force got her to the other side but there was no sign of Charlie in the ante-room, or the next one, or the gaming room.

Back in the hallway, she weaved through the procession and was climbing the main staircase when someone called her name.

Ana.

"Sophie, you must help me."

"What kind of help?"

Ana dropped her voice. "I can't tell you here. Come, we go upstairs and I tell you my plan."

"I don't have time for your plans tonight, Ana. Where's Charlie? If he's here, he's in danger. Venn's not going to put up with him any longer. We have to talk him into never coming back to the club."

Ana grabbed Sophie's arm. "Please, Sophie, I pray you: listen to me. I need your help so much."

"Ana, what are you doing up here?" said Venn, who'd appeared on the top step.

"There is no people down there," said Ana.

"I don't care. I said I wanted you in the Sussex Room all night. There's a lot of high rollers about. Now get your arse down there."

Ana threw Sophie one last imploring look before leaving.

"Having a good time, yeah?" said Venn.

"It's a blast. But I'm looking for Hugo or Charlie."

"Charlie's around somewhere. He's busy – there's more things to fuck up tonight than usual. I don't think Hugo's here yet but don't worry, lover boy's coming."

"I'll try his suite."

"He won't be there. There's nothing going on in The Gathering Place. I couldn't afford a Roman blow-out on every floor. The party's all down here, babe. And anyway, don't you remember what I told you about Hugo being on the way out?"

Venn put an arm around her. She gently eased herself free and Venn laughed. "Still the Girl Guide when you want to be. Listen, I've got to go and see some people. Maybe you'll be more in the mood for getting close later. 'Cos we've never really got close, have we?"

Sophie was scared, convinced he was trying to put her at ease now he'd worked out she was the spy.

"No," she said. "I guess we haven't."

She watched Venn leave and remembered what he'd done to Amber and Chowdry and how he would do the same to her. But would he really kill her on the night of his beloved party? Maybe he would. What could be easier than luring her to the deserted Gathering Place, sealing it off using the tunnel override codes that only he and Hugo possessed, killing her and getting Terry to drive the body away...

Forget that for now. Just get Charlie out of here and keep searching for Hugo.

The lantern room had been transformed into a series of interlocking tents. The single gangway snaking across the room led to an improvised Roman bath – fully serviced by staff bringing tubs of hot water – at the far side. The sheer number of people impeded Sophie's progress, as did the copious number of bodies writhing on the floor.

Curving around the bath, a mini-amphitheatre offered a grandstand view of the couplings in the water. The audience were naked, many of them fondling each other as they watched the others. Seated at the back, in the shadows, an obese man wrapped in just a towel aimed a home movie camera at the action. Sophie felt repulsion and fear as she realised it was Gerald. He aimed the viewfinder at her and grinned.

The same camera he used on the Echo night. But don't react. Don't give him the satisfaction.

She was heading for the exit when Charlie appeared in the doorway. She was about to call to him but saw that he was with someone, a shortish woman in a linen tunic and cloak, her face concealed by a tragic mask. Some alarm sounded in Sophie and she ducked behind a pillar without knowing why.

Charlie was doing his tour schtick but he sounded weak and confused and his emperor's garb – obviously thrown together in a hurry – hung awkwardly on him.

"This is an authentic bath, we went to great trouble," he was muttering. "It's heated constantly. Ah, they're bringing some more water now. It's... it's, you know, heated constantly..."

Sophie peeked at Gerald, the Cheshire cat, who still had the camera trained on her. He'd guessed that she was hiding from Charlie, and that if he kept pointing that thing at her, Charlie was going to spot her. The last thing she needed was his mischief making.

She mouthed *fuck off*. With a little wave goodbye, Gerald did as he was told, redirecting the camera on the bath.

Charlie had one hand on the small of the woman's back and was ushering her into the tents.

Why the hell was the chick wearing a mask? Maybe she was shy and just coming to check it out, or maybe just famous and not ready to be spotted yet. But why was Charlie giving the tour on the busiest night of the decade? Was he trying to enrage Venn in the hope of prompting some final battle?

"Why don't I leave you to look around?" Charlie was saying. "I have a few things to attend to. Come and find me later. There'll be a big scene in the hallway at midnight. I'll be there."

The woman nodded and now she was alone, a tiny figure amid the monstrous carnal show.

Go after Charlie. You've been looking for him all night. Why are you so hung up on this woman? The coke's screwing up your head.

Coke. Yes, she needed it more than all the other nights put together. It was the only thing that was keeping her from dropping asleep on the spot. She wanted the kick, too, and she wasn't going to even think about the implications of that.

Right next to her, laid out on a pedestal, was a row of lines and gold tubes. Without missing a beat, she snorted the fattest one.

The stranger still hadn't moved. Why was she so nervous?

You were, too, on your first night, Sophie reminded herself. The poor girl obviously couldn't believe what she had walked in to. The last days of the Roman Empire was pretty far out, even by the Erato's standards.

The woman crept into the city of tents and began observing a foursome from a discreet distance. Was this turning her on? Maybe she was just a quiet nympho, waiting for Charlie to leave so she could get her kicks.

228

A beefy blond guy with a flowing mane of hair, who had been a slave earlier in the night but was now down to just the spiked collar, appeared behind Sophie and slid his hands over her arse, his fingers moving round to her crotch. Before he could get there, Sophie turned and kissed him, the long, drawn-out embrace a perfect cover for watching the woman. And not without its own pleasures. If only she didn't have to tail this woman, she'd maybe stay with this guy a little longer.

The quarry was leaving lantern city.

Sophie moved away from the slave and his protests were swallowed up in the babble of groans, chatter, whips, chains being applied, strained against...

The gallery was the scene of frantic activity as a film crew, trapeze artists, fire eaters, jugglers, girls painted gold and a host of men wheeling cannons and what appeared to be industrial fans all raced to get their piece of the performance ready. The woman squeezed herself in among the spectators lining the balustrade for the midnight show downstairs.

Sophie checked her watch: ten to midnight.

She entered the shadowy area between the gallery and the cocktail bar. It was here that Danny and Isabelle had performed their tango, with Gerald playing voyeur. That night, the space had been deserted; now it was packed with insanely drunken couples screwing on couches and with young girls who'd passed out in bergeré chairs, their hair stuck to the gold paint that made the seats into thrones, their designer heels resting in vomit and the lake of melted ice that flowed from the champagne buckets. Littered all around were used condoms, spent amyl nitrite poppers, sex toys, broken glass.

Sophie leant against a sideboard carved with a mask of Bacchus and trailing vines, and waited.

Still with her back to Sophie, the stranger removed the mask to fan herself. When she turned her head to one side, Sophie saw who it was and knew she hadn't been paranoid.

She reached out to clutch a handful of velvet curtain, suddenly feeling faint... and then she experienced an intense anger, the desire for revenge. Hatred would drive her in enacting it. She'd witnessed enough violence at this club and how it resolved things quickly without the bullshit that the straight world put itself through. And now she wanted some for herself.

The woman moved from the balustrade and, in a delicious stroke of luck, actually stepped into the shadows, brushing close to Sophie, who stayed concealed behind the curtains.

The woman's eyes were wide, trying to come to terms with the shock of the depravity in here.

Sophie said: "Good evening, Saffron."

The woman spun round too quickly and slipped in the muck, sprawling on to an unoccupied couch, her mask dropping from her face.

Sophie stepped into full view. Wrapped around her hands was a length of chain with leather cuffs at each end. "I should have known that Michael Challoner wouldn't be the last exclusive you'd try to steal from me."

"Sophie!" said Saffron, wide-eyed with fear. "Oh my God..."

"I really am pleased to see you. Because it means it isn't me that's been rumbled. It's you."

Saffron tried to sit up but Sophie's one-handed shove kept her in her place. Now Sophie stood over her, letting the chain go slack and then yanking it tight.

"It also means that I haven't been betrayed by an old friend of mine." She hated herself for having ever suspected Eamonn. "Which is a first..."

Saffron tried to pipe up but her words came out as funny little squeaks that made Sophie laugh.

"Congratulations on your double exclusive, by the way: *'My afternoon with hospital killer Bernie Littlechild'*. Challoner picked me as his contact and Littlechild nearly murdered me but *you* got the story – you always pull it off, Saff. At least someone came out of it smiling. And congratulations on the other exclusive – stealing David."

Saffron's eyes darted around as she looked for a way out. Sophie pressed a knee down on Saffron's thigh, trapping her on the couch.

"Do you know why Charlie asked you here?" asked Sophie.

Saffron looked confused by how much Sophie knew. "No. He called me a few days ago. I came here last night for the first time. He said he had some grievance with the owners, that he wanted a big story in a magazine. The truth about the Erato."

"I bet he did. He'll do anything to trash Eddie Venn. But the reason *you're* here is he asked me who was the best journalist I knew – and I said you. Our relationship has never been short of ironies, has it?"

"Sophie, please, just get off me. There are so many things I want to say to you."

"Oh, and me to you, Saff."

Saffron tried to lever herself off the seat but Sophie lashed out with a fist, the chain wrapped around it, and revelled in the satisfying crunch and the sight of blood from Saffron's mouth.

Saffron was screaming and lashing out but the coke made Sophie feel invincible. She straddled Saffron, pinned her, adjusted the chain, her mind crazed with a dozen questions, torments. Saffron whispered some pathetic little mantra, an appeal for mercy.

Some of the people who had been watching this scene unfold were now scurrying away, probably to find help, and that meant Charlie. Which meant Sophie didn't have long.

"Just let me go," said Saffron, crying. "I'll leave the club. You can have whatever story you're doing. I won't tell anyone you're here undercover."

"Who said I was still undercover?"

"What do you mean?"

"Maybe I just like it here, bitch."

From behind, two hands grabbed Sophie's shoulders and yanked her backwards. She sailed through the air and landed hard, cracking her head on the parquet floor. Dazed, she looked up and saw that it was Charlie.

"What the hell's going on?" he barked.

Saffron was already halfway across the gallery.

"Yeah, that's right," called Sophie. "RUN!"

"What the hell are you playing at?" said Charlie.

The shove had knocked Sophie for six and she held her head in her hands. "I think that's what *you* need to tell *me*, Charlie."

"What are you talking about? She's just a new member."

"Don't mess with me, Charlie." Sophie started laughing again and found it hard to stop. "*She stole my fucking husband.*"

"Jesus. How was I supposed to know that? I asked you who was the best in the business and you said Saffron Honey."

"So you sneaked her in here to write a big story? Did you really think that some scandal in the papers would make Hugo kick Venn out of here? That you could bring back the old days?"

Charlie let out a roar of blind fury and upturned the couch, sending it thudding into a wall. Now it was Sophie's turn to be terrified.

"Would that be so bad?" he bellowed, no longer the weak old man. "What would you know about how it used to be? They've ruined this place. The dream's over. It could have been beautiful. And for the record,

I didn't do it just out of spite – Saffron's magazine is paying me, too. I need every penny now."

"Why? What are you talking about?"

A surge in noise from downstairs – a roll on the band's drums, premature poppers, calls for everyone to gather in the hallway.

"I have a feeling you're about to find out," said Charlie. "Come on. I don't want you to miss this."

"Miss what? Charlie, *just tell me*."

But he was hurrying away.

The party sounds grew more urgent. Sophie picked herself up, wiped the worst of the mess from her tunic and followed after him.

***

CHAPTER THIRTY-FIVE

The hallway was packed tight with bodies; people were even crowded up the stairs for a view of Summers and Venn, who had been granted a tiny island of floorspace for their address, which was under way. Sophie jostled to the front and tuned in to their improvised double act of bawdy jokes and good-natured insults, the men bouncing surprisingly well off each another.

This crowd would lap up *anything* right now, thought Sophie. Even without the mountains of booze and top-quality drugs, they'd be starstruck in the presence of these two big hitters, the tycoon and the gangster, who had the power to turn this club into anything and take everyone along with them.

Five to midnight.

Above everyone's heads, a series of pulleys operated by the slaves delivered dozens of bottles of champagne to anyone who could reach up and pull them free from their harnesses. Tozer, Rat Eyes, the Italian and the scarred man pulled hard on the rope, laughing hysterically as it looked ready to collapse. Only a blast of profanities from Venn stopped them. Tozer blew him a sarky kiss.

Behind Venn and Hugo stood their ice sculpture doubles: the crook as a young boxer; the tycoon debonaire in a dinner jacket, his head tilted in contemplation. Flashbulbs popped as the flesh and bones versions posed with their likenesses: Venn striking a fighter's stance, toe to toe with himself; Summers relaxing with an arm slung lightly around the doppleganger's shoulders. A ruddy-faced, handlebar moustachioed sculptor proudly stepped forward to take a bow.

Summers saw there were just three minutes to go and hollered for any remaining empty glasses to be charged. He and Sophie locked eyes, he acknowledged her with a smile and then silenced the hubbub with a whistle.

"All right, all right, it's all over!" said Venn. "The Sixties are over. Best decade in the history of the world so let's see it out in style. I want everyone to raise their glasses: TO THE SIXTIES!"

The toast came back at him as a roar.

"I'm just so emotional tonight," he said. "Emotional to be here, in this fantastic club. The Erato, there's nothing like this place, and I want to thank Hugo—" – Hugo patted Venn on the back – "for being... just the guy that he is. We may be from different worlds but let me tell you, this man is my friend, my business partner and I want to thank him, publicly, for bringing me in to this place, 'cos this place is..."

"Ours!" shouted Tozer, eliciting a chorus of groans – and another filthy look from Venn.

"Because this place is going to be the centre of the universe," said Venn. "And now over to my friend, Hugo Summers, for some very special news."

Sophie raised herself on tiptoes to look for Charlie. She spotted a concerned Mitzi doing the same thing.

"Friends, Romans, Arabs, lend me your cocaine," said Hugo, to massive cheers. "I thank my new friend, Eddie Venn, for his kind words. That man has injected more energy, more creativity, into the Erato than I – and my father before me – could ever have dreamed possible. Some people, I know, think we should have kept the club as it has always been: for the elite, the privileged, a museum piece. But forgive me a certain pride if I say that I have always embraced progress, always believed in new ideas, whether in art or business, and that what Eddie intends to do with the club next, well, I envy his vision and he has my full blessing.

"So what I'm trying to say is, we're ready for the next stage. Some of you have been asking why all the the outfitters, the lawyers – what's been going on? Well, I'm sorry for the secrecy, but it's been necessary. I can now reveal that as of midday today, the Erato and The Gathering Place upstairs – " – he kept them hanging there, the place silenced – "are entirely and officially... the property of a consortium headed by Eddie Venn."

Pandemonium: cheers, catcalls, boos, missiles sailing overhead, Tozer and his mates leaping up and down wildly, simultaneously opening three bottles of champagne, spraying the room. No wonder they don't kow-tow to Venn, thought Sophie – the partnership made them equals again.

Summers tried waving down the fuss, wanting a little more time to finish.

"You all know Venn," he boomed. "He's a man of flair and he can't wait to get started on a major refurb, which is within his powers now that for the first time he has a *financial* interest in the club. More than an interest: this place belongs to his consortium. And as for me, well, I'm moving to the States. Despite what you will have read in the papers, nothing is definite yet but I'm certain that New York is where the future of my business lies. My thoughts are at risk of becoming stale and so I'm turning to a young country to make them young again. And now I see that we only have a couple of minutes until the new year. The new *decade*. So please join me in a toast to... the Seventies!"

"THE SEVENTIES."

A scuffle had broken out among Tozer's party. The hallway was so crowded that people were climbing on to the piano. Abuse was shouted as a hall porter ordered them to get down.

It was no surprise that Hugo was getting out, thought Sophie; none of his lot were left. It was anarchy in here...

She turned a full circle, still looking for Charlie. No wonder he'd been keen to contact a journalist with some muscle: not only did he want to do the dirty on the club out of spite, but he needed some cash, too – because he knew Venn's first job would be to sack him. Charlie wouldn't have a job by the time the night was over.

A new, angry voice above the din turned Hugo's happy expression to granite.

Charlie was barging through, glugging from a bottle of champagne, his costume swapped for slacks and white shirt, more befitting whatever bitter finale he had planned. Mitzi vainly tried to hold him back but he'd dreamt of this moment and nothing could stop him.

"I wish to raise another toast!" he called, as he planted himself between Venn and Hugo and threw his arms around them. It was the first time that Sophie had seen Venn look really uneasy.

"Sophie, take this, please."

It was Ana. She was trying to press a piece of folded paper into Sophie's hand.

"Not now," snapped Sophie.

"Please. *Take this.*"

Ana forced the paper into her grasp and disappeared into the crowd. Sophie slipped the note into a pocket she'd sewn into the costume.

"Ladies and gentlemen, I give you Charlie Dryden," said Hugo, which got a small cheer. "There's just time for a quick toast before 1970. But you'll *have* to be quick, old friend."

"Haven't I earned a few words, Hugo?" said Charlie. "I appreciate that my appearance isn't in the script

Venn's written for you tonight. He's been writing the scripts for quite some time, hasn't he?"

A couple of hundred boos came back at him.

"Oh, come on, Charles," said Hugo. "Not now."

"I'm not here to bury you, Hugo, but to praise you," said Charlie, projecting to the back row. "*Salute* you. You bankrolled my plays, even when two, three, four of them flopped, didn't you? Because you are a good and loyal friend. That's right! We were friends once. Perhaps you can share what the next chapter will be for Charlie Dryden, once the new management has done away with him. And you, Hugo, what will become of you now? I don't quite believe you about the new beginning. I think you're running... What does everyone else think?"

Charlie pulled a big pantomime expression; he was now so deluded that he thought the audience were with him. Couldn't he see that he had no friends here any more?

Venn had had enough and shoved Charlie away but Charlie stormed back.

"You got seduced, didn't you?" he demanded of Hugo. "What happened to the poets, the writers, the actors? This was the home of the bohemian. That's what you told me it would be when you asked me to be your manager, back in those wonderful times before I had to share the job with a gangster."

Venn lunged and shoved Charlie again. This time he struck a pillar head on and thudded to the floor.

"Shit," said Venn, noticing the time. "*Ten!*"

Summers wore a convincing smile, too much of a cool customer to let anger show.

Everyone: *nine*.

Enraged, Charlie struggled to his feet and began weaving around Venn and Summers like some mad terrier. People were throwing food at him and a lot of it was hitting Summers and Venn.

Eight.

Charlie, at top volume: "Well, in the spirit of the era, I would rather burn out than fade away. And so would you raise your glasses, please, to the death of the Erato, and the eternal torment of The Gathering Place!"

Seven.

A wall of jeering – then cheers as Terry pushed through and dived at Charlie, who hurled the champagne bottle at him, the distraction buying him vital seconds to vanish. He was halfway up the staircase before Terry even spotted him again.

Six.

Venn shouted for Terry to let Charlie go. He passed a full bottle of champagne to his lieutenant. "No rush, Tel. We'll get that wanker later."

Five.

Sophie was bobbing up and down with the rest; there was nothing else she could do at this moment. Hugo held out a hand, imploring her towards him but she was a link in what would imminently be an *Auld Lang Syne* chain and the people either side of her wouldn't release their grip.

Four.

Then she saw him: Gerald, coming up behind her, but she could tell he wasn't heading for her but for Summers. He was puce with anger. What had he just heard that he didn't like? That Venn was taking over? But isn't that what he wanted? Hadn't he made that possible?

Three.

Gerald was thwarted, unable to push through the throng. He got pulled into a chain.

Two.

Charlie's words: *I think you're running. What does everyone else think?*

One.

Bernie. David. Saffron. The last month.

Summers' smile. His eyes on her.
Everything those eyes had ever seen.
Don't hunt what you can't kill.

***

SEVENTIES

CHAPTER THIRTY-SIX

Indoor fireworks – catherine wheels, rockets and waterfalls – went off in each corner of the room, and Sophie and everyone else ducked as two of the gold-painted girls swooped down on trapezes, criss-crossing one another as they sailed through the blizzards of snow being pumped from the huge fans up in the gallery.

As soon as *Auld Lang Syne* was over, Gerald fought his way towards Summers, who'd seen enough and was taking off.

Sophie followed them and caught: "You betrayed me, Hugo! I was lied to! You never told me you were leaving the country. You said the New York rumours were being put about by the competition to undermine Summers Steel."

"Did I, Gerald? I have a very poor memory these days. Well, with respect, you can't do a thing about it, old boy."

"I can do *everything* about it, Hugo."

"So you intend moving to the States and following me around, Gerald? I don't think so. And I can't see you instructing your lawyer to turn on the heat on, can you? *What would you tell him without incriminating yourself?*"

Summers had reached the lobby and was calling a lift.

"Please don't follow me, Gerald, or I shall have you removed."

"Are you so blinded by ego that you think that's possible, Hugo? I delivered this place to Venn. Do you think his boys would lift a finger against me now?"

Hugo stepped into the lift and the uniformed operator shut the doors.

The cage between them, Gerald smiled, eyes twinkling. "I told you – I've found him now. You leave me no choice but to bring him into play."

Sophie tried to catch Hugo's reaction but the lift was rising. He was going to The Gathering Place.

"Didn't you see the photo I put under your door?" shouted Gerald.

Sophie shrunk back out of sight as Gerald re-entered the hallway, passing within inches of her.

Venn's men would capture Charlie any minute now, and they weren't going to let him off with just a beating. If she didn't find him first, she'd never get a chance to ask what he'd meant about Summers "running". And she *had* to find out: Charlie obviously knew more than she'd ever suspected, and tonight he'd tell her.

But where would he have gone? There was no way he'd try to get into The Gathering Place, where he'd run straight into the arms of his killers. And he didn't know the codes either. Would he have left the building, just stumbled out and found a pub somewhere? Maybe he was drowning his sorrows in the cocktail bar. Seemed a good place to start. If he wasn't there she could try the–.

"Sophie, thank God, somebody sane," said Mitzi. She was sweating wildly and covered in fake snow, having just battled across the madness of the grand hallway. "Have you seen my Charlie?"

"I'm looking for him."

"Oh, please, please find him. I'm beside myself, darling. I had no idea he was going to pull that crazy shit. We gotta get him outta here and make sure he never comes back."

"It's okay, Mitzi, we'll find him together and get him home, okay? Why don't you search this floor? I'll try the mezzanine. He could be in the cocktail bar, it's always been his-."

"No, no, no, honey. Jesus, I *know* where he is. There's only one place he's gone."

"Where?"

"The upstairs. Didn't you hear what he said? He hates that place. Everything was good around here until Venn showed up and built it."

"But Charlie doesn't know the codes."

"He got them off someone yesterday. I think he bribed that dago bitch with the scar."

"But he still can't get in there. They have two guards watching that place..."

"No. Terry and those other guys are racing round the building looking for him. There's no-one guarding that joint. It's just how he planned it."

Charlie, you clever bastard.

"Baby," said Mitzi, pulling Sophie's face close to hers. "Please get up there and save my Charlie. He thinks The Gathering Place is evil and I know he's going to do something stupid."

***

CHAPTER THIRTY-SEVEN

Even the mad noise on the two floors below did not penetrate The Gathering Place.

Sophie stood in the lounge, alone but for the sounds of the manmade stream and the revolutions of the wall panels. They cycled through their city nightscapes and sunset beaches and mirrors. It was creepy in here and she hurried from the room.

As she approached Hugo's suite, Charlie's righteous anger filled the corridor.

She knocked, looked up at the camera and was quickly let in by Charlie.

Hugo stood by the windows. Charlie was wild haired, sunken eyed. Neither man acknowledged her.

"I'm sorry that you feel I owe you a living, Charlie," said Hugo.

"I never said that. But it would have been nice to know that you were planning to fuck off to America. You know as well as I do that Venn will sack me; Christ, *murder* me."

"Venn gave me assurances that he'll keep you on. I couldn't do much better, Charlie. I'm sorry, but I've had more pressing things on my mind."

Charlie held out his hands. "We were friends, Hugo."

"Your outburst downstairs, *implying I have things to hide*, and your trespassing on to this floor, demanding entrance to my private suite, are they the acts of a friend?"

"A real friend would have given me the codes to the tunnel years ago."

"Regrettable, I admit, but one of Venn's demands. And I am a man of my word."

"Well, bravo, Hugo. I'm welling up. But you know, you didn't *have* to let me in here just now."

"I would hardly leave you in the corridor, which brings us to a more pressing point: did it occur to you *why* The Gathering Place might be empty tonight?"

"That's just the way Venn wanted it. Concentrate the party down in the Erato, he said. And that's been hard enough. I've been crazy trying to fix up snow storms, circus performers, costumes, all those props. It's not even like-."

"Charlie, just shut up for a minute, old boy. Don't you think it's strange that Venn has kept this place empty for the biggest night of the year?"

"I don't follow."

"I imagine that despite his assurances to me, he intended to lure you up here at some point in the early hours. But you've walked into his trap. Now it's just a matter of when the heavies will arrive. My guess is soon. I would leave the building if I were you and not come back."

"All right, I'll leave you alone, Hugo. I know when a friendship is dead. But do me one last favour – tell me why you went in with him."

"I'm a businessman, Charlie. We may find people like Venn despicable, but business isn't about being friends. Perhaps if you'd ever been in business you'd understand. Upstarts like him are the future. That's the real lesson of this hideous decade."

"No," said Charlie. "That's not it. It doesn't add up. The Summers name, the club, the tradition, all spunked away to some poor man's Kray twin? It's all about Gerald, isn't it? He turned the thumbscrews until you let Venn buy in here. And now he's handed Venn the whole thing. What's Gerald got on you? Is it *Emily*?" He cast a quick, sideways look at Sophie. "Or is it Puymirol?"

"Go fuck yourself, Charlie."

"The cheek of the man to say that after *my* loyalty," said Charlie, righteous anger driving him. "All those

246

lies I told your society pals about your 'breaks in the country', covering up your depressions so the banks didn't get the jitters. And how I've turned a deaf ear to the tittle tattle, what those pals thought happened to Emily, and Abigail Wilman. Yes! *Abigail.* I've nearly pieced it together myself, the whole story. I wonder what you might tell me now if Sophie wasn't here."

Summers swept every bottle and glass from the bar.

"Get out, Charlie! GET OUT OF HERE!"

"And I can read," Charlie said. "*Puymirol?* That's in the *history books,* Hugo."

Summers made no reply, merely opened and shut the glass doors distractedly. He said: "Sophie, would you mind going to the lounge?"

"Actually," she said, "I don't think I can."

All eyes turned to the monitor, which showed three blurry figures in the corridor. Sophie knew those shapes by now: Terry. Lenny. Jack.

The entryphone chimed.

Nobody moved.

"Well, it looks like you were right about Venn reneging on his promise not to touch me," said Charlie. "Unless those guns under their clothing are for my protection, of course."

"Can they get in here?" asked Sophie.

"Yes," said Hugo. "Venn and I have the codes to everywhere on this floor." He threw open the sliding doors. "You can climb over the wall to the next balcony, and then on to the roof garden. You can get back to the corridor from there. Once I've let these three in here, I'm going to lock the doors. They won't be able to get out. That'll give you enough time to get away. But I won't be able to hold them forever. And Charlie, don't go home and don't come back."

"Are you mad? They'll kill you," said Charlie.

"They have no beef with me. Just you."

247

"Well, bollocks, I'm not running from them. We'll fight them together."

"You're not running," said Hugo, placing a hand on Charlie's shoulder. "You're making sure Sophie gets out of the building safely. Because no-one is safe tonight."

Sophie knew this was a ploy to soothe Charlie's ego but it worked, because seconds later she and Charlie were on the balcony. Hugo shut the doors on them and drew the blinds.

In the suite, Hugo straightened his bow tie, finished his whiskey and soda and palmed a small knife from a drawer in the bar. Then he crossed his arms and waited.

A series of urgent chimes.

On the monitor, Terry tilted his head to look at the camera.

His hand moved to the keypad.

The door clicked open.

The new arrivals entered casually and formed themselves in a triangle, with Terry at the front.

"I'm sorry to do this, Hugo," he said. "We've come for Charlie."

"Well, firstly, as you can see, he's not in here. And secondly, would you mind getting the fuck out of my suite?"

"I'm sorry, Hugo. Venn's orders."

"Then kindly go and remind Venn that this is my suite."

"It's his suite now. His *club*. And we have orders to deal with anyone who tries to stop us."

Hugo nodded, arms still folded. The small knife from the bar that he'd palmed pushed into his flesh.

"All right, boys, have a look around," said Terry.

"This is absurd," said Hugo. "What makes you think he's in here?"

"Just a quick look round, then we can all get on with having a few drinks, eh, Hugo?"

Summers' smile was as guilty as black ice.

"It's *Mr Summers*, boy," he said, hitting two buttons on the wall, the first locking the doors, the second killing the lights.

Terry tore in for a quick attack and walked into a powerful blow that plunged the knife into his heart. His death was so sudden that he didn't even scream. In the dark, Lenny and Jack assumed it was Summers that had gone down. But after a body thumped to the floor, Lenny and Jack were shocked to hear the voice that then spoke.

"Who's next?" said Summers. "Guns not much good in here, chaps."

He darted in as if to attack, then retreated just as swiftly. He kept moving, his footwork nimble, his hands held up close to his face in a boxer's stance. Sometimes he passed across the light filtering through the blinds, sometimes he ducked below it; whatever he knew would confuse them. He chuckled, then barged straight between the two of them, jolting them off balance with vicious elbow swings, before vanishing again. Taunting them. Daring them.

Winded, they pulled themselves together, angry now, which, of course, is what he wanted.

They came for him.

***

CHAPTER THIRTY-EIGHT

Charlie helped Sophie over the stone trough dividing the last balcony from the roof garden and they hurried to the tunnel's doors.

"Take the lift to the underground passage in the basement and walk across to the car park," he said. "It's not you they want but we can't take chances. Go to Piccadilly or Park Lane and get a cab, okay?"

"Where are you going?"

"Don't worry, I'll be out of here in five minutes. But it's dangerous for you to stick with me. Go!"

"No, Charlie. I promised Mitzi I'd find you."

"I've got one last job, Sophie. And then I'm done."

The important thing was getting *herself* out of here, she thought. She certainly wasn't safe now that Saffron had seen her and could feasibly rat her out to Venn.

"What are you going to do?" she said.

"What I should have done years ago. Torch The Gathering Place."

"You're going to *burn it down?*" She pounded his shoulders with her fists but he had a new strength and hardly even registered them. "Are you insane? *You'll kill everyone.*"

"Then your job is to get them out."

He turned and strode into the shadowy corridor leading to the lounge.

Sophie stood there for a while, paralysed with indecision, before keying in the code and entering the tunnel.

***

CHAPTER THIRTY-NINE

Charlie was again awestruck by this beautiful thing that Venn had created. It was only the second occasion he had been in The Gathering Place's lounge – the first was earlier today. He felt emotional as he thought what might have been, had Venn recognised his talents, and had Venn's heart not been so corrupt.

And then he pictured how the rest of the evening would unfold, and his mood brightened. He would take the lift to the basement, slip away from the club via the underground passage and walk to his other club, The Anderson. There he would buy drinks for whatever friends he found there, and phone the Erato's reception to ask his old pal Bob to locate Mitzi and discreetly instruct her where she could meet her husband.

Now, in the lounge, he opened a deep drawer concealed in the wall and removed the two plastic bleach bottles he had placed in there that afternoon, when the staff and members were absent, gathering strength for the big party. He unscrewed one of the caps and began tipping the petrol on to the carpet.

***

CHAPTER FORTY

On her way to the ground-floor lobby, Sophie slumped against the wall, exhausted but relieved that she still had the power to make sound decisions. She had decided to tell the hall porter what Charlie was doing and instruct him to whack hell out of the fire alarms.

But when she got down there, Bob just nervously opened and closed his fob watch and shook his head.

"I can't do that, miss," said the proud Yorkshireman. "You see, for some time now, George Tozer and his mates have been setting off the fire alarms when they're worse for wear. It's got us in terrible trouble with the police, not to mention the fire brigade. They don't find things like that at all funny. Mr Venn has given me his orders: the fire brigade are not to be summoned without his express permission. Or Mr Summers' or Mr Dryden's. But no-one else."

"You must be kidding," said Sophie. "Charlie's going to burn this place down!"

"Then we need to find Mr Venn or Mr Summers and ask them if-."

Sophie grabbed a carriage clock from a side table and rammed it into the nearest fire alarm. The glass shattered but no alarm sounded. She kept thumping at the button but to no avail. Finally she turned to Bob, who was shaking his head.

"I was about to say that Venn ordered all the alarms to be switched off, miss."

"Then I'll go across the road and call the fire brigade from a phone box. Jesus!"

Clack clack clack from the fob watch. "That won't do any good. The fire brigade won't come out to us unless Charlie, Venn or Hugo give them the call, miss."

"What?"

"I'm sorry, miss," said Bob. "It's nothing to do with me."

Sophie slapped the counter in frustration and returned to the first floor, where things were getting out of control. The Roman musicians' instruments had been commandeered by Tozer's associates, who were wringing vile noises from them and hurling them around. The spit-roast pigs had been stolen and set on fire by Rat Eyes, who watched the flames with a demented glee; the older mate of Tozer's was trying to push over the Christmas tree; acid casualties lay slumped in the middle of the floor; a woman staggered around, sobbing and wearing nothing but a musquash coat; a man in a Victorian nightgown was painting the floor purple, and all dancing at the ballroom disco had been replaced by a seething mass of group sex, fucking against walls, heads beneath hoisted skirts, faces contorted in ecstasy...

Like a trapped rat, Sophie made desperate circuits, looking for Isabelle, Danny or Mitzi or anyone else she had befriended, but recognised no-one.

It was time to search the mezzanine. Mitzi might have settled in the cocktail bar in the hope that Charlie would seek her out there. Sophie realised she was out of ideas and started to panic.

***

CHAPTER FORTY-ONE

Terry and Jack were dead.

Lenny was sure of that, even though he couldn't see them in any great detail. He knew that Terry was on the floor, Jack on the bed. He knew what death sounded like, recognised the noise made by snapping necks, the jettisoning of blood from vital arteries. He'd dealt that finality to others and now it was time for it to be dealt to him. This Summers was an expert at death, but the three of them had learned that too late.

Now that there was no danger of hitting one of his own side, Lenny emptied his 9mm Mauser in the direction he believed Summers to be.

But when the ringing in his ears died away, there were no cries of pain, no falling bodies, just the reek of cordite.

Terrified, Lenny hurled the gun in the hope of getting lucky and heard it smack harmlessly against a wall.

He fumbled in his pocket for his flick-knife and clicked it open.

"Okay," he said. "I'm going. Just let me go, yeah?"

Maybe Summers would reply, giving away his position... but somehow Lenny didn't think so. Summers was clever, very clever. He was clever with that knife that did for Terry, who lay on the bed, his corpse pitter-pattering blood on to the carpet.

And when that first murder had left Summers unarmed, he had despatched Jack with a series of punches that put him to the floor quickly, where – as far as Lenny could see – he'd snapped his neck with a single kick.

Okay. So Lenny wasn't going to try to kill or capture Summers. It was time to get out of here, and to hell with what Venn would say.

Yes, for fuck's sake just run.

Lenny clambered over the bed and Terry's bloody corpse and hurled himself at the door, where his bloody palms just slipped hopelessly as they tried to grip the handle. Finally they got some purchase but the door was locked.

Lenny hammered his fists against it and began crying: "No, please" over and over. And then he was very briefly aware of some cold presence behind him.

***

CHAPTER FORTY-TWO

Charlie emptied the last of the petrol from the second bottle and dropped the container to the floor.

The lounge was covered in lines of fuel that crisscrossed the floor, snaked over every piece of furniture, splashed up walls and led in a single trail to the corridor, where he now stood, match in hand.

He tried to think of some final witticism for his own amusement, and found he couldn't. Witticisms were a luxury that could get him killed. He just had to get away quickly before whoever Sophie had recruited for help discovered him.

Within the half hour he'd be drinking at the Anderson with Mitzi. They would check into some London hotel for a few days and then, when the heat was off, disappear into the Continent. The south of Spain would be a good bet.

Of course, he hadn't told Mitzi any of this, but he had her passport in his pocket, along with all their savings. She'd go along with it if he told her that's how it had to be.

A bold strike of the match. The flame threw an orange glow over the corridor.

He dropped it and savoured the satisfying *whumf* as the line of petrol caught alight and spread back into the lounge.

There. That should destroy The Gathering Place. It might destroy the Erato, too, but as Venn owned that as well now, all the better.

Charlie ran.

***

CHAPTER FORTY-THREE

The ice sculptor stood guarding his masterpieces, which had been taken from the crowded grand hallway to the relative safety of the mezzanine floor. He gave Sophie an oily smile as she passed him on her way to the cocktail bar.

In the bar, she spotted the grandee who had lent her the cigar that so effectively injured Venn. Now he was in raucous conversation with Pippa.

"Pippa, have you seen Venn?" said Sophie.

"Yeah, I know *exactly* where he is. Driving my husband's Lotus around the streets. They're so wasted they're going to crash it."

Shit. That meant she couldn't even go and get *Venn* to stop Charlie. And as for Terry and Jack and Lenny, what had they done with Hugo upstairs? Hugo had promised he'd try to hold them in his suite for a while, but surely they'd be out of there by now?

Another idea: recruit *Tozer* and his boys to stop Charlie, if it wasn't too late. They might be crazy but if they had some share in the club, as she suspected, they wouldn't want anything happening to it. And if *they* wouldn't help, she'd have to go back and stop Charlie herself...

***

CHAPTER FORTY-FOUR

Charlie felt a sense of justice as he keyed in the codes and stepped into the tunnel. Venn had thought he was so clever, keeping the upstairs clear tonight so he could lure Charlie there. But that plan had backfired, and the floor's desertion had meant Charlie could carry out his own plan undetected.

And given that Ana – Venn's own personal whore – had sold the floor's access codes to Charlie, Venn really wasn't very smart at all, was he?

Charlie began whistling the theme tune to *They Might Be Heroes* as the doors swished shut behind him. The footlights faded up to show the way along the catwalk. He ran his hand over the cushioned walls, marvelled at the tubular design and wished he'd been able to spend more time here. But no, he hadn't been one of Venn's chosen few.

Or Hugo's, for that matter. He could have talked Venn into going a bit easier on you these past few years. But what Gerald has over Hugo is bigger than your friendship.

As Charlie neared the end of the tunnel, he saw the glowing tip of a cigar.

***

CHAPTER FORTY-FIVE

Tozer and his gang had disappeared. She would have to get everyone out of here now. If Charlie had bottled out of torching the place – or simply been bullshitting – she'd just have to live with the consequences. She'd be expelled from the club and her big exclusive would be ruined but at least she wouldn't have a few hundred dead people on her conscience.

Sophie dashed from the sauna and bumped straight into Mitzi in the gallery.

"Sophie, *where is he?*"

"He's upstairs. I think he's done something stupid."

"Like what?"

"I don't know. I'm going back up there to check. But I'm pretty sure that-."

A knot of people were hurrying from the cocktail bar. At the same time, a large group were pushing their way out of the lantern room and hurriedly throwing on their togas, tunics and armour.

The sculptor and a helper had grabbed the ice statue of Hugo and were taking it down the staircase, double quick. Where were they all going?

Sophie looked at the remaining statue, the one of Venn, and noticed how slick it was, how ill-defined the features.

"Jesus," said Mitzi. "I'm sure that thing's not supposed to melt yet. It's just so hot in here..."

She was right – it was roasting. The plaster on the ceiling was bubbling and boiling.

"We gotta get people outta here," said Mitzi. "And I've gotta get Charlie."

"No way," said Sophie. "You don't have the codes to the tunnel and I'm not telling you. You're leaving with everyone else. Charlie told me he'd be out of there in five minutes. That means he's already out of the building." Two black stains were appearing above their heads. Growing.

Danny and Isabelle emerged from the lantern room. Danny shrugged at Sophie as if to say what's going on? Sophie pointed to the ceiling.

"The Gathering Place," she said. "It's on fire..."

***

CHAPTER FORTY-SIX

"Hugo, you startled me," said Charlie. "What happened back there in your suite?"

"I killed them."

A nervous laugh. "But not really, right? You didn't really?"

"Yes, I did. Because I'm a good and loyal friend, Charlie, despite what you think. But before I left the suite, I saw something on the monitors. I saw you setting fire to the lounge. And I wondered: is that the action of a good and loyal friend?"

Charlie opened his mouth to protest but no words come. He was more concerned with the fact he couldn't just barge out of here – the second set of doors hadn't opened. And Summers stood blocking them.

"And asking me about Emily and Puymirol, in front of Sophie, was that the best time to raise these questions?"

"That was a mistake, Hugo, and I apologise. Look, you know I'm an arse. A fuck-up. Let's just get downstairs, call the fire brigade and talk things through, eh?"

"It did occur to me to dial 999 before I left the suite, Charlie. But as the club is no longer my property, I'm *more* worried about those questions of yours."

"Puymirol? Just rumours. People who know you, gossiping in the cocktail bar when they're drunk. The same with Emily."

"My wife committed suicide, Charlie."

"Yes, I know. Bloody hell, it's hot in here, Hugo. The walls are melting."

"That's because Venn made this floor out of plastic, perspex, flammable fabrics. Anyone trapped in this tunnel won't die from the flames, they'll die from the hundreds of deadly gases created by the toxic chemicals that will flood in here. They'll have time to observe their own death, second by second, as total suffocation kills them. Now: *Emily*. What do they say?"

Charlie turned and saw flames licking at the doors he'd just come through.

"Oh shit. *Shit shit shit*."

"*Emily*, Charlie?"

"That you killed her!"

"And Puymirol?"

"Why aren't the doors opening?"

"Because as soon as you stepped into this tunnel, I changed the codes. You're stuck in here until I get some answers."

"Oh come on, Hugo, Puymirol's in the history books!"

"*What do they say?*"

"They say about you and Abigail, that's what they say. You can *guess*, Hugo. Please, I beg you, let us out of here!"

Charlie charged at Hugo, who winded him with a single, effortless punch. Charlie fell to his knees.

Hugo's fingers danced over the buttons and the doors opened.

"I *could* let you out of here, Charlie, but the problem is I'd be letting all those questions of yours – all those *secrets* – out, too. Goodbye, old friend."

Charlie clawed his way along the catwalk on hands and knees but the doors closed inches from his face.

***

CHAPTER FORTY-SEVEN

The evacuation of the mezzanine floor had been orderly to begin with.

Drunken guests, alerted by the sudden rise in temperature, had moved on to the gallery and made their way down to the grand hallway, which quickly became as crowded as it had been at midnight.

But then the numbers fleeing the lantern city, the cocktail bar, the sauna and pool and the seating areas on the gallery had grown so great that a bottleneck formed at the head of the stairs. Even then, the operation was undertaken with a sense of order – until the gilded ceiling above the grand hallway bowed, first in one spot, then another, and panic took hold, with people losing their footing and tumbling down the steps.

Gerald stepped over the fallen and used all his bulk to bully his way to the first floor, then to the ground-floor lobby and out to the street.

The crush in the hallway became serious as those fleeing the mezzanine were joined by those piling out of the ballroom and away from the gaming tables and other first-floor rooms. The chaos was aggravated by the abandoned chariots, thrones, shields, swords and tables piled with banquet food.

The largest of the bulges gave way, dropping a torrent of plaster that knocked half a dozen people to the floor. A broken water pipe poked through the hole and began drenching the hallway. The first tentacles of flames were visible then, dancing on the ceiling, spreading, joining with others.

Sophie had helped Mitzi down the staircase before the rush and handed her over to Isabelle, who promised to get her safely outside. Now Sophie spied Tozer and Co skulking away from the gaming room and falling in with the other evacuees.

The lift doors opened.

Venn and Jerry piled out, both laughing.

Then: Venn's mouth wide open, his mind denying what his eyes were seeing.

Belatedly, the alarm bells began ringing.

"What the fuck's happening?" demanded Venn.

"It's Charlie," said Sophie.

"I sent three blokes up to get him. What happened?"

"Hugo stopped them before they could do it."

"What do you mean *stopped them? I sent three of them.*"

A cacophany of sirens from the street.

"I don't know. It doesn't matter. But Charlie did *this.*"

Sophie didn't know why she was telling Venn this now: it was too late for him to stop it. Did some part of her want Charlie out the way?

Dazed, Venn wandered across the hall, directly below the flaming ceiling. Sophie looked up and saw what everyone else has seen: that the chandelier was dropping down on its chain, one jolt at a time. In the next heartstopping moment the entire fitting burst from its mount and Sophie launched herself at Venn, shoving them both to the floor.

The chandelier exploded on the floor right next to them, showering them in hot glass. Venn instantly got on to his knees and asked Sophie if she was all right. When she said yes, he helped her to her feet. She cried out as the boiling particles started burning through her dress to the skin. Venn quickly brushed them from her clothing, turning his hands bloody.

"Just get out," he said.

"Don't worry, I'm going. Come on."

"I'm going to The Gathering Place," he said. "*I've got to open the safe.* Everything's in there, all the screening pictures. *Everything.*"

"Don't be stupid, it's an inferno. Are you blind?"

"I've got to get to the safe. *Fuck!*"

The two of them were alone in the hallway. A flaming wooden joist fell, landed on a chariot and set it ablaze. Venn headed for the stairs in the elevator lobby then stopped when he saw large folds of black smoke banking down. He *had* to get to The Gathering Place and the only route left was via the mezzanine. Dodging falling timbers as the entire ceiling began to disintegrate, he tore across the hallway and up the glass spiral staircase.

On the way to the ground floor, Sophie passed a fire crew and gave them a stuttering account of what she knew: that it was arson on the top floor, and that the new owner was probably up there.

In the lobby, Danny made sure the last person was safely out the doors and then took Sophie's hand and led her into the cold of Arcadian Gardens.

***

CHAPTER FORTY-EIGHT

Hugo was right when he said the poisonous gases would kill Charlie before the fire did. The tunnel had only just started to fill up with them and already his lungs were in agony.

He squatted in the centre of the catwalk. It was the only position left to him: the walls were too hot to lean against and the temperature at the ceiling made standing equally impossible. But now his leather soles had become so scorching that he had to start hopping and squatting.

He wondered if his blood would boil while he was still alive.

The other lobby − the one he left ten minutes ago, confident that he was on his way to the Anderson − was howling with flames, a blast furnace.

All around him were the sounds of the club ceasing to exist: walls bowing, glass shattering, tiles, fittings, picture frames and furniture popping, banging. Those noises, terrifying as they were, gave him a shred of hope that the sides of tunnel would somehow spring apart and allow him to escape.

But when he saw the tunnel filling with black smoke he broke down, wide-eyed and beaten, and with each sob he sucked in hot oxygen. Within moments, visibility was down to zero and he crashed to his knees, body wracked with sobs. Images of Mitzi flicked through his mind, but he was too confused to really know who she was.

His heart gave out, finally affording him the relief of death. Charlie Dryden died with his palms stuck fast to the melting acrylic glass doors.

There was a new sound, a low rumble as the gases lingering near the ceiling reached their ignition point, that moment when every particle of smoke and oxygen turns to fire. A yellow flicker turned into a deep yellow glow, blossomed... and then the "rollover" struck: a huge orange fireball that plunged from the ceiling to the floor and popped open the door like a cork from a champagne bottle.

Windows blew out, sending showers of glass down into the street. The gases flooded the steel lobby and the process started all over again, except that the lobby was ten times as big as the tunnel, and the next time a rollover struck it would be ten times as powerful.

***

CHAPTER FORTY-NINE

Venn crossed the gallery, so wound up that he made no attempt to even look out for the torrents of falling plaster and rafters. He pushed on towards the spiral staircase, blind to the flaming balustrades and the pain in his feet as his soles stuck to the boiling floor polish.

So much of his empire resided in that safe, and nothing would stop him reaching it – and from killing Dryden, if he was still up there.

"Fuck!"

The staircase was melting and riven with cracks but there was enough of it remaining to reach The Gathering Place.

Taking care not to touch the handrail, he ventured up a few steps to see if it would hold his weight. When it did, he began a swift ascent, praying that he would make it all the way.

Without warning, the staircase broke from its mountings. Venn had just enough time to grab hold of the rail before the entire structure pivoted round on its remaining fixtures and crashed into the wall.

His fingers sank deep into the melting glass, inflicting a pain that shocked even Venn. Knowing he was about to fall, Venn looked down and saw that the bottom half of the staircase had become detached from the upper part and lay about thirty feet below him.

He could do nothing to save himself and dropped towards a huge, jagged shard of glass...

***

CHAPTER FIFTY

Arcadian Gardens was like a warzone.

The half dozen police on the scene were struggling to push back several hundred clubgoers and passers-by to establish a cordon.

But when the rollover struck, windows shattered, chunks of window frame and lengths of flaming curtains began raining down and the officers didn't have to issue any more orders: everyone bolted for side roads, Sophie among them. Three more fire engines droned into the street and stopped in the space vacated by the spectators.

Sophie edged back towards the cordon, trying to see if she could spot Hugo or Charlie at the top floor. But the writhing orange flames that licked from every window told her there could be no survivors up there.

"Will you *get back* behind the line!" a policeman yelled.

A reef-blue Jensen Interceptor roared out of the underground car park across the road, mounted the pavement and squealed to a halt in front of her. The driver threw open the passenger door.

"*Get in the car, Sophie*," said Hugo.

Two more ambulances sped into the street. A furious police officer was shouting for Hugo to drive on or face arrest.

"*Get in*," Hugo ordered Sophie. "It's not safe to be around here now. We have to go."

"What happened to Abigail Wilman?"

"What?"

"Charlie mentioned Abigail Wilman. What's she got to do with you?"

"I don't have time for this! Get in!"

The police officer bellowed abuse at Hugo. Sophie noticed someone else, too – watching from the pavement: *Gerald*.

"Why?" she said. "Because Charlie said too much tonight? Because I'm a loose cannon now I've heard about Puymirol and Emily? *Tell me about Abigail.*"

"Why do you care?"

Sophie knew her read on Hugo was spot on – he feared what she'd heard tonight and wanted to get her away from the police before the questioning began. Of course she'd go with him, but he didn't know that. This was the time to squeeze him.

"Because I know that Abigail came to see you," she said. "I know that you were the last person to see her alive. And I want to know what happened to Caroline Havelock."

She saw the inevitability of what she was going to say next. Saffron would be seeking revenge tomorrow anyway, blabbing to the Old Bill and every newspaper that would listen that the magazine journalist Sophie Miller was undercover at the Erato. Sophie's cover was blown. There was nothing to lose.

"MOVE THAT CAR NOW!" barked the copper.

"What the hell are you talking about?" Hugo shouted at Sophie.

"I've been investigating her disappearance," she said. "Investigating *you*. I'm an undercover journalist."

Hugo shook his head in disbelief. "I should have known. You never fitted. Look… Abigail came to see me, *years ago,* to pay back some money on behalf of the Havelocks. She was scared. I think the Havelocks were using her in some kind of sex game. I have a theory on what happened to Abigail. You'll have to come with me if you want to find out what it is. So will you just get in!"

Three police officers were striding towards the Jensen. They'd had enough. One of them said: "*Do not attempt to move, sir. Stay where you are.*"

Sophie cast one more look at Gerald. Even in the dark street, with the fire raging, he appeared to be smirking.

She got into the car.

One of the policemen tried to open Hugo's door and found it locked. The Jensen pulled away sharply, spinning him, ditching him on to the asphalt.

As they reached the end of the road, the final rollover struck, blowing The Gathering Place and the roof into the sky in an immense orange fireball. An awesome weight of Portland stone, brick, wood, slate and glass thundered down into the streets around the building. And then the screams started but when Summers floored the accelerator it was clear he wasn't thinking of going back to help.

It was several minutes before either of them spoke.

"What happened to Charlie?" she said.

"I don't know. You saw him after I did."

"That was him back there – his *explosion*. My God, I wonder if he got out..."

"And Venn?"

"He said he was going back upstairs to empty the safe."

"Bloody fool," muttered Summers. As the Jensen turned on to Park Lane, he said: "Come to New York with me. Until we can sort this mess out."

"Yes," she said. "Okay."

"Tell me where you live. We need to get your passport right away."

"Head for Portobello Road."

Sophie patted her tunic pockets for her cigarettes. They had long since been lost but her hand closed around a piece of paper.

Ana's note.

Fuck Ana. She'd been a bitch to Sophie all along. She just wanted to use Sophie because she sensed she had a heart, that she was someone who could help her to get her daughter back.

Sophie unfolded the note. "VENN SAYS SALVO WANTS SELL MY DAUGHTER. I MUST GIVE VENN £1,000. HE GIVE TO SALVO. SOPHIE HELP ME PLEASE."

Sophie didn't want to think about that now. Instead, she thought how she had a new addition to the list of people who had let her down, disillusioned her. The new one was Charlie, betraying his friend Hugo for a fistful of cash.

Before him had been David, of course; arranging his secret assignations with Saffron.

And before him had been her father, who in a roundabout way had got her into this whole thing.

Sophie peered at Summers. As flawed as any of them. Worse, probably. But also more than any of them: he was a survivor. Wasn't that what she was, too? Is that why he'd pursued her? She had detected something else in him, something which only now she could put into words – a desire to do the right thing. Not always, of course, but enough of the time.

She looked down and realised she had ripped up Ana's note.

"What was that?" said Summers.

"A note from a friend. Someone who wanted help."

"And you've torn it up? That doesn't sound very... Sixties."

Sophie wound down her window and let the shredded paper go. She watched in the wing mirror as the pieces fell over a band of revellers staggering into the road. They cheered and jumped up, swatting at what they thought was confetti.

Sophie found a wrap of cocaine in her handbag and dabbed what was left into her gums. She closed her eyes, and smiled.

"Fuck the Sixties," she said.

NEW YORK

CHAPTER FIFTY-ONE

Manhattan
January 1970

Tony Corsaro took a big bite of his cheese danish and thought again how he'd feel about killing a guy. Really *feel* as he stuck the knife in or pulled the trigger.

And then he thought about something else: whether he could *do it*.

In the next instant, he'd thrown away that thought because he *knew* he could do it. He'd pictured it so many times and never once had he pussied out. Yeah, not only could he do it, but it would definitely happen at some point.

His friends said he was crazy to be screwing around with legbreaking and protection when he could make a million dollars drawing portraits. You sat for Tony and bang, he'd get you down on paper in fifteen minutes. He could do you straight or funny, whatever you wanted.

Tony wasn't so sure about the million dollars. Beyond sketching faces from the neighbourhood or stiffing passers-by for a few dollars, he didn't know where it could lead. And chicks wouldn't go for an artist; not the kind of chicks he wanted to go with anyway.

He took a swig of chocolate milk, missed his mouth and felt a stream of it hit his 501s. *Fuck.* Now he was not only cold and bored, but covered in a brown streak as well.

He checked his watch – ten o'clock. He'd still be in bed with Teresa now – well, if he was still seeing Teresa. Tony indulged in a quick flash of her body... Yeah, still good. Had to be better than standing around on this little patch of Central Park West for the third morning in a row.

If the dame stuck to her routine – and she'd been very regular – she'd be stepping out of that castle across the road any moment now. What was it called again?

The Bentley Hotel.

"Luxury living", that's how they sold these things to the rich pricks. Well, there wasn't no luxury going on inside now: it was empty. The uniformed stiff on the door had confirmed as much when Tony had waltzed up to the entrance and asked some innocent questions.

The Bentley's closed for a re-fit, buddy, he'd been told.

Closed. That meant the dame lived there on her own, like some little princess with no-one to play with. And Tony knew *where* she lived. Last night he'd driven past and there was just one light burning in the whole place – up in one of those pointy turrets on the top floor, like a single-eyed demon. It had given him the shivers just thinking about her being alone in there. Yeah, they might be packed with luxury penthouses but all Tony got from those nineteen storeys of brick and sandstone was bad vibes.

You can shove your make-believe French chateau, I'm happy on the Lower East where I can walk out for a six-pack.

He stamped his feet hard on the icy sidewalk. You didn't need to be a genius to see it was going to snow.

This was the kind of low-grade job they'd give him if he joined the family business. Except Uncle Petie didn't want him to join the family business. Stay in college then start something legit of your own, he always said. Well, fuck that. If Tony's cousins had all gone into the family business, then why couldn't he? Petie would break eventually.

A Lincoln Limo nosed out of The Bentley's underground garage up to the entranceway.

Action time.

Tony balled the danish's wax wrapper and dropped it into a trash can like his mother had always told him. He slung his rucksack on to his back, climbed on his beloved sky-blue Honda P50 and pushed down through the pedal until she was humming.

He'd been in big shit on days one and two of this job for having lost the limo. On the first day, the lights were red and he couldn't jump them because there was a cop car up his ass, and yesterday he'd hit black ice and come off the bike, bruising his arm to hell.

Well, he couldn't screw up on day three as well or Tony wouldn't get paid. No, today he had to take some good photos of the broad and make a list of all the places she stopped. He had been reluctant to accept this job when he'd been approached in the pool hall, but he was broke right now and a job was a job.

Okay, here they came, the stoned princess – hidden behind her usual camouflage of mink coat, Jackie O sunglasses and headscarf – and on her arm her escort, the Jew undertaker, or whatever that wiry-haired character in the dark suit really was.

Tony had a hunch that beneath the disguise, she was a real piece of work. A stuck-up white bitch but a horny little number who needed it double bad because Hubbie was busy shining the boardroom table with his secretary's ass. Jackie O had the blues sitting around in the chateau, which is why the undertaker kept her zonked up to the eyeballs.

Yeah, that's what was going on. Definitely.

A liveried doorman held the back door of the limo open and the undertaker helped the mystery woman in, muttering stuff all the time.

The limo pulled out on to the road. Tony waited until it had turned on to the street, and then he pulled out, too. He knew what happened next: they'd head for 59th Street, where they'd stop at Bloomingdale's. The driver would act like his pants were on fire, jumping in and out of the car and peering into the store whenever she was gone longer than five minutes. That guy was under some pretty heavy orders not to let anyone get to her. Or to stop her getting to anyone.

After Bloomie's, the driver would drop her off on 5th Avenue for more clothes buying and her morning bagel. This is the point where Tony had come off the bike yesterday. But today, he was going all the way – wherever she went he'd be there with the Polaroid camera, and tonight he'd hand over the snaps, give his report, take the money and be done with this shitty job for good.

***

CHAPTER FIFTY-TWO

Tony Corsaro's mystery woman did her best to keep up with the bagel shop guy's comic routine but was pleased to scuttle back to the car.

She wasn't exactly up to witty repartee these days. Maybe when the treatment was finished she'd go in there and wow him with the old Boyd charm, but lately all she felt like doing was shopping and sleeping.

And so she bought stuff: dresses, winter coats, handbags, lingerie, LPs she played once and books she stared at without getting past chapter one. She shopped on auto-pilot, buying things that gave her no pleasure. It was all just a routine, and the routine offered some comfort. And so she shopped.

The daily excursion (closely minded by Rudy, the driver) was the one compromise Hugo had allowed her, to stop her from going mad in captivity. Or what he called "care".

Today, Sophie had bought two pairs of shoes and the Simon and Garfunkel album, *Bridge Over Troubled Water*, which had hit the shelves just that day. Her flirtation with Venn's rock music was over – it was time to return to who she really was.

Lastly, she grabbed her morning copy of the *New York Times* and got back in the limo, where she started to flick to the business pages. To her surprise, the story she was looking for had made the news section: "JOURNAL DEAL ON AS TYCOON IS CLEARED OVER BLAZE".

The story read: "Steel and press tycoon Hugo Summers' plans to buy the *New York Journal* Group were back on track today following news that he would not face criminal charges over the blaze that wrecked his private members' club.

"Through his lawyers, Summers said he was 'relieved this harrowing and unnecessary ordeal is over and I can return to my adopted home country with my family name untarnished'.

"There is now nothing to stop Summers finalising the small print on a deal that had looked dead in the water a month ago when London police issued a warrant for his arrest. At the time it was thought he had vanished after the fire to prevent any police investigation harming his imminent purchase of the *Journal* and its four sister titles, including the *Los Angeles Observer*.

"The 55-year-old issued a statement through his lawyers on 4 January claiming that he had left Mayfair's Erato Club before the blaze to fly to New York, where he had isolated himself in his apartment for rest due to physical exhaustion. He claimed not to have kept up with the news media and had been unaware of the fire but agreed to help with police inquiries. However, it was not until he was threatened with extradition two weeks ago that Summers finally returned to England for questioning by Scotland Yard.

"Great secrecy surrounded membership of the Erato Club, whose members included many powerful figures from the business world. The Erato and its top-floor offshoot – known as The Gathering Place – were completely destroyed in the fire, which police believe was started by their manager, Charles Dryden, a former film director, whose burnt remains were found in the building.

"Summers tried to buy the Journal Group five years ago but pulled out, citing the predicted slump in the advertising market. However, the straight purchase from his friend Doyle Raymer is now said to be a certainty, with Summers' line-up of backers remaining the same as on his last attempt. They are believed to be two other friends: Maurie Golds, the investment banker, and Bob Tomko, owner of Tomko Discount.

"Yesterday's statement by London's Metropolitan Police ended a sensational chain of events which began when Dryden drunkenly harangued Summers in front of new year revellers, moments after the tycoon had announced he was selling the club to businessman Edward Venn. Dryden is said to have been involved in a feud with Venn, who suffered an injury in the fire and was also questioned by police. He disappeared on 7 January and has not been seen since.

"Along with Dryden, magazine journalist Sophie Boyd, 34, is also thought to have died in the inferno, although one club member, Danny Flack, 29, claims to have guided her out to the street shortly before the club exploded. The forensic search for her remains has so far drawn a blank. Police are looking into the possibility that Boyd was writing an undercover exposé of the Erato and are questioning another journalist, Saffron Honey, in relation to this. In the tangled web that grows by the day, Honey is rumoured to be a close friend of Boyd's estranged husband."

Sophie closed the newspaper and curled up in a ball on the back seat. She just wanted to sleep. To be tired was better than to be addicted, Dr Lazar kept telling her, and although she trusted Hugo and Lazar she now wanted to know when the treatment would be over.

"Are you all right, miss?" asked the chauffeur.

"I'm fine, Rudy," she said. "Just tired. Take me home, okay?"

Cocooned under her chinchilla coat, she watched the first flurry of snowflakes rush up to the windows and sweep balletically over the roof. The car passed a huge billboard which read: "WAR IS OVER! If you want it. Happy Christmas from John and Yoko." It was good that someone still believed in it all. And then she thought of Moog outside his record shop, quoting *Easy Rider* that day: "*We blew it.*"

Three cars back, a sky-blue Little Honda kept its distance. Nothing was going to shake it this time.

CHAPTER FIFTY-THREE

A blizzard was falling by the time the car arrived back at The Bentley.

Dr Lazar was standing beneath the canopy, hands in pocket, making awkward conversation with Andy, the concierge. Apart from the workmen, Lazar, Hugo and Sophie were the only people the poor guy had had to speak to since the hotel shut for its re-fit eight months earlier and he was bored out of his skull. Sophie always tried to engage him in a little conversation, but that usually ended with Lazar hurrying her inside. She didn't like Lazar, but as Hugo's personal physician she trusted him. Kind of.

Sophie got out of the limo and paused to turn her face to the sky. She savoured the feeling of those cold flakes cutting through her barbiturate-induced numbness. It reminded her of childhoods on the beach at Clacton, when she and her brother had lain in the sun for as long as they could bear it before running into the sea. The delight of those two extremes came back to her now and she smiled at the memory of that beach, at the pleasure of being somewhere other than the strange, terrible world of fear that was her home now.

"Quite a blizzard," said Lazar, jerking her from the daydream.

She tried to read him but as usual found it impossible. That permanently downturned mouth would suggest displeasure had she not known that it was always part of his expression. And it was impossible to study his eyes as he wore tinted, prescription sunglasses whether he was indoors or out. Even in bright sunlight, they would have looked wrong on him... Too flash for a doctor; creepy, somehow.

Lazar's shiftiness was enhanced by the fact that at this point in the morning's routine, his eyes began darting all around, checking out who might be watching them. It was important that she wasn't seen, as he always reminded her.

"The snowflakes looked pretty against the windows," she said.

"Yes... Yes, I imagine they did. Let's get inside, shall we?"

Sophie offered her friend Andy an apologetic smile as he opened the doors to The Bentley.

The Bentley.

It still made Sophie smile to think that Hugo had named the place after his favourite car and that most guests never realised this.

Crossing the hotel's famous lobby, she held her breath − as always − because she felt the hotel was sleeping and didn't want to wake it. Not that it looked very famous at the moment, with nearly every surface covered in white sheets.

She hoped that one day she would get to see the lobby as it was meant to be, rather than this eerie shell in which motes of dust swirled endlessly in the winter light. Instead of the thud of chisels and the drone of generators, she longed to hear the gentle sounds of an afternoon quartet; instead of paint and varnish she wanted to smell the fine foods from The Bloomsbury Grill.

Sophie trailed her hand over the dust sheets covering the grand piano and fountain, and then stepped into an elevator, whose wire-glass mirrors and mica ceilings had been covered, too.

Sophie wanted to ask Lazar something, but couldn't quite come out with it. And so she remained silent as the cab creaked its way to the penthouse. Each floor was deserted − she never even spotted any workmen on them − and illuminated only by the low-power emergency lighting.

The lift stopped at the penthouse level and they stepped into a lobby filled with packing crates.

"What's all this?" said Lazar.

"It looks like some more of Hugo's stuff from England," said Sophie, examining a label. "Yes... These are the pictures he wants to go up in the board room. They've just dropped them off on the wrong floor."

The doctor nodded as he fished a bunch of keys from his pocket.

"Dr Lazar, I was wondering..." said Sophie. "When my treatment would be complete?"

He opened the apartment door's top lock, then grimaced as he took care of the dead bolt, which was always stiff.

"Is two locks really necessary?" she said.

"We've been over this."

"Who are we expecting? The Mansons? I feel like a prisoner."

"Yes, you've said that, too. Please don't be difficult. You know the situation, Sophie – everything is for your own protection."

"It's really quite..." she began, but couldn't find a word – the drugs he gave her had messed up her thinking.

Once they were in the apartment, Lazar locked them in.

Sophie threw her coat on to her bed and hurried through the Renaissance-themed lounge, passing the bedroom, on one side of the space, and the study and kitchen, on the other side. She poured a glass of Chateau d'Yquem in the kitchen and took it to her "turret", one of the eight pointed pinnacles ranged around the top storey. Hers was one of two on the side of the building that overlooked Central Park, which was already speckled with snow.

"Alcohol will just make you feel drowsier," said Lazar.

"Yeah, well, I wasn't planning on entering any spelling bees."

Lazar didn't even feign a smile to humour her. His was such a heavy presence that when he left each day, it was like a weight off her shoulders. But he never left until Hugo returned home around eight – she had to be watched at all times because she was considered a suicide risk. They never called it that, they called it "ensuring her safety".

And so she was stuck with Lazar, and he with her – his sole patient, it seemed. He fiddled about and watched TV in the study, or whatever the hell he did in that locked room, the only one she wasn't allowed in to.

Visibility was so poor on Central Park West that the traffic was down to a crawl. Sophie felt a muffled thrill of excitement; she wanted to get out there and play, just as the old Sophie would have. But the old Sophie didn't exist – she was dead.

Lazar was digging around in his medical bag.

"Don't tell me," she sighed. "More pills."

"But you're fresh out, right?"

"Yeah but I'm not a druggie, doc. I won't go back to coke. It was just something that happened at the club. A one-off, okay? Well, a one-off over six weeks. I want to be able to think again. I want the old *me* back."

"That's exactly what we're trying to achieve. But to find the old Sophie we must first cure the new Sophie. And the new Sophie is an addict. It's only been a month since you were using cocaine heavily every day. The treatment is working. It's cleansing your body and your mind of the narcotic. It's setting the counter to zero."

Lazar handed her the usual pill (an antidepressant) and a small bottle of "cleansing tonic" (just an over-

285

the-counter vitamin drink, she guessed). He was there in the morning to make sure she took them, then again when she returned from shopping and when he left each night.

She downed the tonic before popping the pill with a swig of wine. He shook his head disapprovingly, which gave her a little kick — it was reassuring to know that she hadn't become an entirely compliant prisoner.

The doctor then found another key and let himself into the study. Shortly after, she heard the sounds of the TV; some sports game.

Sophie crept to the bathroom and quietly threw up the pill. She'd done the same the night before, too. She changed out of her Missoni knit dress into jeans and a sweater. Each day she dressed up to go shopping, only to slip into comforting woolens upon her return.

She scooped up a blanket and padded back to the turret to sit in her Chesterfield armchair for a first listen to the new album. She wondered if Hugo would be home before it got dark. When it got dark, the workmen left and even though she never really saw them, it was comforting to know that they were around on the floors below or on cradles at the side of the building. She didn't like to be alone in The Bentley with just Lazar.

She was cold. It was always cold in here. Hugo had asked the maintenance guy to ensure there was full power and hot water on their floor, but the radiators never gave out more than a faint heat. Luckily, the turreted apartments had fireplaces and she got theirs going now with the last few logs. She'd have to ask Hugo for more. Here she was in one of the world's most opulent hotels and she was having to beg for firewood like a peasant.

For the thousandth time, she thought about how she had got here. New York City. About how she might have played things differently, had she been given a chance to think when Hugo had pulled up in his car on new year's eve.

Would she have gone with him, knowing what she did now?

She thought long and hard.

Yes, she would. That was where the story was going. There was no story without Hugo. She'd had no choice but to get in the car and do as he said.

But would she have allowed herself to be kept a virtual prisoner in one of his secret flats for three days while he schemed for her to fly from Biggin Hill to LaGuardia, with a false passport? Would she have obeyed his orders for her not to contact her family and let them know that she had survived the fire?

Again, she thought that she would. How could she live with herself knowing she had got so far in cracking the mystery of Hugo Summers and Abigail Wilman, only to give up when the going got tough? For the rest of her life she'd be a joke on Fleet Street and to herself.

And now... And now she had allowed herself to be cooped up in here for a month, playing the reluctant patient while she waited for some blinding revelation that would explain Hugo's history with Abigail.

But of course, Hugo was much too clever to reveal anything other than his official version. And so it had become a game of cat and mouse, with Hugo wearing her down with questions and drugs to find out what she knew, and Sophie biding her time, hoping that Hugo would make some slip as she made him tell and re-tell his line on Abigail.

She was sure that Lazar had administered sodium pentathol, the truth drug, to her on one occasion soon after her arrival at The Bentley. Thankfully she had given nothing away as he had given her too big a dose and she had passed out, but afterwards she had fought and kicked and screamed and threatened to escape if Hugo tried anything like that again (Hugo had vehemently denied any sodium pentathol had been used).

But she would have it out with Hugo tonight, she would really push him hard. And then she would decide once and for all what she *really* believed about his Abigail theory, and about why she was being held in this place, drugged out of her skull.

And if she didn't like whatever conclusion she drew, she would escape.

Snowflakes hurled themselves at the window, speckling the glass until the lights on the other side of the park were just a faint blur. Eventually it got dark and she drew the deep rose velvet drapes on the world. She found her pad and pen and stared down at the first page. *"Once upon a time there was a princess who lived all alone at the top of a beautiful snow palace..."* There were pages of it. Writer's block no more.

The next thing she knew, she was being woken in the dark by the sound of someone opening the front door's two locks. She tensed as he crept stealthily through the suite to the turret, without switching on any lights.

He stroked the back of her neck and leaned over to kiss her.

"Darling," he said.

***

CHAPTER FIFTY-FOUR

While Hugo changed out of his suit, Sophie heated up the shepherd's pie she had made the previous night and they sat down to eat with a bottle of Chambolle-Musigny. Sophie did a food shop several times a week and usually cooked in the evening. Sometimes they'd order a take-away and Andy the concierge would bring it up to the suite. Most evenings they played an ongoing game of five-card stud. They had started with $500 each of Hugo's cash and Sophie currently had about $800 of it.

Hugo related in detail the trip to London and how he had faced days and days of gruelling questioning about the club and the night of the blaze.

"How about Venn?" said Sophie. "Today's newspaper said he was still missing."

"Yes, everyone seems to think that he's been done in by his merry band of investors: Tozer and those other three who'd started hanging around the club. I hired a private detective to put his ear to the ground. Just out of curiosity, really – I have nothing to fear from Tozer, given that the club had legally left my hands by the time the fire broke out."

"It was a close call, though."

"Admittedly. But all the contracts had been finalised that afternoon. I was no longer the owner of the building."

"I hope Tozer sees it that way."

"It's true that he was screaming blue murder when Venn told him there wouldn't be any insurance pay-out. He only went in with Venn because he thought the Erato would be a nice little earner and a bit of prestige. Tozer blamed Venn for not having sacked Charlie a long time ago. He demanded Venn buy back his share of the club or stump up the repair bill all by himself."

"So why would he *kill* Venn, if it's his only chance of clawing back what he's lost?" said Sophie.

"Maybe he's found out that Venn just doesn't have it, or doesn't intend to pay."

"I didn't think Tozer had the clout to bump off Venn."

"You'd be surprised. A lot of Venn's soldiers were just old muckers of Tozer's that Venn had picked up. When push came to shove, their loyalties reverted to Tozer. Venn had grown too fast, hadn't really built a solid power base. He thought he was invincible but most of his operatives deserted him after the fire when they realised it was going to be war."

"And what about the screening pictures? Won't Venn be using those to blackmail people for some quick cash?"

"I'm pretty confident that Venn is fertilising the bluebells in Epping Forest. But in any case those pictures all went up in flames in Venn's suite. The heat was so intense that everything in the safe melted or turned to ash."

Sophie breathed a sigh of relief.

"You're safe now," said Hugo, placing a hand on hers.

He asked her what she'd been up to and she spelt out the tedium of her days and her aching desire to phone her mother to say that she was alive. When he sidestepped this with some vague comments, she decided it was time to strike.

"Tell me again why I'm being kept here, Hugo," she said.

Hugo slapped his cutlery down on his plate. "How many times must I answer the same question, Sophie?"

"I'm sorry. It's just…"

"*Just what?*"

"That I need to trust you. I'm a bloody prisoner in here and I want to know for how much longer."

290

"You're here for your safety, Sophie."

"*For my safety, for my safety*. I'm sick of hearing that. Safety from whom, Hugo?"

"We've been over this a hundred times since you came to New York. You're still at risk from *Gerald*. The screening pictures may have gone up in smoke but you can bet your life that Gerald has still got that film of the Japanese girl you told me about. He'll use it to squeeze every penny he can from you but he won't be able to as long as he thinks you're dead. He'll do anything for money – the man practically went bankrupt when he lost all his directorships. He'll also be thinking that you and I are involved and that he can use that film to settle the dispute *I* have with him."

"Which you won't tell me about."

"It was a misunderstanding over some property many years ago. I've told you that, too."

Sophie pushed some food around her plate while she thought about this. She was getting nowhere; it was time to really provoke Hugo. She took a deep breath.

Say it.

"I'd be happier if you'd just admit you've been keeping me here because you're scared of what I know," she said. "You're petrified I might go mouthing off to the cops about Abigail and de-rail the whole *Journal* deal."

Hugo stood up from the table and took his glass of wine to the turret. The window was a sheet of crystals.

"Yes, okay," he said. "That was my reason for bringing you here. There, I've admitted it. Happy?"

"I knew it. You've been keeping me hostage until the takeover is done and dusted. Because I'd be a liability if I was out there. But thank you. It's good to know the truth for once."

"I'm sorry. I really am, Sophie. But you have to understand what's at stake here. I plan to sell off most of my other interests in the next few years to focus on making a real go of the *Journal* Group. If the deal falls through again, everything I've planned for the next ten years of my life falls through, too. And anyway, it's not *all* about the takeover. Once I'd brought you here, I thought about Gerald and the lengths he would go to and I knew that you weren't safe out there in the real world. And there's an even more important reason that I wanted to keep you close, wasn't there? Your problem with the drugs? And we've nearly cured that."

"Have we, Hugo? Because I don't think I had a problem at all. Two weeks of pick-me-ups? That's really all it was. Okay, I got a little frazzled at the end but that's hardly surprising, considering what I'd been through – starting with Littlechild and David."

"Lazar knows what he's doing, Sophie. He has cured many people."

"Oh please, Hugo. He's just feeding me downers and some vitamin drink! There's no 'cleansing' going on, I'm just being kept strung out – on your orders, presumably."

"I've given him no such orders but very well. I'll talk to him tomorrow, see what he says. Okay?"

"Okay. Thank you. Now one last thing: tell me about Abigail again."

Hugo dropped his head. "Not again, Sophie. Please…"

"One last time, Hugo. I've gone along with everything you've asked me to do since you brought me here. I've put up with being double-locked in a cold suite for twenty-two hours a day. In return, you can tell me your story one more time."

Hugo returned to the table. "Fine," he said. "But can we finish dinner at the same time? I'm ravenous."

***

CHAPTER FIFTY-FIVE

"Abigail made an appointment to see me in late 1946," Hugo began. "She said that we shared a mutual acquaintance in Caroline Havelock and that it was a highly confidential matter."

"How did you know Caroline?"

"I met her and her husband Tom at a party before the war. He was an occasional stage actor, a stand-in, and she did some set designs. They ran some tinpot magazine – leftie nonsense but we got on well through our shared love of the theatre. When they told me they were on Queer Street I paid their mortgage for a year, plus the arrears. The arrangement was that they could pay me back as and when.

"And then, as I say, in '46 Abigail requested a meeting. She told me that Tom Havelock had killed himself and that Caroline had been blinded during the Blitz. The Havelocks had used her in some kind of sex games before the war and now Caroline was blackmailing her, threatening to ruin her if Abby didn't give her money and act as her assistant. She was scared that if she didn't carry out Caroline's demands, her life would be in danger."

"But Caroline was blind. What danger could she be?"

"Maybe there were others working the scam with her. Maybe there were others who had been involved in the *games*. I never found out. But Abby came to see me on two other occasions, asking me to protect her."

"And what happened to Caroline?" Sophie had got Hugo to tell this whole story at least half a dozen times, but it had become her obsession to see if he would one day contradict himself on some detail.

"Suicide. Found dead at the bottom of cliffs at St Dunstan's."

Sophie poured them both some more wine. "No. Too convenient."

"Convenient? Her husband had topped himself and *she* was blind. I imagine Caroline thought it was highly *in*convenient. And besides, this blackmail attempt of hers was clearly the act of a desperate woman. When she realised it wasn't going to work, and that she'd most likely wind up in jail, suicide probably seemed the only way out."

"Why did Abby come to you for help?"

"Because she knew I'd fallen out with the Havelocks over the loan and thought I might have some ideas on how to defeat Caroline."

"Why did you fall out over a small loan?"

"Because Tom was a fool with money. He came to me begging for a lifeline and then got very cavalier about paying it back, making jibes about capitalism and how I must get a kick out of rescuing a commie. It led to a big row and I instructed my solicitor not to let him off the hook. It was purely a matter of principle. Christ, Sophie, it was so long ago."

"And what happened to Abigail?"

"You tell me. My theory is that she threatened to expose Caroline, who had her bumped off."

"Surely that would have been a dangerous strategy for Caroline? She must have guessed that Abby would have confided in someone else about the blackmail."

"Yes, but Caroline was at the end of the road; she probably didn't much care what happened any more. And the day after Abby was killed, Caroline either threw herself off the cliffs in remorse or was pushed off by some accomplice. I've always imagined it was the former."

The wind moaned around the hotel's steeply pitched roof and there was a loud *schluuuumf* as a pile of dislodged snow dropped past the windows, startling Sophie. Hugo didn't flinch.

"And so *did* you help Abby?" said Sophie.

"I gave her what advice I could and sat her down with my best lawyer for an informal chat. But I didn't want to get involved with someone else's blackmail. When you're running a huge business you have to take great care over things like who you associate with."

"And why was she spying on you from the restaurants in St James's?"

"Ah, your friend Scottie's theory? Well, he was right: she *was* spying on me. When I told Abby I couldn't help her any more, she became persistent. Started stalking me. Anyway, the next thing I knew, MI6 were knocking at my door: Abby was missing and Caroline was dead…"

"Did you sleep with her?"

"No. I don't sleep with everyone, Sophie. And anyway, she came to me very disturbed, depressed. Our handful of meetings weren't exactly on a romantic footing."

"If MI6 came to you, how come your connection with Abby's disappearance was never made public?"

"Because my old paymasters MI5 made sure of it. Try to understand how damaging it would have been for them, Sophie. Even though I had nothing to do with Abby or the blackmail, the fact that she had come to me for help just before her disappearance would have mired them in scandal.

"The same went for MI6. Their decision to have hired Abby – a woman who'd subsequently been blackmailed over some mucky menage a trois – would have made them look very stupid indeed. The whole way that Abby had run her resistance networks would have been re-evaluated by the press and by historians. So MI6 decided not to make it public that this missing woman Abigail Wilman had been one of their agents. That didn't come out until that stupid book, *Avenging Angel*."

"In which you are conspicuously absent?"

"Yes. Thankfully, my link with Abby has never been uncovered. Until now."

Sophie broke eye contact and went to sit in her Chesterfield.

"Last thing," she said, lighting a Marlboro. "Tell me what Charlie was talking about in your suite. 'Puymirol' and 'history books?'"

She had never asked Hugo this before and was glad her back was turned to him.

"I swear I have no idea," said Hugo. "I wish I'd had more time to find out myself but Venn's boys were knocking on the door, I seem to recall."

Wind was howling around the turret like a banshee. The sound usually made her feel very isolated, but not tonight. Tonight she was communicating with Hugo properly for the first time since his depression had returned a week ago, practically turning him mute.

"Honest?" she said.

"I swear."

"And Scottie…?

"All I can say about your friend is that I know nothing about it. He sounded highly unstable. I'm afraid you may just have to come to terms with the idea that Venn had him killed."

Hugo's blurred reflection appeared in the glass. She hadn't heard him approach. He caressed her neck, let his fingers roam to her throat, stroked her chin, her face.

"I need to make contact with my family," said Sophie. "Just to let them know I'm alive."

"Soon," he said, twisting her hair around his fingers and pulling her closer. "But first, you have to come clean with me."

"What do you mean?"

"You know what I mean."

"I don't know anything more. I've told you everything I know about you and Abigail."

"You're holding things back. You're a journalist, Sophie, and a very good one. You wouldn't tell me everything. You still want to get to the bottom of the Abigail mystery and you think I hold the key."

Still pulling her hair, he was leaning right over her upturned face now. He put his lips down close to hers. She knew that with one snap he could break her neck but she trusted him. Or was it just that she *wanted* to trust him?

Hugo said: "All that hanging around with Gerald and Charlie, two men who knew quite a lot about me... They must have told you things. What were they?"

"Nothing you don't know. I don't have anything else up my sleeve, Hugo. Nothing that could wreck your precious deal."

"Oh, Sophie. You're wrong... I *care* about you... Care very much..."

They kissed and for the first time in weeks she felt the first stirrings of lust when Hugo began touching her. Now the drugs were fading in her bloodstream, her sex drive was returning, as was mental capacity. She now believed Hugo about Abigail. Maybe soon she would tell him that she had stopped taking the medication.

There were still things he was holding back from her, but she couldn't expect a man like Hugo to tell her everything about his life. Even so, she was desperately curious as to who his nocturnal visitors were, the men he let into the suite just as her bedtime drugs were putting her to sleep. Sophie hated these muttered conversations in the study, or hated the fact that she was locked into her bedroom and unable to creep on to the landing to eavesdrop.

Anyway, she was still holding on to a few secrets of her own: the photo that Gerald had pushed under the door; the fact that she knew about the mystery surrounding Gerald's naming of The Gathering Place; and how she had gone along to Brick Lane and thwarted the firebombing. Gerald was the only person Hugo was scared of, and right now those little secrets were the only bargaining tools she had.

Hugo lifted her up. Her foot caught on a wing, sending the chair thudding to the marble floor. Suddenly she wanted him. Even when she had been at her most suspicious of him and his motives for keeping her here, her feelings for him had still continued to grow each day. It wasn't just that they were two broken people, there was real…

She pushed the word from her mind. As he carried her to their bedroom, she began unbuttoning his shirt.

Hugo had secrets, dark secrets that could still make Sophie famous. But for the first time, she truly believed he hadn't killed Abigail, and that was all that mattered for now.

***

CHAPTER FIFTY-SIX

Tony Corsaro thought: *the timing is going to be a bitch.*

Did he make his move as she walked from the car to the bagel shop or when she was inside (where her driver wouldn't be able to see her) or when she was heading back to the limo?

He didn't know but he'd try out the advice his uncle had given him yesterday: make a decision and then make that decision work. Uncle Petie had repeated his usual stuff about how Tony should stay in college and then get his own business or else do something with his "artistic shit". But just before Tony had walked out of his uncle's restaurant, Petie's face had broken into a big smile. And that's when he'd said the stuff about making a decision.

Tony could read between the lines. His uncle was saying: okay, I've tried my best to get you on a straight life, but if you ask me again I'm not gonna turn you down if you want to get involved in the non-pizza side of the Corsaro Pizza Company.

So today, Tony felt better about life. Surer. But that didn't make this job with the mystery woman any easier. She was late for her morning bagel and copy of the *Times*. Maybe she was getting her legs waxed. Maybe she was getting her pussy waxed.

Tony snorted at his own joke. He was so bored with watching the bagel shop and pretending to read the same comic book that he'd laugh at anything. It was still colder than a witch's tit and he'd skidded badly on the drive here this morning. He'd given up tailing the limo from the hotel – the dame always came straight for her bagel, and so he'd come straight here today. Yesterday he got some clear photos and made a good list of her routine. He'd handed them over last night. Today was the last day of the job and it just involved more of the same. He couldn't wait for it to end.

Tony heard a swoosh and saw the limo pulling up to the opposite kerb. Time to jaywalk. He started crossing the road.

The driver came round, helped the porcelain princess out and watched as she entered the shop. Tony slowed down as he hit the sidewalk so as not to arouse the driver's suspicions. Inside the shop, he saw there were two men ahead of her in the queue. That was good news – he had a few seconds before she got served.

Tony sidled up and stood to her left.

"Sophie Boyd?" he said, quietly. "I've got a message for you."

"I'm sorry?"

He was expecting that. People always made like they hadn't heard something when they weren't expecting to be spoken to. He repeated what he'd said.

"You've got the wrong person," she said.

The two customers in front of Sophie turned round to see what was happening.

"You two got something I can help you with?" said Tony. They decided they didn't. "Yeah, yeah, we met at Sal's the other week," he said to Sophie. "That party, you know." He linked his arm through hers and steered her away from the counter to a vacant booth. Sophie looked around for help but none was coming. Tony sat next to her, trapping her in.

"I'm not who you think I am," she said.

"I don't think you're anyone," he said, quietly. "I'm just being paid to give you a message so quit feeding me lines, okay?"

She nodded.

"Ana sent me," he said. "Spanish Ana's here in the city and she says your life is in danger and she can help. She says there's stuff you need to know. Did you get all that?"

"What do I...?"

"You have to meet her tomorrow at the Pine Bank Bridge. Half ten in the morning. You'll need to get away from the driver 'cos he keeps you on a short leash, don't he? Can you do that?"

"Yes. Tell her I'll be there."

"The Pine Bank Bridge. Know where that is?"

"No."

"Central Park. Just east of the West Drive at 62nd Street. That's half ten tomorrow morning."

Sophie repeated the address twice then said: "Who are you?"

"Just a messenger for hire. Forget you saw me."

"How did you find me?"

"I've been following you for three days. Nearly broke my goddamn neck on some ice, too."

The two customers from the queue were talking to the manager and pointing to the booth.

"Broke your neck?"

"Yeah. Motorbike."

She had a crazy idea. "If you're just a messenger, can *I* hire you?" she said.

"For what?"

"I might need some help. Someone who can give me a lift, some transport... I don't know. I just need people on my side. I've got money."

"That'll do it."

"So will you help me?"

"Maybe. Why don't you take my number until you work out what the hell you're talking about?"

Sophie found a pen in her handbag and Tony scrawled down his first name and number on a scrap of the comic book. Without another word, he was out the doors.

"Are you okay, miss?"

The manager stood beside her. She muttered that yes, she was all right, thank you, and then she left, too.

CHAPTER FIFTY-SEVEN

Sophie was still shaking as Lazar helped her out of the car.

Ten thirty tomorrow, Pine Bank Bridge. Just east of the West Drive at 62nd.

She was already panicking over how she could talk Rudy into making a detour and then give him the slip to meet Ana.

Ana.

The thought of seeing her had stirred up mixed emotions. Ana would be seeking what she was always seeking: help. Now that Venn had gone to ground, Ana probably saw Sophie as the only person who could help her to rescue her daughter. How did she know that Sophie was alive? Ana had the power to wreck Sophie's plan of staying holed up at The Bentley until she had found out everything she could about Hugo. The problem with that goal was that over the last week, Hugo had all but stopped communicating – his depression had returned with a vengeance, and none of Lazar's pills was helping. Even when he lay in bed, curled up in a ball, Hugo would tell her only that Gerald would be coming to find him soon about the debt, and that he was worried it could blow the *Journal* deal out of the water.

Lazar and Sophie took the elevator to the penthouse floor. As he unlocked the door to the suite, Lazar said: "Hugo asked me this morning how long your treatment would last. He said you were anxious. I told him the end of next week."

"That's great news," she said, but she knew that one way or the other, everything would be over by the end of next week – she would either have escaped or be dead.

Lazar discovered the deadbolt was unlocked.

"Hugo must be home," he said.

Sophie found him reading through some papers at the dining table.

"Don't tell me the negotiations are over," she said. "Is it signed?"

"Not quite," said Hugo. "But I have something more important to attend to. Would you care to follow me to the top floor? I'd like your opinion."

"I thought this *was* the top floor."

"Ah, then you've obviously never been to the board room."

***

CHAPTER FIFTY-EIGHT

Dust swirled in the light slanting in through the board room windows.

Despite an elaborate skylight, the room's dark panelling and ornate vaulting made it seem more like a haunted house than a place to do business, thought Sophie.

"This is the only room in the hotel that's not covered in white sheets," she said. "Isn't it getting a lick of paint, too?"

"Yes, it will do. But I removed them so we can complete the negotiations up here."

"The takeover? The newspapers said they were being held at the Plaza."

"They were, but the press interest in me has been so intense because of everything to do with the fire. We can't go for a leak at the Plaza without someone shoving a microphone in our faces. Doyle Raymer and I have agreed to come here for the final talks as from tomorrow. The press won't suspect we're at The Bentley. It's closed. But that's not why I asked you up here."

He gestured to a huge mahogany table, on which lay a dozen or so rectangles. Sophie stepped closer and found herself looking at oversized cromalin prints of a glossy magazine cover and some inside spreads. The magazine was called *Sensual* and featured a radical design – brightly coloured backgrounds, skilful montages for the "celebrity spot" pages and an elegant sans font that Sophie had not seen before. The coverlines: "Women who beat their husbands", "I met my hubbie at an orgy", "Make every time like the first time".

"What's this?" she said. "Part of your masterplan?"

"Yes. We've got very big plans for *Sensual*."

"So what's it got that *Cosmo* hasn't?"

"Bigger writers, bigger news, an edgier sexual content, at least sixty extra pages and associated lines in everything from fashion – that's clothing shops on both coasts – to business and social networking events. Plus a lot of *very* interesting noises from high-end advertisers, and some big campaigns, kicking off with equal pay and sex discrimination."

"Winnable campaigns, or just token noises?"

"Winnable and very high-profile. We've already got a massive story on Westerley's car plant on sexual harassment, and someone undercover at Applegreen Foods who's dying to spill the beans on how the board is holding back female employees. Rebecca Shepherd's going to be our news editor."

"Wow. You got the best. But wait a minute – news editor? Is this a women's mag or a newspaper?"

"The best of both."

"I'm not sure that's going to appeal to a mass readership."

"Our market research says otherwise. As you should know by now, I don't do anything by guesswork."

A phone at the far end of the table was ringing.

"Sit down," he said. "We've spent months doing dummies. I'm very interested to hear what you think."

"Me, too. When's the launch planned?"

"March."

"Don't you think you should sign the takeover before you start planning the empire?"

"It's as good as done."

The phone was still ringing but Sophie had too many questions. "Who have you got lined up as editor?"

"Possibly Janine Hamilton, but keep it under your hat."

"Wow." Hamilton was journalism royalty, a tough-as-hell, motormouthed New Yorker who'd been a war correspondent before making the leftfield move to edit

Vogue. She'd quit a few years back to write a couple of trashy, mega-selling novels.

"And the deputy?"

"I was thinking that you might fit the bill," said Hugo, answering the phone. "Summers."

She leant over the table and pretended to study one of the spreads, but really she was feeling dizzy.

Deputy editor.

She placed her hands on the table for support. She wasn't thinking of the future but the *past*: the failed magazine launch, the injustice of her career being blown off course and the way she had resigned herself to never coming that close again.

Deputy editor of what would be one of the biggest magazines in the world. Everything she had ever dreamt of (more or less).

A second chance.

When she began to regain her senses, Sophie was aware that Hugo was losing his patience on the phone.

"I'm sick to the back teeth of all this *harassment*," he was saying. "I was informed by Scotland Yard that I would not be facing any charges. You can direct any more questions to my lawyer, who will be very interested to hear of..." Hugo looked at Sophie and shook his head despairingly. Then his expression changed from anger to bemusement. "I see... I see... In that case... In that case, come over at three. Yes, she's with me here now. I'm staying at my hotel, The Bentley. You know it? Good. The concierge will tell you where to find me."

Hugo hung up. "So, any thoughts?"

"Are you serious?"

"Yes. It wasn't just Venn that I asked my private detective in London to investigate. It was you, too. You've had an impressive career and it's a pity you got shortchanged by those shysters when that magazine didn't launch. Prove yourself and I don't need to tell you that it could lead to the top job or another editorship in the group."

"How would it work?" she said, laughing. "I'm dead!"

"My plan was to stick you in this rehab place I know and say you'd been there since the night of the fire. But it looks like that's out the window. That was Scotland Yard on the phone. They're coming over this afternoon. They know you're alive."

***

CHAPTER FIFTY-NINE

Half an hour before Scotland Yard were due, Hugo's head American lawyer burst into the suite, a whirlwind of energy.

"We'll sue them for everything they got," screeched Joe Ciaffone, sticking out a hand and introducing himself to Sophie. She sat back in her armchair, entranced as the tiny man paced the room, speaking in big statements. "You don't wanna speak to these cops, Sophie? Then don't speak to them – *ever!*" and: "This is the most disgusting case of persecution since Herod heard about that baby!"

The news that Scotland Yard were coming over had put Hugo into one of his blackest moods; Sophie recognised the faraway look in his eyes. He sat quietly at the dining table, making notes, which he would occasionally pass to Ciaffone, who would either agree vehemently or attack them with a ballpoint.

Following one particularly heated outburst from his lawyer, Hugo looked at Sophie and offered an apologetic smile.

"Joe and I met when I needed some urgent legal advice back in '49," he said. "I'd come into father's fortune and thought I'd make my mark by expanding into America. Some tenement blocks came on the market and–."

"And they were a terrific idea for his bank balance but a terrible idea for his longevity," said Ciaffone.

"What he means is, another party had eyes on the same buildings," said Hugo.

"AKA *the mafia*. It's a good job you've had me around these last twenty years, Hugo."

"So what happened?" said Sophie.

"Well, I'd already *bought* the tenements when these chaps took an interest," said Hugo. "Of course, I refused to sell, not knowing who they were. Luckily Joe here negotiated for me to stay alive."

The internal phone was ringing. Hugo answered it and exchanged a few words with the concierge.

"They're here," he said.

"Now remember, Sophie – don't say a word, okay?" said Ciaffone.

Hugo went outside to the lobby and shortly ushered in three men: a louche man in his fifties, Detective Stevenson from Special Branch; a younger, boyish-looking man in his forties from MI6 called Phelps and a hangdog-expressioned lieutenant from NYPD, Detective O'Hanrahan, who had a jaded air about him. It was easy to imagine that if someone had offered him ten dollars as a pension, he'd have retired on the spot.

Stevenson had a suave and aloof air, similar to Hugo's, and by his manner obviously considered himself the most important of the three, although who had seniority over whom was not spelt out. He and Phelps perched on the recamier while O'Hanrahan eased his bulk into an armchair. They all faced Hugo, who stood in the turret, arms folded.

"I'm just here to keep an eye on things," O'Hanrahan announced to the room. "American jurisdiction, you know? As far as we're concerned, no crime has been committed on our soil."

Sophie took coats from the men and hung them up, then made fresh coffee. There was an awkward silence as she passed the tray around. Ciaffone drummed his fingers on his Dictaphone manically, spoiling for a fight. Finally he placed it on the edge of the dining table and pressed record.

"Okay, let's get down to it," said Stevenson. "So we now know that Miss Boyd is alive and that you, Mr Summers, were lying when you told us in London you didn't know where she was. We've been to Biggin Hill and LaGuardia, we've spoken to your flight crew and a lot of other people and we know that you smuggled her out of the country. You've perverted the course of justice."

Hugo just kept looking out of the window. It was snowing again. "Go on," he said.

"We could charge you right now. Not so good for that deal of yours, which I'm guessing all this deception was designed to protect?"

"How did you know she was here?" said Hugo.

"Gerald Masters tipped us off. He saw Miss Boyd getting into your car on the night of the fire. He's desperate for money, as you no doubt know. He went to see some of his old fascist bully boys to see if they would come and find you."

"And extort you," added Phelps.

"By 'old fascist bully boys', do you mean Venn?" said Hugo.

"No. We believe Eddie Venn is dead. George Tozer turned on him when he found out there wasn't going to be any insurance payout for the fire. He blamed Venn for allowing Charles Dryden to work at the club. Anyway, these other thugs came to us. They were on bail over some nastiness and wanted to cut a deal. For the last month they've been recording all their conversations with Masters and passing them on to us."

"What does Masters have on you, Mr Summers?" said Phelps.

"That's a bullshit question," said Ciaffone, pointing a figure at the MI6 man.

Phelps smiled benignly, stood up and switched the Dictaphone off.

"Perhaps it is, Mr Ciaffone. So why don't we all cut the bullshit and just have a non-bullshit conversation? Or perhaps you'd prefer me to take Mr Summers down to the station for a more formal Q&A? But if I did, he wouldn't set foot outside of a cell for the next eight to ten years. This is lovely coffee, Miss Boyd – so much better than the instant stuff we drink back home, isn't it?"

"Okay, boys, what's the deal?" said Hugo.

"We have no desire to upset your takeover," said Stevenson. "That's nothing to do with us. We want Masters. We know you have some kind of feud with him and we're hoping we can use that to finger him."

"We want everything you know about him," said Phelps. His hair was damp with melted snow and he carefully smoothed it back with his fingers. "He's been growing a very significant fascist organisation with the purpose of striking against immigrants."

"What you might not know is that Masters was behind the murder of a Bangladeshi man about a month ago, an Amir Chowdry. Venn and Tozer did it for him."

"Well, Venn is dead," said Hugo. "You'll have to nab Tozer."

"We will, if we can link him to it. But Masters is our priority. We want all the dirt; we want you giving testimony."

"Hypothetically speaking, if Mr Summers did help you, what's your end of the deal?" said Ciaffone.

"Hypothetically, we won't bring any prosecutions against him," said Stevenson. "Plus we'd help to resurrect Miss Boyd here from the dead."

"Meaning?"

"We'd let you come up with whatever story you wanted – that she'd run off after the fire, or whatever. And we wouldn't contradict it."

Bored and redundant, O'Hanrahan fingered some fleck of food from his collar, then looked up to admire the ceiling.

Hugo sighed. "What would I have to do?"

"Work with us," said Phelps. "The same goes for you, Miss Boyd."

"Me? I don't know anything about Masters."

"But you associated with him at the Erato?"

"I *saw* him on two or three occasions there, nothing more. I found him repellent." She felt sick as she recalled the night she had thwarted the first firebombing attempt. She had never told Hugo about it, even when he'd pressured her to reveal everything she knew about Masters. But now these guys were saying the only way to keep Hugo out of prison *was* to reveal everything...

As if reading her thoughts, Stevenson said: "And we do mean everything, Miss Boyd. If this reaches court and Masters' lawyers come up with some piece of information that we don't know about, they will be very clever indeed at using it against us. Especially if they can show that our witnesses withheld secrets from their own defence team. Do you understand?"

"She understands," said Hugo.

"And I'm sure you understand, too, Mr Summers," said Phelps. "You understand that your stint in charge of the *New York Journal* might be the shortest in history if you're charged with kidnapping a-."

"Yo, yo, that's blackmail!" shouted Ciaffone, springing to his feet.

"For God's sake, sit down, Joe," said Hugo. "They're right. The deal would be over as soon it had been done. I'd be ruined."

O'Hanrahan caught Sophie's anxious expression and raised an eyebrow at her. He spotted a copy of the *New York Times* under the recamier and slid it out to peer down at the sports.

Stevenson said: "Play it our way and you get to look a hero, putting Masters behind bars. Unless, of course, there's stuff you've done that you don't want going to court."

"Are you a fascist, too, Summers?" said O'Hanrahan, his eyes still on the sports.

"Certainly not," said Hugo. "I used to be on good terms with Masters, many years ago, until we had a falling out over some money. He wasn't such an extremist when were friends; that came later. I'd be happy to see him locked up."

"And how about you, Miss Boyd?" said Phelps. "Is there anything in your association with Masters that could compromise our prosecution?"

Sophie remembered that Ciaffone had said she didn't have to speak. But maybe it was time to tell, before things went any further. And she'd feel safer admitting to it now, those little things about Gerald that she'd been keeping from Hugo.

It was at times like this that she wished she were a more devious person because she couldn't help looking guiltily at Hugo.

"Well?" he said. "Is there, Sophie?"

No. Wait and tell Hugo about it later. It won't be too late. Hold on.

"Because we must know now," said Phelps. "For your sake and for Hugo's."

Tell them now. Tell them about that photo. Tell them it's in the decorations box in your bedroom at Notting Hill. If the London police haven't already found it, these guys can go and get it. Tell them about the night at Brick Lane.

She opened her mouth and what she heard was: "No. I know nothing more about Masters."

Nobody spoke. She knew this was one of their tactics – hoping she'd feel uncomfortable in the silence and say something.

Finally, Stevenson slapped his hands down on his thighs, making her flinch. "Right. In that case let's set up the first proper interview session. I suggest tomorrow. We'll just need *you* at first, Mr Summers."

"Yes, all right. Speak to Ciaffone about the details."

"You're doing the right thing," said O'Hanrahan, as the three guests stood to leave. Sophie didn't know if he was addressing her or Hugo or both of them. "But what the hell do I know? I've had an ulcer for fifteen years."

CHAPTER SIXTY

Sophie slept for only a couple of hours that night.

Once again, there had been the midnight visitors. She couldn't tell how many. Hugo had let them into the suite and they'd all crept along the study to begin their murmured conversations.

This time, she had been able to listen in for longer than usual because she felt no overpowering sleepiness – she'd thrown up the bedtime pill again. It had been two days since she'd taken medication. She felt shaky – the mood swings were intense – but she had no choice but to ride it out.

But however hard she strained, she could make out none of what they said. After a full hour of trying, she got into bed but was still awake when Hugo came in shortly after.

They lay there, not moving, listening to the shrill wind. The TV news had said the snow was going to thaw later today.

Today. Today was going to be tricky.

Had she done the right thing by holding back those snippets from the police? It tortured her... Why had she done it?

Instinct.

Scottie had always told her about instinct. When you had gathered as many facts as you could, you had to use instinct. And he had said her instincts were good.

But still, she didn't know why she had lied. If this case against Gerald came to court, could it backfire? Maybe she should confess to Hugo, get him to take her to Phelps and Stevenson and lay everything bare...

No. She had to be strong, like Abby.

Abby. She was the key. That's what this was all about. What would she have done?

Sophie drifted off to sleep at about 6am. When she awoke, Hugo was gone and Lazar was standing at the

315

foot of her bed. She took the morning pill and "tonic" and ordered him out. He waited in the lounge while she slipped a snakeskin-lined fur coat over a Cossack-style silk shirt and flared jeans.

Duping Rudy was easy.

He had been instructed not to let her go into crowded places, which meant no shopping. These were Mr Summers' orders, he said. Sophie's blood pressure soared at this, but of course Hugo had left for the day and she had no way of disputing it.

All his rhetoric about trust. He was making sure she couldn't do any harm so close to the deal. *The deal...* The paper had said it was imminent. It was probably being done today.

Now, in the limo, Sophie acted as if she was about to blow up in a big way, and began haranguing Rudy, finally getting him to agree that she could buy her morning bagel. He could watch the entrance of the bagel shop easily.

When she had done this, she got back in the car and said: "Hey Rudy, I'm sorry I shouted at you. How about a visit to the park?"

Rudy mulled this over before replying: "I guess we could do the park. But I gotta come with you. Whereabouts?"

She told him to park on 5th Avenue.

***

CHAPTER SIXTY-ONE

Sophie had memorised the layout of Central Park from one of Hugo's guide books and took the lead, heading for Bethesda Terrace, where she knew there were toilets. If she could get into the ladies, she could maybe slip away from Rudy long enough to meet Ana.

First she decided to work up a bit of theatre, staring at the banks of snow and frozen lake like she was still whacked out on the pills. It wasn't a very difficult acting job – going cold turkey again had made her weak these past few days. It seemed to work – Rudy's body language suggested he wasn't in the least worried about her bolting.

"So pretty," she said, her eyes on some vague point in the distance.

That'll do, Boyd. You're not gunning for an Oscar.

They carried on walking, awkwardly, like two teens on a first date, Rudy whistling, hands in pocket, and her staring everywhere but at him. She was almost enjoying the acting job.

There they were. The toilets.

She tried not to quicken her pace or look at her watch.

"Rudy, I've got to use the ladies."

"Okay, but no climbing out the window, okay?"

"Deal."

And then she had some luck. Because just as she was walking up the path to the block, Rudy turned his back against the breeze to light a cigarette, and in that moment she veered across a snowy verge and ducked behind the building.

She waited a few seconds. He wasn't coming for her. She raced away.

***

CHAPTER SIXTY-TWO

She arrived at the elegant Pine Bank Bridge with five minutes to spare, so wracked with nerves that her arms shook as they gripped the ornate handrail. Looking out over the bridle path, she despaired at the circumstances that had brought her to this fabulous city she'd always dreamt of visiting.

The good news was that there was no sign of Rudy. The chances of him stumbling across her were slim, unless he roped in some policeman to search for her, which seemed unlikely.

The sound of children playing in the Heckscher Playground floated across to her. She and David had been planning children but she hadn't even thought about children since he'd left.

She looked at the buildings surrounding the park and thought: *I could just run now. Run to the British Embassy. And then spend the rest of my life looking over my shoulder for Hugo and Gerald and Tozer. Always worried that Masters would turn up on my doorstep with that film of the Echo night, demanding that-.*

"Hello, sweetheart," said a rasping voice right by her ear, a voice with the power to bring back all the horrors and pleasures of 1 Arcadian Gardens.

As Sophie started to move, the monster grabbed her around the waist from behind and pulled her close to him.

"Walking in a winter wonderland," he sung, dancing her around in the snow. "Did you miss me?"

Sophie was transfixed by the melted skin down the left side of his face, at the ruined, half-closed eye, at the huge area of red raw scalp.

"Didn't your parents teach you it's rude to stare?" said Venn. "I know it ain't pretty. I guess we'll never get intimate now, will we?"

She opened her mouth but nothing came out.

318

"Ana couldn't make it," mocked Venn. "Now, I'm going to let you go. With these busted hands of mine, I can't hold on to you. And with these busted legs, I couldn't catch up with you." He opened his overcoat to reveal a bulging shoulder holster. "But these bullets could."

Venn released her and Sophie half collapsed against the latticework. The small exertion had exhausted Venn, who stood wheezing, bandaged hands on hips.

"You're looking a bit pale yourself," he said. "It must be like seeing a ghost. Did you think I was dead? You and the rest of the world. Lucky I've got a few mates left who could get me over here or I'd never have got the chance to say hello."

"Who's been patching you up?"

"The NHS for the first few days. Until I had to discharge myself when Mr Tozer's demands became a bit urgent. I've been relying on some bent quack to bandage me up."

"So what happened to you after I left you in the hallway?" she said.

"That designer of mine didn't build the spiral staircase to withstand the towering bloody inferno, that's what happened. I was halfway up when they collapsed. Landed on a broken step." He opened the coat all the way this time to reveal a blood-soaked shirt. "Two hundred stitches and still it won't stop bleeding. Three blood transfusions. Lucky for me the place was swarming with firemen and ambulance blokes by then. They pulled me out. And lucky for me that Gerald saw you driving off with Hugo, too. Pretending to be dead? Crafty."

"Makes two of us."

Venn gave a chuckle that sent him into a coughing fit. He dabbed his mouth with a handkerchief, which was mottled red. "The smoke scorched my lungs, closed 'em all up.

319

"So what do you want?" Sophie said. "Let me guess: money."

"Us criminal types are so predictable, aren't we? Tozer's got it in for me. He went psychopathic when he found out there weren't going to be no insurance money for the club he'd just bought. He held me responsible, said I should have sacked Dryden, which is funny because that's the very same grievance I've got against Hugo. Tozer wanted me to settle the bill. When I told him to fuck off, he declared war. And right now, it's a war I'm losing." He stepped in close to Sophie. "And he's not the only one I've got a grievance against, Miss Bigshot Journalist. I wasn't too happy myself when I read that you'd been doing an undercover job on my club. If I don't pay off Tozer and his mates, I'm as dead as Charlie Dryden, and that is very fucking dead. So you're going to help me get out of this hole."

"What do you want me to do about it?"

"Get me into that castle of yours on the other side of the park. I can talk Hugo into settling up." He tapped the gun beneath the coat. "Then I can get square with Tozer."

"Why not just kill him?"

"He's too strong. His boys would rub me out, guaranteed. But trust me, somewhere down the line, killing Tozer is *very much* the idea. You catch on, Sophie. Pity you never wanted to be on the team."

"Wait a minute. It was legally your and Tozer's club by the time the fire broke out. Hugo doesn't owe you a penny."

"I'm sure that's how a jolly hockey sticks girl like you sees it but I don't. And seeing how it was Hugo what kept Charlie on at the club, it's Hugo what can pick up the bill."

"He won't pay."

"Just a few mill; spare change for Hugo, but worth it to save his old mate Eddie Venn, eh? Anyway, I thought you'd want to get your own back. Why's he keeping you in that place? Don't tell me it's because he loves you and wants to protect you from the cruel world. That's the kind of bullshit Hugo comes out with, just before he lets some poor girl go. He knows you've got stuff on him, doesn't he? And he's got you under lock and key until he can find out what it is. Pretty clever move: I wouldn't want some hysterical journalist running around loose, just before I bought the biggest newspaper in the country."

Sophie dug into her handbag and found her cigarettes. Venn held out his hand for one. "Go fuck yourself," she said. When she had lit up, she said: "Okay, you're probably right about Hugo. How did you know I was here?"

"When Gerald saw you roaring off with Hugo, I knew you'd be wherever Hugo was going next, and everybody knew that was the Big Apple. I've had you tailed."

Tony, the messenger boy. Not working for Ana but for Venn. Of course.

"I got that kid to tell you Ana wanted to meet you," said Venn, grinning at his own cleverness. "I had my doubts about him but he must have done a good acting job because you're here."

"You still haven't given me a good reason why I should get you into The Bentley," she said.

"Well, why don't we start with your screening pictures – and work our way up to Gerald's home movie of you and Echo?"

"Everything in your safe was burnt in the fire. Even I know that, Venn. You'll have to try harder."

Venn lit his own cigarette and smoked it with the tiniest of drags. He stamped his feet in the snow and couldn't stop himself beaming.

"Okay," he said. "Your screening pictures are gone. But the film… the film was never *in* the safe. Gerald kept his sweaty little hands on that. And what a film it is: you and Echo, kissing on the sofa… Then suddenly, whoops, Echo's having a fit. Oh no, someone's given her an OD…"

"But it can't show me giving her the injection because I didn't do it."

"Let's just say Gerald's shaky camerawork makes things… ambiguous. Ambiguous enough to ruin the rest of your sweet life. Your friends and family'll never *really* know what happened, and the phone ain't going to be ringing from them posh mags you work for. You'll be stacking shelves in the Co-op."

"So what's the deal?"

"I can tell you stuff about Hugo. Stuff Gerald has fed me. Stuff you need to know for whatever story you're writing."

"Go on."

"Gerald's been searching for some old geezer, someone Hugo don't want to see. And now Gerald's found him."

It had to be the old man in the photo. And the man Gerald was threatening Hugo about on new year's eve: *I've found him now. You leave me no choice but to bring him into play.*

"So who is he?" she said.

"I tell you that once you've got me into the suite. That's the deal."

"What do I get – a name?"

"A name, and what it's all about. The whole thing. And it's juicy. Boy, is it fucking juicy…"

"Juicy enough for me to risk everything?"

"Well, how's about this for a taster? Does the name Abigail Wilman mean anything to you?"

Sophie shut her eyes for a few moments. "Maybe."

"Yeah, I had a feeling as soon as Gerald told me about this that it must have been your angle. I bet Abigail's the reason you came to the Erato in the first place, right? Hoping to meet Hugo, solve the mystery, get famous…?"

In the playground, some children were singing a nursery rhyme.

"How do I know you won't shoot Hugo if I get you in there?" said Sophie.

"I would have thought that would have been a blessing for you."

"What do you mean?"

Venn removed a square of newspaper from his pocket and handed it to her. "You journalists want to keep up with the news more."

At that moment, she spotted Rudy in the distance. It was obvious that he'd been pushing his bulk as fast as it would go because steam was billowing from his mouth.

"That's my driver," she said. "He's seen us."

"Open it."

Sophie unfolded the square and saw that it was from the business pages of that day's *Times*. In her excitement between the bagel shop and the park, she hadn't bought a copy. The down-page lead story was about the *Journal* deal.

"It says Hugo's deal is being done *tonight*," said Venn. Rudy was closing in on the bridge, panting like some rabid dog. "He's been keeping you prisoner so you can't balls up the deal. But once that ink's dry, you're expendable, darling. That's why you've got to get me into that castle of yours right now. *I'll* get my money and *you'll* get the last piece of the jigsaw."

"And then what do I do?"

"You come with me. We'll work something out. You're a goner if you stay in that place."

323

She looked at Rudy; listened to the nursery rhyme; felt the weight of the buildings around the park; saw Abigail's face...

"Okay," she said. "Let's do it. When I get back to the hotel, Lazar will phone Hugo to tell him about me running off in the park. He'll come home; he always has when I've played up."

"What if he doesn't? He's got his hands full with the takeover."

"Then I'll pull something big so he *has* to. Bring a box or a crate and the concierge will let you in. People are always making deliveries for Hugo. We're on the nineteenth."

"And when I get up there?"

"Lazar will let you in. Say it needs a signature. He'll have me locked up in my room by then."

"All right," said Venn. "I've got a car. I'll follow you. Once you get to The Bentley, I'll give you ten minutes, then I'm coming in. Best of British."

And Venn turned his back and limped away, moments before Rudy arrived on the bridge. With one hand he pointed an accusatory finger at Sophie and with the other he clutched his chest.

"Oh my God," he said. "Oh my God. Where did... where did you get to?"

"I got bored, Rudy, so I went for a stroll, okay?"

"No, not... not okay at all. You know I'm gonna have to tell Lazar about this."

"Yes," she said, pulling the fur collar around her neck as a chill breeze blew up. Venn had vanished. "You do whatever you've got to do."

***

CHAPTER SIXTY-THREE

Things moved quickly after that.

Rudy sped her back to The Bentley, muttering all the way, his face streaming with sweat. Sophie felt guilty for having tricked him but one day he'd know the truth about Hugo Summers and the mystery woman.

Throughout the journey, she tried to spot Venn. Her eyes flicked from burgundy Plymouth Valiants to white Chrysler Imperials to Buick estate wagons and a sea of sedans and coupes. But she couldn't see him. Not that it mattered – he knew where she was heading.

The Bentley. That's where it was all going to end, she thought, as the limo cruised down Central Park West. The workmen on their cradles looked like insects stuck to fly paper.

An ashen-faced Lazar was pulling her from the limo before Rudy had even switched the engine off. There followed an ugly exchange, with the doctor saying the driver had disobeyed his instructions, and the driver bellowing that the instructions hadn't been explicit enough.

The row didn't last long as Lazar was eager to get Sophie into the hotel. He shoved a big note at Andy as he did so. Sophie wondered how much the concierge was being paid to open a couple of doors each day, make sure the builders weren't walking out with the fittings and keep his mouth shut.

In the elevator, Lazar couldn't look her in the eye. Was he angry with her or was it just that he was afraid of what Hugo would say when he learned she had gone missing?

The doors opened and Lazar manhandled her towards the suite.

"I'm going to phone Hugo," he said, pushing her into her bedroom. She sprawled on to the bed. Lazar's

325

last words as he locked the door were: "He must hear of this."

"This 'setback to my treatment'?" she yelled, going to the door. "How long before I'm weaned off my coke habit? Do you think another year will crack it, doc?"

She stood there, listening, and sure enough, about a minute later, she heard the faint *ting* that meant Lazar was picking up the phone and putting in a call to whatever meeting room in the city Hugo was in.

Perfect. Now she just had to hope that Venn with his horror make-up could get past Andy downstairs.

Of *course* he'd get past him. He had a gun and *his* life was on the line, too.

A second ting indicated the call was over. Good. A longer conversation would have meant Hugo was asking questions, testing whether he really needed to come home. He'd obviously decided in a hurry that he did.

Sophie put on some platforms – the closest thing she had to shoes that she could run in. She was leaving. Dying or leaving – one way or the other she was checking out of The Bentley. She scraped together her money from various hiding places – nearly a thousand dollars she had squirrelled away – stuffed it in her purse, and thought about what she needed to do.

There was nothing. Nothing to do but wait.

She felt like a condemned woman, waiting for the executioner. Except Venn was supposed to be her saviour. She didn't know whether he was right about her being expendable as soon as the deal was signed, but it would be too dangerous to disbelieve him. It was definitely time to get the hell out of here.

She thought about Abigail. Tried to draw strength from those pictures of her, the Sten Gun slung around her shoulders. The stories of her bravery.

Sophie told herself: *you've come so far.*

She heard Lazar shuffling around in the lounge. Pouring himself a drink.

She heard the distant honk of taxis. She looked to the windows and saw the first drops of melting snow sliding down the panes. The thaw was here.

Long minutes passed.

In the lounge, the internal phone was ringing. *The concierge.*

"Yes, yes, I'll sign for it. Send him up," she heard Lazar say.

She held her breath. The acoustics changed ever so slightly in the room: the elevator was rising through the shaft.

Venn was coming.

She heard Lazar open the front door. Heard the lift doors opening. Lazar was saying something, issuing some charmless order. Then he seemed to repeat it, louder, as if it had been ignored. Venn shouted for Lazar to get back into the room.

"Have you called him?" Venn was demanding.

"Who? Who are you?"

"*Don't play games with me* – is Hugo coming here now?"

A scream from Lazar. "Yes."

"How long 'til he gets here?"

"I don't know."

Smack.

"Fucking guess, then!"

A series of thuds as Venn laid into Lazar with his fists. Lazar screeching like a girl. Some searing feeling of bloodlust rose within Sophie. She realised she was whispering Venn's name over and over.

They were fighting back.

"Okay, okay," said Lazar. "He said he'd be home in about an hour."

There was a cracking sound that made Sophie wince. The image of Amber and the knuckledusters popped into her head.

No more noise from Lazar.

Venn unlocked the bedroom door and stood there, grinning.

"Well, that worked all right, didn't it?"

She stepped out and saw Lazar lying face down.

"What did you do to him?"

"Little kiss on the back of the head," said Venn, holding up the gun that she'd glimpsed in the park. "Takes a bit of practice. Reggie Kray taught me."

"Will he be all right?"

"Who cares? Here, grab his legs."

Sophie did as she was told and they managed to drag Lazar into her room and lock him in.

Venn strode into the lounge. "Not exactly been slumming it, have you?"

"Yeah, I've been having a whale of a time."

Venn turned a three-sixty, looking for something. "So where does Hugo keep his moolah?"

"If he has any here, it'll be in the study."

"Men like Hugo always have readies," said Venn. He tried the study door and found it locked. He tapped the wood to test its thickness.

"I thought the plan was to wait 'til he got home then *ask* him for the money," said Sophie.

"It is, but once a burglar, always a burglar. And I want everything he's got."

Venn walked to the opposite side of the room and turned sideways on, bracing himself for a charge.

"For God's sake, Lazar has *keys*," said Sophie.

Venn laughed. "That's a relief. I'm not really up to strong-arm stuff right now."

He went to unlock the bedroom and returned with Lazar's key ring. Moments later he was in the study, tossing ledgers, diaries and papers over his shoulder.

Sophie stood in the doorway watching. It felt good to see Venn ransacking this place that had been forbidden to her. He turned his attentions to a mahogany case clock and then fruitless examinations of various *objets d'art* including a pair of sphinx hurricane lamps, a stick barometer, cane stand and pair of globes. Last, he pulled the emptied drawers from the mahogany writing desk and searched the cavities behind them.

"Nice one, Hugo," he said, withdrawing his arm and throwing something to Sophie.

"My passport! My false passport, anyway."

"Stick it in your handbag. You'll need it when we get out of here."

Sophie did as he advised. "Who said I was leaving with you?"

"Oh, what? You're going to stay here once I've got my money? Even though Hugo will know it was you what got me in here? You're brown bread, babe. Uncle Venn's your only ticket out of the crem. Pack what you need because we're leaving within the hour."

"So you think Hugo's just going to write you a cheque and you can walk out of here?"

"That's exactly what's going to happen. The cheque will clear, believe me. And once you've heard what Gerald has on Hugo, you *will* believe me."

"So let's hear it."

Venn peered at Sophie through an antique telescope.

"Stop messing around," she said. "We don't have much time."

"Yeah," he said. "And it's time for a drink."

He poured himself a brandy and settled in Sophie's Chesterfield armchair in the turret, turning it so it faced the door to the suite. He held the Walther PPK with some difficulty in his bandaged right hand.

Sophie sat on the recamier. The room was silent except for the ticking of the clock from the study and the trickle of snow melting on the roof.

Venn said: "Sophs, come and sit here with me."

"I'm fine here."

"I want you to."

"Get on with the story, Venn."

"Ah yes: Abigail Wilman. As a kid, I always found her disappearance fascinating, and to think that now I know the truth..." He tapped a hand on one of the armrests in invitation. Sophie sat down.

"*Tell me*," she said.

"Yes... Abigail, Abigail..." Venn tilted his head to the ceiling, as if trying to dredge up some distant memory. "You and I, Sophie, we never did get intimate, did we?"

"No, Venn, we never did."

He was running the barrel of the gun up and down her spine.

"You always wanted to be with me," he said. "I saw the way you looked at me sometimes. Come with me today, we'll go back to England. We're Brits, for Christ's sake. We don't belong out here with these phoneys. And what's happening to me now, that's just a setback. I'll be bigger than ever. It'll be like Tozer never existed."

Sophie turned and looked at his ruined face and even though it was hideous, there was something else, too: the fascination of being this close to a man who had killed.

Three loud thumps made Sophie jump to her feet.

"Easy," said Venn. "It's just the doc. He's woken up." He reached for Sophie's hair, twisted it round his fingers and gently pulled her back to the armrest.

When he saw that Sophie was preoccupied with Lazar's hollering from the bedroom, he bellowed:

"Shut the fuck up in there, or I'll put a bullet in your head!"

The noise stopped.

"You will come with me, won't you?" said Venn.

"Maybe," she said, her eyes on the clock. Anything to humour Venn because she couldn't run the risk of Hugo coming home before she'd found out the Abigail secret.

"Will you?"

There was a rumble from somewhere in the bowels of The Bentley. They both froze, thinking it was the lift. Venn raised the gun, pointed it at the door.

"Workmen," said Sophie, releasing her breath. *"Tell me about Abigail."*

Venn reached into his trouser pocket and passed her something. A photograph. Before she even looked at it she knew what it was going to be, and she was right. It was the old man in the picture that Gerald had put under Hugo's door that first night she'd spent with him. But it was a different snap. In this one, the subject was in his wheelchair outside a building clearly signed as Heathrow Airport. She could just make out that the date on the newspaper he was holding up was January 23, exactly a week ago.

"Who is he?" she said.

"He's the one man who can ruin Hugo Summers. Hugo's terrified of this old gipper, and that's why he fled to New York."

"Fled..." said Sophie. "That's what Charlie said on new year's eve – that Hugo was running."

"Yeah, Charlie obviously knew a lot more about Hugo than we realised. But whatever Charlie knew, Gerald knows double."

Venn showed her another picture. This was a close-up of the old man's hands holding a document titled simply "Puymirol". Below the heading was a typed list of names but the camera was in so close that only the first few were visible.

"Puymirol," said Sophie. "*That's the place Charlie mentioned.* Hugo denied he knew what it meant."

"Okay, what I'm going to tell you dates back to the war. And you're not going to believe *what* I tell you, because it could bring *Gerald* down, too."

"Why would Gerald want that?"

Lazar resumed his banging on the bedroom door. He was shouting for help at the top of his lungs.

"Because he doesn't give a shit any more," said Venn, ignoring the din. "He lost his reputation and his money a long time ago. Gerald's a poker player – he thinks he can push all his chips in and Hugo will fold, and he's right. If what I'm about to tell you goes public, Hugo will be ruined. Gerald's already ruined; things can't get any worse for him. And he *hates* Hugo – he'd be happy to fuck *himself* over if he thought he could bring Hugo down."

"And it's all about this money that Gerald says Hugo owes him over some property?"

"Let me out of here!" Lazar was shouting, over and over.

"Yeah, except it ain't nothing to do with property," said Venn.

"So what is it?" said Sophie.

"Take twenty-five years off nineteen-seventy and see where that leaves you."

"The end of the war?"

"Correct."

"Stop playing games, Venn. Did Hugo kill Abigail or not?"

"You're coming back to London with me." He pulled her hair, made her gasp. But she didn't try to struggle free. "I want you," he whispered.

Sophie jerked her head forward, painfully breaking from his grip. She got to her feet and leant over Venn, grabbing his shoulders and shaking him.

"WHAT HAPPENED TO ABIGAIL?"

"All right, all right! What happened was that Hugo–."

Sophie felt some presence behind her and realised in that moment that Lazar's noise had covered up the opening of the front door. She hurled herself to the left. As she was in mid-flight, there was a deafening boom, as if the whole room had been detonated. A hole appeared in Venn's forehead and a fine spray of blood, brain and armchair stuffing rained down on her. Sophie screamed and kept screaming.

When the noise of the gunshot had died away, Hugo said: "I knew it was a good idea to tell Lazar I'd be an hour. Bought me the element of surprise. What did Venn tell you?"

"Nothing."

"I don't believe that."

"You're going to kill me anyway, so why do you care what he told me?"

Hugo regarded her for a few moments. Then he removed the Walther PPK from Venn's grip and went to unlock Lazar. There followed a short conversation, in which a hysterical Lazar tried to justify his decision to let Venn into the suite. Hugo asked questions in a voice so calm that Sophie could only intermittently hear what he was saying.

Lying to the side of the Chesterfield were the two photos. She scooped them up and shoved them into her back pocket.

"Get in there and do what you've been paid to do," Hugo was telling Lazar.

Sophie clambered to her feet and went to stand in the turret so she didn't have to look at Venn and the brain-spattered wall.

"I'm finalising the deal in twenty minutes upstairs," Hugo told Lazar. He was only just hanging on to his cool. "I've moved the last knockings of negotiations to the board room for some privacy. Now do what we discussed: make it look like an accident. Take the gun and do it."

After a pause, Lazar said: "All right."

Hugo peered around the wall and looked at her. They locked eyes. And then he let himself out of the suite.

Lazar stepped into the room. The gun that had killed Venn was now pointed at her.

"Sophie, please come with me," he said.

"So you can kill me?"

"No, I'm going to sedate you." His eyes tried not to flick to Venn, and failed. He looked like he might throw up. "Please, come with me."

Knowing how nervy Lazar was, Sophie made no sudden movements as she walked past him into her bedroom.

She sat down on the bed. If strength wasn't in her now, she would die.

Careful not to turn his back on her, Lazar opened his medical bag on the bowfront chest, and with the hand not holding the gun removed a syringe from its restraining band.

Sophie recalled *Avenging Angel* saying Abigail had once defended herself against an attack on Primrose Hill. A scuffle with a tramp that had alerted her to her latent powers. Among those powers had been bravery. Sheer guts...

Lazar was plunging the needle into a vial of what she guessed was the sodium pentathol. But he wasn't gearing up for a truth session this time. For the first time since she'd known him, he removed his sunglasses. The gleam in his eyes told her he couldn't wait to get his revenge on her for having humiliated him.

"Roll up a sleeve," he said, the syringe in one hand, Hugo's revolver in the other.

Sophie began doing as she was told, but slowly, with trembling hands. She noticed the swelling on Lazar's forehead where Venn had hit him.

And that glazed look in his eyes…

Lazar was vulnerable.

"What's this all about?" said Sophie, putting on a weak voice even though every muscle and sense was primed for a fight. "Why not just shoot me?" When Lazar didn't answer, she said: "Oh, I get it: Hugo's planning to fly my body back to London, make it look like I OD'd. Plenty of members from the Erato to testify that I was a coke user, right..?"

The dose was ready. Lazar began taking tiny steps towards her.

Abigail in the park. What had *Avenging Angel* said about that? That she'd grabbed the guy's wrist, found a pressure point?

Should have paid attention, Boyd.

The needle.

"This will just make you sleepy..." he said.

"Okay, doc," she said. "Okay..."

***

CHAPTER SIXTY-FOUR

Doyle Raymer blew cigar smoke towards the board room's domed skylight. He'd been patient but now he'd had enough of the English lawyer's drone.

"Listen up, guys," he interrupted in his broad Texan accent. "I don't really think we need to be getting bogged down in the likely depreciation of the printing press roof at Seattle at this stage, do you?"

The lawyer who had been interrupted placed a finger in his report and looked up. The three other men on Hugo's team also stared across the table at Raymer to see what maverick approach he was going to take now. His negotiating style had been so tough that every man in the room felt drained, including his own team, who sat facing Hugo's.

"Or the state of ten delivery trucks," continued Raymer. "Or whether the goddamned post boy at the *LA Observer* needs a new pack of rubber bands!"

Nobody spoke. Instead, all eyes turned to Hugo, who had spent the past half-hour staring at a miniature New York Stock Exchange ticker machine, encased in glass. Staring at his *reflection*, more like, thought Richard Protheroe, the man who had been reading out the report. Like everyone at the table, Protheroe's nerves were frayed, his patience long since spent in trying to get this deal done.

It had been murder trying to get Hugo focused on the talks. Protheroe knew that it was the depression. *Every man* around the table knew it was the depression.

"Forget about the roof," said Hugo. "Joe, I've known Doyle for fifteen years – we can forget about the roof. If it leaks, I'll come round and mend it myself. Put it in the contract."

The room burst into laughter and Joe Ciaffone crossed something through in his yellow legal pad. Raymer chuckled long and hard, the folds on his 65-

year-old face breaking into more folds. He blew another smoke ring towards the skylight, which had been left open to accommodate his penchant for Monte Cristos. Everyone was chilled to the bone, apart from Raymer, who benefited from the insulation of a white stetson that he never removed.

"Screw the roof," said Raymer. "Thank God… I thought I'd be in a seven-card stud game in Houston right now. I told my buddy to stick in my antes and he called me this morning to say I already owe him three thousand dollars. Now, gentlemen, what do I have to do to get to that game, huh? Anyone? *Hugo?*"

But Hugo wasn't laughing any more. He was looking along the length of the table towards the doors. And so was everyone else.

Raymer waved away a cloud of his own smoke and saw an attractive if haunted-looking woman holding a gun.

"Gentlemen," she said, in a voice so quiet that the men at the far end of the room leaned towards her. "I'm sorry to break up your meeting, but there's something I think you should know."

"Everyone, this is Sophie," said Hugo, in a voice full of tolerance, as if a child had just run in. "I'm afraid I turned her down for an editorship in London a few years ago and she's been rather problematic ever since. She's never actually pulled a gun before, though."

Joe Ciaffone and a couple of the other men chuckled uneasily. The others couldn't take their eyes off the intruder.

"Well, hell, you should give the lady a second chance," said Raymer. "Your newspapers are going to need a strong team, right, Hugo?"

With her arms held out straight in front of her, Sophie alternated her aim between Hugo's team and Raymer's, so no-one could make a sudden move.

Hugo stood up. "Sophie, did you forget to take your medication? You're in no state to be handling a gun. They require great skill, too – fire at me and you'll hit one of these poor men here."

"I bet you that's the gun we heard fired about half an hour ago," said the man to Raymer's left.

"*I* told *you* that was a gunshot," corrected Raymer. "What's going on here, Hugo?"

Sophie spotted an atypical face among the sea of identical middle-aged men with brown flannel and plaid suits, thick-framed glasses and receding hairlines.

"Mr Stevenson," she said. "I see you've quit Scotland Yard for Hugo's legal team. I'm sure that's a very profitable move."

The man adjusted a pile of papers. "If you're talking to me, young lady, my name is Maurie Golds. My business is investment banking. Perhaps you can explain what you mean about Scotland Yard."

Sophie turned her aim to the man next to him. "Ah, Mr Phelps. You've changed careers, too."

But the one she knew as Phelps shook his head. "My name is Protheroe, and I'm on Mr Summers' legal team."

She shifted to train the muzzle on his neighbour. "And don't tell me, you're not Detective O'Hanrahan?"

Raymer's team burst into laughter.

"Detective O'Hanrahan!" roared Raymer. "I always knew it! Bob Tomko has been moonlighting all these years! Sack your partner at once, Hugo, godammit!"

Hugo was laughing, too. He said: "Sophie, those gentleman, in order, are Richard Protheroe, one of my lawyers, Maurie Golds, my good friend from Golds and Weinstein, and Bob Tomko, owner of Tomko Discount, also an old pal. Maurie and Bob are my partners in the purchase of the Journal group."

"Well, they can always go to Hollywood if it doesn't work out," said Sophie. "And I *knew* I recognised them from somewhere else – they were watching that show at the Erato with the girl in the wedding dress, weren't they? *The yanks*... I'd bet a dime to a dollar that they're the midnight callers who've been creeping into the study after I've been sent to bed. Understandable – you've had a lot to plan, haven't you, boys?"

Hugo pushed his chair back, and Sophie saw that he aimed to use this moment of confusion to disarm her.

She closed her eyes, turned the gun upwards and squeezed the trigger.

A gigantic bang was followed by a showering of plaster from the ceiling on to the table, shattering Hugo's ticker machine. Every man at the table except for Hugo and Raymer leapt to their feet.

"Everybody sit down!" said Sophie.

Nobody moved, they just looked at each other as if wondering whether to charge her.

"Sit, boys," said Raymer. He stubbed out his cigar.

They did as he said. Now she had their attention, Sophie began to realise how out of her depth she was. When the dust had settled, she said: "My name is Sophie Boyd. I'm a journalist. I've been kept a virtual prisoner at this hotel since Hugo sneaked me into the country on a false passport. The reason he's done this..."

Her voice was faltering. Raymer raised an eyebrow at Ciaffone, who just shrugged.

"The reason he's done this is because I've been investigating his part in the disappearance of Abigail Wilman, a former British secret agent, and he thinks I know things that could wreck this deal if I ever made them public. He's been using every trick up his sleeve to get me to reveal what I know, including using the services of these three men, who he got to impersonate members of MI6, Scotland Yard and the NYPD. He also told me I would be deputy editor of a new magazine called *Sensual*, but I now see that he was using emotional blackmail, doing everything to get me on his side. And he's been using a Dr Lazar to sedate me round the clock and-."

"Lazar?" scoffed Raymer. "Not Bobby Lazar by any chance, that freak who wears those shades indoors?"

"Yes, that's him!" said Sophie. "I'm afraid I had to incapacitate him with a kick to the balls and a bump on the head."

"Goddamn it, Hugo," barked Raymer. "I fired Lazar as my personal physician eight years ago! He tried to touch up my wife! Don't tell me he's on your payroll?"

Hugo was pinching the skin at his temples. "Just for prescribing me with some... Look, I'll tell you about it later, Doyle, okay? Once we've got rid of this maniac woman. Just put the gun down, Sophie, all right?"

"Not until you tell me the truth about Abigail."

Hugo got up and began walking ever so slowly in Sophie's direction. She took a step back.

"You've fired that thing once," he said. "I didn't think you would. I was wrong, okay? But next time you'll hurt somebody." He held one hand open, palm up, and kept moving. Sophie kept retreating. She was almost back at the door.

"So come on, Sophie," called Ciaffone. "You've slandered Hugo to the eyeballs, let's hear the accusations."

"You cowards," she said. "You think I'm going to back down because you start ganging up on me?"

"It's a thirty-eight special," said Hugo. "A present from the New York chief of police. He'll be very upset if you shoot me with it."

"Then just stop where you are."

"What you're holding is called a smooth presentation grip. It's not really meant to be fired, so the grip can get a little sweaty. Do your palms feel sweaty? Your chances of hitting me are about one in four, I'd say. On those other three occasions, you'll miss and I'll snap your neck."

Sophie hadn't thought about the gun until now, but Hugo was right: the grip was slippery in her grasp. And her arms were aching, starting to droop.

She reached into her back pocket and threw Venn's two photos on to the table.

"I don't know what Hugo did with Abigail, but it's to do with something called Puymirol in the war," said Sophie, her voice cracking. "And it's maybe something to do with The Gathering Place. Not the club he used to own but the name, the name itself: *The Gathering Place.*"

"Jesus," said Ciaffone. "Just grab the fucking gun, Hugo."

"I don't see *you* volunteering, Joe," said Summers.

Sophie was pressed up against the doors. "Get back, Hugo," she said, tears glistening in her eyes. "There never was going to be a new magazine, was there? Or maybe there was, but not with me on board. After I told you about my dad and how he'd made me so ambitious, you knew exactly which buttons to press, didn't you? I was so stupid…"

"Just wait a minute," said Raymer.

Hugo halted.

Sophie's arms were in agony.

"What is it, Doyle?" said Hugo, through clenched teeth.

"*Just wait, goddamn it.*"

Hugo turned to look at Raymer, who along with one of his team was studying the photos.

"I know that name," said the Texan. "*Pweemeeroll,* yeah. Heard enough about it when I was leading the 20th Combat Engineer into Normandy. Goddamn Nazis shot up a whole bunch of French civilians there.

You kill one of ours, we'll kill ten of yours. Yeah, they rounded them all up in the town square and shot them French guys one by one."

"Abigail was never based anywhere near those places," Hugo whispered to Sophie. "The game is over. Give me the gun."

"You know what, Hugo," said Raymer. "She may be stark raving mad but I'd like to hear what the lady has to say. I think I owe it to my boys in the 20th Combat and to my left leg." He put a hand on his thigh and rapped on wood.

Hugo stood just inches from Sophie. She was terrified of him but couldn't help looking into those mesmerising eyes, maybe for the last time. She thought she could read him now; maybe that was a skill of his that had rubbed off on her.

"I don't think so, *Doyle*," he said.

"Why not? If you've kept the gal cooped up with that pervert Lazar, and been feeding her drugs, I want to know what else has been going on. And then there's the slight matter of her being called Sophie. Now, with me being a betting man – although I'm kinda resigned to missing that game of stud – I'm guessing she's the same Sophie that the papers say disappeared in that fire of yours. Call me a man of principle, Hugo, but I want the newspapers I've been building up for the past thirty years to go to the right person. A person who doesn't have a bunch of skeletons in the closet. I'm cautious like that."

"No, Doyle. *Sophie, give me the fucking gun.*"

She drew on the last ounces of energy and lifted the revolver up to point at the centre of Hugo's chest.

"Sophie," said Ciaffone, "how about a compromise? Let's all take a break, huh? A temporary ceasefire?"

She was being offered a way out. She had done all she could, put as much doubt into these men's minds as was possible with the information she had. It was time to escape with her life.

She pushed open the doors and ran.

CHAPTER SIXTY-FIVE

She ran and ran and only stopped when she thought she was going to throw up. She checked in to a cheap hotel and passed off an American accent. She didn't want questions about passports, even though she had the false one in her bag. All she wanted was shelter, and for twenty bucks that's what she got.

She ordered four bottles of beer from room service and drank them in rapid succession. For the past two months her mind had been filled with thoughts of Abigail, the Erato, Venn and Charlie. Now none of those mattered – it was all over. All she could think about was Hugo.

Somehow, she fell asleep. When she woke, the first shades of dawn were lightening the room.

All her evidence seemed ridiculous, far-fetched. She had ruined Hugo's reputation with absolutely nothing.

What if you got it all wrong?

**

In a taxi cruising down Central Park West, Sophie watched nervously for the first sight of The Bentley.

"You sure you want The *Bentley*?" said the cabbie. "That place is closed."

"Just go there," she said, hoping that Andy was asleep in the lobby and could be woken.

Sophie paid the cabbie and found the entrance doors locked. Peering in, she saw her man stretched out on a leather couch, covered in one of the hotel's fine quilts. A few taps on the glass were enough to stir him.

"Hey, miss, what you doing out there?" said Andy, bleary eyed. "I thought they never let you out."

"I'm sorry to wake you, Andy."

"It's okay. What time is it?"

"Half six? I'm not really sure. Listen, I need you to tell me something. Is Mr Summers upstairs?"

"He came in at midnight then left about half an hour later."

"And he couldn't have slipped back in while you were sleeping?"

"No, only I've got the key."

***

CHAPTER SIXTY-SIX

The suite smellt of Hugo's cologne.

Lazar had long since fled. He had been as weak as she had anticipated and had screamed like a girl when she'd delivered one well-aimed kick to the balls. He'd curled up on the floor, a sitting duck for a whack on the head with the thirty-eight that had put him out for good. It had taken all her self-restraint not to give him his own injection, but she didn't want a murder rap added to her troubles.

Venn's body was still in the chair and she went to the phone without looking at him. She found Tony the messenger boy's scrap of paper in her handbag and dialled his number. It rang for ages.

Finally, a voice said: "What the fuck?"

"Tony?"

"Yeah. Who's this?"

"It's Sophie. The woman from the bagel shop."

"Holy shit. It's… I don't even know what time it is."

He hung up. She dialled again and this time when he answered she cut off his volley of abuse with the words: "Three hundred dollars to take me to JFK and wait with me until I get on a flight."

"Will it be dangerous?"

"I doubt it."

"I don't want to get in trouble over some job for a broad. I got college and some artistic shit coming up."

"Three hundred. Bring a gun, just in case."

There followed a lot of sighing and puffing and clearing of throat from Tony. Then he said: "Okay. But I've only got the Honda. Where and when?"

"In front of The Bentley. As soon as you can. But don't let me down, Tony. The guy who paid you to follow me is dead, so don't try to be clever and tip him off."

"Jesus…"

"Three hundred, Tony."

"I heard you first time. Gimme half an hour."

He hung up. Sophie stood in the turret and looked down at the park.

Flickering blue lights.

She strained to see what was going on but the pinpoints were distant and it was too dark. But she could just make out the shape of two police cars.

She turned to leave the suite and that's when she noticed the white envelope on the floor.

**

Dear Sophie,

You had the measure of me, in the end, and I applaud that. I know there are enough doubts in Raymer's mind now that he will never sign his company over to me. He may have enjoyed all the fun and games at The Gathering Place that night but when it comes to business I'm afraid he has high ideals.

Few people have ever stood up to me the way you have.

There was one notable other, of course. Abigail did not come to me because she was being blackmailed by Caroline Havelock. She came to repay some money I had loaned the Havelocks before the war. The two women had lost contact when Abby left The Affairs, but Abby sought out her friend after the war and found that Caroline had been blinded during the Blitz. Vulnerable, Caroline wanted to settle the old debt to allow her peace of mind and asked Abby to act as the courier.

As for my relationship with the Havelocks, there were 'sex games' – in a sense – but they were of my making. Tom and Caroline were not the instigators but the victims. And Abigail was never involved.

After my friendship developed with the Havelocks, I became infatuated with Caroline, had to have her so much that I ended the relationship with my lover, a Polish woman called Rena. Rena became difficult and when she tried to attack me with a knife, I murdered her. Caroline knew none of this when she left

347

Tom and moved into my Hampstead home, but subsequently had her suspicions. One day, Tom showed some rare courage and came to rescue her.

I let her go – I didn't want some ugly thing that could hurt the Summers name and besides, I was petrified that if the police got involved they would uncover Rena's death.

Then came the war, and the most shameful episode of my life. Understand that I was a different man in those days, Sophie. I was a fascist, pure and simple, a Nazi sympathiser. I believed that only they could crush the Communist conspiracy that was defiling the world.

My title might have been MI5 case agent, but in reality I was a double agent for the Germans. I had found a kindred spirit in a young MI6 officer, Gerald Masters, and we formed a lethally effective partnership. He would get wind via his SOE networks in France of Nazi infiltrators operating in Britain, and I would make contact with these people and give them what support I could, setting up safe houses and tipping them off when they were in danger of being exposed. Reversely, Gerald was in a prime position to alert the Nazis to the movements of those SOE groups he controlled, hence the massacre at Puymirol and in many other towns and villages.

After the war, I began to regret my actions and started to suffer from the depression that has afflicted me ever since. I became convinced that my treachery would one day be uncovered and to this end I attempted to burn the SOE records at the Baker Street HQ, partly succeeding.

Later that year, Abigail came to see me with Caroline's trifling sum of money and I intrigued her. I discovered that she had been a great SOE agent and I could tell that she sensed my evil (although I must stress she had never been in any of Gerald's networks, nor had she even heard of him or me during the war).

She did all she could to stay in with me, knowing what would charm and interest me. Abby knew that I wanted to seduce her and of course she never let it happen. She was a bored SOE girl with no war to fight and so I <u>became</u> her war. Once she learned that I was friends with Gerald, she must have investigated him, too, and discovered the high rate of SOE deaths in the circuits he controlled.

One night at Hampstead, I killed her, bludgeoned her with an axe handle when her back was turned. The next day I eliminated Caroline Havelock, too, pushing her off the cliffs at the blind home at Ovingdean. That was much harder to orchestrate and involved a large bribe to one of her carers. Abigail's and Rena's bodies are buried around the large oak just outside the southern perimeter fence of The Church of the Holy Innocents, High Beach, Essex.

Over the next decade, Gerald stepped up his right-wing activities, just as I began to scale mine down. He saw me as a traitor to the cause, but I had been deeply affected by the Moscow Three and Seamus Knutt debacles, when my newspapers' witch hunts had gone terribly wrong. And then there was the death of Emily, my first wife...

Emily's death came about because Gerald had become convinced I was withholding his share of the money we had been promised by Franz Strasser, a German spy we met regularly in England during the war. Strasser had told us we would be rich men when the war was over and the world was under Nazi control. When the tide began to turn against the Germans, Strasser fled back to Germany and we never re-established contact with him.

After the war, for some unknown reason Gerald became convinced that Strasser had paid me and that I had pocketed all the money, which was nonsense, of course. But Gerald was increasingly obsessive, even coming to the house and telling Emily exactly how we had betrayed British agents. When Emily confronted me and threatened to go to the authorities, there was only one solution. I killed her but made it look like she had gassed herself in the car.

Since that day, I have tried to immerse myself in work and push the past from my mind but Gerald has prevented that. I even allowed Gerald's henchman, Venn, to buy into the club in the hope it would appease Gerald, but of course such people are never appeased. That decision to make Venn my partner was also

349

motivated by the realisation that I would one day move my operations to the States as I loved the country and would stand a chance of leaving Gerald and his demands behind forever.

Recently, he has gone to the absurd lengths of tracking down Strasser, who is the old man in those pictures you gave to Raymer. Gerald is desperate for money and has been threatening to spring Strasser on me for some time. Of course, by now Strasser will have told Gerald the truth – that he never gave me any money, but Gerald is apparently oblivious to this and is steaming ahead with his blackmail anyway. As for Strasser, the unrepentant old Nazi can only be in it for a share of the cash and will no doubt happily back up any claims Gerald cares to make to the press. How they hope to get away it, I have no idea.

Maybe I should have just paid Gerald off a long time ago but I couldn't bring myself to. If I had paid him off, my terrible actions during the war would have gone with me to the grave. Actually, that's not true, is it? Because your friend Scottie had done such a good job of raking up the past. Too well – when he came poking around at the Erato, I had to use Venn's boys to take care of him, too. But you have done him proud.

And as for The Gathering Place… That's what Gerald named the upstairs club when I was away on business – another tactic to pressure me into paying up. He thought that I would panic, having one of my own clubs named after the locals' nickname for the town square in Puymirol. The scene of our darkest deed. It is a blessing that the diseased Erato and Gathering Place burnt down, something for which we have Charlie to thank. Alas, Charlie had otherwise become a liability and I took the opportunity to prevent his escape on new year's eve by trapping him in the tunnel.

As for Protheroe, Tomko, Golds and Ciaffone, they were innocent but naïve pawns in my endgame. I fed them a script and assured them that if they played their roles correctly, the deal would go ahead and we would all be rich. They knew nothing about Abigail Wilman until a few days ago, when I gave them just enough information to pull off their acting jobs. I think Bob Tomko as the NYPD 'tec was best, didn't you?

These last few weeks I have often taken a walk beside The Lake in the park across the road. My depression has been severe of late, as you know, and instead of finding comfort in the stroll, I picture the firing squad, see the villagers toppling one by one against the wall they used for screening movies outdoors. Bleeding, screaming. I wasn't there that day but I can picture the terrible events that I helped to engineer, and the many others like it. And some voice keeps telling me that it is time for me to join those people so that judgement can finally be passed on Hugo Summers.

I have greatly enjoyed knowing you, Sophie. It's just a shame that you found me as my life was ending. Yours, I believe, is about to begin.

All my love,

H

***

CHAPTER SIXTY-SEVEN

"Whoa, you can't go there," said a cop.

There were three police cars, and officers with torches and dogs and crime scene signs.

Sophie saw that she wasn't going to be able to bluff this one and said okay. She walked away down the street before ducking behind a row of bushes and clambering with some difficulty over the wall into Central Park.

She trudged through the slush towards the arc lamps being set up around The Lake. It only took a few minutes but it was the longest journey of her life.

The dazzling lights picked out the figure in the icy water, turning a slow circle. The face drained of colour, the double-breasted suit spread behind him like some vampire's cloak.

She'd seen enough. Seen enough of everything. She walked away.

The cops never even noticed her.

***

CHAPTER SIXTY-EIGHT

West London

Sophie parked the Roadster in front of the New Regency Hotel in Bayswater. The best thing about her daring mission to sneak back to her home earlier that day had been finding her beloved MG in the street. It had been given a thorough search by police but after a bit of spark-lead help from a fellow motorist, it was back in action.

Now, a jetlagged Sophie walked up the path to the hotel, not believing what she saw: the whole place boarded up. A selection of chairs and framed pictures had been dumped in the front yard and a cat sat on top of an abandoned fridge.

She thought back to the night she had come here for her first meeting with Venn. The wheeler-dealer men and the prostitutes and the room with the two-way mirror…

She was about to turn away when she saw that some enterprising individual had carved a small hole in the board over the front door. Squatting down, she peered into the lobby. The reception counter had been burnt and somewhere deep inside the building, people were arguing.

**

Where the chandelier had hung, there was bare flex; where the bar had been there was a hole in the floor. Wires, glass, needles, syringes and blankets were littered everywhere, all mixed in with puddles of excrement and urine.

Sophie held her breath, crossed to the red door and pushed it open, finding herself in the narrow corridor once again.

The doors had been removed from the rooms. There were people in each one, cooking up or passed out. The ones who were conscious looked amazed to see someone so smartly dressed in here. She kept moving, muttering "Buildings Inspectorate" as a mantra to reassure them.

She crossed the wooden boards that bridged the hotel with the one next door. It took her a while to find the room from the screening night. The mirror had been shattered many times and was covered in graffiti.

Ana lay on a bed, staring at nothing.

"Hey," said Sophie. She perched on the bed and stroked her hair. Ana was rumpled and teary eyed but otherwise looked okay.

"What happened here?" said Sophie.

"They came."

"Who?"

"Tozer and his men. They say Venn owe them money. They take everything, sell it off to make quick money. They kill Venn."

Sophie nodded. She would give Ana the real story about Venn later. Now she just had to get her out of this place. She could hear the junkies shouting and coming down the corridor, looking for her.

"Why did you come here?" said Ana.

"To find you."

"Why did you think I'd be here?" said Ana.

"I didn't, but I had nowhere else to start. This place is the Hilton compared to what the Erato looks like now. How long have you been here?"

"Not long. Two days… It's better than the streets."

Ana propped herself up on one elbow. Sophie half expected to see needle marks on her arm but they looked clean. An empty bottle of white wine on the floor told her that Ana's old familiar addiction was taking care of her just fine.

"So what now?" said Ana.

"We're going to Spain to rescue Carmen."

Ana make a kind of spitting sound. "You're crazy."

"I'm serious. And we don't have to worry about the screening pictures any more – they were all burnt in the fire. It's over."

***

CHAPTER SIXTY-NINE

Sophie bought Ana a bite to eat at a nearby café and related everything that had happened.

"And what will happen with Toad?" said Ana.

"Well, at some point soon I'll have to go to the Old Bill and put *all* my cards on the table. Then they'll have to arrest him. Hugo's suicide note will get the ball rolling. All of Gerald's operations in the war will be raked over. He doesn't stand a chance."

"But he still has the film of you and Echo?"

"Yeah, but I didn't touch her. It won't look good but hopefully people will understand that I was undercover. And if they don't, well..." Sophie looked at her watch. "Come on, we're going to miss that ferry."

Black clouds hung over them on the drive to Dover and the air was heavy with ozone.

Sophie said: "Tell me about this place where your daughter is. Why do people go there?"

"Nobody goes there, except Vicente Salvo's men. They take the drugs there, from Morocco. Then they take them all over the country, all of Europe."

"But how could *we* get in?"

Ana said nothing and Sophie thought she had gone into a sulk. Then she said: "The food truck."

"Good." Sophie pulled out and overtook a lorry so fast that Ana gripped the edge of her seat.

"But we need money to bribe the driver," said Ana.

"Don't worry about that," said Sophie, thinking of the money she had hoarded from her shopping trips and poker games with Hugo. She'd brought back nearly three thousand dollars, which she was exchanging for sterling in dribs and drabs. "We've got enough. You just worry about keeping quiet when I'm driving on and off the ferry."

"*I told you* I'm not going in the boot. I hate dark places."

"Do you have your passport?"

Ana rolled her eyes. "You know I don't."

"And do you want to see Carmen again?"

"Yes, of course."

"Then you're going in the boot. Are you sure you know how to get to the hacienda?"

"Yes, I'm sure."

"Then that's all we need," said Sophie. She was now using the slow lane to overtake cars in the fast lane. Anything to get an edge; time was short.

"It's going to rain," said Ana.

"We'll be fine," said Sophie. "Just fine..."

Up ahead the clouds were parting, and sunlight spilt from the gaps like feathers through a slashed pillow.

*****

The author would like to thank Joan Johnson, Caroline Sullivan and Lisa Batty for their help in the writing and marketing of this novel.